MOWIN' THE HEAVENLY LAWN

MOWIN' THE HEAVENLY LAWN

Kirk Hiner

Writers Club Press
San Jose New York Lincoln Shanghai

Mowin' the Heavenly Lawn

Writers Club Press
an imprint of iUniverse, Inc.

For information address:
iUniverse, Inc.
5220 S. 16th St., Suite 200
Lincoln, NE 68512
www.iuniverse.com

ISBN: 0-595-23683-9

Printed in the United States of America

The author would like to dedicate this book to Claude Clayton Smith, Jim Jividen, and Andy Prieboy for education, motivation and inspiration. You guys can fight over who did what.

Seriously. Three-way ladder match for the IC strap, July 25th at Red Rocks, live on pay-per-view.

"The world is a comedy to those who think, a tragedy to those who feel."

—Horace Walpole
18th Century Philosopher

"There's what's right and there's what's right and e'er the twain shall meet."

—H. I. McDonough
20th Century Philosopher

Contents

Acknowledgements

This book was started during a period of my life when it was easy to be spiteful, and was severely delayed by long bouts with happiness. Throughout it all, I received plenty of help and encouragement.

Thanks to my parents for buying me my first typewriter even before I knew how to use one. Next time, I'll try to write a book you'll like.

Thanks to Dave Larson and the group at Nisus Software, Inc. (**www.nisus.com**) for creating a word processor that actually makes it *easier* to write. Yours was the best of the four used to author this novel.

Thanks to Joe Ryan at Applelinks (**www.applelinks.com**) for giving me a forum and an audience to keep me in practice.

Thanks to Kristi Hiner for proofing the book while I was off having my picture taken with M11.

Thanks to Jim Jividen for giving me the good jokes and for being my editor, researcher and "audience of one."

And thanks to Tieraney for continuity, criticism, and for all that happiness mentioned above.

CHAPTER 1

The Kidnapping of Holly Hobbie

*M*y name is Guy, and I once killed somebody.

There. See? I said it. That wasn't so hard. Certainly not as hard as actually performing the act, no matter what the psychologists and reformed criminals say. Yet, despite my acceptance of the situation, I was always hesitant to confess my crime. Not because of fear, I don't think, but because I simply never found reason to: not to job interviewers, not to coworkers at the Steak 'N' Shake (drink the shakes, avoid the steaks), and not to late night radio psychiatrists.

Actually, that's not entirely true. There was one opportune moment when I did admit to having killed somebody. After all, it's quite difficult to keep something like that bottled up forever. It's something unique to impart, something to generate interest, and every now and again I had to refrain from becoming the hit of the party. I was compelled to generate such interest during my first freshman orientation class in college. Our professor stood behind a rickety, wooden podium at the open end of a tight horse-shoe of desks. She told us to state from where we came and something interesting about ourselves. I watched as the students hurriedly scoured their lives to find that one nugget of personal data that, at once, provided the requisite degree of interest while simultaneously being devoid of any meaning whatsoever.

❋   ❋   ❋

This exercise was not new to me. The first time I recall having to introduce myself to a crowd of strangers was in kindergarten. Back then, I stood and said, "My name's Guy Lindsey, and I'm five years old."

It was easy when I was five, as the only interesting thing about me was my age. There were no great "life stories" to tell, no worldly experiences to share and no baggage to display, and Lord knows I hadn't yet killed somebody. Although, now that I think about it, that would've made for some big discussion in the teachers' lounge come lunchtime.

"One of my new kindergartners stood up today," Mrs. Piper would've said from behind a thick, gray cloud of cigarette smoke, "a boy named Guy Lindsey, and he said—"

"Yes, I know his parents," Principal Steele would've smiled, carefully nodding his head in that polite, principalesque way. "Fine people. Salt of the Earth."

"Well, their boy stood up in my class today, and he said, 'My name's Guy Lindsey, and I once killed somebody.'"

"Hmm." Principal Steele would've still been nodding his head, practicing for parent/teacher conferences. "Interesting life, for a five year old. Did he say who he engaged in this inappropriate behavior with?"

"'With *whom* he engaged in this inappropriate behavior,'" Mrs. Piper would've corrected.

As the semicircle of freshman confessions worked its away around to where I was sitting, I wondered how they would handle mine. My classmates were saying things such as, "My name's Kerry, and I hope to produce propaganda for the Democratic Party," or "My name's Shawn, and my goal in life is to become co-editor of the *Phi Beta Kappan*." I guess they were still under the impression that college prepared them for work of this sort...or, in fact, work of any sort. Damn English majors. Even before I'd completed my first and only entrance application, I knew my money would be better vested in a digital camera or a nice wristwatch. One with that Indiglo, perhaps. Shiny.

See, the thing is, I cared about as much for these people and their goals as I did about...say...little Terry Hogan back in kindergarten when he announced who he was and that he, like everyone else in the classroom, was five years old. I completely forgot Terry Hogan's name until about a week later when he pointed out we had the same style shoes. That Terry Hogan was five made no particular impression, but the fact we both wore brown Hush Puppies was something concrete upon which a five-year-old could base a friendship.

To cement this, I offered him a Life Saver. Life Savers were like medicine to me, and had been since I could remember. And not those fruity kinds. I hated that crap. They never tasted like they were supposed to. Cherry didn't taste like cherries, it tasted like red. Grape didn't taste like grapes, it tasted like purple. Orange didn't taste like oranges, it tasted like...okay, but I've made my point. Even worse was the next trend towards fake flavors. I guess the scientists in the Life Saver and fruit drink labs couldn't get their products to taste like anything at all, so they started inventing flavors or smashing them together in weird and unnatural ways. Watermelon-grape! Tangerine dream. Super Berry Sensation. What the hell is a super berry? Forget all that crap. Flavors cannot be invented in a lab. I mean, pity the child on Parents' Day at school…

"My mom's a scientist, and she's working on a cure for cancer."

"My dad's a scientist, and he helps to launch the Space Shuttle."

"My dad's a scientist, and he invented the flavor Super Berry Sensation."

It's just wrong.

For great tasting Life Savers, there's just one simple rule; the name must have an O. Pep-O-Mint. Cin-O-Mon, Wint-O-Green. I explained this to Terry Hogan, he understood, and we became best friends until just before sixth grade when he moved to Toledo.

Good thing, too. He'd never have to learn that I would end up killing somebody. Not that anyone else did, really, save for the murderee, who has since forgotten, I'm sure. Oh, and that person to whom I confessed, and who has certainly also forgotten by now. But I maybe could've confided in Terry. Honesty is a curse of friendship, which is why I now try vehemently to avoid making friends.

It was almost my turn to offer an interesting life tidbit to the other college freshmen, so I prepared for my first public announcement that I was, in fact, a killer. I guess I always found it much easier to be honest with total strangers. No one would've believed me anyway, and they would've forgotten my name within a week.

When it was nearly my turn, the guy sitting next to me stood and claimed, with a peculiar lack of emotion, "Name's Papa Shango, and Papa Shango know voodoo."

That was the first and only time he referred to himself as Papa Shango. I mean, yeah, it was obvious he was lying about his name, but his real name was equally odd—the Arbiter. And after that day, the Arbiter was the only moniker he'd use.

I was so flummoxed by the whole Papa Shango thing that, when it was my turn to stand up, I could only say, "My name's Guy Lindsey, and I'm five years old."

❧   ❧   ❧

Honestly? I was much happier when I was five. Life was good when I was five. My mother, having just given birth to her second son, was happy. My father, having just been promoted to department chair at the college where he taught physics, was happy. My little brother, having just been born and therefore having no clue yet as to what was going on, was happy. And because everyone around me was so happy, then hell, I was happy too!

And then I was introduced to corporal punishment.

I remember it as clearly as some can recall where they were upon learning that President Kennedy had been spanked…I mean shot—although I'm certain many can recall where they were when Kennedy was spanked, too. As for *my* spanking, I was in kindergarten, sitting unassumingly in the third row beside my new best friend Terry Hogan. The other students didn't like to sit beside Terry because he was born with a cleft lip and palate. He still had a scar above his upper lip, giving him a minor speech impediment. This bothered the other kids, and even Mrs. Piper seemed to grow impatient with him when he spoke. I didn't understand their actions; Terry was a good guy.

Certainly not the kind of guy who would kill somebody.

On the other side of me was a girl with long, flat brown hair and legs like broomsticks. She would eventually turn me down for a date in junior high because, she explained, her mother told her she wasn't allowed to go out on single dates until she was sixteen. She would eventually get pregnant at fifteen and drop out of high school. I certainly hope *that* hadn't been a group date. Either way, I believe she's now working the accessory counter of some department store in the local mall, and despite (or maybe because of) all the makeup she wears, looks twice her age. Her legs no longer look like broomsticks, though. Very nice. I just can't help but think of how much better her life could've been if she'd gone to see that movie with me.

I wish I could remember what movie it was.

When she was sitting beside me in kindergarten, she wasn't pregnant. She was just looking at me with that "Aaawwwwwwmmmmm, you're in trouble" look all five-year-olds get when someone just did something heinously wrong and everyone else is glad it wasn't him…or in this case, her. My crime was what Mrs. Piper would constantly refer to on my grade card as "speaking out of turn." Imagine if, throughout life, people could only speak when it was their turn. If someone swore, would he then lose a turn? Could someone go twice in a row if she said something particularly nice? That'd be pleasant, as only polite, interesting people would get to talk a lot. No more presidential addresses, no more post game interviews with professional athletes.

I felt the desire to line-jump when Mrs. Piper drew a line across the chalkboard. In little boxes beneath this line, she wrote all twenty-six letters of our alphabet. I don't know why, but the boxes reminded me of clothespins, and I felt compelled to let the whole class know. As Mrs. Piper was leading us through the lesson, I simply stated, "It looks like my mother's clothesline." What's the big deal about that?

Well, Mrs. Piper sure thought it was a big deal. She was over me like a hawk on a field mouse, and before I could find an old tire or cinder block under which to hide, I was bent over her knee, looking at shoes that were nothing like mine. Actually, the hawk analogy is somewhat inaccurate because Mrs. Piper looked more like a crow. Despite being at least in her sixties, she had jet black hair and sharply angled glasses that formed a perfect triangle with her pointed nose. With her manner of dress, she would've looked more at home as a 19th century school marm, or at least a guard at an East German female prison. She spanked me six times, but it wasn't the pain that made me cry. It was the humiliation. Not even my parents had the nerve to spank me in public, yet this woman had somehow been authorized to humiliate me in front of my peers as if we were back in medieval England and I'd just denounced the King of Bretagne.

I knew right there that I would never call Mrs. Piper "friend."

As it came to pass, I ended up considering very few teachers to be friends. In first grade, I was spanked now and again because, as far as I could tell, things that I found to be funny, others didn't. I wonder how people such as Andy Kauffman made it through first grade. It's been said that laughter is the best medicine, but apparently only when it's prescribed by teachers or parents or anyone else in authority. When the teacher laughed, we all could. But when it was just me, it was "speaking out of turn;" a spanking offense.

I finally learned this lesson by second grade. Like all the kids who got citizenship awards at the end of each week, I sat at my desk in the third row and never said a word and minded my own business and only spoke when given authorization by the woman with the wooden ruler at the front of the room. I thought I finally had the system licked, but then my report cards started claiming something else that greatly disturbed my parents; the "speaking out of turn" comment was replaced with "lacks concentration."

There's just no way to win in second grade.

Although my parents would constantly discuss this with me, I never got spanked for it. Thus, I avoided corporal punishment all through second grade.

Well, nearly, but I separate this spanking from all the others I received in school because this one actually taught me something. With this spanking came the most important lesson I've ever learned.

It happened like this. It was during the spring, and although the sun was just starting to shine on a regular basis, it was still fairly cold outside. Therefore, as grades one through three returned to the building from lunch recess, most kids were still wearing coats, hats and gloves. Upon entering the hallway, all the boys removed their hats. I was still cold, so I kept mine on. No sooner had I reached my classroom when my teacher, Mrs. Garvin, a slightly younger, tighter version of Mrs. Piper, scolded me in front of some other kids for leaving on my hat. She delivered a well rehearsed speech about how it's common courtesy to remove one's hat when indoors, but she never explained why. She then yanked the hat from my head and said I couldn't have it back until the end of the day. I didn't understand that punishment because I was inside now, and I wasn't going to need it, but I didn't point this out. I was afraid it might be deemed funny, and I didn't feel like getting spanked.

Once the scene was over, we all headed to the back of the class where the cloakroom was located. I was hanging my "cloak" when I saw a girl still wearing her hat. I can't remember her name, but I can remember that her hat was a hand knitted, blue and white atrocity that covered her ears and the back of her neck. Having just been taught this lesson, I felt I should spread the good word and promptly relieved this girl of her fine chapeau. Just as I was about to explain it's not courteous to wear one's hat indoors, I suddenly got that strange feeling of being a mouse again, this time trapped between the floor and the downward arc of a broom. Before I could react, Mrs. Garvin grabbed me by the arm and marched me out into the hallway.

"Whaddid I do?" I yelped, still holding the girl's hat in my hand. "You said we ain't allowed to wear hats inside."

"*Are not* allowed, and that rule's for boys only," Mrs. Garvin explained as she spun me around the doorway. I tripped over a pile of boots and lunch boxes and slammed my shoulder against the wall. "You should know that. Now you stay in this hallway until you feel you can behave as a good young man."

She then tore the hat from my hand and stormed back into the classroom. Before she shut the door, locking me out of her cell, I saw that the girl who owned the hat was crying. What's up with that? It pissed me off. I mean, look, I had no problem with getting yelled at, and I preferred it when my punishment was sitting in the hallway.

But that girl really got on my nerves, crying over something that stupid. All the injustices in the world—already apparent to a second grader, even—and she was bawling over a stupid little hat that was pretty ugly to begin with. It angered me to the point that I wasn't content to just sit there and lack some concentration for a while, enjoying a fine Life Saver. I hated crybabies, and I was going to let her know. After searching around, I found her lunch box nestled in with the others. I knew it was hers because she was the only one in school with a lunch box that promoted Holly Hobbie. I remember this because, in first grade, it was one of the things for which I got spanked for finding funny.

Making sure that Mrs. Garvin couldn't see around the cardboard cut-out of the little, red-headed leprechaun that guarded her door, I picked up the vintage, metal Holly Hobbie lunch box and hid it behind the large cooler that chilled the milk for the kindergarteners. I then slumped against the wall and waited for Mrs. Garvin to come out and end my "punishment."

I don't know if I thought that would be the end of it, but it of course wasn't. The brat started crying again the next day, and Mrs. Garvin explained to the class that the girl had lost her lunch box and would be in trouble with her parents if she didn't find it. She then asked for volunteers to help in the search, and I—like the chump I was—raised my hand. Yesterday I just wanted to see the crybaby suffer, but here was my chance to be her hero. Mrs. Garvin was clever and didn't pick me right away, but I was eventually chosen to join Holly Hobbie's search and rescue party. We were let out to the hallway where, after pretending to search around a bit, I found the lunchbox. I marched triumphantly into the classroom, the prize held high above my head as if it were the Stanley Cup.

It didn't take me long to realize my mistake. No sooner had I relinquished the prize when Mrs. Garvin turned on me like a revolving door.

"I knew it was you, Mr. Lindsey. I felt you might have hidden it yesterday when you were in the hallway," she scolded. "You just cannot seem to stay out of trouble, young man."

Mrs. Garvin always called me "Mr. Lindsey" and "young man" when she was yelling at me. I think she believed that if she referred to me as an adult, then she could punish me as an adult and not as a seven-year-old child.

"I chose you to find that lunchbox because I was sure you would go right to where you had hidden it, and I was right." Actually, she was wrong. As I mentioned, I purposely pretended to look in some other places before I looked behind the cooler. She could've at least given me that much, but I knew there was no use arguing. She was too busy revealing her evil plot like the villain in a James Bond movie. All she needed was a cat to stroke. "Before I send you to the principal's office, I want you to apologize to Pussy Galore."

Okay, Mrs. Garvin didn't really didn't call the girl with the hat Pussy Galore. I'm sure that grade school teachers are strongly cautioned against using the word "pussy" in the classroom. But for lack of a name better than "girl with the hat," I thought I'd carry the James Bond analogy one step further.

"I'm sorry for finding your lunchbox," I apologized to Pussy (see what I mean?). I thought my joke was kind of funny, but Mrs. Garvin sure didn't think so. Neither did anyone else in the class. They all sat stone-faced as Mrs. Garvin again marched me to the hallway. I wished my best friend Terry Hogan had been in my class that year. He would've laughed. Even though our shoes were no longer the same, he still would've laughed. As it were, I was now aware that I was to be spanked. I'd just told a joke, after all, and I needed to be brought swiftly to stern justice.

Mr. Steele was very calm about the whole thing. I sat in his secretary's office and listened to Mrs. Garvin's muffled babbling as I watched the secretary beat out punky rhythms on her old, dark green, metal typewriter. She had really long, dark red fingernails, and she typed very slowly so she wouldn't break them. Either that or she was just a really lousy typist.

Mrs. Garvin soon left the office, shooting me a wicked look as she walked past, and Principal Steele asked me to come in. He told me to close the door, then ordered me to sit in the chair across from his desk. I did both, popping a Wint-O-Green Life Saver in my mouth; I needed something to enjoy throughout all of this. Mr. Steele then repeated the events of the day, and asked if they were all true. I said, "I suppose," and kind of shrugged.

"You suppose," he repeated. "Then how do you suppose I should punish you?"

I was going to tell him that he should spank me, mainly because I knew he was going to anyway and I at least wanted to get something right out of all of this, but I instead just said, "I don't know."

"You don't know." He repeated. He was doing a lot of that. "Well, I have a good idea."

He opened his drawer, and I knew he was going to pull out a paddle. I wanted to see what else he had in that drawer, to see what else principals considered important enough to store with their paddles, but he was too quick. He was walking towards me before I had time to get up from the chair.

"You're wearing a Cub Scout uniform," he pointed out. He was right. I was. "Would you care to tell me what it means to be a Cub Scout?"

"I don't know," I told him. I really didn't know. I only joined because my best friend Terry Hogan did. And in Cub Scouts, everyone wore the same shoes.

"You don't know." He was driving me nuts. I felt I was about to be punished by a parrot. Polly want a spanking? "Well to me, being a Cub Scout means being honest and trustworthy."

I almost started to laugh. I didn't know that Mr. Steele, at his age, was still a Cub Scout. He should've at least earned his Wolf Badge by now.

"Do you think that hiding [that girl's] lunch box was an honest and trustworthy thing to do?" he continued.

"I don't know," I said, knowing he was about to repeat my answer. He did, but he also told me to lean over my chair. Again, I did as I was told.

Principal Steele was unique at my grade school in that he seemed to spank kids with intent to inflict pain rather than to just make a point. I was crying after the first hit. I lost my Life Saver after the second. By the forth, I couldn't even remember why I was there. As Mr. Steele climbed up to five…six…seven whacks, I learned the most valuable lesson of my entire life:

After doing something wrong, no matter how horrible and no matter what the reason, never admit it to anybody. Ever.

Before I left the principal's office, my butt burning red through my well pressed, navy blue Cub Scout pants, Mr. Steele told me he wanted me to write a paragraph on what it meant to me to be a Cub Scout.

I wrote the paragraph that night.

I quit the Cub Scouts the next day.

CHAPTER 2

The Red Rooster

I rarely saw the Arbiter throughout my first year at Floodbane College. This is surprising, as Floodbane wasn't all that big a school. It enrolled only about fifteen hundred students, fifty percent of whom were freshmen. Funny thing is, only about half these students survived that first year. Floodbane always took in more freshmen than it could house and feed, knowing many would drop out. At the open forum with the president of the college (an event held the second week of each school year because the president believed the students wouldn't have yet found much about which to complain), the question as to why the college grossly over-enrolled freshmen was invariably asked. In fact, because it was only the second week of the school year, it was pretty much the only question asked.

"…and that's why there never have been and never will be spoons in the cafeteria," President Tunney enforced, pounding his fist against the podium. He then lowered his head to stare over the top of his bifocals, out at the twelve or so students who gave up their Saturday night to voice their concerns. That was another belief held by the President; schedule the open forum at ten o'clock on a Saturday night when most of the students were otherwise engaged in their weekend vices. In fact, it was rumored that to ensure this result, the

President bribed the bar owners to offer twenty-five cent pitchers of beer, and he reduced security by half so there was less chance of the frat boys and sorority girls getting themselves caught in positions that would require them to attend a school hearing, thereby forcing the President to leave the solitude of his mansion more than his customary once or twice a year. It all worked so beautifully.

"Now I'll open up the floor to your questions," the President said as he waved his right hand before him, sweeping it across the podium to indicate that his "your" meant us. With this gesture, the twelve of us suddenly became highly uncomfortable, cowering away from any questions we might've raised as if asking them would result in some sort of electric shock zapped through our chairs or a two ton weight dropped on our heads. So, instead of voicing our concerns, we stared at our laps or scratched the backs of our necks or performed whatever eccentric habits we'd developed to help us cope with such situations. And those of us who had no eccentric habit developed one on the spot. Mine became squeezing my palms together quickly, thereby producing a flatulent sound which would've gotten me spanked quite often back in Mrs. Garvin's class, I'm sure. I should point out I only resorted to this nervous habit because I had no Life Savers handy.

Finally, one girl stood up. She wore large, round glasses and had a large, round butt that seemed to sigh with relief when all the pressure was released from it as she stood. Looking at the girl, I'd never felt so sympathetic towards a butt before. But I so respected her for having the courage to stand before the President that I didn't think it fair or polite to place all my attention on her ass.

"I have a question, Mr. President," the girl began. "I'm currently liv—"

"Please, miss lady," the President interrupted. "You need not be so formal as to call me Mr. President. You can call me just President."

The girl stopped for a moment then turned to look at the rest of us to see how we were responding to this request by "President." We weren't responding at all, and she wouldn't have been able to tell if we had been because we were seated so far apart. The forum was being held in the one thousand-plus seat theater that was named after President—President's Performing Arts Theatre for the Performing Arts—and those of us in the audience were a good fifteen to twenty feet away from one another. Compounding this, the lighting had been brought down so far that it only served to show us how large was the butt of the person talking.

Realizing she was getting no feedback from the other audience members, the girl struggled onward. "President, I'm—"

"Thank you," President interrupted once again.

"Excuse me?" the girl asked.

"Thank you," President repeated. He didn't even change his inflection. He repeated it so solidly that he sounded like a wax dummy in a history museum—a Ben Franklin or a Fonzie—who did nothing more than say "Thank you" each time some youngster pushed his button. "Thank you for calling me President."

"You're welcome?" the girl said with hesitant politeness. She then stared about her again as if trying to remember what she wanted to ask. I was relieved that her eccentric habit didn't involve the production of flatulent noises.

After another second or two of uncomfortable silence, she remembered, "President, I'm currently living in a room with three other girls, whereas…now don't get me wrong, I love them and we get along very well, like sisters…but the room is designed to hold two girls. There are only two beds, two desks, two chairs, two closets."

"Why do you only have two of everything if there are four of you in a room?" President asked. He seemed awfully concerned.

"The room only came with two of everything," the girl explained. "That's all we were assigned."

"Then why do you have four girls living there?"

"Because that's what we were assigned."

"I thought you just said that you were only assigned two."

"Right. Two of everything."

"Then you were assigned two roommates?"

"No. Three."

"So there are only three of you living there?"

"No. Four."

"How do you get four?"

"I have three roommates, plus me is four."

"How many roommates do *they* have?"

"Well, they each have three as well."

"All three of you have three roommates?"

"All four of us have three roommates."

"If four people have three roommates each, then that's...what? Twelve girls in one room?"

"No. Mathematically, that'd actually be sixteen girls."

"How can you fit sixteen girls in one room?"

"We can't! There aren't sixteen of us! There are four of us in one room!"

"And you're upset about that? Think of the girls who have sixteen roommates." A pause. "I know I will. Why, they'd have to share a—"

The Dean of Students quickly stood up, whispered something in President's ear, then returned to his seat. President looked ahead and said, "Let me understand this. There are four women living in one room, none of whom have any roommates. Is that correct?"

"If I say yes, will you understand that there are four of us living in one room?"

President answered, "Yes," as if that should've been obvious.

The girl was trying so valiantly to keep her cool through this. "Then yes," she said, holding out the S like a snake hissing.

"So then what's the problem?"

"The problem, as I stated before, is that the room is designed to only hold two girls!"

"And yet you're living with four girls?"

"I'm not! I'm living with three!"

At this point, some guy in the very back sung out, "Where the kisses are hers and hers and hers and hers…" I didn't get the reference at the time, but only because the conversation between the freshman girl and President had me captivated. I sensed she was about to blow her cool and pull a gun from her purse and kill everyone in the room, and apparently the Dean of Admissions sensed this as well; he stood once more and asked President if he could speak. President agreed and, although he didn't leave the podium, he did push the microphone over so the dean could be heard.

"We in the admissions office, located on the first floor of Admissions…if you ever need to discuss any problems you're having about financial aid and class scheduling, or if you just need help adjusting to college life or need a friendly ear onto which you can pour out all of your problems onto, we're always there for you between the hours of nine and eleven in the morning and from one to four in the afternoon by appointment only except for Tuesdays, Wednesdays and Fridays.

"We at admissions realize that there's usually always a student housing problem during the first semester. To keep the rising costs of tuition down, we over-enroll to compensate for the students who quickly realize that college life is not for them. Because our dropout average averages half of our freshman dropouts, we over enroll so that those who stay will not be left without a roommate."

"But why do so many students drop out?" the girl asked.

"Inadequate housing accommodations, mainly."

And so it went at the yearly President's Forum at Floodbane College. Nothing was ever really discussed, so nothing was ever resolved. In fact, most of the students didn't even know that the forums existed because they were never promoted. I only attended that one my sophomore year because I happened by the theater the night it was being held. My original intention was to go to the student union to play some video games, but the game room was closed.

The game room in the student union was a peculiar enough place. It sported two bumper pool tables, a skeeball game (the prize tickets from which could only be redeemed for more skeeball tokens), a 1980 *Flash Gordon* pinball machine that was missing the left flipper, and two video games—Crazy Climber and Dig Dug—from the early eighties, both of which suffered from intense phosphor burn-in. And although Floodbane refused to buy more up-to-date machines, it did have technicians come in to install the anti-drug message that comes up at the end of most video games. It's the one the player reads after losing the game which reminds him or her that, "Winners don't use drugs." I always found this to be quite curious. Having just *lost* a video game, children all across America were being told that *winners* don't use drugs. Do the math.

Anyway, when I asked why the game room had closed so early on a Saturday, I was told by the janitor that President was on campus. To celebrate, the student workers who ran the place decided to shut down early and go out with their friends to get drunk on quarter pitchers and maybe take a couple of girls back to their frat house. I asked the janitor if President Tunney's (I didn't yet know to refer to him only as President) visit was cause for this type of celebration. He just shrugged and continued to mop as he explained that it made more sense than the previous week when the boys decided to close down early and go out with their friends to get drunk and maybe take a couple of girls back to their frat house in honor of the cafeteria adding chipped beef gravy on toast to the breakfast menu that morning. I disagreed with the janitor on this one; that chipped beef gravy on toast is good eating.

After I became aware of what a debacle the forums were, I realized the only way the Floodbane system could be changed was if people were to actually attend these things. And the only way to accomplish this would be to publicize them. To do that, I'd have to get on the newspaper staff.

And so it came to pass that, two nights later, I made this suggestion to the newspaper's advisor at the organizational meeting. Having no idea who I was or what I was doing there, he asked, "Do you really want the whole campus to know that you had absolutely nothing better to do on a Saturday night than attend President's Forum?"

Thus, the revolution was quelled. I slumped back in my creaking, wooden seat and watched as the advisor listened to the other pitches and systematically reject them. Of course, most of them were pretty bad. One student proposed doing a semester long study of the differences between male and female college students ("Because they're funny," was his justification, "like females get drunk to party and males get party to drunk...get...dr...you know what I mean."), and another thought a whole page of Mad-Libs would increase sales...despite the fact that the papers were already free. But good ideas or not, most students quickly realized they'd rather be out getting drunk than scraping for a position on *A Daily Planet*.

I never did find out why the paper was named *A Daily Planet*. It perplexed me not because of its relationship with Perry White's paper (Floodbane dropped *The* from the name and replaced it with *A* in order to avoid a lawsuit from DC Comics, which came anyway after naming the campus literary magazine *The Aquaman*), but instead because *A Daily Planet* was published only once a week. Always had been. Any logical thought would've led to the paper being named *A Weekly Planet*. As I was quickly discovering, logical thought wasn't part of the curricula at Floodbane College.

The few of us who refused to retreat from the meeting were assigned positions by default. The editor and his main assistants were given positions based on previous experience on the paper because, as the academic advisor stated, "They're used to the threats." The rest of us were assigned our duties completely at random. This is how I became co-copy editor with the Arbiter.

As we were filing out of the room, I found myself side by side with the guy who told my freshman orientation class that he knew voodoo. My curiosity piqued; had anything more exciting happened to him since then? Despite the fact we sat next to each other throughout the duration of that freshman class, we never once spoke. I saw him occasionally in the cafeteria or walking around campus, but even then I never stopped to talk. He was usually surrounded by a group of people, and I hated groups of people. Groups of three were actually too large for me. Any more than that and I'd usually just sign off like a UHF channel after midnight (I wouldn't sing the National Anthem, though). I rarely left my dorm room and certainly didn't participate in any of the social mixers on Friday and Saturday nights. It was probably because of my reclusive nature that my dormmates would throw beer bottles at my window and yell at me for no apparent reason. Their actions upset me at first, and I went through many packs of Life Savers, but I quickly turned them to my advantage; it was impossible for me to hold onto a roommate. I went through three in my first month, and then managed to keep a single room for the rest of the year. Even as some freshman were sleeping on floors in rooms with three other students, I was by myself. It took me a while to convince the Housing Department of the Admissions Department that this was for the best, but after someone attacked my door with an aluminum baseball bat one Tuesday morning at about four, I was able to persuade them by using the personal safety clause in the College Handbook. I was a health hazard. I later learned they allow homosexuals to live alone, but I chose not to use that excuse. I was sure my dormmates would then take the baseball bats to my head instead of just my door.

Incidentally, the drunken freshman who attacked my door tried to tell the resident assistant that I had attacked my own door. Imagine that. I didn't even own a bat.

Because of my social status, I was surprised when the Arbiter struck up a conversation in the hallway of the student union.

"Hey buddy," he greeted.

I turned to see if he was talking to me, then replied with, "Yeah?"

"Going to be partners," he said, offering his hand. "Name's the Arbiter."

For some reason it surprised me that he introduced himself this way. "I thought it was Papa Shango."

The Arbiter stared at me blankly. "Why would you think that?"

"That's how you introduced yourself in freshman orientation last year," I explained.

He continued to stare at me for a moment, then eased his expression. "Wonder why."

I shrugged. "My name's Guy Lindsey."

"Guy Lindsey…wait. You *were* in that orientation class. You sat two feet away and never once said, 'Hi,' or 'How was your weekend,' or 'If that freak teacher doesn't shut her bulbous mouth I'll scream like a little school girl in a carnival fun house,' or anything."

"That's because you were sleeping most of the time," I explained.

A smile curled in the corner of The Arbiter's mouth. "Think the only time you spoke all semester, in fact, was when you introduced yourself."

"That's probably true. I can't remember back that far. I try to forget the past."

"You know they say if you forget history, you're doomed to repeat it."

"They also say that ignorance is bliss."

The Arbiter thought about this a moment. "You know, when you think about it, they really do contradict themselves a lot. They also say 'don't throw good money after bad,' and then they turn right around and say 'in for a penny, in for a pound.'"

"Or 'all that glitters is not gold,'" I added. "They've had a lot to say over the years. And besides, history is going to repeat itself no matter what. It's those who remember it who are doomed."

The Arbiter raised his eyebrows, then turned back ahead. When we reached the end of the hallway, I threw open the door hard enough so that he and I could both get through before it closed. The early fall wind greeted us immediately, lightly cleansing us with sprinkles of mist from the fountain in front of the student union. To the left of the fountain was a sign which said simply "Student Union." The building, like most others at Floodbane, had no formal name.

"Can even remember what you said at orientation," the Arbiter told me as his white shirt began to glow a fluorescent purple in the electric-blue light of the fountain. "You said, 'My name's Guy Lindsey, and I'm five years old.' Thought it was hilarious."

I didn't recall anyone finding it hilarious. "I don't remember you laughing."

The Arbiter thought for a moment. "Papa Shango no laugh."

"Well, whatever," I responded. "And how about you? Do you still know voodoo?"

The Arbiter did laugh this time. He laughed quite heavily in fact. He had an honest, genuine laugh that made me feel like he really did find my question funny. It'd been a long time since I heard a laugh like that, and it kind of made me happy…even though I was expecting Mrs. Piper to swoop down on me from out of the darkness for making someone laugh without first getting her permission. I could see now why the Arbiter always had so many people hanging around him.

Although he was by no means muscular, the Arbiter was in pretty good shape. He stood nearly six feet and looked to weigh about 180 pounds, only slightly chunky around the middle. His face was stern, accented by eyes that were blue. Not light blue or midnight blue or any other variation of the color. Simply blue. His dark brown hair was neatly trimmed and combed on top, but tattered wildly behind his neck, causing it to sprout forth from behind his ears like weeds from under a fence. I couldn't tell if that was natural or had gotten that way from lack of grooming.

Looking at him, I could tell the Arbiter was the kind of guy strangers wouldn't hesitate to approach for directions.

"Hey listen, you got any plans tonight?" the Arbiter asked.

I was shocked as hell. No one at Floodbane had ever asked me to do anything. I was starting to worry.

"Why?"

"Just wanted to see if you wanted to hang out."

"You're not gay, are you?" I asked.

Again, he laughed that genuine laugh of his. "No, but there's a lot of life ahead yet. It's just that most people are out at the bars tonight to take advantage of the 'free beer for every pitcher' deal."

"How much are the pitchers?"

"Seventeen bucks."

"Seventeen…! Do they get to keep them?"

"No."

"Hardly seems like a deal to me."

"People don't need deals to get drunk, they need excuses. But anyway, everyone out will already be drunk, and it's only fun to hang around drunks if you get to watch them get there, you know?"

"No."

"Once saw some guy get a shot glass stuck in his mouth. The moron was trying to do a blow job, only the glass slid inside his teeth. His lips wrapped around it like a snake swallowing an egg, and the suction held it there for the next five minutes or so. Almost had to call the fire department to get it out. You just can't write a joke better than that."

"So if it's so funny, why don't you want to go tonight?"

"Wrestling's on."

"You're a wrestling fan?"

"Yeah, why? You know someone who isn't?"

I can't say I was surprised by this. His reference last year to Papa Shango certainly indicated he was a longtime fan. Yet most people don't readily and proudly admit to being fans of professional wrestling. No matter how high it may climb in the peaks and valleys of its popularity, wrestling will always be considered the "fake" sport. A second-rate or even third-rate form of entertainment geared towards juvenile and immature audiences. To the "educated" or "real athletes," wrestling fans were like drug users; they acknowledged their existence and may have even known a few, perhaps dabbled in it themselves in college, but really hoped none of them were relatives.

Yet there I was outside of Student Union Student Union at Floodbane College, and I felt like I was about to come out of the closet. "I love wrestling! Who's your favorite wrestler?"

"Hate them all."

I stopped walking for a moment. I needed my brain to sit perfectly still so I could try to figure this guy out.

"Then why watch it if you hate all the wrestlers?" I asked.

"Love wrestling," he explained. "Just hate wrestlers."

"I don't understand," I confessed as we started walking again.

"Sure you do," the Arbiter reassured me, "you just don't know that you understand."

"I don't understand that, either," I confessed again.

"That's understandable."

I accepted this, and the two of us continued up the sidewalk until I could no longer hear the fizzing of the fountain water splashing into itself. We were quiet for a moment before I was suddenly overwhelmed by my total lack of comprehension of what the Arbiter had just told me.

"No! You mean to say that you watch wrestling every week and yet you hate every wrestler?" I asked, knowing that this wouldn't help anything at all.

"Exactly," the Arbiter said.

"Isn't that kind of like watching another TV show week after week and hating all the characters?" I continued, thinking I was cornering him in his own philosophy.

I wasn't, and I would have to get used to that.

"It's also like enrolling for classes here and hating all your professors," the Arbiter added, "or voting for president and hating all the candidates."

Up ahead, a sports car turned onto the road and headed towards us. I think it was playing some kind of heavy metal or rap music on the radio…I could only hear the bass and the drums.

After it passed, I turned back to the Arbiter. "You've never liked any wrestlers?"

He thought for a moment. "Well, no. Not since the Red Rooster left."

"The Red Rooster?!" I almost yelled. "All the thousands of wrestlers throughout history and the only one you pick to like is Terry Taylor?! Why?!"

"No, hated Terry Taylor. Liked the Red Rooster."

"It was the same guy," I explained.

"Know that," the Arbiter explained. "Hated the man, liked the incarnation."

"Why?"

"Felt sorry for the Red Rooster," the Arbiter said. "He had to play such a pathetic role. All the time clucking. Ain't no grown man should have to cluck for a living."

I stared at him for a good ten seconds, but he didn't return my gaze. Instead, he merely said, "Suppose you liked Hulk Hogan."

"The greatest of all time. Well, before he went south…then came back north," I replied. "The Immortal Hulk Hogan. 'I got something deep inside of me. Courage is the thing that keeps us free.'"

"The immortal prima-donna showboat. He only knew six maneuvers, and two of them involved cupping his hand to his ear," the Arbiter argued. "You only liked him because everyone else did."

I started to laugh at this point. There we were, two college students who had never held a conversation before, and five minutes into our first we were arguing about professional wrestlers, one of whom had the same name as my best friend in grade school. Close enough, anyway, as Hulk Hogan's real name is Terry Bollea. I don't know what my friend Terry's real name was. Instinctively, I looked down at the Arbiter's shoes. They were white Asics…exactly like mine.

The Arbiter was wrong about why I liked Hulk Hogan, however. He was my best friend Terry Hogan's favorite, and he and I used to get together every Saturday to watch wrestling on cable. We started watching it in third grade; one year after I'd been spanked for hiding Holly Hobbie and three years before I would get spanked for the last time in my life.

❀   ❀   ❀

It wasn't my parents who smacked my adolescent butt for the final time; it was Mrs. Patera, my sixth grade teacher. It was kind of sad because, until that day, Mrs. Patera had been my favorite. I bet her a quarter every Friday throughout the fall that our community's high school football team would lose. They ended up 2-8 on the season, so I cleared one dollar and fifty cents.

I can't remember on what I spent my winnings, but I'm sure I don't have it anymore.

It was all a big joke to me and Mrs. Patera, and it gave my dad and her something about which to laugh on Sunday mornings in church (as if the children's bell choir weren't already enough). I soon came to realize that most of my classmates didn't share the humor. I guess it was because some of them had older brothers on the team. One kid even served as the spit boy…or whatever they call the chump who runs the water bottle out to the players while they're in the hud-dle.

The student who harbored the most animosity towards me was Heath Millard. His dad was the John Stuart Mill High School health teacher and, therefore, coach of the John Stuart Mill High School Fightin' Golden Sandies. There was apparently a rule at JSMHS that all health teachers had to coach football…or maybe that all football coaches had to teach health. Either way, both positions were always filled with incompetence.

The Fightin' Golden Sandies claimed only two victories a year for something like eight consecutive years, and never from the same teams. We managed to beat every high school in our conference, just never during the same season. The head of the athletic department was constantly hiring new health teachers to try to take care of this problem, but it was all for naught. Our boys just seemed to have it burned into their flunking-but-still-eligible-to-play minds that they were only required to win two games. If they won them early on, they'd slack off the rest of the season. If they lost the first eight, they'd defy the odds and close the season by beating teams they had no right to beat. I realize now I should've bet Mrs. Patera much more than just that quarter. As a kid, however, betting more than a quarter would've probably led the school board to think I had a gambling problem and, therefore, a lack of parental supervision which would've landed me in a home, my parents in jail, and my story on a Lifetime movie with Meredith Baxter stretching her acting wings by playing the lesbian social worker who saves me despite a broken home and an alcoholic father who hasn't been able to forgive his wife for dying of a brain aneurysm seven years before.

Because of the lackluster football, the highlight of each game was the marching band show. John Stuart Mill had one hell of a marching band. They had won so many area marching competitions that the only way they could get invited after a while was as "featured performers," removed from competition so another school could win. To see the John Stuart Mill High School Marchin' Fightin' Golden Sandies Marching Band was the only reason I ever went to the football games, and it was my dream to one day be down there on the damp, evening grass, looking up into the stadium lights as they reflected tiny, shimmering crosses off the brass of my very own Conn trombone.

To admit this dream to anyone, however, would have achieved the same results as if I were to…oh, wear Mrs. Patera's underwear to school one day, especially with Heath Millard in class.

It's not really like Heath and I hated each other…yet. I doubt anyone even really hated another student in sixth grade. Well, maybe Hitler. Hitler probably hated people in sixth grade.

> "Mrs. Fraulich! Mrs. Fraulich! Do not call on zee second row, only zee sird row! Zee people in zee second row are weak unt shtupid! We in zee sird row are superior at zee arithmetic unt zee shpelling!"

Heath and I were complete opposites and had absolutely no business even belonging in the same phylum, let alone classroom. Unfortunately, the few friends with whom I was left when my best friend Terry Hogan moved away to Toledo were better friends with Heath. And because Heath was the coolest sixth grader around, I had to pretend to like him in order for his friends to pretend to like me.

I think Heath was aware of my true feelings, which may be why I was always the target for his jokes and snide comments. I had to take them. I had to suffer through them in order to suffer through his friendship so I could remain friends with people who really weren't worth it. I was in sixth grade, and kids who don't have friends in sixth grade get sent by the school board to homes they've never seen as they watch their parents sign those aforementioned Meredith Baxter movie deals with Lifetime executives…assuming Lifetime has executives.

Now that I think about it, I could've single-handedly jump started Meredith Baxter's career.

Want to know how bad it was between me and Heath? He ate fruity Life Savers, the freak. The few similarities Heath and I did share began to dissolve in junior high when the unpopular were finally weeded out from the popular, and they completely eroded in high school when he became a Fightin' Golden Sandie and I became a Marchin' Fightin' Golden Sandie. Our differences were accentuated by the fact that he excelled in everything while I wallowed in mediocrity. Only a sophomore, Heath Millard was already the starting varsity quarterback. At that same time, I was still the last chair trombone player. This made no sense to me, either. I spent every free moment I had practicing that damn trombone. I practiced in the band room during study hall when I should've been studying. I practiced in my bedroom at night when I should've been sleeping. I practiced at the dinner table when I should've been eating a pork chop.

I marched in front of the mirror and down the hall. When mom called me to dinner, I'd march to the table. I stood at attention when spoken to, and I stood at parade rest when I wasn't spoken to. When I walked to school, it was in beat with the John Stuart Mill High School fight song (a highly militant arrangement of "Onward Christian Soldiers"). When I took notes in class, they were in the key of B flat. I realized early on, I think, that this was all for naught, but that only made me work harder. I often wonder why the band director didn't just kick me out. Maybe he liked my dedication, or maybe—like most everyone—he simply didn't know I was there. There was little else I could do, anyway. Trombone was all I knew, so I clung to it like Captain Lawrence of the Chesapeake barking, "Don't give up the ship!" as the British took it in the War of 1812.

But then came Ann Penella.

It was at the beginning of my sophomore year—immediately after I'd again scored last chair in try-outs—that my destiny with Ann began to take shape. Because I was in the practice room running over the tryout piece again, trying to figure out just what the hell went wrong, I missed the sign-up for bus seats to the away games. By the time I got to the list, the band buses had all been filled.

It didn't surprise me, really. I mean, I got along okay with some of the other musicians, but it's not as if we ever hung out. I certainly could not have expected them to save me a seat. It would've helped if I'd had some enemies, they might have assigned me to another bus just to make sure I didn't end up on theirs. Instead, I was completely forgotten by everyone. Although the band probably wouldn't miss me, the spectators would surely see a hole in the marching line if I weren't there. Realizing this, I took my dilemma to the band director.

Mr. Bravo's door was open after class had ended that day, so I slowly stepped in. The room smelled like that musty area of the basement where dad kept his *Playboys* (do all dads purposely do a terrible job of hiding their smut?), and there were scores of music sheets scattered about his desk and the shelves behind it. The afternoon sun shone in from the single window behind Mr. Bravo's desk and reflected light off the spot on his head from which his hair was cowardly retreating.

Hearing the music scores slide beneath my feet, Mr. Bravo turned around. He looked at me quizically, then picked up his grade book.

"Guy Lindsey," I pointed out, trying to save him the time.

Mr. Bravo didn't reply and instead picked up his sectional listing.

"Last chair trombone," I continued.

Mr. Bravo still made no sound, but raised a pudgy finger to run across his two chins. He then grabbed the chart for that week's marching band show.

"Number thirty-nine," I added.

His eyes immediately lit up. "Ah, yes," he beamed. "Nice glide step."

"Thank you," I smiled, knowing he was probably mistaking me for someone else. "Mr. Bravo, I have a bit of a problem."

"You're not satisfied with your tryout?" he asked. He definitely wasn't confusing me with someone else.

"Well, no, I'm not satisfied, but that's not my problem," I explained. "All the buses are full, and I didn't get a seat."

"Well, I'm not driving you home."

"I mean the band buses…for the away games."

Mr. Bravo once again adopted a look of confusion and moved his finger from his chins to scratch just behind his right ear. "How did this happen?"

"I was rehearsing and everything just kinda filled up," I shrugged.

"You rehearse?" Beat. "Well, what bus are your friends on?"

I paused. "They're…uh…they're scattered about."

Mr. Bravo stared at me for another moment, then stood up. "Well, let's go check those rosters," he suggested. He pointed for me to exit his office, then followed, stopping for a moment to straighten the picture of John Philip Sousa that adorned the wall beside the door.

The sign-up sheets had been taped to the chalkboard behind the conductor's pedestal. When we reached them, Mr. Bravo again brought his hand up to his chins and rubbed them slowly, enjoying the percussive sound his fingers made as they scratched against the stubble beneath his bottom lip.

After staring at the sign-up sheets for a few moments, he pointed out, "You're not on any of these."

I was suddenly worried that someone else may be watching this. Rehearsal had been over for a while now, however, so the room was empty.

"No, sir," I replied.

"They're full, too," Mr. Bravo pointed out.

"Yes sir," I agreed.

"Well, I don't think we can justify getting you your own bus, could we?"

I was going to answer him when, in one fluid motion, almost as if he were conducting "Durango" or another piece from the opening show, Mr. Bravo turned his head just a bit to the right, grabbed a pencil, wrote my name on a piece of paper, then headed back towards his office.

"Now you're on a bus," he said as he disappeared back into the hallway that led to his sanctum. I just stood there a moment, staring blankly at the area where he'd been standing just a moment before. I envied his power to completely rid himself of problems with a simple flick of the wrist. For a moment, I thought perhaps I should become a band director upon graduation. But the remembrance that I couldn't play a single instrument with any sort of effectiveness muted this thought.

Sighing dejectedly, I stepped forward to see onto which bus I'd been placed. The sheet he'd signed had been taped up separately from the others, so I should've realized immediately that something was amiss. I also probably should've noticed a problem when I began to scan up the list to see with whom I'd be riding. They were all girls. When I reached the top of the paper and saw that the heading read "Cheerleaders/Dance Troupe," I shouldn't have been shocked.

But I was.

There I was underneath eighteen dancers and…

    ✿   ✿   ✿

"…twenty cheerleaders!" The Arbiter yelled from the second floor lounge of Sophomore Male Male Dorm. I flushed the toilet of the lounge restroom, quickly washed my hands and walked into the TV room that forever reeked of the beer spills that had dried into the carpeting.

"What?'

"That stage must be jam-packed with twenty cheerleaders!" he exclaimed, thrilled with his discovery. "Look at them up there, all flipping around!"

"So?" I asked. "What happened to wrestling?"

The Arbiter turned to me for only a moment. "Listen. All for watching a bunch of fat, hairy, sweaty men jump all over each other in the middle of the squared circle, but this…" He pointed up to the TV. "Go…" he squinted to see the name on the banner behind the two tiers of shapely legs stacked across the screen, then added, "Hiedeger High Orangemen cheerleaders!"

"What is this then?" I asked, flopping down on the dark blue couch beside the Arbiter, causing dust to erupt forth like ash from Mount Vesuvius.

"National Cheerleader Championships," he explained. "ESPN2. Orlando. Florida. United States of friggin' A." He seemed enthralled.

I watched a few moments, but failed to see anything more than a bunch of teenagers throwing each other around a room to some messy synthesized beat.

"Oh, come on! That was a terrible basket toss," the Arbiter shouted out, using the new terms as quickly as he learned them. "Let's see some height! Let's get tight, girls! Big 'G' little 'o'! Go! Go! Go!"

"I don't see what's so interesting about this," I continued to gripe. I had this thing against cheerleaders. "Look at 'em all, smiling and shouting like they actually care about what's going on. They don't mean it. They're probably all a bunch of skanks."

"They sure are, God bless 'em," the Arbiter smiled. "Each and everyone of them. Can you imagine it? Thousands of high school girls converging on Sea World in Orlando to flip all over each other…oh man! It's hard to be humble when you can jump, cheer and tumble!"

"I think you're enjoying this a bit too much," I pointed out, but the Arbiter was oblivious to my comments.

"Can you imagine what it must be like to be a guy cheerleader down there?" he asked, not taking his eyes off the girls in the short blue and yellow skirts, which seemed an odd choice of colors for a sports collective called the Orangemen. "Can you imagine what it must be like to be away from home, probably for the first time in your life, and you're surrounded by thousands of great looking girls—the crème de la crème of high school Homecoming Queens all across this nation—and they love you just because you're a guy and you're a cheerleader and you can execute a basket toss! V-I-C-T-O-R-Y! That's the Orangemen battle cry!"

"Yeah, but most guys only become cheerleaders because they're gay and aren't interested in girls," I offered.

I was thinking back to the guy who played the Fightin' Golden Sandie mascot in high school. No one knew what a Golden Sandie was, so they dressed this guy up like a blonde, Swedish Girl—the kind of woman who was more suited to a butter label than a football helmet—and gave him boxing headgear. The head gear proved to be a blessing, as he was beaten up often. High school kids will do that to a guy who looks like a Swedish butter churner. If he wasn't gay before that, the constant beatings for it would certainly convince him he was.

I was also thinking of that cheerleader school bus I rode in high school, and the incident on it that set off the chain events that lead to my killing somebody.

The Arbiter brightened at my generalization of the sexual orientation of male cheerleaders. "But that just makes it better for those who aren't! There are probably three guys there who were just sitting around one day in study hall, maybe in the cafeteria after finishing off some pizza and green beans, trying to figure out what activity they could do in order to get scholarships, something like volunteering at the nursing home, transcribing repeats of *Murder, She Wrote* to the deaf, and one of them jokingly suggests they become cheerleaders! They're hitting each other on the shoulders like guys do, and they're laughing because they know they're going to get to cop a lot of cheap feels, and yet the girls all think it's so...no wait! One of the guys joins because his girlfriend's a cheerleader and they split up on the bus on the way down so now he's got all week and thousands of girls to use to get his old girlfriend jealous! Oh man! God bless that boy! God bless that boy and all those girls around him! God bless everyone on the TV screen right now! God bless TV! God bless pixels and cathode rays and Philo T. Farnsworth!"

"Can we just go back to wrestling?" I pleaded.

"Sure," the Arbiter replied as he flipped the remote back to World Wrestling Entertainment. He dropped back in his chair as if the channel had never been turned in the first place and immediately started to write something in a hard, gray folder that he always carried with him. I remember first seeing him with it in that freshman orientation class, but I just thought it was a regular notebook. After the semester was over, he still had it with him. Even when I saw him in the cafeteria, he was still carrying it, sometimes writing in it as if documenting what he was having for dinner that day. The thing never left his side.

The wrestling match on TV eventually ended, and I asked the Arbiter if he wanted to turn back to the cheerleaders.

"Hate cheerleaders," he replied.

My sophomore year became rather important to me, as it was then the Arbiter became my first real friend since Terry Hogan moved to Toledo. The Arbiter and I worked exceptionally well together on the newspaper staff, and it was assumed the two of us would serve as co-editors when we were seniors. Most would've been satisfied with just the Arbiter taking the position, but he made it quite clear to everyone that he and I were a team. As he often explained it to them, "Got things that need to get done here, and Guy's the only one who can help." And unlike some other people in my past, he didn't hang out with me out of pity. He wasn't ashamed to be my friend.

Oddly enough, no one seemed to mind when the Arbiter insisted he'd only work if I worked with him. He had somehow achieved the type of status where just about anything he wanted was okay by most others. If not, it was futile to oppose him. Maybe it was his brutal honesty that made it seem he never had any ulterior motives. People seemed to respect that even as he criticized them. But although he'd achieved this power to influence others without trying, he didn't abuse it.

I still wonder if this was because he was just a nice guy or if he really just didn't know he could have.

The drawback to all this was the Arbiter's popularity. He was never at a loss for people with whom he could hang out. That's not to say everyone liked him, but those who did liked him a lot. On the other hand, those who didn't flat out hated him. These people always seemed to be the extremists. Stereotypes, the Arbiter would call them.

"Stereotypes are there for a reason," the Arbiter explained to me one night while we were lying on the fifty yard line of the football field for the Floodbane College Football Players.

An aside. "Football Players" actually was the team name for the Floodbane College football team. No one really knew why. As with just about everything else at Floodbane, there was no documentation on how the team name came about. The theories were as numerous and varied as the explanations on the disappearance of the dinosaurs, the most popular of which was that Floodbane just neglected to choose a mascot. I mean, that's the Floodbane "Football Players" theory, not the dinosaur theory. I'm sure no one believes the dinosaurs became extinct because Floodbane neglected to choose a mascot.

Anyway, the name "Football Players" was then assigned by opposing teams because they needed something to hang on their banners to announce who they were going to destroy on Saturday. The alternate choice, "Talent Enhancement," just proved too difficult to chant.

It had been proposed numerous times that the name be changed, but this never got any further than a letter to the editor of A Daily Planet. The suggestion was always rebuked with the same argument, which usually came as a form letter from the current president of Floodbane:

Dear Student:

Thank you for your suggestion regarding the changing of our team mascot for the Floodbane ~~Normal School~~ College Football Players. After careful consideration, we regret to say that the mascot cannot be changed at this time as it is economically unfeasible. The money we save by simply using a third string defensive lineman as the sideline mascot instead of investing in a costume were our mascot, say, a penguin or a lug nut, is being invested in special endeavors which will ultimately keep the tuition down for you and all the students of Floodbane ~~Normal School~~ College...~~the first students in the history of this fine institution.~~

Please understand that, as we receive hundreds of suggestions a month, we are unable to send you a personal reply. This rejection is in no way a reflection of the quality of your suggestion, and we encourage you to send suggestions to other heads of things at Floodbane ~~Normal School~~ College in the future. For ~~10¢, 50¢, $1.50, $5.00, $5.05, $15.75,~~ $50.00, we will critique your suggestion and offer pointers on how to make other suggestions that may or may not get implemented in the future. Simply enclose a check and a photocopy of the suggestion in the enclosed envelope. Be advised that suggestions will not be returned and become the sole property of Floodbane ~~Normal School~~ College. Good luck, and study hard!

Yours,
President

Naming the team Floodbane College Football Players paid off in other ways as well. Swept up in the political correctness myth of the early nineties, Floodbane College sued their longtime rivals, the Ramirez College Night Stalkers, after they posted a banner which read "Kill the Floodbane College Football Players!" Representatives from Ramirez College claimed the banner was only meant as a battle cry to inspire their football players to victory and that they didn't intend to actually kill anybody, but the courts didn't see it that way and decreed that the banner violated the Floodbane College speech code. Ramirez College was forced to forfeit the game. However, no one at Floodbane bothered to document this, so the game still showed up as a loss for the Football Players.

Incidentally, the Night Stalkers were taken to court four other times that year by animal rights activists after posting banners that read "Club the Gein College Seals," "Harpoon the Chikatilo University Whales," "Net the Albert Fish College Dolphins" and "Cage Up the Chase College Calves in Cramped Quarters So That Their Meat Stays Tender, Lean and Red."

Yeah, Football Stadium was rife with scandal and ignominy. Perhaps that's why the Arbiter insisted that we go there every now and again, just to lie down on the fifty yard line and talk about things such as stereotypes.

"All stereotypes have concrete foundations," he continued. "Women are considered to be bad drivers because many of them are. Men are considered to be insensitive because many of them are. Blondes are considered to be dumb because many of them are. That doesn't mean that every blonde is dumb or that all women are bad drivers."

"Or that all men are insensitive," I added.

"No. They all are," the Arbiter corrected. "Only it doesn't matter because they just don't give a damn. You'll never see a million men marching on the White House lawn because they're portrayed by the media to be insensitive. Four hundred thousand, tops, would march. The rest just don't care. Too much wrestling to watch on the TV."

I found Orion's Belt in the stars as the Arbiter continued.

"The problem with stereotypes is that some people use them to judge individuals. You can't think a woman's a ditz and a bad driver just because she's a blonde female, but once you actually learn that she *is* a ditz and a bad driver, you can shrug it off and just say, 'Well, she is a blonde female after all.'"

Hearing him say this, I suddenly realized how true this philosophy was to the Arbiter's life. Girls who belonged to sororities always had fun with the Arbiter. Sorority sisters retched at the sight of him. Guys who played sports thought the Arbiter was great. Athletes abhorred him. People who worked for Floodbane College respected the Arbiter. University faculty and staff wanted him expelled. And amazingly, the Arbiter looked at all these people with indifference. He greeted his friends and enemies with equanimity.

When I first brought this up to him, he replied with, "What's it matter, anyway? They're all just ants." I didn't know what he meant by this, but that's the way it was with the Arbiter. I could never fully comprehend the guy, and wasn't entirely sure I wanted to.

It was his enigmatic nature that most pleased him, I think. Like Cicero, the guy had complete control over every faction of his life. Because of this, he inadvertently found himself in control of a lot of other people as well. The one exception to this was Rhonda Vorhees.

I was there when the Arbiter spoke with Rhonda for the first time, and I remember recalling that if they ever got married and had children and grandchildren, they'd have a wonderful story to tell them about how they met.

It was a Tuesday morning in late September, not even a month into our junior year of college. The Arbiter and I were on our way to Student Union when we saw a woman approaching us. I recognized Rhonda because she'd been in a couple of my classes. It was more than that, though. *Everyone* knew Rhonda. She was the girl about whom all the guys fantasized while they masturbated at night. The next day, as these future captains of industry would plod down to the lobby and slump lifelessly onto the cigarette burned sofas, they would brag about how great Rhonda had been the previous night. The guys returning from the shower would agree, saying she was just as great for them, and they'd then call their buddies back in the dorms to see if Rhonda was good for them, too. According to the guys at Floodbane College, Rhonda Vorhees was having sex at a frequency on par with the Romans under the rein of Bob Guccioni's Caligula, or at least on par with Gene Simmons of KISS.

All the sororities, therefore, did everything within their power to get Rhonda to pledge just so they'd be able to get more boys over to their houses and, in turn, more pledges. The fraternities tried to convince her to become their "Little Sister" just so their fantasies would be more believable than the next frat's. But Rhonda never entertained these offers. She turned them all down with languid and non-malicious ease, and had therefore developed many enemies across campus.

But this did not turn Rhonda into a bitter person. She was pleasant in class, and those who actually knew her always spoke highly of her character. Yet it was difficult to get to know Rhonda. In a way, her affability had built around her an impenetrable barrier.

I liked this about her. She was wonderfully gregarious with complete strangers who merely wanted to find the time or discuss the weather, but when the questions slithered on to "Hey, what's your major?" or "What are you doing this weekend?" she'd pull away as if she'd just been offered a piece of candy if only she'd climb into the El Camino. Rhonda never judged people by their actions, but by their intentions. I was sure she was the one person who wouldn't label me "killer" just because I'd killed somebody. Perhaps this is the reason, as our friendship would grow, I would become strongly compelled to confess to Rhonda that I had once killed somebody.

Well, one of the reasons.

Rhonda was a great judge of character, too. She seemed to only have to listen to one sentence from people to know from where they were coming. First impressions were everything with Rhonda Vorhees. It certainly would've saddened me, I'm sure, to see the impression I had made, but I was dying to see how the Arbiter fared.

"Who *is* she?" he asked in almost a whisper, heavily stressing the "is."

I was kind of caught off guard by this. As I mentioned, even though Rhonda had reclusive tendencies, everyone knew who she was. This is why I didn't answer the Arbiter's question.

"Isn't she something?" I said instead.

"Who *is* she?"

"She was in my art class my freshman year. I used to slide my desk over closer to hers during the slide presentations just so I could pretend we were at the movies."

"Who *is* she?"

"She was also in my biology class last year. She always—"

I was interrupted by the Arbiter's hand clenching my shirt just below my right shoulder. I turned to look at him to see what he was doing, but he was still staring fixedly at Rhonda. "*Who is she?*"

"What, are you serious?" I asked. His lack of a reply indicated he was. "Her name's Rhonda Vorhees. She's a junior with us. She hasn't been in any of your classes?"

"Would've flunked them if she were," the Arbiter replied as he let go of my shirt.

Recognizing his sudden obsession with her, I decided that I'd save him the trouble. "Forget it. She's not known to be the socialite."

"It sure is a beautiful day, isn't it," the Arbiter pointed out.

He was right, it was, but it had been all morning. I couldn't understand why he chose now to point it out. "I suppose," I agreed, looking up at the cloudless, blue sky. The last scents of the damp, morning grass were just now starting to fade from the air, and a light, fall wind was gently brushing the flowers and trees. "Kind of cold, though, I think."

"No, it's perfect," the Arbiter stated, still watching Rhonda as she came closer to us. "It's a beautiful day."

I guess I should've known he hadn't been talking about the weather, but I'd never seen the Arbiter act this way before. I'd seen him around a lot of other women, some of whom were just as physically attractive as Rhonda, but none had ever evoked this melodramatic response. In fact, other than hyper excitement, this may have been the first emotion I'd ever seen him display.

"She does have a great body, doesn't she," I offered.

"Body?" the Arbiter asked. "Haven't made it past the hair."

It was long, red and curly. Striking, but I played it coyly. I'm not sure why. "What about it?"

"That red," the Arbiter continued. "Haven't seen a red that absolute since that last Arizona sunset."

"When were you in Arizona?" I asked.

"Never," he replied.

I didn't believe in love at first sight. Even with Ann back in high school, it took me nearly a year to fall in love with her...or to at least realize I had. The whole concept of love at first sight just seemed ridiculous. Love was too multifaceted to be achieved in one meeting; a fleeting glance across a crowded room. To me, love at first sight was a notion created by romance novelists so they could skip the courtship and get right to the sex. Observing the Arbiter at that moment, however, had me reconsidering my beliefs.

Rhonda was now only about thirty feet away from us, and I'm sure she could tell the Arbiter was staring at her. She seemed to be making an effort to look away, but her eyes kept coming back. I looked almost perversely forward to the encounter. I was sure the Arbiter was about to say something so romantic and honest that it would completely demolish every wall of the beautiful, Bavarian castle Rhonda had built to protect herself. He probably would've too, had it not been for the bicyclist.

He had been coming up from behind her quickly, and, upon catching up to her, lowered his hand to grab her ass. She jumped at his touch, and he laughed as he sped by her. It took Rhonda only a second to compose herself, but by then all she could effectively do was call him a "Jerk!"

That made me smile; a woman who still chose "jerk" over the more familiar expressions available to college students at the time.

At her comment, the bicyclist looked back at her and laughed harder. He was still laughing when he turned forward just in time to ram his face hard into the Arbiter's gray folder.

The bike continued to roll forward before veering into the grass and flipping over next to a well manicured shrubbery. The rider, however, was lying on the concrete at the Arbiter's feet. He grimaced with pain as he rubbed both his backside and his nose for a moment, then looked up at the Arbiter with a face as red as Rhonda's hair, almost camouflaging the sliver of blood that trickled from his nose.

"The fuck you doing?!" he barked. I believe he was trying to sound intimidating, but—as he was still lying on the concrete, rubbing his butt—it was hard to be threatened.

"You wrecked your bike," the Arbiter helpfully pointed out.

"I'm gonna wreck your ass," the bicyclist barked as he painfully climbed to his feet.

"That's fine. It's insured." The Arbiter was completely unfazed by his threat even though the bicyclist stood a good six inches taller than he. That's not to say the bicyclist was a muscular guy, but he was in good shape. His black hair sat flatly atop of his head and was cut down to stubble around the ears and in the back. There was something odd about his face. He wasn't disfigured or anything, but he just didn't look...right. Kind of like how a skull never really seems to be in the shape of an actual human head. He was wearing a fraternity sweatshirt with plaid shorts that didn't match and deck shoes with no socks. He looked like the kind of guy the Floodbane College Public Relations Office for Relating Public Matters to and for the Public Relations—easier remembered by its initials FCPRORPMPR...well, perhaps not—would photograph incessantly for the brochures that were sent to prospective students, leading them to believe that only casually cool people attended Floodbane.

I had never seen the bicyclist around campus before, so I didn't know his name. Yet his demeanor left me uncomfortable. I had this ominous feeling the Arbiter had just made a mistake.

My fears were temporarily put to rest when the guy retreated to his bike instead of following up on his threat. Rhonda had reached us by that point, so we three stood side by side, watching as the frat boy picked up his bike and turned back to us.

"Let me just say this; if you assholes broke somethin' I'm gonna report you to my dad and he'll sue your townie asses for everything you got." He then gingerly stepped onto the bike, whiped his bleeding nose off on his sleeve, and started to ride away…being careful not to sit down.

The Arbiter turned to Rhonda who announced—quite emphatically, "I can fight my own battles."

The Arbiter raised his eyebrows a bit. "I don't doubt that for a second."

I was dying to see how his first words impacted her. The response wasn't quick in coming, however. The two of them stared at each other for a second, then the Arbiter smiled. Rhonda didn't change her expression, but she also didn't turn away. Not even when she said, "Hi, Guy."

I was shocked that she remembered my name. "Huh? Oh…uh, hi, Rhonda." I suddenly felt as though I should introduce the two of them. "Rhonda, this is—"

"I know," she interrupted. "You call yourself the Arbiter."

"No," the Arbiter countered. "That's what everyone else calls me."

Something suddenly struck me as odd, as if I were listening to a record I'd heard a hundred times before, and it just now skipped.

"Then what do you call yourself?" Rhonda persisted.

"Me. I. Myself. Whichever is grammatically correct."

Finally, Rhonda smiled. And when she did, that may have been when I…well, her hair *was* a majestic shade of red. Deep orange, really. I don't know why I hadn't noticed it until the Arbiter pointed it out. Her skin was pale, but only to the point that it highlighted her hazel eyes which slanted slightly inward towards her nose as with heroines in Disney cartoons. Her face was soft and comforting like a mother's voice as she sings her child to sleep, and I suddenly felt ashamed and sexist for only noticing her body before. Then I started to feel guilty for lusting for her face now. I was so overcome with guilt as I looked at Rhonda that I started to blush and had to turn away.

The silence made me nervous, so I tried to think of something clever to break it. I couldn't find anything, so I just stared at the concrete and kicked at a couple small rocks.

After a moment or two, Rhonda finally spoke, "It's good to see you again, Guy. We should go to the movies again soon."

"Yeah," I agreed, then stopped. "Huh?"

"Art class."

I was floored. Completely floored. "How did you…"

"During rococo, you asked if I wanted some popcorn." She then turned back to the Arbiter. "It's nice to finally meet you Arby," she said with that sweet smile. I thought for sure the Arbiter would be offended at her bastardization of his name, but he instead seemed encouraged by it.

"I'm glad to have met you also," he beamed. "Maybe I'll clothesline someone again for you sometime. Clothesline, DDT, northern lights suplex…whatever draws the big pop."

"It's a date," she said as her smile widened and she turned and continued her walk. After a moment, she turned back towards the Arbiter. "A date or a pay-per-view."

He and I watched her walk away, and I again felt remorse for staring at her this way.

"Let's go," I suggested as I turned away from her, blushing again.

"Not yet," the Arbiter insisted, not moving.

"Why not?"

"Watching the sun set."

The Arbiter's courtship of Rhonda was a joy to witness. I think this was partly because I knew that she was eventually going to feel for him the same he had immediately felt for her. It was like watching a critically panned Hollywood blockbuster; the good guys were pleasant to look at and easy to love; the bad guys were bumbling idiots and very funny, and no matter how convoluted the plot, there was always the underlying awareness that the hero and heroine would end up together.

The other reason I enjoyed watching the Arbiter romance Rhonda was because he appeared to genuinely be in love with her. I'd seen this type of behavior from guys before, but there was rarely ever love involved. And sadly, most of the women they were romancing were so wanting that they were never able to see the actual intention. But the Arbiter was genuine (Rhonda would've burnt him at the very start had he not been). There was no deception here. No hidden motive. No intent to inflict pain as Heath Millard wanted me to do to…well…

❧   ❧   ❧

It was during the spring of our sixth grade year, and we were all out at Heath's house for his birthday party. Heath was always having parties, but this was the first one to which I'd been invited. I didn't want to attend, but my parents were thrilled I'd finally been invited somewhere. Anywhere. They RSVPed Mrs. Millard a mere moment after opening the invitation.

Although Heath's birthday fell on a Thursday that year, the party took place on Saturday morning. I can remember the trepidation I felt as I walked up his driveway, carrying his gift (for under $5.00, read the invite) in one hand as I turned to wave to my mother with the other. She waved back, and, once the front door swung open for me, backed the car onto the country road and drove away.

Mrs. Millard was the woman at the door, and her tight, leathery face cracked a smile so loudly that it frightened a flock of robins from the telephone wire above.

"Hello there, young man," she greeted me, reaching out her hand to take my gift. I didn't like her smile. It was too much like Heath's.

"Hi."

"The other boys are already inside," she explained as I passed her and stepped into the house. It reeked of cats and cigarettes, but was otherwise exceptionally clean. The floor was a polished, light brown wood with assorted rugs spread throughout. Every corner had some type of stand sporting all manners of country home knick-knacks, and each wall was decorated with family pictures (mostly of Heath), paintings or clocks. It was obvious they'd been living in this house for a very long time.

I never saw one cat to explain the smell, but ashtrays were abundant. As Mrs. Millard directed me through the hallway and onto the back patio where Heath and his friends were playing a game, I passed three ashtrays with cigarettes still burning. No one acknowledged me as Mrs. Millard scooted me through the screen door, Heath's friends were too busy watching some small kid whom I'd never seen drop a clothespin into an empty, two liter Sprite bottle.

"Come on, moron, drop it," Heath chastised.

"It's too hard for me," the boy whined as if he'd been explaining that all day.

"Everything's too hard for you," Heath insulted. "That's how come you're still in fourth grade."

"I'm in fourth grade because I'm small," the boy explained with false pride that was obviously instilled by his parents.

Heath wasn't going to let him hold on to that. "Sure, that's what your Uncle Vince told ya because you're stupid and you believe it. You know you're stupid, right?"

"I guess so," the kid shrugged.

"Tell you what," Heath offered. "If you get the clothespin in the bottle, then you're not stupid. But if you miss, you're the biggest moron on the Earth. Deal?"

"But you missed," the kid pointed out.

"But I'm allowed to because I'm not stupid. Because you're stupid, you're not allowed to miss. Now drop the damn clothespin. You're the last one, and we can quit this stupid game after you're done."

The kid nervously stood over the bottle and stared down past the clothespin to the opening of the bottle like a B-17 bombardier down to a German armory. Although I didn't know the kid, I was pulling for him. I knew what it was like to be on that end of Heath's hostility. After a few moments, he let the clothespin fall. It hit the lip of the opening and bounced off to the right, much to the glee of the other boys at the party. They were all making fun of him now, but the kid looked like he'd heard all this before. I think it was only because I didn't join them that they finally noticed I was there. Seeing me, Heath asked if I wanted a turn at the bottle.

"Aren't ya done?" I asked.

"Yeah," Heath replied.

"Then why'd I wanna play?"

"If you're not gonna play with us, then why'd ya come over?" Heath demanded. He sounded angry with me.

"But you're not playing anymore," I explained, trying not to hurt his feelings.

"That's 'cause you're being such a wuss," he stated as he looked around to the others. They were all taking his side, of course, even the small kid who seemed relieved there was someone else for Heath to attack. "You ruined the game for all of us."

All I could really do at that point was say, "Sorry," even though I had no idea for what I was apologizing. That's another lesson I learned early on in life; apologize often but never change. I wish I knew who'd taught me that so that I could thank him or her...or them.

After a few more minutes, everyone had arrived for his party. I was surprised there were no girls there, seeing as how Heath was so popular with them, yet I wasn't going to ask him about it. I didn't intend to talk to him at all. After the first conversation had failed, I decided to just sit in the background and wait for my mom to pull back into the driveway.

Once everyone had arrived, Heath asked his mom if we could play in the woods behind their house. She seemed to purposefully glance at all the birthday decorations—which I'm sure she paid for and hung up herself—then sighed deeply.

"Go ask your father," she suggested with a shake of her head. Her raspy, heavy, tired voice indicated she'd realized the same thing I had; it was just no use arguing with Heath Millard.

Heath brightened at her response and immediately led us all downstairs to his father's den. His dad was sitting in a tall, leather chair, reclining back so his head was almost level with the television set in front of him. The room was paneled with a fine, polished, fake mahogany, and the carpeting was deep red, casting a somewhat dreary, musty feel over the entire area. It smelled as if they'd finished the basement without bothering with waterproofing. The ceiling was low, and aside from the TV, the only light in the room came from a trophy case along the back wall. There were three shelves inside the cabinet, each of them about four feet long. On each one were two trophies. Save for the bottom one that only displayed one trophy and a ribbon. I almost started to laugh when I saw it; such a huge treasure chest and so little treasure. It seemed that Mr. Millard was about as successful an athlete as he was a coach.

I was about to go over and look at the trophies when Heath asked, "Dad, can we all go play in the woods?"

"What did your mother say?" his dad questioned after a long pause, not turning away from the golf tournament on TV.

"She said it's okay with her if you didn't mind," Heath replied, smiling over to one of his other friends.

"Then I don't care," Mr. Millard replied. He still didn't turn from the TV set. He was watching a middle aged man in pale, yellow slacks sink a putt for birdie.

"Thanks, dad," Heath said as he turned to head back up the stairs. Before he did, though, he grabbed me and positioned me between his dad and the TV. The man already seemed annoyed with my blocking his view, but Heath compounded this by saying, "Dad, this is Guy Lindsey. He's the one who was always bettin' against the Fightin' Golden Sandies all last year."

Heath chuckled to himself as he and the others went back upstairs. I couldn't seem to leave. Mr. Millard's angered eyes were holding me there as if in a tractor beam from a sci-fi movie. I guess that power came from game after game of glaring at referees, players, parents and such. He was also that odd combination of fit and fat at the same time...like John Belushi or Meatloaf. I wonder if either of them ever coached.

After a moment, Mr. Millard finally said, "You don't like my coaching?"

I was twelve years old. What did I know about coaching?

"I'm not really—"

"You think maybe my switch to a four-three defense wasn't a good move, maybe?" he persisted. "Well listen, I had gaps to fill, son. Every now and again in this life, a man...well, he's got some gaps to fill."

"Sir, I really don't—"

"We had to get some deeper penetration into the line. Our weak safety was getting exploited on the crossing routes, so we took the weak side backer and flipped him over...made him an elephant. You see, son, every now and again a man's gotta become an elephant. Gotta fill them gaps."

"Maybe I should—"

"Then we took the interior lineman, stunted with the weak side end." At this point. Mr. Millard was using the remote control, a couple beer bottle caps and a matchbook to diagram the play on the coffee table. Throughout his description, he would periodically glance around for another item that could represent a halfback, a lineman, or whatever. Unable to find anything, he'd tear another match out of the matchbook. He did this three or four times, and he seemed newly surprised each time that he couldn't find another bottle cap. "That gave us a match up advantage in case they decided to come off the corner and allowed us the time to red dog with our strong side corner. You see, son, every now and again, a man's gotta be his own dog."

"What's that mean, sir?"

"You're all a bunch of armchair know-it-alls," he spat, still working out plays on the coffee table. He seemed to be taking out an awful lot of frustration on this sixth grader. "You all think you can do a better goddam job than the coach. Everyone's gotta get his two cents in, but no one ever wants to drive the bus. You understand me, kid?"

"Yes sir," I lied. I found myself scavenging my pockets for a roll of Life Savers, but found nothing. By this point, I just wanted to get out of there.

"Then they expect me to be a good coach while they give me that goddam health class to teach," he continued. I didn't think he was talking to me anymore, so I started to slip away. "How the hell can I be expected to coach a football team when I've got five classes to coach? Huh? How can a man concentrate on the nickel package when he's gotta worry about whether or not little Johnny Blue Jeans understands about goddam spirochetes?"

Mr. Millard faded away as I cleared the top of the stairs and softly shut the door behind me. Mrs. Millard was nowhere around, but a new cigarette was burning openly in a cereal bowl serving as an ashtray on the kitchen table. There appeared to be some crusted corn flakes along the side of the bowl. I scooted out the back door and watched Heath and his gang disappear into the woods.

Although I could barely see them through the trees, I could hear them yelling excitedly. I'd heard Heath talk about the creek that ran through the woods behind the house, so I assumed they were playing in there. I decided to follow them. I mean, what else was I going to do? Talk stunted weak sides and syphilitic bacteria with Mr. Millard?

It didn't take long for me to regret my decision. No sooner had I stepped into the woods when my chest suddenly felt as if I'd been stung by a wasp. I began to scream and swat at it frantically. I was spinning and stumbling around trees until I eventually caught my foot on a root or rock or something and fell hard to the wet, dead leaves on the woodland ground. The sharp pain in my chest wouldn't go away, so I didn't quit swatting at it until I made damn sure that wasp was dead. After a moment more of this, I noticed the gang was approaching me, laughing. I quit slapping my chest and just laid there, panting and crying, until the others were standing directly overtop of me. The only one I was looking at, however, was Heath. And I wasn't even really looking at him, I was looking at the BB pistol in his hand.

"Some shot, huh Guy?" he asked as he knelt beside me. "Where'd I get you?"

I didn't say anything. I was trying too hard to stop crying.

"Shit, you're not gonna tell my parents are ya?" he said, suddenly pulling away from me. Heath was the only grade school kid I knew who sounded effective when he swore. "Aw man, ya can't do that! They'll take my gun away! Fuck, Guy, don't narc."

I couldn't believe the situation. He was standing over me with a BB gun, I was lying flat on my back, and yet *he* was afraid. For the first time since I'd known him, Heath was afraid.

"Please, Guy," he nearly cried. At any minute, I expected him to drop down and just start bawling. "Please, don't tell, man. My parents'll whoop my ass and they won't lemme have anymore parties. Come on, Guy! They'll take the gun away!"

He showed me the gun up close. Or at least the barrel of the gun. I realized that Heath's plea was more of a threat. It worked; I was scared.

"I won't tell," I said weakly. The pain in my chest still made my voice crack.

"Cool," Heath said with a cocky laugh, his fear disappearing in an instant. He then waved his gun in the air and turned back in the direction from which he came. "Come on! Let's go find that frog."

All the others followed him, leaving me alone again. I was still lying on my back, looking at the trees all around me. They'd just recently sprouted their leaves, so they were still that perfect shade of green against the blue, late morning sky.

Once the guys had all left, I pulled up my shirt to see how bad the wound was. The BB hadn't lodged in my skin, and it didn't even leave a hole in my shirt. This upset me because now, if I did want to tell on Heath, I would have no proof aside from the mark on my chest. There was a small white circle where it had hit, and the skin surrounding it had turned bright red, but this would soon fade away.

After spitting on my fingers and rubbing the saliva—the elixir of childhood—into the wound, I pulled down my shirt and stood up to see where the others had gone. They were back at the creek where they'd been before I was shot, so I also headed in that direction. When I reached them, Heath shocked me by handing me the gun.

"What's this for?" I asked.

"Shooting things," Heath explained.

"Why'd I want it?"

"Before you got in the way, we had this frog we were gonna kill. Now we can't find it."

"So why are you giving me the gun?"

"'Cause you're gonna shoot my cousin Mick over here."

Heath pointed to the small kid of whom he was making fun during the bottle game.

"No, I'm—"

"No, see, it's because of you that we can't kill the frog. We already shot you, so that's no fun no more. So we decided that you should shoot Mick 'cause you already got shot."

"I'm not going to—."

"We could always just shoot you again," Heath threatened.

"I don't wanna do it," I whined. I didn't mean to, but that's how it came out.

Heath was all over it. "'*I don't wanna do it*,'" he mocked, multiplying my whining by ten. "Quit bein' such a fuckin' baby, Guy. Come on, Mick likes it. He likes to be hurt, dontcha Micky?"

Mick smiled and nodded, "Shoot me. Bang bang!" The other kids all laughed.

"Come on, Guy, quit bein' such a wuss. He wants you to do it. It's not gonna kill him or nothin'."

Heath was right. It wasn't going to kill him, but it would hurt. Believe me, I know. Still, I tried to raise the gun, pointing the barrel in Mick's direction. But then I turned to look at Heath, and I saw that smile on his face again.

It was at that moment that I felt hate for the first time. I hated every boy who stood there and watched as Heath tried to talk me into purposely hurting some kid I'd never even met. I couldn't understand this. Why was this fun to them? Then I began to wonder what Heath was thinking when he shot at me. Moreso than the pain, I found myself hurt by the thought that they all laughed at me, that hurting me was entertainment to them. And even better than that was the entertainment of making me inflict the same pain on someone else.

At that moment, I fully understood what kind of person Heath was. I knew he had no compassion or respect for anything around him, and my anger turned to fear. I wanted to attack Heath right there and point that gun in his direction, but I was afraid. I was afraid of my anger and of the hate, and I just wanted to get away. I threw the gun down and ran as fast as I could, and I could hear them calling after me.

"Guy! Guy!"

They didn't want me to come back, they just didn't want me to tell on Heath. They were afraid I'd run to Heath's mom and show her my chest and tell her about Mick.

"Hey Guy!"

I wasn't going to narc, though. I'd just have to deal with the problem even more, which would entail dealing with people. I was suddenly afraid of everyone. I was afraid of Heath and his friends. I was afraid of his dad. I was even afraid of his mom and her cracking face. I couldn't trust anyone anymore.

"Guy, come on!"

I ran right by Heath's house. If I slowed down, another BB would sting my back, I was sure. In one afternoon, Heath Millard destroyed my faith in everything I'd been taught by those in whom I was supposed to have trust. If one kid was capable of this, wasn't everyone?

❦   ❦   ❦

"Guy! Guy, are you coming or not?!" the Arbiter shouted from outside my room. I looked over at the door, then said, "Yeah, hold on," as I stood and grabbed my purple and black "Billy Bishop Goes to War" varsity jacket. I'm not sure why I had it, or even who Billy Bishop was. All I can figure is that he never made it back from war or else I wouldn't have his jacket. I opened the door, and the Arbiter was standing there, tapping his foot and his watch in synchronized jest.

"Cripes, man, what were you doing in there?" he asked. "Been standing out here screaming your name like some kind of freak. What'll your dormmates think."

"They'll wonder why you don't have a baseball bat," I smiled as I shut and locked the door. The Arbiter and I left the dorm and walked to President's Performing Arts Center for the Performing Arts to see the opening of the Floodbane College production of Sophocles' *Antigone.*

Rhonda was playing the title character.

CHAPTER 3

"The Far Side of Crazy"

*B*ut before I get to *Antigone*, there's one more thing I'd like to explain about the Arbiter. Well, not really explain, but simply mention, since I certainly could not explain it.

Of all of the Arbiter's peculiarities, there were two which I'm certain would've crystallized every single thing about him had I been able to figure them out. One of these was his incessant desire to climb radio towers, which I'll get to later, and the other was that he wrote critiques of the performances of dead actors and sent them *to the dead actors themselves.* Not to "the estate of" or to a surviving family member. No, these were letters written directly about the dead actor and mailed directly to the dead actors…well, as directly as that's possible, anyway.

It was this trait that most perplexed me, perhaps because I had to discover it on my own. The Arbiter seemingly wanted to hide it from me. I knew he preferred to watch old black and white movies over anything current, but that didn't seem too odd. A lot of people lock themselves in their houses with their fifteen cats and sip a fine four or five glasses of brandy while watching Blondie marathons on AMC or TMC or whatever. I think all the shiny colors in modern movies confuse them. But unlike most others, it ends up the Arbiter chose black and white movies because it was almost guaranteed that at least one of the actors was now performing on the silver screen in the sky. In fact, he wouldn't watch any new movie until he learned that at least one of the actors had passed on.

I believe *Poltergeist* was his all-time favorite.

I hadn't known the Arbiter for long before I began to notice he always disappeared after the movie was done, and I wouldn't see him for at least half an hour afterwards. The whole thing intrigued me. I knew if I could figure out what he was doing after the theater lights came up or the VCR started to rewind, then I'd finally understand what made him…him.

Of course I was wrong, because when I did find out, it only confused me all the more.

I uncovered the mystery the weekend after he'd first met Rhonda at the beginning of our junior year. He had been noticeably distracted since that day, so I guess I shouldn't have been surprised that he slipped up so badly that Saturday night.

We had just finished watching Laurel and Hardy's *Their First Mistake* on AMC when the Arbiter grabbed his gray folder and climbed up from the floor to sit at his study desk. He sat there for quite a while listening to some classical piece on the Aiwa stereo that sat on his dresser along with his jarred collection of high-bouncing balls; the type that can be bought in supermarket gumball machines for either twenty-five or fifty cents, depending upon the state of purchase. The Arbiter had over a hundred of these substantial orbs of potential energy, all seeming to strain against the various sizes of jars that confined them.

"Grieg," the Arbiter suddenly exclaimed without looking up from his writing. "'Peer Gynt Suite Number 1, Opus 46.'"

He was referring to the music on the stereo. The Arbiter announced every piece that came on when he was listening to symphonic music, feeling it was his duty to educate me in the classics. It kind of worked, I suppose. I mean, if somebody played me a piece of symphony music, I wouldn't be able to tell him what it was. If he said, however, that he was going to play me Allegro ma non troppo from Symphony No. 6 in F major, Op. 68, Pastoral, I would say, "Ah! Beethoven!"

I'm the same way with Life Savers. Tell me I'm getting a Pep-O-Mint, and I can't exactly recall the taste. But pop one in my mouth and I'll announce, "Ah! Pep-O-Mint."

Perhaps Beeth-O-Ven would've made a good flavor of Life Saver. Beeth-O-Ven, Tchaik-O-Vsky, R-O-Ssini.

I suppose that after nearly seven years of trombone playing, I should've been more adept at recognizing the classic composers and their works. Unfortunately, my ear was about as bad as my tonguing, and all classical music just kind of ran together. Actually, pretty much all pieces or songs within any specific genre of music sounded the same to me.

As the Slovak Philharmonic Orchestra was finishing the second movement of Grieg's suite ("Death of Ase," to be exact), the phone rang. Answering it, I wasn't surprised that it was a woman calling for the Arbiter. I was shocked as hell, however, to hear exactly which woman.

"Yes, is Arby there?" the woman asked.

"Rhonda?" I guessed. I knew the Arbiter had spoken to her a couple of times, having gone out of his way to make sure he would run into her on the sidewalk or in the cafeteria or beside her car in the parking lot, but neither of them had made any sort of contact with one another over the phone.

Hearing her name, the Arbiter dove out of his chair and landed beneath the phone, denying me the chance to momentarily pretend she was really calling to speak to me. He kneeled there with his head bowed and his hand outstretched for the receiver as if he were about to receive Communion, so I handed it to him saying, "This is the call of Rhonda. Take and speak in remembrance of her."

"Hello, Rhonda?" he greeted as if he'd been expecting the call all day. He was still on his knees and remained there for the entire conversation. "Nothing much, I was just writing a letter...No one important, really. How about you?...Doesn't sound like...Really? For what play?...Of course. Sophocles. It's the third of the Theban Plays...I'm full of useless information. I'm a bastion of useless information. For instance, did you know that in the Academy Awards in 1983, *Ghandi* beat out Disney's *Tron* for best costume design?...No, I've never seen either movie. I'm not sure if I can yet...Sure...Sure...Sure I have, but not since high school...I got kicked out...No, it wasn't anything like that. The director kicked me out because I skipped a rehearsal to attend a Lions Club father/son banquet...No, my dad wasn't a member...Can't remember his name. Food was good, though. Swiss steak and mashed potatoes at Perkins...Absolutely not. Why?...You mean now?"

Men often talk about how the birth of their first child was the most incredible event they ever witnessed. Seeing the expression on the Arbiter's face right then is still mine.

"Of course it's not a problem! I'll be right over!...No, that's okay. I know where you live...Because I've been stalking you since Tuesday. I've stolen your toothbrush, and I've been dressing up like a clown and hiding in your closet so I can watch you sleep...Yeah, that was me. I'll be there in five minutes...Okay, bye."

The Arbiter hung up the phone, let out a whoop and a yell, then grabbed a jar of high bouncing balls and threw them up to the ceiling. They careened all around the room, and the Arbiter nearly fell over them as he scrambled to get to the door.

"What's going on?" I managed to ask before he got out of the room, preceded by four or five balls.

"She wants help memorizing her lines for *Antigone*," the Arbiter beamed. He then repeated himself slowly and quietly. "She wants help memorizing her lines for *Antigone*."

Then he was gone.

As soon as he shut the door, I turned to look at his desk. His gray folder was still sitting there, open to what he'd been writing before the phone call. It took me only a moment to overcome any reservations I may have had. I sat myself in the Arbiter's chair and, as the high bouncing balls continued to roll about my feet, I started to read what was written before me:

To: STAN LAUREL
From: the arbiter
Re: *THEIR FIRST MISTAKE*

Comedy is a messy business.

That's probably why comedy teams tend to turn so viciously on each other. Abbott and Costello. Martin and Lewis. Laverne and Shirley. With drama, there are enough intrinsic shadings within a given performance to afford an actor(s) the opportunity to plausibly claim a modicum of artistic success regardless of the apparent objective merits of such a belief.

With comedy, they either laugh or they don't.

Every day becomes a referendum on your very soul. Nowhere to run, nowhere to hide. But if you are part of a collective—specifically, one-half of a two man team—how can you not yield to the overwhelming temptation to start looking at the other guy? He's all the time bumbling through the set-ups and then stepping all over your punches. His timing has gotten worse than the fellow's who stopped by the Presidential box at Ford's Theater to ask, "Other than that, Mrs. Lincoln, how was the play?" His idea of contributing to the writing process is saying that you ought find a way to inject more references to Joan of Arc at the top of the act.

He thinks you need to use more puppets.

But not you and Oliver Hardy, Mr. Laurel. You seemed to have a real genuine affection for each other that transcended professional respect. It's a tricky dynamic to capture, isn't it? But you always seemed to add just the proper amount of...whimsy to your line readings sufficient to keep your relationship with Mr. Hardy from becoming condescending or mean-spirited.

Maybe the best example of how this closeness manifested itself on film was in this sweet scene from *Their First Mistake*;

Mr. Hardy played a newlywed whose bride was upset with the amount of time that he was still spending with you:

> **Laurel:** What's the matter with her anyway?
> **Hardy:** I don't know. She says I think more of you than I do of her.
> **Laurel:** Well you do, don't you?
> **Laurel:** We won't go into that.
> **Laurel:** You know what the trouble is?
> **Laurel:** What?
> **Laurel:** You need a baby in the house.
> **Laurel:** What's that got to do with it?
> **Laurel:** Well if you had a baby...you could go out nights with me.

As the film unfolds, Mr. Hardy and his wife do, in fact, adopt a baby; however, she eventually files for divorce with the claim that your character is the "other woman." You and Mr. Hardy wind up raising the baby yourselves, lying in bed together with the baby strategically placed between you. Finally, you deftly reach into your pajama top and pull forth a baby bottle which you have been warming against your breast.

It's...huh. Mr. Laurel, there is sort of another interpretation of this picture, one that perhaps can be taken up at a later time.

Before I could get the letter back in the folder, the door swung open and there stood the Arbiter, looking down on me like an executioner with ax in hand. He suddenly appeared more physically imposing than usual. He always was muscular, yet slightly paunchy; like a Greek statue. His peculiarly blue eyes scanned the room and, like always, led me to believe he was thinking of hundreds of things and trying to decide which thought was most specifically calibrated for this particular occasion. Choosing one, he walked over to the desk, picked up his gray folder and—smiling all the while—said;

"Touch that again—"

❈   ❈   ❈

"—and I'll put your head through that window," Heath threatened, standing over me a second more to make sure enough band members, cheerleaders and dancers standing outside the school bus witnessed my public humiliation.

But let's backtrack, as I wouldn't hear this particular threat from Heath until our junior year of high school, quite a few years after the party for Heath's eleventh birthday. I only bring it up now because it's a prime example of how life with him did not get any easier. Oddly, as the sixth grade school year went on, Heath seemed to become more embarrassed by the fact that someone deserted one of his social gatherings. It was almost as if—at the age of eleven—he already had enough cognitive awareness to be insulted by someone leaving him at the altar, even if the bride was someone as insignificant as myself...not that I ever considered marrying Heath; although, I do look strikingly crisp in white. Anyway, Heath started to insult me behind my back instead of just to my face, therefore causing my friends-by-proxy to ignore me on purpose. This actually made me feel better about myself. At least now I was worthy of being ignored as opposed to just forgotten.

As my already minute social life became all but defunct, my self-image greatly improved. My fear had turned to feelings of superiority. I believed myself above all these people; above all my classmates, their friends, their brothers and sisters and cousins. I was better than all my teachers, from Mrs. Piper to Mrs. Garvin to Mrs. Patera. I was better than Mr. Steele who taught me to never tell the truth. I was certainly better than that girl who sat beside me in kindergarten and turned me down for a date in junior high then got pregnant when she was fifteen and dropped out of high school to end up working in a department store at the local mall. I should give that girl more credit, though, as she was an instrumental link in the chain of events which led to both the greatest and worst moments of my life. Yet she was hardly pivotal to my life in sixth grade. In sixth grade, she was only a moron. They were all morons. Especially Mrs. Patera, who—with only a month to go in the school year—deemed me a troublemaker who deserved to be spanked.

She pulled me into a small room across the hallway from her classroom and quickly shut the door. The walls of the room were constructed with brown bricks, and the floor was black linoleum. One bare, dim light bulb was fastened high on the wall above a large, thick, wooden table which held scientific gadgets and books far beyond the reading level of grade school students and probably most grade school teachers. There was a shelf against the wall opposite the table, also containing numerous books that were stacked haphazardly. I had the feeling no one had used these materials in years, and I began to wonder if anyone had even used the room. In all honesty, I didn't even know it existed until Mrs. Patera marched me in there with her paddle jabbing into the small of my back like a pistol. I half expected a one-eyed German named Gunther to come in and proclaim, while smacking a riding crop into his palm, "Vee have vays to make you tock!"

It wasn't the spanking I was fearing so much as the aftershocks I knew would rumble up behind. As I have mentioned, Mrs. Patera went to my church and was a good friend of my dad's. They were going to talk about this, then my dad would talk to me. This spanking was going to be a problem for a good while to come.

What bugged me most about the whole thing was the thought that, whereas I was going to be spanked, Heath Millard was sitting on his candy-ass at his little desk, laughing with his friends about my fate, smilingly sheepishly at the better looking girls; the future cheerleaders who secretly yearned for the day when he'd catch up with them and reach puberty so they could lose their virginity to him out behind the football locker room of John Stuart Mill High School.

If I seem bitter, it's because I am. I get that way when I haven't had a Life Saver for a while. They freshen the breath *and* the heart.

"I don't understand what came over you," Mrs. Patera scolded, still expecting me to explain why I chose to fight Heath Millard on the playground that day instead of play four square or cartoon tag like all the other good boys and girls. I wasn't about to explain this to her. She wouldn't understand. She was a moron.

Therefore, "I don't know," was all I said.

Mrs. Patera seemed disappointed in me. She frowned and looked as if she were actually going to apologize for what she was about to do. She didn't though. She just tried to make me feel guilty by saying, "I expected better of you, Guy. Wait here."

She left me alone with the dust and dirt that layered the artifacts abandoned in the small room. I think she was pulling on me what my father always used to when punishing me. After I'd done something wrong—something like lowering my little brother down the laundry chute with an extension cord or cutting the pictures out of his *Playboys* and selling them to the neighborhood kids—my dad would send me to his room to think about what I'd done. I hated that more than the spanking. He was always fair, though, my dad. He never punished me without just cause.

I wonder if he would've spanked me for killing somebody.

All I could think of as I waited for him to come in and spank me was which belt I was going to have him use. That was my dad's cruelest child rearing habit, forcing my little brother and I to choose the belt with which we were going to be spanked. It was an awful scare tactic that would've caused the child psychologists to "go ape shit," to borrow my dad's own expression. They would've written books about my father and used him as a prime example of how not to raise children. I don't know if they were right or not, but I do know that when dad spanked me for doing something wrong, I never did it again.

This couldn't have been what Mrs. Patera was up to, though. She only had one belt, and I'm sure she wasn't about to take it off in a private room with a sixth grade boy. I mean, it's not like I was attending a Catholic school or something. I never found out what she did when she left that room, not even six years later after I won the church scholarship to help pay for a couple books at Floodbane. She stopped me after the service to congratulate me, and we joked about how—after teaching for nearly thirty years and raising two children and one grandchild—I was the only person she spanked in her entire life. Even then I didn't ask her why she left the room for those few minutes before she came in and whacked me five times for punching Heath Millard. I really didn't care.

Likewise, Mrs. Patera never really found out why I punched Heath. I don't even know if Heath ever fully understood what made me snap that day, even though he purposely provoked it. All I know for sure is that he learned nothing from it. Maybe I should've had him pick which fist I'd use to hit him.

We were out at recess when it happened. The other kids were on the playground, behaving as kids should, but Heath and his friends managed to convince me to sneak behind the bus garage with them. Apparently, Heath had been back there a couple of times before and had set up some sort of hut with old tires and cardboard boxes. There were a few empty cans of Pabst Blue Ribbon lying nearby, but I have no proof as to whether or not they were his.

As we approached the boxes, my "spider senses" started tingling. Why was I back there? I wasn't particularly fond of these people, and I'm certain they didn't care much for me. Maybe I was just trying to prove a point, trying to let Heath know I was a man and I was ready to take him on anytime, anywhere. Yeah, and maybe I was an albino lingerie model.

When we got closer to the box, I could hear the soft, unmistakable mewing of a kitten. It actually sounded more like crying, and it sort of frightened me. Knowing that Heath had set this all up, I was sure the kitten's future would not be all that glamorous. I felt as badly for the kitten right then as I eventually would for all the girls in high school who went out with Heath; even that girl who sat beside me in kindergarten and turned me down for a date in junior high. Although she was no friend of mine, I wasn't about to wish upon her an evening with Heath.

Oh, there's another philosophy of mine which I'd learned by early high school: nothing brings people together faster than a common enemy; for instance, the Indians siding with the British in the Revolutionary War because they hated the Colonists, Stalin joining Churchill and FDR to stop Hitler, or Michael Hayes teaming with Tommy "Wildfire" Rich to fight Terry Gordy. Or was it Terry teaming with Tommy to fight Michael? Or did Michael or Terry team with Steve O. Or Steve Keirn? Hell, all I remember is someone smashed someone's tin cup, and many piledrivers ensued.

Away from the wrestling ring and back behind the playground, Heath did not seize the kitten by its neck and swing it high above his head to slam it onto a log as did young Noboru in Yukio Mishima's *The Sailor who Fell from Grace with the Sea*. Instead, he carefully picked it up and held it against his chest. He let the others pet it, then he pet it himself. The kitten clawed at his shirt, trying to gain a foothold higher up his body. Heath let it have some slack and the kitten managed to get up on his shoulder. It balanced itself precariously, shaking as I had after Heath asked me to shoot his cousin. The others all laughed at the kitten's pitiful display, and Heath pulled it reluctantly off his shoulder then put it back in the box.

"Come on, guys," he said as the kitten started to cry again. "We can't get caught back here."

The others agreed and took one last look at the kitten before we all started back around the bus garage. I didn't understand why Heath bothered to take us all back there, especially me. None of them were talking to me anymore. I was beginning to think maybe this was Heath's way of making up for all those months of treating me as if I didn't exist. Maybe he just wanted to show me that he could be a humane guy. I was beginning to feel kind of embarrassed for the way I'd acted at his house, and it actually occurred to me that maybe I should apologize to him. The kitten's constant crying wouldn't let me do so.

"That cat sure sounds unhappy," I said. The others smiled at my comment. I didn't understand that.

"Yep," Heath agreed, not turning to look at me. "I haven't fed it since Monday."

I stopped moving as the others started to snicker. It all was obvious to me then. The only reason Heath took me back there was to piss me off. I obliged him.

"I'm doin' a science project for the science fair," Heath continued. "I'm doin' a project to see how long it takes to starve a cat to death. Whadda ya think of that, girl?"

I didn't have an answer for him right away, as I wasn't really thinking of the kitten at that moment. I wasn't thinking of any of the other guys there. It was just me and Heath. That's the way he wanted it. If I hated him the day he shot me and asked me to shoot his cousin, now I despised him. I loathed and abhorred him. At the same time, I feared him worse than any nightmare or unexplained shadow in my bedroom at night. I feared him because he was real and I couldn't call my dad in to scare him away. My mom couldn't turn on the night-light and make Heath disappear. I had to confront this fear myself, and I had to do it now.

Heath and his friends had cut around the garage, laughing at my inability to do anything about the situation. They quit laughing a few seconds later when I was suddenly on Heath's back, swinging my fists at the back of his head. One landed hard enough to knock him to the ground, and I dug a knee into his back as I continued to punch him in the side of the head. I wasn't saying a word all this time; I was only crying. I cried harder as I hit him harder, and it never occurred to me that when he fell forward we came into sight of all those on the playground. The teachers were running towards me, but I knew I had a few more seconds to let him know I wasn't going to take this anymore. His friends could've ended it much more quickly, but for one reason or another, they chose to not get involved.

I continued to pummel Heath until a large pair of hands yanked me off of him. I was still swinging and kicking and crying, but I was connecting with nothing but air. Voices were yelling, and it sounded as if some were cheering, but I could not make out who was doing what. All I knew was that I was shaking like that frightened kitten, and I had this overwhelming feeling that although I was going to be severely punished for it, I'd just done something great for mankind.

Have a nice day.

Good or bad, I had finally taken control of Heath Millard. In that brief moment of violence, I had shown him that he couldn't just push people around and play with their emotions and get them to do whatever he wanted. I was proud of myself, and as the red heat cooled from my face and I was set back on the ground, I found that I wasn't afraid of the punishment that lie ahead.

The crowd that had gathered around was now quite large. There weren't a lot of fights in grade school, so the few that did take place were PPV size events. Everyone would be talking about it for the rest of the day, and no one would again place Heath so highly on the social pedestal. I'd exposed him for the coward he was.

Wrong again, Guy.

Once Mrs. Patera had picked him up, Heath immediately turned to me. I expected him to be in tears, hopefully even bleeding. Instead, he was smiling. I'd just given him the beating of his life, and he was smiling.

And then it all sank away. There was no glory, I wasn't the victor. He hadn't hit me once, yet he somehow won the fight. Any control I thought I'd gained was a mere illusion. Heath had probably planned the whole thing. He'd most likely even set up the entire kitten scenario just so I'd attack him and get in trouble. With one, twisted smile from Heath, I had become the bad guy.

He even went back to get the kitten before we were taken inside. He claimed he'd found it back there before I attacked him.

"I don't know what Guy was trying to do," he said as he stroked the kitten's soft back. Even the kitten wasn't coming to my defense. It was purring and rubbing its head into Heath's chest as if it had been in on the plan from the very start. Damn cat. I hate cats. "But all I know is I found this kitten."

"He was gonna kill it!" I nearly screamed. "He hasn't fed it since Monday! He's starving it for the science fair!"

"Mr. Lindsey," scolded Mrs. Garvin, the other recess supervisor that day. It was the first she'd spoken to me since second grade. "The science fair isn't for another three weeks. The kitten would be dead by then."

Okay, was I the only one getting the point, or was I the only one missing it? Perhaps Heath's intentions weren't as he stated. In retrospect, I probably should have considered that most grade school science fair projects are about something like photosynthesis or vitamin C absorption; not many eleven-year-olds make it to districts via Tabby's carcass.

But truth or not, I knew any argument I could raise was futile against Heath's charm and his lies. Everyone had flipped over Heath's valiant deed, especially after Principal Steele—as if wanting the kitten to serve as my scarlet letter—agreed to let it live in our classroom until we found a good home for it. Heath was a hero, and I had become the village outcast. The only dignity I could salvage came from not again explaining "what came over me," as Mrs. Patera had put it. She wouldn't understand the reasons for the intense hatred I harbored for Heath. No one would have believed my stories, anyway. They would've thought I was lying to save face, just like that girl who turned me down for a date in junior high did after Heath got her pregnant.

We grew to have so much in common, that girl and me. I wonder if she has ever killed somebody, and I still wonder to what movie I wanted to take her.

The spanking was supposed to teach me a lesson, I suppose, but all it did was reinforce my belief that I should never admit my wrongdoings to others. I had, in my anger, explained to Mrs. Patera out on the playground why I attacked Heath, and it brought me nothing but the disapproval of my peers and a spanking from my teacher. My story was truth, but this still didn't matter to anyone. The truth is only that to the person who tells it. Everyone else does with it what he or she wants.

This is why, justified or not, it took me so long to admit having killed somebody.

And this is why, despite my growing desire to do so, I still couldn't confess my killing to the Arbiter and Rhonda. It felt odd, wrong, like my peculiar desire to try LSD, but the itching to talk to my new friends grew slowly more intense. Looking back at my freshman year, I'm sure I wouldn't have been able to announce it in that orientation class even if the Arbiter hadn't thrown me with his Papa Shango introduction. Not to those morons. And speaking of morons…

Ends up that the apartment Rhonda would take during our senior year was directly above the guy's whom the Arbiter had smacked in the face with his gray folder one year earlier.

His name was Jayson Fayme. Jayson Alexander Fayme; the type of name that would look great on a framed, juris doctorate degree hanging on a law firm wall. I think the best way to describe Jayson is to insert his name into a generic joke I had heard at the beginning of my college career:

Jayson Fayme was at a party, and he goes up to this guy and asks him, "Why does everyone hate me before they even meet me?"

"Saves time later," the guest replied.

That's the way it was with this guy. I kind of felt guilty for hating him the first time I saw him. I mean, all he did was what everyone else on campus had always wanted to do, that being to grab Rhonda Vorhees' ass. Jayson at least had initiative. But the more I got to know him, the more I realized I had no choice but to hate him. He was a living example of the Arbiter's theory on stereotypes. He fit them all. Drunken frat boy, spoiled rich boy, prejudiced white boy, sexist male boy…outside of his fraternity brothers (and even their friendships were conditional), I don't think there was one person on campus who liked Jayson.

Save for President, of course.

President adored Jayson. More accurately, President adored Jayson's family. President adored any family that sent a total of seventeen members to his school, seven of whom came within the last fifteen years. The only buildings on campus that had actually been assigned proper titles (save for President's Performing Arts Center for the Performing Arts, of course) were named after the Faymes…buildings in which they had never been! Entire pamphlets were dedicated to the Faymes and circulated about campus, the town, the state and the country. A popular Floodbane myth rumored that a C-130 Hercules cargo plane full of Fayme family pamphlets dumped its cargo regularly over third world nations that held reincarnation as a hallowed belief, just in case the natives should come back in their next lives as the children of a wealthy Floodbane College alumnus.

Because of his family's reputation on campus, Jayson was exempt from all Floodbane rules and regulations. He passed every class without attending, he won athletic scholarships without participating in any sports, and he was even absolved from the sacred Floodbane Speech Code. It was perfectly acceptable for him to ride his bike around campus and grab the ass of whomever he chose. Hell, he probably got credit for it as an independent study.

Still, despite Jayson's multitude of character flaws, he did have one miniscule, yet slightly redeeming quality.

The boy was totally harmless.

No one paid him any mind. His professors conducted class as if he weren't really in the back of the room blowing bubbles in cans of beer through a straw in his nose. His peers continued their conversations as if he hadn't just jumped into the middle of their group and belched, laughing hysterically. Even his frat brothers ignored him when he'd attempt to French kiss the TV while watching porn tapes, fashion shows, or the occasional rerun of *Double Trouble*. They had only allowed him to pledge because he had such good standing with President, after all, and President secretly agreed to have any and all current charges against the fraternity dropped if Jayson became a member.

But when he reached junior status, it finally became impossible for me, the Arbiter and Rhonda to ignore Fayme. For it was during that year that he swiped the editing job at *A Daily Planet* away from the Arbiter and me, it was during that year that he rented the apartment beneath Rhonda's, and it was during that year that his stupid, grade school crush on her became an obsession not unlike those displayed in graphic detail in direct to video movies starring Gabriella Hall or Kira Reed.

I guess I could understand the crush part, for I'd had my fair share of crushes before I swore off relationships with women. My first and still most dear was on Penny Robinson from the old TV show *Lost In Space*. I'd always watched repeats of the show in grade school with my best friend Terry Hogan before he moved to Toledo, and I'd quickly developed an intense crush on the young, pure, neglected Penny. Although I continued to have more crushes on more women—mostly TV and movie stars, of course—I never really got over the fairer of the two Robinson daughters until I met Ann Penella on the cheerleader bus on the way home from a high school football game.

❆   ❆   ❆

It was the closest I ever came to love at first sight, the kind the Arbiter experienced with Rhonda. Actually, that's somewhat inaccurate with my situation; it was closer to love at first sound or love at first action. The night it seemed that everyone within a stone's throw was throwing the stone at me, Ann spoke to me, even shielded me. Yet I couldn't even manage to thank her, and that's how I knew I was doomed.

It was on the school bus on the way back from our first away-game my sophomore year of high school. The ride to Nietzche High to take on the Fighting Orange was uneventful enough. I just sank down in one of the swamp-green seats about midway back, staring fixedly out the window the entire trip. I could hear some of the girls complaining that I was on the bus while others opted to make fun of my hair or my acne or anything else they could see over the seats, but I ignored it well.

As I've said, they were all morons.

Young, pretty, nubile, extremely shapely morons.

On the trip back, however, the cheerleaders and dancers got vicious. After the Fighting Golden Sandies had just been humiliated by the Fighting Orange, I made a break for the bus, believing if I got the back seat I'd at least only be susceptible to attack from straight ahead. I'd played Risk™ enough times with my family to know it's pointless to try to fight a two front war. Well, that and to attempt defending Europe, but that strategy isn't really conducive to analogy.

It didn't take long for me to realize my mistake. The chaperons had sought quieter haven in the center and front of the bus, and the girls who had become cheerleaders and dancers because they had school spirit and not because they wanted to get laid more often were up front with them. Thus, I was trapped in the back with the Arbiter's stereotypes.

The girls were giggling and yelling and singing, snapping each other's bras, flipping each other's skirts and flirting with lesbianism as they showed one another how their boyfriends kiss. There was no way I could just look out the window this time, and no thoughts of nuns or dead puppies could stop my erection.

Two of the girls saw me staring at them, and they started to giggle even harder. They then stood up and strutted to my seat. One girl reached over, hovering her not-quite-yet-developed breasts in my face while she grabbed my trombone case and passed it up to the girl in front of her. All the girls were watching now, laughing and cheering them on as if at Chippendales. I was petrified. Literally.

"You're kinda cute," one of the girls said as she dropped herself on my lap, running her fingers through my hair that'd become flat with grease from wearing the band helmet for so long. She gasped in disgust and rubbed her hand on her friend's uniform.

The cheerleaders howled.

Her friend was one of the dancers, so she was wearing shimmering, nude tights under her skirt. I know this because she sat down next to me and grabbed my hand, placing it on the inside of her thigh. She then clamped her legs together around my hand, rocking back and forth while moaning in mock ecstasy. I thought for sure that the chaperones would hear her and put an end to all of this, but the noise was either drowned out by the laughter and the hip hop music blasting from some boom box or else they just didn't give a damn.

Cars were passing by, spinning their lights around the bus like a strobe light flashing on a mirror ball in a Tokyo nightclub. It was enough to let the girls see the sweat that was pouring down my face.

"I can feel how hard he is!" the girl on my lap yelped. She sounded overwrought, but she didn't move.

At that comment, the girls in the surrounding area started laughing about how turned on I was and what the two girls should do next. I heard something about my sweat, then the cheerleader lowered her face to my neck. I could feel the moist heat of her breath, and it made me shiver. She quickly pulled up and made the same noise of disgust she had earlier, this time sticking her finger in her mouth as if to induce vomiting. The other girl, with my hand still viced between her thighs, reached over and placed her hand on my knee. She inched it up slowly between my leg and that of the cheerleader on top of me, and it was driving me nuts. I hated both these girls. I hated them all, but I was too damn excited to do anything about it. I was in every teenage boy's wet dream, and it was a nightmare to me. This was the first physical contact I'd had with a woman, and I had no idea what to do.

A car passed us as the dancer continued to slide her hand up my thigh, and in one brief moment I could see her face' as clear as day. It was the girl who sat beside me in kindergarten and turned me down for a date in junior high, and who later became pregnant with Heath Millard's baby and dropped out of high school. She displayed total revulsion as her hand slid further up my thigh. I was too weak to stop her. I felt like I was about to explode, and everything around me became all hazy. I could no longer feel the girl's hand on my thigh, just this pulsating sensation in my lower abdomen, as if my heart had fallen into my pelvis.

In the background, I could hear someone saying to cut it out, that enough was enough. The laughter had started to die out, but the girls kept moving and the pulsating didn't stop. It was getting uncontrollable now, and I could no longer make out any faces or even shapes. I think I heard the dancer announce that I was going to "spurt," and then the cheerleader jumped off my lap. The other girl was still making her way back to us, still trying to get everyone to quit. I focused all my energy on her and managed to make out that she was also a cheerleader, not a chaperone as I'd expected. I felt relief for just a second as my guardian angel flew closer, then I felt the dancer's hand on my groin.

Then I ejaculated.

Then I passed out.

When I awoke, I was still in the back seat of the bus. My trombone case was back on my lap, pressing something damp into my groin. I touched the wet area of my band pants, and then I remembered what had happened. I was too humiliated to move. The last thing I wanted was to face the girls who'd done this.

They had shut the radio off now and were no longer singing and giggling. Most of them seemed to be asleep, the others continuing to talk softly to one another. Taking advantage of the sudden peace, I rested my head against the back of the seat and shifted my position to try to pull my wet underwear away from my skin. I could hear the sound of the tires spinning on the asphalt and the gears grinding when the bus driver turned or applied the brakes. I closed my eyes and pretended I was again five years old in the back seat of my parents' car with my baby brother sleeping in the child seat next to me as we returned home from Grammie and Pop's, listening to some pop song on nighttime radio. It comforted me, and I soon fell back asleep.

When I woke up again, we were back at John Stuart Mill High School, and most of the cheerleaders and dancers had already disembarked. The few that remained were in the front, waiting for everyone to get out of their way. I watched as they all stepped off the bus, wondering who'd eventually come back to make sure I hadn't died or something.

It ended up being the bus driver.

He was halfway down the steps when he turned and saw me, then sighed heavily and trudged his way back. He stood over me for a second as if he couldn't even tell if I was alive, but then decided to find out by saying, "Hey, son, we're home. Ya gotta get off."

"I know," I said. "I'm going." I grabbed my trombone and stood up, causing my sticky underwear to again press up against my skin. It was making me sick.

"You sure is a lucky son of a bitch, ridin' this bus with all them girls," the driver said as he turned around and walked to the front.

"I sure am."

I avoided everyone for the rest of the night; as I didn't want to explain the dark spot on my band pants. People already had enough reason to make fun of me. I was pretty sure the girl who'd made me ejaculate realized what happened, but I thought I'd play it safe just in case she did pull away in time. I waited until everyone was out of the band room before I put away my trombone, then I waited until everyone was gone before I called my parents. The band director normally had to stick around for the last student's parents to arrive, but that never seemed to be the case with me.

As I sat on the curb of the high school parking lot, all I could think about was how Heath Millard would've handled what had just happened had he been in my place. Or what about my best friend Terry Hogan who'd moved to Toledo? I kept running through the event over and over, only I kept replacing me with other people. I didn't want to have any part of it, but I sure wanted everyone else to. I knew they all would've fared better than I.

Suddenly there was someone behind me. Before I had time to even fear that it was another cheerleader, I heard, "Hi Guy." The voice was soft and hesitant, like a child's when approaching a frightened, abandoned dog. I turned to see who it was, but her face was blackened out by the floodlight behind her, casting a halo of light around her head.

I didn't say anything.

"I'm sorry about what happened on the bus," she continued after a moment. "They can be real immature sometimes."

I still didn't talk. I was afraid of what would come out.

"They're okay, though, most the time. They didn't mean anything by it. They were just trying to have fun."

Hearing this, I turned away. Now I didn't even *want* to say anything.

Sensing this, the girl sat down beside me. "Who am I kidding? They're bitches, right?"

I looked back at her, and now I could see her face. She was smiling at me warmly. I really believed she felt bad for what had just happened, and I felt safe for the first time that night.

"I'm Ann," she greeted. "Ann Penella."

I knew that. Everyone in school knew Ann.

"I'm Guy Lindsey."

"I know," she said. I looked at her inquisitively, so she added, "I saw your name on the bus list. I was wondering what kind of moron would sign to ride the cheerleader bus."

She laughed lightly at her comment, so I smiled. I continued to look at her, but I couldn't find anything to say; I was afraid I'd look like a...well, like the fool on the bus. I was spared the awkward moment when my father pulled his restored, forest green 1970 Chevy Impala into the lot. He rarely took it out, so I was quite surprised.

"That's my dad," I said with relief.

She continued to smile. "Take it easy, Guy."

"Thanks," I said as I stood up. I felt as though I should add something, so I did. "You too."

"I will," she agreed, standing as my dad stopped the car in front of us. "And Guy? Get off that bus before next week."

I smiled, got into the car, and shut the door. My dad asked who she was, so I told him it was just some girl who didn't want to wait alone. He seemed disappointed it wasn't something more. I couldn't tell him why she was talking to me, as I didn't really know myself. I also didn't know why I wasn't able to talk back to her. I guess I just wasn't that good at conversation. I hadn't been good at it in grade school, I still wasn't in high school, and I never even acquired the art in college. Perhaps this is one of the reasons why I became so impressed with the Arbiter. He always seemed to know exactly what to do and say no matter what the situation.

Thus bringing me back to the night when he and I went to see Rhonda in *Antigone*. He had visited her on and off a couple of times beforehand, mostly to help with lines and once or twice just to get something to eat at Panthemom's Pizzeria and Restaurant down the road from our dorm. But he hadn't yet taken her out formally, and he had yet to kiss her or even hold her hand. All they'd done was talk, yet each time the Arbiter came to my room afterwards he was more in love. Each time I went to his room, there were more high bouncing balls on the floor.

We took seats close to the front of President's Performing Arts Center for the Performing Arts. Although I was a junior, it was the first time I'd been in there for an actual theater production, having before only attended that forum of President's my sophomore year. I didn't like theater too much because it didn't seem real to me. There weren't enough graphic depictions of sex and violence for it to accurately reflect life in modern America. Not enough bus chases and full frontal prostitutes and sword fighting skeletons and the like. There's not one play by Edward Albee, Stephen Sondheim, or even Rogers and Hammerstein that couldn't have benefited from a good bus explosion.

"Oh what a beautiful morning/Oh what a beautiful—"

BOOM!!!!!

Now *that's* theater.

So I confess I wasn't looking forward to Floodbane's production of the Sophocles classic. All I knew about the story was that this one woman insisted on burying her brother properly even though they dug him up at one point after she'd already buried him. Rhonda played this woman. I liked that concept, but I was sure she wouldn't end up getting hit by a bus.

The Arbiter, on the other hand, was waiting for the play to start in much the same way that a father waits for his daughter's name to be called at graduation. He seemed so proud of the whole thing, but not in a patronizing way. He was in love, after all, and as I sat there in the maroon-colored theater, lit up brilliantly by the three chandeliers, numerous stair lights and the Floodbane College Coat of Arms projected onto the main curtain, I realized I could no longer remember what love felt like.

That made me feel safe.

"Did you send her flowers?" I asked the Arbiter. Although I didn't participate in theater, I still knew some of the traditions.

"Of course," he replied, staring intently at the curtain in front of him. "Always on opening night."

"No other nights?" I asked. I was just making conversation.

The Arbiter turned to me with a "get real" type of look. "It's love, not obsession," he explained.

"You're the one using her toothbrush," I joked, referring to his first phone conversation with her.

He laughed.

"What did you say on the card?" I continued to pry. Most people would've thought this to be a rude question, but I knew the Arbiter wouldn't mind. His life was open for anyone who cared to look. He knew most people wouldn't.

"Not much," the Arbiter replied. "Just said, 'Good luck, Macbeth.'"

I laughed. "Really."

He shrugged.

"That's bad luck to say 'good luck,'" I reminded him. Along with knowing the traditions, I also knew the superstitions. None of them made much sense to me, and the 'good luck' vs. 'break a leg' well-wishing made the least. But actors are a passionate lot, and the superstitions, no matter how ridiculous, are always taken as gospel. In fact, "Hell, it's bad luck to mention *Macbeth*. You've cursed her!"

He smiled. "Pretty eager for the play to start. Dying to see what'll happen."

I dropped my head into my right palm and shook it back and forth. I was suddenly terribly frightened for the entire troupe, but...I was also much more interested in seeing the play. I'd grown so used to feelings of impending doom that it had become one of my favorite things. And maybe now that bus accident really would happen.

But no, the play came off without a hitch, and Rhonda was great in it.

> *"Rhonda's performance made me want to bury my dead brother!"*
>
> —Kerry Von Erich, *A Daily Planet*

Aside from the fact that no one screwed up, I sort of enjoyed the play. I mean, there were no sword fighting skeletons or anything, but the whole play was centered around the nobility of death and how people react to it, so I guess that was good enough for me. It made me think that perhaps the person I killed in high school shouldn't have been buried. Some people just aren't worth the effort.

When the play was over, the Arbiter and I waited in the lobby for Rhonda to meet us. I was sure she'd be mad at the Arbiter for the note he had left with the flowers, but I was again way off the mark. It took her a while to emerge from the hallway that led to the dressing room; she had to remove her make-up and hang up her costumes and all. When she finally did come out, she walked right up to the Arbiter, put her hands on his neck and—for the first time—kissed him full on the lips.

The Arbiter was pleased.

"Hi Guy," Rhonda greeted me as she released the Arbiter. I don't think he wanted quite yet to win back his freedom.

"You did a great job tonight," I said. "I mean it."

"Thank you," she gracefully accepted, and then turned to look squarely into the Arbiter's eyes. "And thank you, Arby, for the flowers. They're beautiful."

"I'm glad you liked them," he smiled. She was still holding onto his neck.

"And your note was hilarious," she continued. "The others were all freaking out. They were ready to cancel the whole show because of you!"

"Told you," I smirked to the Arbiter.

"I can hardly wait to see the tape," Rhonda added. "I'd like to see if anyone kept looking into the rafters for fear of falling sandbags."

I was puzzled. "I thought plays weren't supposed to be filmed."

"They're not," Rhonda agreed, "unless they're either bad productions of Andrew Lloyd Webber musicals on PBS or potential enrollee recruitment films for second rate theater departments at small colleges. Anyway, you guys will have to watch the tape with me sometime."

"That's not likely," the Arbiter stated.

"Why not?" Rhonda didn't seem hurt, but she was taken aback.

Knowing of the dead actor rule, I was curious to see how he'd be able to satisfy Rhonda without lying to her.

"Same reason I won't watch wedding or vacation videos," was his reply.

"Fair enough," Rhonda smiled.

Unbelievable.

"Guy, you'll watch it with me, won't you?"

"Sure," I shrugged. "Although I'd be more interested had a few sandbags actually fallen."

"We've got a few more performances, Guy. Don't give up hope. Oh, that was hilarious, Arby. They all hate me now, I'm sure. Only you forgot to mention whistling, so I just whistled away!" Rhonda started whistling a tune I didn't recognize, again mocking theater superstitions.

Apparently, the Arbiter didn't either as he asked her, "What piece is that?"

"Song," Rhonda corrected. "'The Far Side of Crazy.'"

"Must be Mozart," he said.

"Wall of Voodoo," she added, as if that was supposed to explain something. "They're not together anymore."

The Arbiter and I looked at each other blankly.

"You wouldn't like them, Arby," Rhonda told him, reaching over to shake his chin. "They're a rock band."

"I thought you don't like rock music," the Arbiter questioned.

"Not so much," Rhonda confessed, "but Wall of Voodoo is good."

"Why Wall of Voodoo?" I asked. I knew this had to be some kind of character defining trait that would help me understand her that much more.

She sang her reply.

"'In a circle, we place ourselves. It's the human thing to do
It's a cruel play, a lifelike stage. Tell me it's the same for you.'"

So much for understanding her. No wonder she and the Arbiter hit it off so quickly.

"When I die, are you going to see that I get a proper burial?" the Arbiter asked. Kind of a maudlin question, I thought, but Rhonda didn't seem to mind.

"Will people try to stop that?" she asked.

"One never can tell who will hate me by the time I'm dead," the Arbiter pointed out.

"Well, maybe I'll die first…then I won't have to worry about it," Rhonda smiled.

The Arbiter finally got off this subject with, "Well, on that note, I'm hungry. Want to get something to eat?" the Arbiter asked.

"Sure," Rhonda replied.

The Arbiter then turned to me and asked, "You coming?" in a manner that answered his question for me.

"No, you two go ahead," I said. "I have to go back to my room and find something to do so that you two can be alone."

They laughed.

As I watched them leave, walking hand in hand through the marbled lobby of the theater, I found myself laughing at the almost surrealistic aura that surrounded them. I mean, it made sense they would hit it off, but not so suddenly, and not in such a big way. Not in a theater lobby after he'd just written her a note that—in the mind of most actors—could have caused the entire theater to crumble down faster than the walls of Jericho. I mean, I had at least offered her popcorn, right? Love like this just didn't happen…unless of course a bus were about to hit them both.

But they didn't need to hear my prophecies of doom. Maybe it was just me. Maybe it was just because of the way my only romance had ended a mere year and a half after it began.

It ended with blood in the grass.

CHAPTER 4

Beggars Can't Be Choosers

*R*honda would eventually play for us the CDs by the band who wrote "Empty Room," the song she whistled after her performance in *Antigone*. Some of it was pretty good, most of it was very bizarre, and all of it was very dark. One song in particular stood out in my mind, the chorus of which went like this:

> And I'll remain on the far side of crazy
> I'll remain a mortal enemy of man
> No hundred dollar cure will save me
> Can't stay a boy in no-man's land

When I confessed to Rhonda I liked the song, she responded, "That makes sense." I'm not exactly sure what she meant by it. I mean, even though I was a recovering killer, I hardly think that qualified me as "crazy." And I say recovering killer in much the same way that a man will say he's a recovering alcoholic. It's a tricky label, really, and one that's not altogether fair. I mean, if an alcoholic quits drinking, he can't just be normal? There's no label for former alcoholic, so they just tag him "recovering." I killed someone, and I hadn't done it since. So, by the same logic, I was a recovering killer.

But again, I wasn't crazy. Certainly not like John Hinkley, Jr. the guy who tried to assassinate President Reagan, and about whom that song was written. And especially not like the Arbiter. He was the one, after all, who wrote letters to dead actors and climbed radio towers.

The first time I saw him climb a tower was also the only time I ever followed him up. I can't even say that I did that, really, as I didn't make it nearly as far as he. I don't know if I underestimated the Arbiter's intentions, the height of the tower, or the ability of my legs to proclaim, "Okay, Pappy, this is as far as we go," but I became stranded about thirty feet up while the Arbiter continued to ascend until he was nothing more than a tiny, black spider creeping along strands of red and white metallic webbing.

I remember the event quite well, mainly because I continue to dream about it with frequency. Odd dreams, too…as if there's such a thing as a normal dream.

I've been told that if people hit the ground while falling in a dream, they die. I guess that's what the papers mean when reporting that so-and-so died in his sleep; it wasn't because he was ill or anything, he just didn't wake up before hitting the ground.

In my dreams about the radio tower, I always hit the ground when I fall. Sometimes I slow down and land softly, and other times my feet inflate to clown-like proportions, and I bounce when I hit. One time, I even told jokes on the way down. I was falling and delivering lines such as, "Six hundred feet and all's well," or "Anyone here from the ground? Can I bum a ride home?" There was a crowd of people at the bottom, sitting at small, round bar tables drinking cocktails. They laughed at my jokes and applauded when my feet got big as I landed. Then they turned their attention back to the top of the tower to see who was next. It was Andy Kauffman, and he was wearing his wrestling outfit—thermal underwear and all—from that time he wrestled Jerry Lawler in the early 80s. He didn't tell any jokes, though. He just fell straight down. The audience tittered nervously as he fell, and—just before he hit the ground—I woke up.

Too late to help Andy, unfortunately.

I woke up laughing, as I do from most my dreams. They never scare me, even if I'm facing imminent death. I guess my dreams are the one place where I'm not afraid…unlike on the radio tower that night with the Arbiter.

It was only two nights after we'd gone to see Rhonda perform in *Antigone*. The Arbiter had seen the show twice, but opted against seeing it a third time unless Rhonda would promise him she would somehow work the phrase "ride my majestic frigate" into the show. She wouldn't, so the Arbiter kept the six bucks (student price, of course) and stayed home. I guess that to kill time that evening, he thought maybe he'd try to kill me.

Well, not really. Not in the manner that I've killed, anyway.

Knowing now the Arbiter wrote letters to dead actors, I suppose I shouldn't have been surprised by anything else this guy did. After all, I really didn't know him as well as I sometimes thought. Our conversations never ventured beyond superficial, centering mainly around wrestling, the newspaper, pudding and the like. The Arbiter also had his plethora of friends and admirers, and I wasn't about to acquire his friends as mine by default. I'd learned my lesson from Heath Millard. Still, although I couldn't say we were confidants or anything, I felt I at least knew enough about him so that if I were asked, "Does your friend the Arbiter ever climb radio towers in the dead of night just for the hell of it?" I would've been able to answer, without fear of correction, a resounding, "No."

So, when the Arbiter called me up that Saturday evening and asked if I'd like to climb the WDOA radio tower with him, I said, "What the hell? I've got nothing else to do." He could've asked me if I wanted to launch bottle rockets at cows and I would've said, "What the hell? I've got nothing else to do."

When the Arbiter came to my dorm room and told me to wear something black, I still don't think I was taking him seriously.

As I grabbed a pair of black Levi's and started to put them on, I asked, "Isn't it a little hot for jeans tonight?"

"No, it's cooled down since this afternoon," he said as he threw a black backpack—much like the one currently strapped across his back—onto my bed and walked over to the window. The WDOA radio tower was visible from my room, and he stared at the blinking red light with the intense concentration of a middleweight boxer sizing up his opponent before the opening bell. I kept waiting for him to challenge, "Let's get it on!" although a part of me know he'd never say that. Instead, he merely offered, "Even if it were hot, you'd still have to wear long, dark pants."

"Why?" I asked, digging through my dresser for a black shirt.

The Arbiter turned to me. "What do you think the biggest danger is in climbing a radio tower?"

I paused a moment and looked out to the red light that was perpetually blinking in the distance like some neon motel sign telling truckers that yes, there was room for them. Neon signs always hid something, I felt. They were masks to hide what really attracted the customers. The blue sign that advertised beer in the tiny window of the small town diner was really convincing everyone that this was their chance to escape the revolving credit card debt, the delinquent kids and the Rotary Club commitments for a night. The red lights announcing vacancy in the roadside motel were really stirring up the drivers for the hookers at the other end of the motel phone. The warning light at the top of the WDOA radio tower was really proposing free death for anyone interested in flying into it…or climbing for it.

I suppose I should point out that no one at Floodbane had any idea how the call letters came to be WDOA. I guess it was just bad luck. But despite the unfortunate name, WDOA did have the second highest ratings in the tri-county area. The only station to beat it was WNOD, which was somewhat of a militant radio station that played nothing but gangsta rap. Its popularity still baffles me, what with it being well out of range of any sort of urban audience. I guess it's true what they say; good rhythms and violence geared towards police officers and be-atches really do know no boundaries.

Aside from the metal supports directly beneath it and the other three smaller, fixed red lights at the middle of the structure, the tower itself was hidden by the darkness of the moonless sky. It was as if the lights were nothing but brighter, bigger stars about to swallow up everything that surrounded them. This is why I couldn't take the Arbiter seriously. No one had ever suggested to me that I doom myself to being swallowed by a dying star.

Well, my high school guidance counselor did, but we decided upon Floodbane College instead.

"Death," I finally responded. "Death is the biggest danger."

He laughed. "Death?"

"Well, yeah. I mean…you know…electrocution. Or we could fall off," I explained. Of course, my dreams would teach me that, if this happened, my feet would inflate and save me.

"Do you believe in God?" the Arbiter asked me abruptly.

I furrowed my eyebrows in confusion at this sudden theological twist in the conversation. "Yeah, but I just don't like Him all that much."

"Asked the wrong question," the Arbiter corrected himself after weighing my answer. "Do you believe in Hell?"

"No."

"So then why are you afraid of dying?" he asked.

"I don't know," I said. I really didn't know. "I guess I'm just not ready to find out what's out there."

"Out where?" the Arbiter persisted.

I really had no idea how to answer him. I felt as if I were back in second grade, being pestered by Mrs. Garvin into answering whether "dolphin" is spelled with an F or with a P and an H. I suddenly wished I could just speak out of turn and get sent to the hall to be by myself.

"Out there in...you know...in death," I answered weakly. "Out there in death."

For some reason, I was pointing out the window.

The Arbiter followed my finger, then turned back to me with a smile. "Sounds pretty agoraphobic."

I laughed and resumed my search a black shirt. "Well, that's my new goal, to become agoraphobic."

"Everyone should have a goal," the Arbiter said. "Without goals, there's really no reason to go on."

"What's your goal?" I asked.

"Don't have one," he replied.

As he answered, I pulled out a black sweatshirt that had the phrase "Support the Wittgenstein County Baby Beef Club," inscribed in small, red letters. I'm not sure how the shirt came to be in my possession. I was unaware of the fact that Wittgenstein County had a Baby Beef Club. I didn't even know what a Baby Beef Club was. And where the hell was Wittgenstein County?

The Arbiter nodded at my choice of dark clothing, and I then asked him, "Is there anything you enjoy in life that *isn't* directly related to death?"

Without pausing a second, he retorted, "Rhonda excluded, is there anything in life *worth* enjoying that isn't directly related to death?"

I let out a sigh as I pulled the sweatshirt over my head. I decided to counter his despondency with some of my own. "Is there anything in life worth enjoying at all? Rhonda excluded, of course."

"Yes," the Arbiter responded as tossed the second backpack to me and told me to put it on. It was heavier than I expected. "Miniature golf. Are you ready?"

"I guess," I said, still not really believing we were going to go through with it.

"Then have at it."

As we exited the room, I reached back quickly to stop the door from shutting and locking behind us. I then re-entered the room and came back out with a roll of Pep-O-Mint Life Savers. I showed them to the Arbiter, he smirked, and we headed down the rust-orange carpeted hallway. As we walked, a question he had asked earlier returned to nag me. "You never did tell me what the most dangerous part of climbing a radio tower is."

"No?"

"No. You just said it wasn't death. What could be worse than death?"

The Arbiter turned towards the stairway and bounded down them two steps at a time. When we got to the door, he threw it open and we stepped outside. He then turned to me. "Getting caught."

I was surprised by just how tall the radio tower really was. I'd seen it a thousand times before, of course. Because it was the highest structure in the small town of Floodbane, it was impossible to look west from anywhere on campus and not see it. It was also the first thing people saw when they came to town, which is probably why the Floodbane College flag was flown so proudly at the top. I was always under the impression that the reason for the light at the top of radio towers was to announce to airplane pilots that imminent death stood erect just beneath it, but that they'd be okay if only they'd stay above the light. Yet, up there was the flag, just waiting to wrap itself around a propeller or crash through a canopy. There were even rumors on campus that it was the Floodbane flag which brought down Patsy Cline's plane. Of course, since the Arbiter and I started those rumors, their credibility was suspect.

What made this even more confusing was that Floodbane College's official colors were clear and opaque. Honestly, I'm not making this up. The flag looked like a huge, clear lollipop wrapper blowing free of its stick.

I'm going off on yet another tangent now, if that's okay. As with everything else at Floodbane, the official papers documenting how the school colors became clear and opaque had long been destroyed and forgotten, plaguing the history with rumor and conjecture. The most popular story was that the football team couldn't afford uniforms, so, because they never seemed to have matching shirts, they would play as "skins." This, of course, was not allowed in organized college sports. In order to be allowed to take the field against the Berkowitz College Rambling Rotweilers one day in the early 1900s, they were forced to convince the refs they *were* wearing uniforms and that they were just invisible. The refs didn't believe it, I'm sure, but guys are usually willing to let things slide to get a good game of tackle football going.

The "invisible uniforms" weren't in use by the time I was accepted into Floodbane. For although it cut down on uniform costs and helped to sell tickets, the colors were changed at right about the point when Title IX was passed and female sports started to grow in popularity. Although the athletic department abandoned the traditional clear and opaque stylings, they remained the official school colors.

But the athletic breasts of the Floodbane College alumni were not on my mind as I watched the Arbiter deftly set about getting us over the barbed wire fence surrounding both the tower and the concrete building at its base. Although the barbing was the type to keep cows in a pasture and not that which is used to stop prisoners from gaining freedom or American soldiers from crossing the beaches of Normandy, it still seemed obvious that the people who'd constructed the tower didn't want any stupid college students getting near it. Even the guide wires that reached down from the tower were fenced in with barbed wire where they burrowed into the ground.

The Arbiter, of course, seemed to notice neither the barbed wire nor the…

DANGER
HIGH VOLTAGE

...signs posted on each wall of the fence and of the building, eight warnings in all. Instead, he walked to the fence gate that had been locked shut with a heavy chain and two padlocks the size of my fist. There was a gap about three inches wide between the gate doors, and this is where the Arbiter stood.

He opened the backpack he'd had me carry and removed two large, thick pieces of cloth. After pulling them out, he said, "You can lose the backpack now. You won't be needing it."

"What, don't you have a parachute in here?" I asked as I pulled it from my shoulders and set it against the fence. It was still heavy despite the removal of the cloths. The contents seemed stiff, but I didn't bother checking to see what was in it.

"Parachute wouldn't have time or room to open," the Arbiter explained. He was making no move to open his own backpack that was stuffed fuller than mine had been. Whatever was in there, he obviously intended to take to the top of the tower with him. There was a method to his madness after all.

That is what scared me most.

As I scanned the area to see if anyone was around, the Arbiter jumped onto the fence so his left foot was resting on top of the padlock. His head was now over the top of the fence, and he was placing the two pieces of cloth over the barbed wire on either end of the gap. He looked like a little kid trying to sneak into a baseball game or the country fair. Despite my high hopes, I just knew there wouldn't be a booth on the other side where I could pick up an elephant ear.

"Hope you're watching this," he said as he raised his right foot onto the barbed wire that was buried safely beneath the cloth.

"Yeah," I said, turning to look again for the policemen whom I was sure were hiding just out of sight, waiting for the right moment to jump out and startle us enough so we'd panic and they'd have just cause to shoot us. But there was no one out there. No shadows beyond the floodlight that shone from the wall of the building at the base of the tower. No rustling of the bushes behind the fence or crackling of the stones on the road that led back to the college. The only sounds to be heard were the chirping of insects that hid around the area, the hum of the generator inside the building, and the clanging of the fence as it jiggled beneath the Arbiter's weight.

It took the Arbiter only a second to throw his left leg up under his right in what would've been an excellent breakdancing move in 1983, and then fall forward to the stones on the other side of the fence. He landed on his feet and allowed his legs to buckle so his butt came to rest on his heels. He squatted there a moment like an Olympic gymnast after performing an unsuccessful Russian dismount, then sprang back up and dusted off his hands. He turned to indicate it was my turn. I cursed myself for not taking those lessons from Bela Karolji when I had the chance, or at least renting *American Anthem* a couple more times.

I sighed deeply, then grabbed hold of the fence. I tried to hop onto the top padlock as the Arbiter had, but, being a bit heavier than he, I guess I didn't have his dexterity. After a couple attempts, the Arbiter told me to hold on and stuck his knee through the gap in the doors. I stepped onto his bent leg, then stepped the rest of the way up to the padlock. I stood there for a second, then looked down at him.

"There's no way I'm going to be able to get my leg up there," I said. "I think I'll just go back."

"Not an option," the Arbiter said. "You have to do this. It's for your own good."

"Yeah, you never know when you'll have to climb a radio tower, so it's always good to be in practice," I agreed sarcastically. "More than likely I'll just kill myself."

"That could be for your own good, too," the Arbiter suggested as I continued to balance myself on the padlock. The doors were swinging slightly against the chain, forcing me to shift my weight back and forth in jerky motions. I must've looked like a fawn taking its first steps.

"How so?" I asked.

"Well, for one thing, you won't have to answer the questions the police ask after you're caught because you spent so damn long at the top of a fence with a floodlight shining directly upon you," the Arbiter pointed out in a calm, matter-of-fact tone.

"Oh yeah," I said with sarcasm. "I forgot. Getting caught is worse than falling a few hundred feet and breaking every bone in my body, as you explained."

"Lots of bones in the human body," the Arbiter pointed out. "The chance of breaking every one of them is very slim."

The Arbiter had a habit of missing points like this…or at least ignoring them. "But I'll probably break some of them in more than one place, so that'll compensate."

The Arbiter laughed. "You're kind of funny when you're scared. Now come on."

"I really think I'd rather just wait here for the police."

"Why? Falling is so much quicker than waiting."

"Depends on how high you're falling from."

"This is just enough to kill you, not enough to let you enjoy it."

"You're not doing much to change my mind."

"Don't have to change your mind. You'll change it yourself."

I squinted and looked down at him for a moment. I wanted to tell him he was wrong, that there was no way in hell I was going to cross over the fence and climb that damn tower with him. I wanted to tell him that he was nuts and that I was going back to my room to grow some Magic Rocks or something and would either see him tomorrow or read about him in the *A Daily Planet* obituaries Monday morning.

The obituary section was actually President's idea. It was mainly filled with the names of alumni, revealing in what year they graduated and how much money they left the school so others might be enticed into doing the same. In fact, a Fayme family member was included nearly every week. Unfortunately, none of them was ever Jayson. It was odd, really, because only those who donated to Flood-bane received obituaries. It's as if no one else ever died. Those who didn't contribute to the college coffers achieved immortality.

As I started to tell the Arbiter just where he could stuff this tower, I found myself heaving my right leg onto the cloth over the barbed wire. Knowing I couldn't possibly pull this off with my left leg, I instead swept my right leg the rest of the way over so that I was strad-dling the opening between the gates. I then braced myself on the poles of the gates, hoisted my hips over the top and forced my left leg through so that I was neatly standing on the padlock on the other side of fence.

The Arbiter raised his eyebrows at me, then tilted his head to one side. "Never thought of doing it that way."

"Because you'd rather risk slicing your legs open on the barbed wire," I pointed out as I jumped to the rocks below. Having less distance to fall, I didn't need to buckle down the way the Arbiter had when he landed. "You have no respect for your health. Or life, for that matter."

"Maybe so, maybe so," the Arbiter agreed as he jumped back up the fence to retrieve the two pieces of cloth from the barbed wire. He then hopped back down and led me around the building which housed the generator, dropping the cloths against the building's wall. "But what has life done to earn respect?"

"It's given you Rhonda," I pointed out.

The Arbiter smiled. "For that, it earned loyalty, not respect."

As we passed behind the building on our way to the tower, I became more aware of the deep hum the generator was produc-ing…like the sound of an oboe striking a tuning note for the rest of the orchestra.

Orchestra.

Band.

Ann Penella.

See how that works?

❧   ❧   ❧

I didn't really expect anything to become of my friendship with Ann. I mean, I knew she was different from everyone else—she proved that by defending me during my orgiastic ordeal on that school bus—but Ann was swiftly becoming a popular girl at John Stuart Mill High School. She couldn't jeopardize that by talking to someone like me. This is why I understood when she ignored me during the week after that fateful bus ride. Well, to be fair, I guess I can't say she was ignoring me. She just didn't notice me. As I was with everyone else, I was invisible to Ann.

The only problem was that I didn't *want* to be invisible to her. So maybe it was a good thing when Mr. Bravo denied me the chance to switch buses for the ride to Immanuel Kant Catholic High School to battle the Orange Riders the next week. For although Ann hadn't spoken to me all week, she immediately took a seat beside me when we boarded for the trip. At that point, I realized I had become her charity. When I was being left alone and was in no danger, there was no reason for her to be on patrol. But the moment anyone raised a weapon against me, she would become a shield with which I could defend myself. She had become my Aegis.

I at first felt ashamed for needing her protection. I felt I was an albatross to her, and that, were she given a choice, she would rather have been sitting with her friends, talking about which English teacher was the most boring and which was the best looking…and which was the least likely to blatantly split an infinitive.

Then I felt ashamed for thinking of her this way. She didn't need to help me out the other night, and she certainly didn't need to offer her services again. And so what if she didn't talk to me during the week? My mother had always told me that, "Beggars can't be choosers." If I could be her friend only five Friday nights a year, so be it.

Those Friday nights belonged to me like Saturday nights belonged to beer advertisers.

This is probably why a little over a year after she first came to my rescue, I would choose a Friday night during my junior year to "let down my guard," as they say; why I would choose a Friday night to lower my drawbridge for Ann so she might ride on in and see how comfortable and secure life really was behind my castle walls…and maybe decide to live there with me. I had tried valiantly to fight off these thoughts for a couple months, but knowing she was outside the walls suddenly made me realize just how alone I was inside. The days leading up to my confrontation with her were filled with intoxicating visions of true love and ultimate happiness, watered down by the fear of total failure and the fact that I had been purposely ignoring her for nearly two months. So, although I had finally found the courage to talk to her during the third quarter of a football game our junior year, I still found myself dizzyingly terrified.

Much like when I took my first few steps up the ladder of the WDOA radio tower.

❦   ❦   ❦

At least we weren't on the outside of the thing; the Arbiter had enough sense to climb inside the triangular construction of the tower, which—along with the altitude, I suppose—explained his comment about a parachute not having room to open. The tower tapered to a point at its base, like a pencil or a top. The openings where the triangular portion began to taper were just large enough for us to shimmy through, so I soon found myself crowded inside the tower like one of those girls named Jessica who periodically make the national news by falling into a well. I wondered if I'd be on the news if I got trapped. I wondered if the nation would care for me so much that the wife of our country's president would put off an operation until she was sure that I was safe. God, would that have pissed me off. The attention I could've dealt with I suppose, but not the sympathy from the President's wife.

That's another reason I never admitted I killed somebody back in high school. I could've dealt with jail, I'm sure. I had no friends to miss. I had no monuments to visit or galas to attend. Hell, my sex life probably would've improved in prison…although not in a manner I would've enjoyed. I could've traded cigarettes for protection from some big dumb guy named Smooth, gotten a college degree, improved my miniature golf game and seen college productions of *The Who's Tommy*. But I knew I could never cope with the sympathy. Nobody would scorn or judge me as a killer because I'd be as much a victim as the person I killed. My parents would be blamed for letting me watch wrestling and play video games, and then the media would toss me out like an abandoned baby so the nation could look at me through their patronizing eyes and weep for my lost life. That's what would've killed me, and I'm sure that is what the Arbiter meant when he said getting caught would be worse than dying.

Only how did he know?

I made a mental note to probe into this further, but not at that moment. For although I finally understood what the Arbiter told me earlier, I didn't necessarily agree with it. As I continued to claw my way higher, clutching tenaciously to the metal bars that were wet with the moisture of the evening air and the sweat of my palms, all I could find myself fearing was death.

I tried to think of something else, but it was difficult. It was like trying to escape the situation when those cheerleaders were accosting me on the school bus in high school. How is that possible? When a guy has two women sitting on his lap, one running her hand up his leg, how can he think of anything other than two women sitting on his lap, one running her hand up his leg? Slowly up his leg, applying a little more pressure there, and oh God, don't stop with the neck. Likewise, when he's about to fall to his death, how can he think of anything but?

I wondered how my parents would take my death. How about the Arbiter and Rhonda? Would the Arbiter feel responsible? Would Rhonda blame him? I even went as far back as grade school—back to the teacher's lounge with Mrs. Piper and Principal Steele:

"Do you remember a boy named Guy Lindsey?" Mrs. Piper would've asked.

"Yes, I know his parents," Principal Steele would've smiled, still practicing his ever impressive principalesque head nod. "Fine people. Salt of the Earth."

"Well, he died last weekend," Mrs. Piper would've continued. "Fell off a radio tower."

"Hmm." Principal Steele would've now moved on to rubbing his finger over his lips, wondering if it made him look more sophisticated. "Interesting death for a college student. Better than getting caught by the police, though. Which station did the tower belong to?"

"'To which station did the tower belong,'" Mrs. Piper would've corrected.

The Arbiter, of course, didn't seem phased by the climb at all. It's not that I expected him to be terrified, but I was at least hoping for some kind of hesitance. If he was doing this for the adrenaline rush that usually accompanies risking one's life, then perhaps I would have understood. Hell, he could've gotten himself a bronze in the Xtreme Games. But no, as the full backpack had indicated, he had some kind of agenda. I was beginning to think the guy was fearless. Fearless, and, therefore, completely and totally nuts.

He started out just a few feet above me, making sure that I was safely (?) inside the tower before he began his ascent. He then gave me a couple words of encouragement and proceeded to climb. For the first fifteen feet or so, I kept good pace. Aside from the fact that my back kept brushing the steel bars behind me, and that less than six inches from my body were thick pipes and tubes with more voltage flowing through them than I cared to consider, it was really no different from climbing a ladder to pick an apple. Actually, strike that. It was nothing like climbing a ladder to pick an apple. Dumb analogy. Sorry. It was more like King Kong climbing the Empire State Building. Nowhere to go but down. Quickly. Hard.

It was this thought that finally froze me stiff. My legs and arms tightened up, and I could no longer force them to move. I looked up to see how far ahead the Arbiter had gotten, and it took me a moment to find him because of the distance he'd already covered. I tried to climb higher to catch him; I really did. It's not as if I had to prove myself to the Arbiter, he had never asked that of me, but more as if some kind of prize was waiting up there, something like a cherry pie or tickets to the Royal Rumble. And as I managed to fight my right arm and left leg up to the next rungs, I realized why I had this thought. Some of my happiest high school moments came to me after climbing things. Well, after climbing one thing, anyway; the TV antennae that stood outside Ann Penella's bedroom window.

She lived in the country. Quite a way out, in fact, which I guess was lucky for me. If she hadn't, her family could've pulled in cable and wouldn't have needed the TV antenna that became my stairway to Heaven. But she was *really* out there in the country. Her house was surrounded for miles by farmland, and only one other home could be easily seen from hers. Odd, and somewhat ominous, was the fact that it belonged to Professor Snow.

Al Snow had been a professor of physics at my town's college and was apparently quite a good one. At least that's what the students and faculty had said about him in the papers after his accident. Then again, people rarely have anything bad to say about those who have suffered. That really kind of bugs me, by the way. Like if they were rotten people, then we're suddenly supposed to forget that just because they upped and died. I guess I was just never that fickle. Or maybe I was just never that forgiving. I don't know.

And even worse is when a child dies in a fire or something. I always hate to see that, but I also hate when the reporters get on TV and say, "He was such a happy boy; always laughing and playing. He never had a bad thing to say about anyone." Bullshit. Kids cry and throw tantrums and make fun of other kids and never share their damn Popsicles with others even if they've got the kind that come in pairs. It's tragic that the child died, sure, but why paint him to be an angel sent straight from God? We don't need news reporter melodrama to cheapen the tragedy and the parents' suffering.

I'm not saying Professor Snow never shared his Popsicles. I had never known him—or even heard of him—until after the accident. The story went that he wrecked his car on the way back to his house one evening. The reason was never determined, but his car somehow flipped over a few times and slid a good fifteen feet on its top, coming to rest in a ditch. His wife and two kids were killed in the wreck, and the Professor was thrown through the windshield or the door or something. He apparently laid along the side of the road for the better half of the night. When he was found the next morning, he'd already lost a lot of blood. He was raced to the hospital where they managed to save his life, though I doubt he really wanted them to. He suffered some brain damage, and was, therefore, never fully able to retrieve his life from that dark stretch of country road. The doctors say the brain damage came from the loss of so much blood, but I don't think so. He was reportedly conscious the whole time he was lying on the road. That would make me go nuts, too, lying immobilized, knowing my family was either dying or dead in my car less than thirty feet away and there was absolutely nothing I could do about it. I mean, what must've gone through his head? The panic. The fear. What scared him more, I wonder? The fact that he may die or that his family would. Or was it maybe even just the night. It could get so dark and quiet on those country roads outside of town that I wonder if he didn't think maybe he was already dead.

I would have gone insane, too. Unless, of course, I had a fresh roll of Cin-O-Mon Life Savers with me. They're my favorites, usually.

The worst thing to come from the accident was the fact that Professor Snow didn't go quite insane enough. I guess no one deemed him a threat to society, so they released him to move back into his house. No relatives came around to claim him as their own and take him away, so it ended up that Professor Snow spent his existence on the front porch of his once beautiful house, brandishing a shotgun and listening to a police scanner, threatening anyone who drove this far out of town at night.

He threatened me quite often.

I would drive out to Ann's house usually after midnight, as we'd only visit after her parents were asleep. Even that late, Snow would be outside. When I had the windows down and the radio off, I could hear his screaming from up on the porch.

"It's too late to be out on these roads!" he'd yell. "These roads'll kill you! They don't care! They don't care about you at all!"

I always wanted to shout back to him sometime, "I'm used to that, Professor! There's an awful lot out there that doesn't care about me. But sometimes you have to drive on through to get to those who do care."

"But the roads you go down," I imagined the Professor continuing, "they'll kill them too. People that care, people that don't care. They will all die on these roads."

"Then I'll be sure to wear my safety belt."

But that conversation never happened. He just yelled, and I just drove, as I had absolutely no desire to talk to the man. I wasn't afraid of him, but the whole thing was so eerie; the wind rustling up the leaves scattered alongside the road, the moon casting shadows of isolated trees across the miles of farmland, and this kook standing on his porch prophesying doom while his police scanner cackled and spat out potential situations from back in town. I felt sorry for the guy. He wasn't safe out there. He belonged in a home, but no one was willing to go through the hassle of putting him in one. He would either have to die or kill someone in order to end up in safety, and the irony of that would have made me laugh had it not occurred to me each time I passed his house that I might end up becoming the one he killed. Or end up the one killing him. It was almost enough to make me stop going out there.

Almost.

But if it wasn't for my late night visits, I would've rarely spoken to Ann. I mean, we had spent four Friday nights together on a school bus during my sophomore year, and that was about it. When the football season ended, the charity element was eliminated. Sometimes she'd talk to me when we were alone in the hallway or after school or something, but this didn't happen often enough for me. She kept giving me the same line:

"We never see each other any more. Call me. We'll get together sometime."

But we both knew that sometime meant never. Every time I'd stop her to try to set something up, she'd have to get to class or meet her friends or study something. And there was no way I was going to call her. Telephone calls are so difficult…much more difficult than talking in person. Were I to bump into Ann at the grocery store or Gangrel's Dairy Bar near the park, then we could talk without obligation. But if I called her, then I had obviously been thinking about her and damn well better having something wonderful to say. Not for me, this telephone. Far too much pressure to perform.

So, although I thought of her often, I spoke to her rarely. I would watch her in the hallway and follow her as she floated like a swan from friend to friend in the cafeteria. And sometimes she'd catch me staring and give me a quick flash of smile from behind her curly black hair that so often fell in front of her face, and a small wave of her hand as she brushed the curls back behind her ear. Both the smile and the wave were always just enough for only me to notice. I didn't mind that. I also wanted no one else to see. The gestures belonged to me alone.

That thought is what finally clued me in. The reason she never did anything with me was because her family would have too many questions. Who was I? Did she "like" me? How could I benefit their family? Where did I see myself in five years? The same with her friends. If Ann and I went out together, what would her friends think? In high school, only one thing.

So there was just one possibility. We had to meet where no one else would ever see us. Neither her family nor her friends could know. I guess I should've been insulted by this, but it was too exciting. It was like we were having an affair, and I loved that feeling.

It wasn't long after I'd reached this conclusion that I was afforded the opportunity to suggest it to Ann. It was during sixth period chemistry, and while the rest of the class was learning the difference between water and sulfuric acid, I was staring out into the hallway as I so often did when I wasn't staring out the window. And besides, I already knew the difference. I knew the poem:

Alas, poor little Willy
The boy, he is no more
For what he thought was H_2O
Was H_2SO_4

Because Ann worked in the school office during her study hall (all the popular kids seemed too), she happened to walk by the classroom while running some errand for Principal Brandi. I immediately slipped away from my desk and walked out the door. I never needed to get permission to leave a class because no one ever seemed to notice. There were perks to my apparent invisibility. No hall passes, no truancy slips; I could slip in and out of the girls' locker room…well, okay, not the bit about the locker room. For some reason, women tend to get more wary when they're naked. So do I. I tend to get more wary when they're naked, too.

Anyway, Ann wasn't too far ahead of me when I stepped into the hallway, but I decided to catch up a bit before getting her attention. I had to make sure no teacher came out of her classroom to see who was talking in the hallway. I needed isolation.

"Ann," I practically whispered once I was just a few feet behind her.

She turned to see me, then looked back up and down the hallway. "Hi, Guy."

She said that the same way each time she spoke it; very quickly with hardly any inflection, almost in monotone.

"Hi."

"What're you doing out of class?" she asked. I wondered if she was also a hall monitor now, or if John Stuart Mill even had hall monitors.

"I wanted to talk to you," I replied with a little shrug.

"Well, I'm kind of busy right now," she said with a nod towards the principal's office. "Can we talk later?"

Now normally I would've backed away from her lie and given up; I had never been that strong confronting others. But it was…wait; it was different with Ann, and had been right from that night when we sat on the curb of the high school parking lot. Sure, she was too worried about being popular, but with idiots such as Heath Millard running the show, a pretty high school girl didn't have much chance otherwise. So I forgave that one fundamental flaw in her character simply because she seemed so willing to forgive me all of mine. I'm fair like that.

"That's what I want to talk about," I explained. "I have an idea."

Ann glanced up and down the hallway one last time, then grabbed my upper arm and walked me to the stairway…out of sight of any classrooms. Fine by me. As long as she was touching me, she could've led me into a volcano and I wouldn't have complained. "Okay…"

"Well, I was thinking…you know, that we seem to have better conversations when we're alone. You know, without anyone bugging us. So…I was thinking that rather than…well, maybe…we can just meet…kind of…secretly."

When she didn't reply right away, I immediately added, "It can be someplace safe, just private." I would've popped a Life Saver in my mouth, but I was having enough trouble talking already.

Ann smiled to let me know safety wasn't her concern. "Okay, but where?"

"Well, I came up with the idea," I smiled back. "I was hoping that…I was kind of hoping you'd suggest the place."

She thought for a moment. "Let me think about it."

"You could come over to my place maybe," I offered. "My parents are cool."

She pulled back a little. "I'm sure they are, but I don't think…I don't have my license. Do you?"

"Yeah, but I don't have a car."

"That makes it tougher."

"But still doable. My parents'll let me have it when they don't need it. Like later at night…or something."

"Why at night?" She seemed nervous about that. "Why not like on like Saturday morning?"

Okay, she knew I played trombone, but I wasn't about to tell her I couldn't see her because I had to go to lessons. I may've been a "band fag," but I wasn't stupid.

"I would, but I don't want to miss my favorite cartoon. It's got all these evil leaders from history, like Hitler and Atilla the Hun and Vlad the Impaler, only they're all little kids. They're in a gang now, and it's about their wacky adventures as they grow up." I paused. "Don't you want to know what it's called?"

Ann hesitated a moment, but then she smiled. "Okay, I'm biting. What's it called."

I returned her smile. "Dictator-Tots."

Just as I said that, a student walked by and saw the two of us. I had seen the girl before, but I didn't know her name. Luckily, from the looks of things, she didn't run with the "in crowd." She was wearing a 4-H cap and a t-shirt sporting the phrase, "Help! I'm talking on the telephone and I can't shut up!"

However, the possibility of being spotted suddenly became more real to Ann, so she started back towards the main hallway as she said, "Let me think about it, okay Guy?"

Then she was gone around the corner. Man. No reaction at all to my joke, and I thought it was pretty good. Even worse, no confirmation that we should meet. So, just as I was about to smack my head against the wall, Ann came back around.

"Dictator-Tots," she laughed. Then she looked me right in the eyes. "Okay, I have an idea…"

✺   ✺   ✺

"How about if you go on up ahead, and I'll just hang out here?"

I knew the Arbiter was well beyond hearing distance, but I was talking to him anyway. Or anyone, really. For all I cared, it could've been Andy Kauffman up there and I still would've been talking. Probably not in that pigeon language he invented as Latka Gravis, but talking nonetheless. In many situations, talking is all that can be done.

What upset me most, I think, was that I wasn't even at the tree line, and I was petrified. No matter how hard I fought my legs and my arms to reach up just one more rung, they weren't about to cooperate. I was stuck. I had more success looking up than down, and I saw the Arbiter was now completely out of view. He was past the first ring of three lights, and everything above them was blocked from my vision by their deep, amber rays. He may as well have not even been on the tower with me.

Now normally, I would've been comforted by this isolation; I never minded being alone. But being alone at night while jammed inside the structure of a radio tower? Well, that was different.

I have no idea how long I was stranded up there like a baby bird in its nest, frightened that its mother would not return yet too afraid to go out and look for her. But once I accepted the fact that I wasn't going to get over my fear, I became quite calm. It was a nice night, after all, and the winds that blew up around me seemed to wrap and warm me like a grandfather's hug. The trees waved back and forth as if trying to shake off the insects that chattered amongst themselves incessantly. The insects were quite repetitive, but I guess if I was a bug I wouldn't be too full of conversation either.

"Hey, Henry, how did molting go for you?"

"Eh, same ol', same ol', Phinneas. Same ol', same ol'."

Still, monotonous as it was, I enjoyed eavesdropping on their conversation. It was calm. It was placid. Not like the heavy metal music that suddenly started to fight its way over to us from one of the fraternity houses a couple hundred yards away. The music must have been really loud to be heard from such a distance, but that wasn't unusual. The drunker the frat boys got, the louder the music got. I think that was so they couldn't hear how stupid they sounded. Or maybe so their dates couldn't hear how stupid they sounded. I don't know. Surprising as it may be, I tended to avoid such parties.

After a while of thinking about nothing and enjoying it, I was suddenly aware of a presence above me. It wasn't Andy Kauffman.

"How'd it go up there?" I asked the Arbiter.

"Oh, there you are," he answered. "Top of the tower's thataway."

"Yeah, about that," I started to explain, almost apologetically, "I think I should've stretched before I started to climb. My legs just knotted up, you know? I couldn't move."

"No problem," the Arbiter said. "Didn't get this high the first time."

"You've been up here before?"

"Been up here many times. Practically lived up here my freshman year."

"Even up there, you know, I bet the school still would've made you have a roommate."

The Arbiter laughed. "Are you okay to go back down?"

"I hope," I said, once again tightening my grip on the tower. I'd been hanging there for so long that I'd become content to just rest my back against the bars behind me, bracing myself with my feet. Now that I'd once again grabbed hold, I was reminded of how wet and slippery the metal bars had become with the dew. At least my hands were no longer sweating.

As I started my descent, I looked up at the Arbiter. He was only a couple of rungs above me, but he was being careful to not step on my hands. He paused whenever I did.

"So why do you do this?" I asked.

"Do what?"

I didn't feel as though I had to explain my question, but I did anyway. "Climb radio towers. This isn't typical college student fare."

"Guess that's why."

"Why?"

"Think of my other choices on this campus."

I did. "Good point. But there are other less deadly ways to entertain yourself." Had I been thinking, I would've pointed out that he could have written to some dead actors instead.

Actually, scratch that. That would've been a hell of a dumb thing to say.

"Yeah, just like it up there," the Arbiter added to his explanation.

"Why?"

"Because up there...everything seems so small. Can break away from everything up there. Everybody becomes ants," the Arbiter said.

"Kind of like when you're flying in an airplane," I offered.

"No," the Arbiter countered. "In an airplane, there are other passengers. There are stewardesses and the pilots and monsters on the wing all the time ripping up the engines. Up there," he looked back up to the light, "there's no one. Just stay up there all alone and watch all the ants scamper around and do the same things over and over as if it's all they know how to do."

"And what were the ants doing tonight?"

"Mostly just passing out on the porch of that frat over there."

I laughed.

It wasn't much longer before I was wedging my way through the opening at the bottom of the tower. It was much easier to get out then to get in, and I was soon standing outside the tower as the Arbiter slid out beside me. My quadriceps had tightened up to the point of pain, so I sat down to stretch. From down on the stones, I looked up at the tower and was suddenly embarrassed by how far I'd climbed. Thirty or forty feet looked like an awful lot from thirty or forty feet, but from the ground...

"Don't worry about it," the Arbiter said as if reading my thoughts. "You'll get higher next time."

"Oh no," I countered. "Never again."

"It wasn't that bad."

"No, but many things that I'll never do again weren't that bad," I suggested.

The Arbiter raised an eyebrow, then smiled and reached down to retrieve the cloths he'd left before beginning his ascent. His book bag was fuller now, so he had either added to its contents or swapped them for something bigger. But what *had* he taken up there? I desperately wanted to ask, but I had a feeling it would become obvious enough tomorrow morning. Plus, the Arbiter would've told me if he wanted me to know. What he did tell me was that he forgot the binoculars.

"What binoculars?" I asked.

"The ones in your backpack. Forgot they were in your bag."

I picked up the bag and pulled out a rather impressive looking set of binoculars. "Where did you steal these from?

"Biology department. Binoculars like that, a man can tell the sex of a swallow from five miles away."

"I thought you could tell the sex from the plumage."

"Wasn't talking about the bird."

I aimed the binoculars towards the party house, and suddenly I was right there in the center of the party. "Hey, where's the brew?" I asked one of the guys leaning against the back of the house. I turned slightly to see who else was there, and was suddenly about four houses away. "Whoa!" I laughed as I slowly trained back to the house, this time stopping on a rather attractive brunette. "Well, hello, my beauty. It is such a fine evening. Would you like to watch the stars with me? I understand there is a great view from the bed in Stevie's room."

The Arbiter laughed, so I did as well. I went to hand the binoculars back to him, but he motioned to put them back in the bag.

"Why do you have these?" I asked. "Shoots holes into your ant theory if you're making the ants larger than humans, don't you think?"

"Ants are ants are ants," he replied. "And the ones at the Eta Iota Upsilon house are too far away to see with the naked eye."

"Why them? Why come all the way to this end of campus when the sorority houses are on the other end?"

"Didn't come here to see them," the Arbiter explained as he stuffed the two cloths into the backpack with the binoculars. "Came here to take care of some business. Thought it'd also be a good chance to do some spying."

"Why? What's going on over there?"

"Why do you always ask two questions at once?"

"Do I?"

The Arbiter paused. "Guess not." He zipped up the backpack and tossed it to me. "There's something going on over there."

"Like what?"

"Don't know. Something."

"How can you tell?"

"Ever been over there?"

"No."

"You know how sometimes you have a dog, and you walk into the room and the dog lowers his head and stares up at you like it knows it's about to have Bitter Apple sprayed in its face?"

"You've lost me. What do apples have to do with anything?"

"Guilt. Can't visit that house without every member looking at me as if she'd just chewed up the remote control. Have to find out why."

"Well, have you seen the remote there? Maybe they *did* chew it up."

"Know what your problem is," the Arbiter asked as he heaved himself up onto the padlock between the gate doors. Unlike last time, he wedged his way through the doors as I had before.

"I've got a few of them pinpointed," I said while stretching a bit more.

"Your problem is that you always want all the answers right now. You always want everything solved. Quite often the investigation is more interesting than the solving. The solve…ment. What's the word for that?"

"I don't know. I'll look it up when I get back to the dorm."

"See?"

I think the conversation was exhausting me more than the climb had, so I gave up and climbed back over the fence. We didn't talk much as we headed back towards campus. It was as if we'd just come from Communion or some other somber, holy experience and wanted to spend the time in silent reflection. The Arbiter seemed pensive, but this wasn't unusual. He was the kind of guy who would look pensive while accepting his first sweepstakes check from Ed McMahon:

"Mr. The Arbiter, you have just won *ten million dollars!*"

"Always wondered something, Mr. McMahon. Didn't you ever feel the urge, say during a prolonged segment with Joan Embry, to just reach over and smash Johnny's head with your coffee mug?"

This became especially obvious when we passed the fraternity house from which the heavy metal music was pulsating through the crisp night air. I now recognized it to be old Poison, so it wasn't even respectable heavy metal. The Arbiter and I turned onto the sidewalk in front of the brick house and walked past the porch. It was some thirty feet away, but that was apparently close enough for some drunken girl to notice the black backpacks that the Arbiter and I were wearing. She apparently found this to be a rather dorky thing to have, and was sufficiently inebriated to let everyone in the area know this.

"Nice book bag, geeks!" she shouted out with a sharp laugh. The others on the porch laughed with her. "Can I buy it?"

They all laughed harder. The Arbiter continued to walk, but not without calling back, "Twenty bucks."

The girl on the porch was insulted. She threw her beer bottle towards us and yelled, "Fuck you!"

"That'll be twenty-five," the Arbiter retorted, not skipping a beat. I thought this was hilarious, but the Arbiter didn't even crack a smile. The girl on the porch continued to shout at us as she and her friends started to come our way, but they stopped when one of them passed out and cracked his head on the steps. We would later learn that he had given himself a concussion and had gone into an alcohol induced coma. His friends, thinking he had only passed out, urinated on him at regular intervals throughout the rest of the night. Clearly, had they known his life was in danger, they would have been content to merely spit on him. They were frat brothers, after all, and nothing can break that bond between brothers. The next morning, some joggers passed by and tried to wake him up. They quickly gave up upon realizing how badly he smelled. By mid-afternoon, some-one had come up with the good sense to call an ambulance.

The boy was in a coma for a few weeks, which was good for Flood-bane because it greatly cut down on the bad press the incident received. Had he been able to speak, there would've been a story. Instead, all the press had was a boy who smelled like piss lying in a hospital bed. It was reported that President paid the boy off to play down the event, but the coma kid always denied this…after coming out of the coma, I mean. He'd just say, "I can't afford to talk to you about it," and then speed away in his Lamborghini.

For the next few years, to question how the school handled alco-hol problems, people would occasionally bring up the incident where the frat boys pissed on their intoxicated, coma ridden brother. The college representative would calmly deny that Floodbane had any sort of alcohol problem, but did admit that they were aware of some students who suffered from somewhat of a urinary dysfunc-tion and that they were getting professional counseling from instruc-tors trained in such matters of micturition malfunctions. These, I can honestly say, are twelve steps I hope to never ascend.

This all took place quite a bit after the actual event, of course, so the Arbiter and I had yet to really laugh about the whole thing as we eventually would. Instead, I was laughing only at the Arbiter's quick retort, and he wasn't laughing at all. He was like that. There was something hidden in the Arbiter, and the more I hung out with him, the more I wanted to know what it was. It was like I was jealous of him for having a dark side. I mean, I was a killer, and I didn't have a side that dark. It wasn't fair.

But when had my life ever been fair? Certainly not when I got spanked for kidnapping Holly Hobbie. Certainly not when my best friend Terry Hogan moved to Toledo. Certainly not when Heath Millard was lionized after attempting to starve that kitten.

And certainly not when Ann Penella…well, I really could've used that dark side in high school. I think maybe if I'd had one, then perhaps Ann would have liked me more than she did in ways that she didn't. I had learned from my pubescent habit of reading mom's romance novels that women love men who have dark sides. Dark sides, flowing hair, and a man-tool of love nearly bursting from its cell. Women love to find the dark side (and the man-tool) and help the man come to terms with it (and the man-tool), but not until after they've had a lot of sex (and the…nevermind). Men with dark sides make better love, those romance novels said. They also lean a lot. Ever notice that? Sure, sometimes against a locker or a Camero, but sometimes just Pisa-like, leaning against nothing at all. Could be they get their darkness from an inner ear disorder.

I tried to adopt a dark side, but I just couldn't do it. I tried to become enigmatic so the girls would look at me out of the corner of their eye and whisper, "What is it about that Guy? What's he hiding?" I learned quickly, however, that it's hard to hold secrets from people who don't really give a damn. I could've started wearing Zorro masks, wrestling trunks and moon boots to school and no one would've thought of me as enigmatic. They would have only thought I was a freak. But hell, aren't vampires freaks? And they still get a lot of the good love. I suppose I could've tried to become a vampire, but mine was outdated. I would've been one of those Bela Lugosi types, walking around with my cape spread wide saying, "Bluh, bluh, I von to suck your blood." That just doesn't go over anymore. These days it's all about pretty boys running around with their shirts off, engaging in homo-erotic imagery as they slowly seduce the women of their affections. Give me the old days when vampires simply turned into bats and flew into a woman's second, third, or fourth story bedroom window.

No, I had to face it—I was doomed to be featureless. My life was about as exciting as driftwood, and nothing short of killing somebody would ever change that.

Yeah, like that would even work.

What did, at least for a while, were my late night rendezvous with Ann Penella.

It was her suggestion that we meet late, after her family was asleep. She told me where she lived, so I'd drive out there on Friday or Saturday nights and pick her up. She'd climb down the TV antennae that ran up next to her window, and we'd drive around the countryside…careful to avoid Professor Snow's place because he scared Ann.

We did this throughout our entire sophomore year, sometimes only once a month, sometimes three or four times. We never once actually went anywhere. I never once entered her house. We'd just drive and talk and listen to the radio. I never made a move on her, I didn't want to take any chances. For now, just having someone to talk to—someone who seemed to genuinely like me and who didn't intend to kill any small animals—was good enough for me.

But then the school year ended and the meetings came to an abrupt halt. Ann had grown tired of cheerleading, so her parents put up the big bucks to send her off to dance camp. She left a month after the school year ended and didn't return until a few days before band camp in mid-August. She never gave me her address at camp, but I never asked for it. I knew the rules.

So, instead of spending my summer visiting Ann beneath dynamic moonlight, I spent it watching my little brother. Both my parents commuted into the city for work, so they were gone from about six in the morning until seven at night. They offered to pay me many times, but I had nothing upon which to spend it now that I wasn't using up gas to drive Ann around. They financed my trombone lessons and put money away for my college and things like that, so this was enough for me. Most teenagers would've been pissed at their parents for making them babysit so much. They would've shaved their heads and bought black boots and listened to death metal or folk music, but I didn't mind. I liked my little brother.

I didn't realize that while I was willingly at home all summer, I should've been taking the time to fortify my castle's walls.

I was ecstatic when band camp started up again. I wasn't looking forward to being reminded of how bad a trombone player I was or of the outcast I had become, but rather that I'd be able to see Ann again. This thrilled me...for a couple of hours, anyway.

The first thing I noticed was that she wasn't rehearsing with the cheerleaders that year; she was now with the dancers—as were quite a few of the former cheerleaders. They must've been loving life. Now they'd get to do shows on the field in front of the entire stadium as opposed to just occasionally kicking their legs and flipping around on the sidelines in front of the "Spirit Section" of the stands. And John Stuart Mill High School never sent any cheerleaders to those championships that the Arbiter would later enjoy watching so much. Our girls didn't need to travel across the country to have sex, I guess. The current absence of that girl who sat beside me in kindergarten and turned me down for a date in junior high and was then impregnated by Heath Millard was proof of that.

I still can't remember to what movie I wanted to take her.

I kept positioning myself on the field so that Ann would see me, but she never did. I never got the hidden smile and wave from her. I was going mad. It's not that I needed to talk to her in front of everyone, I just wanted to know that she hadn't forgotten me over the past few months.

When our lunch break rolled around, I threw caution to the dank, summer wind and approached her. I waited until there was no one else around so that neither of us would be embarrassed, then slowly walked up to her as she leaned against the wall beside the door to the band room outside of the high school, apparently waiting for something. I approached her from the front to see if I could pick up on any signals that would either encourage or shun me away.

To my relief, she recognized me...and smiled.

"Guy," she exclaimed as she reached out her arms and ran up to me. I returned the smile but started to back up. She didn't let me get too far before she threw her arms around me and hugged me tightly. It was the first time I'd been touched by anyone since the bus ordeal a year earlier, and although I was thrilled to be near Ann, I cringed at the physical contact.

"How have you been?" she asked, still beaming as she pulled me inside the band room. "How was your summer? Tell me everything!" She was glowing. Honestly glowing.

I laughed a bit. "It's good to see you too."

"I thought about you over the summer," she said.

I was surprised, but I knew better than to let her see that. "I thought about you a lot, too."

"We have to get together for another late night drive," she suggested.

"Yeah, I think we—"

It should have occurred to me, I guess, that maybe her glow might not have originated at the beginning of our conversation. Yet, it never even once crossed my mind that perhaps she was so bouncy and excited not because of me, but because her life in general was just going wonderfully well at that time. The idea had not even formulated in my mind, so when Heath Millard swooped inside the doorway, put his hand on her ass and kissed her hard on the mouth, I was devastated.

Suddenly, I wasn't there at all. Suddenly, Ann not only didn't want to hear about my summer, but didn't even know that I'd had one. She was conscious only of her skin bunching under Heath's dirty grip and his tongue probing her mouth. I just stared at them. I didn't know what else to do. He was stained and sweaty and rough from rolling around on the grass all day with a bunch of other big, dumbass football players, and she was clean and pure and unspoiled from a morning of sitting with the harem of dancers as they talked about boys, geometry and TV. Watching Ann willingly kiss Heath made less sense than if Fay Wray would have locked lips with Kong.

Nowhere to go but down. Quickly. Hard.

When he finally pulled away with a confident smirk, he said, "Ain't that better than writing letters all summer? See you after practice this afternoon, baby." And then he was gone as quickly as he came.

When Ann turned back to me, her face was redder than freshly spilled blood. I wondered if it was from embarrassment or from excitement. She seemed to want to tell me something or explain it all to me, but instead only looked at me sympathetically.

I couldn't talk again. Ann was suddenly as foreign and evil to me as those girls last year who accosted me on the bus. I didn't say a thing as I turned and walked out of the band room.

"Guy," she called after me, but I didn't stop or look back. "Guy, wait, let me explain."

Explain what? That she was in love with someone other than me? Big deal. I could've dealt with that. I wasn't stupid enough to think she would have fallen in love with me over the summer. I mean, I'd hoped, sure, but I long ago prepared myself for the fact that my guardian angel's halo would slip a bit and that she'd fall in love with someone else.

But her halo had done more than slip a bit. It had fallen into a crumpled heap around her ankles. My guardian angel was in love with the devil himself.

CHAPTER 5

The Beetle and the Damage Done

*J*ayson Alexander Fayme. Until the day I die, that name will vex me like some kind of eternal mosquito bite on the knuckle of my soul.

I must reiterate that Jayson posed no threat to any of us, and even he realized early on that intimidation didn't work. The Arbiter feared nothing, I'd grown so accustomed to fear that it now failed to impress me, and it got so Jayson could barely speak around Rhonda without becoming more of an ass than he actually was. All she had to do was smile his way and he'd become as flustered and helpless as a beetle in a swimming pool.

A beetle. A mosquito. That's what Jayson Fayme was; a pest. It was just impossible to get rid of him. Like a mouse or cockroach, we could only frighten him away temporarily—send him scampering into some dark corner where, although we couldn't know what he was doing, he at least wasn't doing it in the dining room where he'd frighten off the guests.

Unfortunately, the pest metaphor doesn't end there. Jayson was sneaky, too. He was a termite. The guy could settle in right beneath people and screw up their foundations before they knew he was there. In fact, that's exactly what he did our senior year at Floodbane. Whether by his plan or by some cruel spin of fortune's wheel, Jayson Fayme managed to take the apartment directly below Rhonda's.

We didn't even know he was there for the first two weeks. There's no reason he should have been; he was only a junior. Not even the Arbiter and I—both of whom managed to live without roommates during our three underclassmen years—could swing off-campus housing. And believe me, we tried. But our numerous requests ended with the receipt of the following form letter:

Dear <FIELD: 1>

As is specified in the Floodbane College Student Handbook, students must live in specified living quarters (campus housing) until said students have reached said students' fourth, perhaps fifth or sixth…or seventh, but definitely final…probably, year. At that point, said students may tender a tender (tender) for specified off-campus housing (off-living quarters) and, if said students' applications meet the requisite qualifications, said students may relocate off campus (off-living) into said specified qualified off-campus housing (off-living quarters).

As Floodbane College professes institutional non-intolerance towards those with alternative lifestyles, however, said gay, lesbian, bisexual, polyamorous, ambidextrous; heretofore to be referred to as HOMOSEXUAL students may live off-campus (off-living) before said HOMOSEXUAL students' senior year. Said HOMOSEXUAL students may live off-campus (off living) during their freshperson, sophomore, junior and/or senior year as said HOMOSEXUALs see fit, provided said HOMOSEXUAL students come to the office of residence life and exhibit said HOMOSEXUAL students' said homosexuality. This can be evidenced through either personal poetry (including SLAM), pornographic (not hard "R") photographs or music CD collections (at least three show tune albums (males) or Melissa Etheridge albums (grrrls)).

As Floodbane College is an equal opportunity institution that does not discriminate against any race, color, ethnic origin, nationality (including Europeans (except for those skinheads), Asians (except for those Taoists), North Americans (except for those pesky Quebecers), South Americans (except for those drug dealers), Australians (except for those dingoes), Arcticans (except for those penguins) and the Antarcticans (except for those of questionable stature)), or sexual orientation, those who would like to experiment with said HOMOSEXUALity can check out above said CDs in the library (Library). CDs are delivered to residence halls of residence (Dorms) discriminately in plain brown wrappers.

We look forward to seeing you soon.

SWAK,
The Office of Residence Life

I always expected the Arbiter to get angry over this rationale, but again…nothing. The last time we received the note, his only comment was, "I wonder what they have against penguins." The matter was never discussed again.

He did, however, hang the letter on the door of his dorm room our junior year. It remained there for quite some time before it was mysteriously torn down one night and replaced with a Bible verse.

"We also know that law is made not for the righteous but for lawbreakers and rebels, the ungodly and sinful, the unholy and irreligious; for those who kill their fathers and mothers, for murderers, for adulterers and perverts, for slave traders and liars and perjurers—and for whatever else is contrary to

the sound doctrine that conforms to the glorious gospel of the blessed God…"

—1 Timothy. Chapter 1, Verses 9-11.

The Arbiter chose to leave this upon his door for the remainder of the year, but not before crossing out the word "perverts" and adding "penguins."

But it was Rhonda's door and not the Arbiter's that was on my mind the night we realized that Fayme was living beneath her. Someone was knocking on it. We ordered a pizza earlier that evening, so, upon hearing the knock, Rhonda bounded down the steps that led to her front door; she never took steps one at a time, but always by two; the carpeting in her stairwell was worn out worse on every other step. Expecting to hear talk of sausage and whether or not there was change to be made for a twenty, the Arbiter and I instead heard the jarring voice of Fayme over Strauss Jr.'s "Overture to Die Fledermaus" that was lightly playing on Rhonda's Sony stereo system.

"Rhonnnnndaaaaaaaaa," Jayson said after she'd opened the door. He made a conscious effort to drag out the two syllables of her name for as long as his lungs would allow.

Rhonda paused a second, then asked, "Where's the pizza?"

The Arbiter had apparently recognized Jayson's voice before Rhonda recognized his face. Immediately after hearing him utter Rhonda's name, The Arbiter threw his head back and smacked his palm onto his forehead, producing a sound like a three wood striking a Titleist for a couple hundred yards.

Jayson's response to Rhonda's question? "In my pants. Wanna slice?"

"Oh no," Rhonda sighed. "Fayme." We could then hear the brown and orange shag carpeted steps creaking as Rhonda started back up them, this time using each one. As she reached the top and appeared around the faux wood paneled wall that separated the living room from the stairwell, she stopped. "Fayme, unless you have our pizza, there's no reason for you to take another step up this stairway."

"Except to see your ass," was his retort.

Rhonda moped her way over to the couch where the Arbiter was sitting. Before she could even sit down, Jayson invaded the living room. As if on cue, the Arbiter and I slouched in our seats as Rhonda plopped down with us. We'd all been in that jovial "waiting for a pizza" mood that people can only be in while…well…waiting for a pizza, and I'd even set my Life Savers on the end table knowing I wouldn't be having any until well after the pizza taste had cleared my palate. But Fayme's presence immediately infested the room with a mumpish (look it up, it's there) plague. Fayme had the same effect on a room that sudden suicides have on New Year's Eve parties; just put away the crab dip and turn off the Foghat, there ain't gonna be no more dancing before sunup.

But if our faces darkened at the sight of Jayson's, his lit up like a house fire. "Hey Ar-*Biter*!" he greeted with a smug smile, stressing "bite." He then turned to me. "I never could remember your name."

"Good," I responded. I don't think he knew how serious I was.

"Good. Good," Jayson started to mimic me, curling his bottom lip underneath his upper teeth. He looked like a mildly retarded beaver. "Good."

The Arbiter started to laugh at Jayson's display, so Jayson began laughing too. I just sat there, fascinated by his stupidity. Something always intrigued me about such public displays of idiocy. I've long been fascinated, for example, how during matches in the United States between international wrestlers (say a Canadian vs. a Japanese), many ringside fans will invariably begin chanting, "U-S-A! U-S-A! U-S-A!" as if the white wrestler just had to be American. And don't even get me started on people who don't use their turn signal. Are they just morons? Do they not know how to use it? Are they afraid of that little bar that juts out from their steering column, and won't touch it for fear it'll blow up the car or maybe even a small European country? I mean, it's not like it's a lot of effort to flip it up or down, is it? Maybe by not using their turn signal, people feel they're sticking it to the man. "He can make me wear a seatbelt, he can make me drive under 65 mph, and he can pass another goddam cell phone law, but ain't no way he's gonna make me notify other drivers of when I intend to switch lanes…dirty rat bastard."

I could see Jayson proudly declaring such independence, just like I could see him suggesting to the Arbiter, "I see you're muscling in on my woman."

"And he's doing quite well, I'm afraid," Rhonda pointed out, reaching her arm around the Arbiter's and resting her head on his shoulder. The Arbiter looked at Jayson as if to smile triumphantly, but he didn't bother.

Jayson didn't accept defeat gracefully, but then, Jayson wasn't graceful about anything.

"What is this shit?" he asked, making no gesture that indicated to what he was referring. He was still bouncing his eyes back and forth from Rhonda to the Arbiter.

"Why are you here?" the Arbiter asked.

"I live here," Jayson responded, rapping his knuckles against the wall as if searching for the stud.

"That's funny. I don't recall seeing your name on the lease when I signed it," Rhonda pointed out. "Fabulous pre-war apartment, fully furnished, two bedrooms, Jayson Fayme, spacious kitchen, eclectic color scheme. No, Jayson, like skylights and air conditioning, you're a luxury I simply cannot afford."

"Neither can my hookers," Jayson laughed, on his own, as always. "I live downstairs," he added as he turned from the wall to look at the stereo. The Arbiter, Rhonda and I looked at one another in disbelief, but were quickly pulled out of shock when Jayson repeated, "What is this shit?"

"You'll have to be more specific," Rhonda asked after shivering a moment as if she'd just walked into a spider web.

"Yeah," I added. "There's a lot of shit going around these days."

"No, that's actually a very perplexing conundrum Jayson has raised," the Arbiter nodded to Rhonda and me. He would never use unwieldy words such as "perplexing" and "conundrum" unless Jayson was around. The boy was so easily confused, and the Arbiter got quite a kick out of it. "Very philosophical. Believe it was Socrates who first asked, 'What is this shit?'"

"Probably right after drinking the hemlock," I added.

The Arbiter laughed, then turned back to Jayson. "You're pretty smart. Are you a philosophy major?"

"You can't drink a hammock," was Jayson's comment.

The Arbiter, Rhonda and I sat there in a stupor, all of us thinking the same thing. It was the Arbiter who voiced this thought.

"What?"

"He just said Socrates drank a hammock, and all I'm saying is that you can't drink a hammock," Jayson explained for us.

"Of course not," the Arbiter agreed. "That's why he died. He choked on it."

"I know that," Jayson pointed out. "I'm not stupid."

The Arbiter held his hands up as if to say, "Didn't suggest anything," but his smile gave him away.

As if trying to spare Jayson, Rhonda said, "Jayson, you still haven't told us your major."

"I don't have a major," Jayson snapped again. He seemed to get overly defensive about the oddest things.

"You have to," Rhonda argued. "Or is your major general studies?"

"I get that one!" Jayson exclaimed with a start. We had no idea what he'd just gotten, but he was quick to explain himself. "Major. General studies. I get it."

"Get what?" Rhonda asked.

"War jokes," Jayson explained.

"War jokes," the Arbiter repeated in disbelief. "War jokes."

"War jokes! War jokes!" Now Jayson was mocking the Arbiter, only the Arbiter was paying no attention.

"Can't recall ever hearing a good war joke," the Arbiter said to us. "You guys?"

"No," Rhonda replied as I shook my head in agreement with her.

While this was going on, Jayson was still repeating the Arbiter as if making fun of someone on a grade school playground. "War jokes, war jokes, war jokes," over and over again. He started speeding up, thereby slurring the words together until they sounded like "Warja, warja, warja, warja." It became harder to ignore him, but none of us were about to give in.

"War just isn't all that funny," Rhonda suggested. "Might be all that death and dismemberment."

"I wouldn't say that," I retorted. "I saw some funny war cartoons when I was a kid."

"War cartoons?" Rhonda sounded appalled.

"What, you mean something like *Babar Crosses the 43rd Parallel?*" the Arbiter asked.

I laughed, and that again seemed to spite Jayson.

"You see, war can be funny," the Arbiter continued. "Listen. Why did the chicken cross the road?"

"I don't know," Rhonda and I replied.

"To kill the Kaiser."

We all laughed much harder than we should have. Fayme, having failed at his attempt to get our attention, started to laugh with us. I doubt he even heard the joke, I think he just wanted to hurry up and belong.

Once we all settled back down, another momentary silence fell upon us. And, as before, it was Jayson who broke it…with the exact same line.

"What is this shit?"

"What are you talking about?!" Rhonda snapped. I don't think it was out of anger, but more out of frustration. Talking for so long to Jayson Fayme was like having to sit and watch one of those toy monkeys bang cymbals together for a few hours, stopping every few moments—teasing that it might be done—but then starting back up again, only louder. It's cute and somewhat entertaining for about ten seconds, but good God, does it get annoying quickly.

"This shit!" Jayson shouted back, pointing to the stereo.

Giving Rhonda a chance to regain her composure, The Arbiter fielded the question. "Right now it's the beginning of Mendelssohn's 'Overture to A Midsummer Night's Dream Suite.' When you first came in it was Strauss' 'Overture to Die Fledermaus.' But that's not why you came up, is it?"

"What the fuck is a 'fledder mouse?'"

"It's German for 'the Bat,'" Rhonda explained.

"No wonder I hate it; it's in a foreign language," Jayson said as he scratched the back of his neck. "Don't you have any real music?"

"Real music?" Rhonda inquired.

"Yeah, real music. American rock and roll! Something like the Stones."

"Will you quit complaining if I put some on?" Rhonda asked as she stood from the couch.

"Will you suck me?" Jayson shot back, witty as ever.

Rhonda turned towards Jayson, and the look she shot him sent chills down my spine. It wasn't particularly intimidating, but I'd never seen her look that way before. The ability to forgive the faults in others was one of her best qualities, I always thought, but it was looking as if Jayson's unfortunate traits were finally pushing her patience a little too far. The Arbiter must've sensed this too, as he stepped between the two of them.

"Jayson, you're a guest here, albeit an extremely unwelcome one, so unless you want to—"

"Arby," Rhonda interrupted, grabbing his arm. She gave her boyfriend one of those, "that's not necessary" looks, but she didn't seem upset with him. It prompted me back to the day when the Arbiter knocked Jayson off his bike for grabbing Rhonda's butt. What had she told him? "I can fight my own battles," I think was it. I had no doubt this was true, but who doesn't like the comfort of knowing the cavalry is just over the hill?

Either way, neither of them said another word as Rhonda went to the stereo that sat in a plywood entertainment console against the wall opposite the stairwell. After a moment, the majesty of the winds and strings was replaced with the raunchy thumping of synthesized drums and keyboards.

"What is *this* shit?" Jayson asked. I'm sure his cockiness didn't mean he wasn't intimidated by the Arbiter's threat, but rather that he was too stupid to recognize it. "I've never heard this shit before."

"It's Wall of Voodoo," Rhonda explained before the Arbiter had a chance to speak up again.

"I've never heard of that. Are they in a foreign language too?"

"Foreign to you, maybe," Rhonda answered.

"I hate music I've never heard before, let me just say that."

We all chose to not point out the flaw inherent in his logic. Instead, I asked, "What's wrong with it? It's rock."

"I told you, I haven't heard it. It must suck if I haven't heard it."

"You would think that, from a guy who listens only to rock music, perhaps he'd be a little more knowledgeable in the genre," the Arbiter pointed out.

"I don't listen to just rock," Jayson said in his defense.

"What else do you listen to?" Rhonda asked.

"Showtunes."

The phone rang.

Rhonda headed to the kitchen to get it, but Jayson was closer. "Jayson and Rhonda Fayme's," he said into the receiver.

The Arbiter moved to grab the phone from him, but Rhonda gently pulled him back with a hand on his wrist. She looked at him for a moment, then he dropped back into his chair, and she onto his lap.

Jayson looked over at Rhonda as he said, "Hell yes, we ordered a pizza. Where the fuck is it?" He then cupped his hand over the mouthpiece and asked, "Did you guys order a pizza?" We responded that we had, and he gave us the thumbs up sign as if he had everything under control. Always looking out for us, was that Jayson, like an angel on our shoulder. God bless his little cheruby cheeks.

After only a second, his nodding stopped abruptly. His eyes suddenly tightened, and his mouth dropped as if his jaw had just been broken. "You're shittin' me."

The rest of us looked at one another, wondering what brought on this sudden change. I figured it was just another of Jayson's miserable attempts at humor, but Rhonda's sudden attentiveness led me to believe I was wrong. She rarely missed in reading people correctly.

"Holy shit," Jayson continued. "Okay." He then hung up the phone and rested against the wall for a moment with his head draped down towards the dark green carpeting that matched nothing else in the apartment.

For Rhonda's sake, it should be noted her apartment came furnished in this fashion. The wood paneling on the walls was actually plastic, and each room had a different color of carpeting; orange and brown shag on the stairwell, dark green in the living room and kitchen, burgundy in one bedroom and orange in the other. I swear I'm not making this up. To make matters worse, the furniture in the living room—a lavender sofa and a light blue chair—worked with none of these colors. Against the wall that separated the stairwell from the living room was a wobbly table, around which sat three chairs that didn't even closely resemble one another. It was horrid to see, and I couldn't believe that Rhonda lived in such a place. She had good—if somewhat common—taste in everything: clothing, music, friends…the apartment just didn't suit her. She explained when the Arbiter and I helped to move her in that the landlord had specified on the lease that she was to make absolutely no alterations, but that he wouldn't explain why. When she asked, he only said, "'Til you spent a night sleepin' 'neath rocket fire and missiles in the jungles of Dien Bien Phu, woman, fingers sweatin' from the pressure of your grip around your machine gun, Charlie watchin' from behind every tree, ya ain't got no right to be tellin' me where to place a throw pillow. Get it?"

As a result, the place looked more like something in which Jayson would live. In fact, he did seem quite at home as he set about telling us what he'd just heard on the telephone. He was being a little too melodramatic for my taste, but Rhonda's attentiveness had me worried.

"What's wrong?" Rhonda asked.

"Guys," Jayson said as he threw his gaze up to the ceiling and breathed out heavily. "Let me just tell you this; I don't think we're going to be getting our pizza tonight."

"*Our* pizza?" I retorted.

My question was drowned out by Rhonda's. "Why not? What happened?"

"That was Panthemom's," Jayson began to explain. Panthemom's was the only pizza place near Floodbane College, but no one minded the lack of competition because Panthemom's pies were so damn good nobody would've gone anywhere else. "They called to say that their delivery guy was in an accident on the way over here.

"He's dead."

I kept waiting for him to start squealing that annoying laugh of his, but it never came. The only sound was a breath of shock from Rhonda. Hearing this, I had to believe that Jayson was telling the truth. Rhonda was simply never fooled by such lies. But the Arbiter wasn't biting.

"Seriously doubt that," he offered.

"It's true," Jayson defended himself. "Call them."

"I think he's serious, Arby," Rhonda agreed, sliding her hand off his shoulder and into his palm.

The Arbiter smiled as if trying to put her fears to rest, then said, "I think he's serious, too. I also think he's wrong. If the driver were dead, management wouldn't call all the people on his route to explain that he had just been killed in an auto accident."

"Sure they would! It's good business practice!" Jayson practically yelled. "When that one guy was killed working on our pool out back of my dad's third wife's summer home, dad called the pizza company right away!" Jayson had suddenly lost the compassion he'd displayed a moment before, and I welcomed this change. He was being an ass again, just like that, and I felt more comfortable with the familiarity of it.

"What exactly did they say?" the Arbiter continued as if Jayson were on the witness stand. Rhonda was watching intently, serving as the judge.

"They said that our pizza would be late because the—"

"Late?" the Arbiter interrupted. He then put his hand to his ear as if it were a phone. "Uh, yeah, this is Panthemom's. Listen. Going to be a touch late with your pizza. Yeah. The driver was just in an accident, and your pizza didn't make it. Driver's dead too. Anywho, another one's in the oven...no, another pizza, so—barring any future fatalities—you should get your pizza in half an hour, with a free two liter of Coke for your trouble."

I was laughing at the Arbiter's bit, and Rhonda was also smiling again.

"That's not what they said," Jayson pointed out, shaking his head back and forth like a little kid presented with a contrary opinion to the existence of the tooth fairy. "Shows what you know, asshole." He then walked across the room to the front window as if he were looking for the wreck. "They said that our pizza's going to be late because the driver's dead in the road. That simple.

"Although a free Coke would fuckin' kick ass."

The Arbiter again had his forehead in the palm of his hand, shaking it back and forth. "They meant his *car!*" he laughed.

Rhonda and I also started to laugh, partly in relief, as Jayson turned back around to face us. "No they didn't. They said—"

"They probably didn't even say, 'Dead in the road,'" Rhonda interrupted. "They probably said, 'Your driver's…Denny LeRoad,' some kind of really bad delivery boy who's notorious for being late."

I was howling, "Denny LeRoad!"

Jayson looked as if he was about to cry. His face had turned deep red again, but this time it didn't go away. We were obviously damaging the fragile Fayme family ego. "You assholes are real assholes," he yelled at us, but we were laughing too hard to hear.

"Next time you order a pizza, request Denny LeRoad to deliver it," the Arbiter suggested over our laughing, "so you can get a free Coke!"

"Fine, then I'm fuckin' leaving, and I'm not helping pay!" Jayson pouted as he headed for the steps. We made no attempt to stop him, and I think that upset him even more. He ran down the steps and slammed Rhonda's door, then slammed his own upon entering his apartment. Some rap music began to pump up through our floor. Or at least I think it was rap. Filtered through floor boards and walls, all rap music sounds to me like Falco's "Rock Me Amadeus." But we didn't care. We were still telling Denny LeRoad jokes.

"Why did Denny LeRoad cross the road?"

"Doesn't matter. He didn't get there."

"How can you tell if Denny LeRoad's been in your fridge?"

"Skid marks in the cheesecake."

And so on.

When the driver did arrive, toting a free two liter of Coke, incidentally, we paid him five dollars to go to Jayson's apartment and introduce himself as Denny LeRoad. He did, but we couldn't hear Jayson's response over his music. We could only see the driver bolt for his car while Jayson threw various household items at him. Lucky driver. He made off with our five dollar tip and what appeared to be Jayson's blender.

Watching all this from the front window, Rhonda suddenly got nervous. "I don't think I like the idea of him living underneath me. He's kind of scary."

"Fayme?" the Arbiter asked. "He's harmless. Comical."

"I don't know," Rhonda continued, still looking out the window. "He's…he snaps too easily. I don't think he has any control."

"He's nothing to worry about," the Arbiter soothed as he pulled her to him and hugged her. "He knows better."

"I'm sure you're right," Rhonda agreed. "I just don't feel that knowing better will stop him."

I didn't like the turn the conversation had taken, so I announced that, "Pizza's getting cold." It was only when we sat down to eat that I looked towards the end table and realized my Life Savers were missing. It seemed obvious that Jayson had taken them, so I didn't bother mentioning their disappearance to Rhonda or the Arbiter. And quite honestly, I didn't miss them that much. I mean, Panthemom's and my two best friends, I was content.

Content. Why always just content? Why, even when safe with friends, could I never get past contentment?

"Are you guys happy?" I surprised myself by asking Rhonda and the Arbiter between slices.

"Crust's a little chewy," the Arbiter replied, "but no major complaints."

"I didn't mean with the pizza," I explained.

"Know that, but it's my answer nonetheless."

"Your happiness is dependent upon the quality of the pizza you're eating?" I asked. "What about Rhonda?"

"Don't have to worry about her, she's never chewy."

Rhonda smiled off the joke as she always did. She either saw through the Arbiter or just knew how to humor him.

"It's all about the moment with Arby," she explained. "You know that."

"Always happy with Rhonda," the Arbiter suggested. "Not always happy with pizza."

"But what about in the bigger scheme?" I continued. "What about beyond pizza and beyond Rhonda?"

"Won't ever pay to go there," the Arbiter said as put down his drink. "Not unless they've got some great miniature golf courses."

"So, that's all you want out of life, to play miniature golf?" I prodded.

"Want a lot of things out of life. Want to get published, to run a tabloid, to bring *Godzilla vs. Monster Zero* to Broadway…got vaulting ambition that'd make Lady Macbeth blush. Right now, however, this pizza sure is tasty."

"What about you, Guy?" Rhonda asked. "The Arbiter's goals lie in journalism, what about you?"

"You first," I suggested. "What makes you happy?"

"Acting," Rhonda replied without hesitation.

"Why?"

"It's the only way we can get people to listen to us. It's odd, really. I can stand here all day and tell children not to judge people by their looks, but no one pays attention. Dress up like an ogre and act it out onstage, however, and every child in the theater will be a better person for at least an hour or two. It's worse with adults. They only listen when the person speaking isn't real. In order for me to make any difference in this world, I have to put on a wig and speak with an accent."

"That may be the saddest thing I've ever heard," I admitted.

"True, though," the Arbiter nodded. "Was better behaved for Smokey the Bear than for my parents."

"So it's your turn," Rhonda again pointed out. "What would most make you happy?"

The answer came to me without hesitation, and I think I almost said it. "To admit to you that I once killed somebody." But I didn't, mainly out of surprise. Up until that moment, I didn't realize how badly I wanted to confess my crime, and I didn't know that I wanted Rhonda to hear it. Can I assume it's because she would have possibly forgiven me? Because she would've cared without patronizing me? Because she would've convinced me with compassion to do the right thing? Or was it because of something else?

I didn't know, and I knew I wouldn't learn that night. Looking at Rhonda, however, I was suddenly completely sure that my secret would not stay with me to my death bed.

"What would make me most happy?" I repeated. "I guess I just want my Life Savers back."

Thinking back on our visit from Fayme, I was reminded of a strong belief of mine which I feel I should now repeat; nothing brings people together faster than a common enemy. The way in which the Arbiter, Rhonda and I had so effectively teamed up against Fayme was yet another perfect example.

Not as perfect, however, as the night I made love to Ann Penella.

Our night together was a long time in the making—the events leading up to it having begun on a Friday evening during my junior year. It was football season, and the Fightin' Golden Sandies were visiting the Aristotle High School Orange Pants. Everyone was in high spirits that night because John Stuart Mill was beating the pants off the…well, huh. Before the Marchin' Fightin' Golden Sandies took the field at half-time, Heath Millard had run a bootleg with no time left on the clock, duping the Orange Pants defense and breaking it thirty-seven yards for his second rushing touchdown of the game. Combined with his touchdown pass and one other run by the half-back, Millard's heroics brought the score to 27 to 6. It was the first time all year the Golden Sandies had even been in the lead, so it looked as if the first of our annual two wins was only one half away…just in time to dampen Aristotle High School's Homecoming Game spirit. Not that it mattered. Win or lose, the dance would take place and the football players would still make out with the cheerleaders. Whether to thrill in victory or agonize in defeat, sex was as much a part of high school post-game activities as the team handshake…the opposition's spit and all.

Puts kind of a perverse twist on those "My son is a Fightin' Golden Sandie" or "A Fightin' Golden Sandie cheerleader lives here" banners that parents so proudly display, doesn't it?

After the halftime show, the band members and the dancers were given the third quarter off to use the restrooms or visit the concession stands or smoke a cigarette behind the locker rooms, provided they were all back in their designated seats by the start of the fourth quarter. It was during these elongated twelve minutes that I knew I had to talk to Ann.

We hadn't spoken since the moment I saw her being willingly pawed by Heath two weeks before school had started. We were now five weeks into the season, so it had been nearly two months. Two months! I'd dreamt about her all summer, yet I'd gone seven weeks without speaking to her. I was baffled by my own anger and cowardice, a combination that had pretty much become the norm for me.

As I approached her near the table that sported the free hot chocolate and hot dogs for the marching band, I tried to justify my confusion and insecurity as a certain strength. I mean, I'd held out for so long. The summer had been good practice, but that was much different. Over the summer, I didn't have to look at her every day. I didn't have to see her name painted on banners in the hallways along with the names of the other dancers, cheerleaders and football players. I only had to think of her when my mind called her up. Once the school year started, I had to think of her upon the order of everyone else.

I tried to hate Ann, but how could I hate my guardian angel? I found it easier to turn away from Jesus Christ back in sixth grade than from Ann Penella. And maybe that's too bad. I could've used Jesus at that point. But like an employee after quitting his job, I couldn't go crawling back to the Son of God. I wouldn't give Him that satisfaction.

And it's not that Ann didn't try to talk to me about it. Sometimes in the hallways or after band practice—always when we were alone—she'd approach me. She'd say things like, "Guy, please," and "Guy, I'm sorry," and once she even said, "Guy, why are you doing this to me?"

"Guy, why are you doing this to me?"

When Rosencrantz and Guildenstern were about to be killed, I seriously doubt they were questioning why Hamlet had tricked them. I'm sure they weren't pleased, but they must've at least understood his motivation. They'd betrayed his trust, and it's all about the trust.

It bears repeating: it's all about the trust.

I must have snickered or something when Ann asked me why I was doing this to her, because she suddenly quit asking. She either figured out the reason or…

Or she stopped caring. That's when I decided it was again time to talk to her. Although I wanted to hate her, I didn't want *her* to hate *me*. The fact that she loved Heath was painful enough. It would've torn me apart knowing that the other extreme applied to me.

So, it was during the third quarter of the fifth game of the season that I decided to break my isolation from Ann Penella. She was the only person I'd ever allowed onto my island, so what was the point in banishing her to the opposite beach?

The night was clear and cool on that last Friday of September. The fall wind had started to kick up around us, but the air was dry. As a result of the cool breeze, most of the dancers were wearing coats. The girls therefore looked pretty much the same, wearing their boyfriends' white and gold varsity jackets. The obvious differences in bodily size between the petite girls and their beefy, football playing boyfriends led to the peculiar visage of these shiny-faced young women swimming in waves of white and gold wool. It struck me that the disproportionately mountainous fabric served to protect each girl not only from the elements, but provided impenetrable barriers which kept each dancer from any physical contact. Sort of the high school equivalent of a chastity belt.

John Stuart Mill High School had chosen white and gold as their school colors due to pressure from the local Baptist Church. They were pure, neutral colors with no evil connotation. The original colors had been gold and black, but the Baptist Church had them changed because, as they explained to the school board, black is "...the color of Satan in the dark." The board wasn't about to upset them any more—losing their big, Baptist booster bucks in the process (them Baptists sure do love their football)—so they stuck with just the gold and white.

For the record, the Baptists had also succeeded in having any sort of Halloween celebrations banned from school by use of the following argument:

> "*Hallow* means *holy. Ween* means *evening.* Therefore, *Halloween* means *Satan's holy evening.*"

Before I reached high school, some of the more perspicacious seniors tried applying the same logic to something they wanted to see banned.

> "*Bio* means *life. Logy* means *the study of.* Therefore *biology* means the *study of Satan's life.*"

It worked, and so there was never any leaf collecting or frog dissecting behind the sanitized walls of John Stuart Mill High School. If the students wanted to learn about the order hymenoptera, they'd have to do it at their weekly goat sacrifice.

Nowhere was the sanctity of John Stuart Mill's school colors more apparent than with the numerous letters on Heath Millard's varsity jacket. He had them in football, baseball, wrestling, basketball...and

I believe there was even one there for lunch. He could apparently eat not just for speed, but for accuracy as well.

But I was doing my best to repress any thoughts of Heath at that moment. Hearing the fans cheer sporadically left me safe in the knowledge that he was on the football field and that he wouldn't again come swooping down from nowhere to grip Ann with his talons and take her back to his roost.

Despite the conformity of not only the dancers' attires, but also their builds, appearances and most likely even thought processes, I spotted Ann instantly. I had spent so much time looking at her that I could've picked her out in Joe Robbie Stadium from the blimp on Super Bowl Sunday.

Before I reached Ann, the girls she was with looked my way and started giggling. To my surprise—as much as theirs, I'm sure—I kept going. These were mainly the same girls from the school bus incident the year before, but I was no longer afraid of them. Ann Penella was in the middle of them all and—although she hadn't done a very good job as of late—she was still my guardian angel.

When she turned, Ann locked her gaze on mine and didn't break it. I was looking into her eyes to find some sort of emotion upon which I could build my strategy, but all I obtained was the feeling she was looking into *my* eyes to find the same. I broke off the stare-down first as I scanned the semi-circle of girls behind her, matching their patronizing gazes with one of complete control. It was as if being this close to Ann again gave me a confidence I had long been lacking, or maybe had never known before. Even as Ann was the source of my nervousness, she was my strength.

An analogy: Christians are taught to both love and fear their God. I don't know how or when Ann reached that status with me, I only know I was ready to be born again that very night.

She and I hadn't spoken since…well, since Heath. We were both confused about where we stood with each other, and I'll concede it was mainly my fault. I knew that, so I also knew whatever I did here could affect whether or not we even remained friends.

Ann was the first to speak. "Guy," she said. That was all. Just, "Guy." I guess she was letting me take control of the situation, so I did.

"Can we talk?" I asked her after a slight hesitation.

She waited about the same amount of time to respond. "We don't have time. I have to get back by the end of the quarter."

I didn't need to look at the clock to know this was just an excuse. "We've got time, Ann."

Her friends started to giggle again, and Ann shrunk from embarrassment. When she looked back towards me, even in the chilly air and the tense moment, her eyes warmed me. I had no idea how I'd managed to go so long without talking to her, but I didn't care about that anymore. I just wanted to talk to her now.

"Ann, please," I said, trying hard to insure my request did not sound like begging. I thought of telling her right then that I needed her, that I was in love with her, but I knew this would ruin everything. She had obviously already realized this from my reaction to her and Heath, and therefore had known it even before I did. Still, she didn't need to hear it from me. At least not in front of her friends. Like me, she was already embarrassed enough.

"Okay," she conceded, but she didn't move.

"Not here," I said, looking up at her friends.

She obviously understood. "I'll be right back," she told her friends without looking back at them. Not one of them replied as she walked past me, towards the fence that sectioned us off from the parking lot. I was left there beneath the stares of the dancers. Like giggling mannequins, their expressions hadn't changed from the moment I'd first approached.

Morons. I was surrounded by morons that evening in high school, just as I would be at the organizational meeting for A Daily Planet the Monday after I first learned that Jayson Fayme would be living in the apartment beneath Rhonda during my senior year of college.

❀   ❀   ❀

The students attending the meeting were pretty much the same who attended every year. There had been one or two new freshman early on, but they apparently became discouraged and left the room. The only faces which didn't belong were those of Jayson Fayme, President and Dean Douglas. Seeing them in the room gave me a tremendous sense of foreboding. It was common knowledge amongst the paper's staff and advisors that the Arbiter and I were going to be appointed co-editors of *A Daily Planet* our senior year, and the thought of having to work with Fayme and under President sounded about as pleasing to me as the prospect of climbing the light tower again with the Arbiter...which he actually asked me to do a few months after I'd first made the attempt.

Which reminds me, I never did close up the light tower story, did I? Ends up the backpack the Arbiter had taken with him during our junior year contained a different flag which he swapped with Floodbane's. Having then stuffed the original flag into the backpack, he climbed down, and we left the scene of the crime. I didn't realize until the next day what he'd done. The new flag was one he had convinced the costume designer of the theater department to make for him, and I must confess it was much more interesting than the original. Rather than simply sporting the school colors, the flag atop the WDOA radio tower was now bright red with bold, white numbering on it. The number was fourteen. That's it. That's all the flag said; "14."

The Arbiter explained it to me the day after the climb. From my dorm room, the flag was clearly visible above and beyond the fraternity houses where the future of our nation lie in comas, reeking of their best friends' urine, and I stared at it as the Arbiter attempted to elucidate his actions. He said it has always been his dream to create the world's biggest miniature golf course. Well, not really his dream so much as his mission. Apparently, for the past six or seven years, the Arbiter had placed numbered flags on various light towers across the country, as well as some large trees, two of our nation's more famous landmarks…and, of course, one obligatory windmill.

I asked, "Are they still up?"

"Hope so," he replied. "They were when last checked."

"Why miniature golf?" I continued. "Why not wrestling? Why not the WWE Intercontinental Belt?"

"Take a look at North America sometime," he explained. "The geography isn't conducive to a wrestling ring. It's shaped all wrong. France would make a good wrestling ring, but not the U.S.

"Besides, miniature golf kicks ass."

I was silent for a minute, then I started to laugh. The Arbiter looked at me for an explanation, so I said, "I just thought of what our forefathers would think. All those sacrifices made, the blood shed…all the lives lost so that we could turn their country into a putt-putt course."

"More useful than the anthill it's become," the Arbiter stated. "And Canada would make for an excellent neighboring go-cart track. Mexico as batting cages should work as well."

Again with the ant analogy, but I didn't feel like going any further with the conversation. I still didn't like to think about the tower. Unfortunately, because the gigantic miniature golf flag had more campus repercussions than even the Arbiter could have hoped, I was forced to think about the tower nearly every day for the rest of my junior year.

It ends up that President—rather than using College funds to have another flag made or track down the original's thief—convinced the athletic department to make the numeral 14 the new mascot. The name would become the Floodbane College 14'ers. In a mad media blitz, President filled the campus gift shop with the new red and white logo and shot wires to every newspaper, radio and TV station within a three state radius. Rumors of the school C-130 started to circulate again as well, this time dropping leaflets across every country club that had ever been graced with President's presence.

The campaign served two purposes; 1.) it sold hundreds of T-shirts, coffee mugs, teddy bears, shot glasses and the like, and 2.) it completely drowned the news of the drunk/urine/coma-boy, which otherwise could have been quite detrimental to Floodbane's image. Oddly enough, despite MTV's big push into celebrating, glorifying and promoting teen stupidity, the American public still tends to frown on college students pissing on each other.

But boy, do they love their putt-putt!

And apparently, President seemed to draw an inspiration from all this that lasted throughout the remainder of the year. He started to attend more campus events and to make longer—although even less coherent—speeches. The Arbiter told me this must be the punishment for his sin, so although he quite often went back up the tower with that set of binoculars, still not explaining why, he never returned the original flag. He wanted to serve his penance, so 14 remained. I'm just glad he never again asked me to climb the tower with him. Nothing short of a major catastrophe would get me up there again…

A catastrophe like what I was about to hear from President at the organizational meeting of the *A Daily Planet* newspaper staff early in my senior year.

I didn't exactly know what he was doing there in the first place. He had never before been to one of our meetings—not even during his media campaign after the flag incident the previous year—and we were pretty sure he'd never actually read *A Daily Planet*. Even the letters he would publish from time to time were written by one of his secretaries or the student help or Dean Douglas if it was important enough. But there he was. I should've put it all together much more quickly than I did. The thing is, I was too geared up for the meeting.

The Arbiter and I had worked diligently for the past couple of years on *A Daily Planet*, taking care of everything from photographing the godawful basketball games to maintaining the Macintosh computer network to willingly providing coverage of the student government elections. (I learned then that the reason mud-slinging is such a popular form of campaigning is because mud is just so much fun to sling.)

After all that work, the Arbiter and I were ensured co-editorship of *A Daily Planet*. Well, unless the women's basketball team had anything to say about it. During a key conference match-up, the Arbiter decided to get some snapshots of the stage band. He started talking to the guitarist, who allowed him to check out his Ibanez guitar. Then, as the Manson College Lady Beetles were lining up for a foul shot, he figured out the hook to Beethoven's Ninth Symphony and started blaring it throughout the gymnasium. When the ref cautioned him to quiet down, the Arbiter threw his fist in the air, made that devil sign that teenagers do, and shouted back, "If it's too loud, then you're too old!"

It wasn't long before he had the entire home crowd participating in the chant, so the referees, in attempt to prevent another Altamont, called a technical. Combined with the foul shots, this was enough to lift the Lady Beetles past our own Lady 14'ers. Or Lady Football Players. I'm really not sure what they were at that point. It's all too confusing.

Despite that incident, I would've rather seen the girls' basketball team at the organizational meeting of *A Daily Planet* than Dean Douglas and President. It threw me, their attendance, but they soon made their purposes known. After Dean Douglas had finally scared away the last of the new volunteers, he immediately went to work on the rest of us.

"Students, now that those who didn't really want to be on the staff have left to not be on the staff anymore, President will get down to appointing positions."

The Arbiter raised his hand, but he wasn't called.

"First off," President began, "the first position I'm going to appoint is—"

"Where's the advisor?" the Arbiter asked anyway.

"Excuse me?" President asked, sounding politely put-out.

"Said, 'Where's the advisor?'" the Arbiter repeated.

"I heard what you said," President pointed out.

"Then why did you say 'Excuse me?'"

"I was being polite."

"Well then thank you," the Arbiter said with a nod.

"You're welcome," President smiled towards the students who were sitting in rows of mahogany wood tables and chairs. The room—adorned in nothing but deep red wood and plush carpeting—normally served as a place where the richer alumni and trustees could dine, far from the cafeteria and the students who ate there…and the food that was served there. Rumor had it that the trustees even got to use spoons, but that was just a rumor.

"Now where was I?" President asked.

"You were about to point out who the advisor will be this year," Dean Douglas told him.

"No, I mean before I came here," President corrected. "My coat smells like perfume and cigarettes."

"Okay, well, I think I'll handle things from here," Dean Douglas jumped up with a start and politely bumped President towards the door. "Thank you, President, for showing—"

"And beer," President continued, sniffing his collar as he opened the door to the hallway. "The wife doesn't drink beer anymore."

And he was gone.

Immediately, the Arbiter stood up and, doing his best Ed Sullivan, announced, "Ladies and gentlemen, how about another round of applause for Floodbane's favorite funnyman, El Presidente! And now, right here on our really big shew, direct from the Boarding House in San Francisco, the Dean of Deans, Dean Douglas!"

Dean Douglas patiently, yet almost cautiously, waited for the applause and laughter to stop, then said, "As President was about to explain before I was so rudely interrupted, there will be no advisor this year."

The Arbiter smiled over to me. The advisors of the past had never really done too much aside from appointing editors at the beginning of the year and occasionally making public apologies for the views printed in *A Daily Planet*, but the official abandonment of any sort of superior gave the Arbiter and me an optimistic outlook for the year.

It was a very short lived optimism.

"Instead, I will be the advisor," Dean Douglas added, immediately pulling back from the table as if expecting to be clubbed. Even if we had armed ourselves ahead of time, we wouldn't have been able to club him. We were in shock; everyone in the room. Everyone except for Jayson Fayme...and the Arbiter.

He was smiling as if something wonderful had just happened. I was wondering if he'd heard something I hadn't, or if he'd just finally lost his mind. I was still clueless, but Dean Douglas's next statement quickly cleared any mud from my head.

"And I appoint as editor, Jayson Fayme. Have a great year." And he was out the door faster than John Wilkes Booth.

For a moment, all was silent. Not even Jayson said anything. He just sat there...smiling. The Arbiter was still smiling, too, while the other students in the room—including me—were dumbfounded.

Then the Arbiter stood once more, this time not bothering with the Ed Sullivan imitation. "Ladies and gentlemen, Dean Douglas! Thank you for coming tonight. Drive safely, and don't forget to tip your waitresses."

But none of us laughed this time. It was as if we'd just seen the President of the United States kiss another man full on the lips during a State of the Union address; we simply had no idea how we were to respond.

After a few moments, Jayson stood up and began to bark orders.

"Now let me just say this. My first order of business is to ban all ad sales to Panthemom's Pizza to be placed in our newspaper. They pissed me off."

At this, the Arbiter burst out laughing. He doubled over, he was laughing so hard, and I half expected him to suddenly jump up in a blaze of anger, foaming at the mouth, and throttle Jayson right then and there. But he didn't. He just continued to laugh at something in which I couldn't find any humor. In his gray notebook, which he'd left open on the table, he'd scrawled the phrase, "Here we go!" I didn't get it at the time, perhaps because I was too tense and confused, much the same as I was that Friday night during my junior year of high school as Ann and I headed off to a solitary place where we could talk.

I could hear Ann's friends start to laugh as I followed her towards the buses we rode to Aristotle High that night. I also heard something about my hair. That made sense, I suppose. The plastic and vinyl band hats seemed to suck the grease from my scalp much like a plunger sucks grime from the bathtub drain. Not only did the dancers have no hats to mess up their model-perfect hairdos, but they also had the entire second quarter to make themselves up before the halftime show.

Their taunts didn't bother me. At the risk of sounding redundant, I point out that they were morons. All that mattered to me was Ann.

As I followed her from the stadium, the night seemed to wash itself of the noise that arose from the screaming fanatics. All I could hear was the wind whistling around and over the parked school buses to which Ann had led me. The black sky was dotted with a thousand stars, all of them shining down encouragement. For a moment, I was struck by how cheesy my thoughts had become; I half expected animated squirrels and butterflies to illuminate the area as they danced about us, adorning Ann's soft face as if she were an orphaned princess.

Once we were safely out of sight, Ann turned to me. She leaned against one of the buses, then suddenly pulled away as if she was afraid of dirtying Heath's jacket. She looked at me for the first time since we had left her friends, and not even the harsh beams of the floodlight above us could harden Ann's eyes.

Before the silence could create an insurmountable obstacle, I smacked it away with, "Would you like a Life Saver? Spear-O-Mint."

"Yes," Ann replied after a pause. I gave her one, being careful not to touch her hand. Ann didn't put the Life Saver in her mouth, she just played with it, twirling the white candy in her fingers.

"Okay, let's talk," she finally said. Simple as that.

"Yes," I agreed. "It's been too long."

"That's not my fault, Guy."

"I know. I'm not blaming you."

"I've tried to talk to you."

"I know. I know." I was speaking as softly as I could. I wasn't about to let her hear any trace of anger in my words. I tried to sound like my mother when she'd soothe me after I'd awakened from a bad dream.

"So why didn't you talk to me?" Ann asked. "What did I do to you?"

I just looked at her.

"Heath?"

I nodded.

"Guy."

"If you only knew."

"Knew what?"

"I mean, anyone but him."

"Why?"

How could I explain to her all the anger that continued to burn inside of me like a funeral pyre? How could she understand his cousin Mick, the kitten and the consequences of all his other actions through the years in which we'd known each other? I couldn't just say, "Oh, he just wanted me to shoot his cousin with a BB gun and he threatened to kill a kitten so we don't get along." They surely wouldn't bring any credit to his character, granted, but they hardly justified my hatred.

"He and I have…somewhat of a past." I smiled at my own words; ends up I had a dark side after all. Bring on the honeys!

"I can't help that."

"And I'm not asking you to. I just want you to understand."

"I do, Guy, I guess. But Heath is really—"

"I'm not talking about Heath. Forget about Heath. I want you to think about just *me*."

She didn't say anything, but I understood her silence. Summoning all my courage, I laid everything out for her. My heart was thumping in my ears.

"I don't pretend to be the most romantic guy in the world (thump-thump), and Lord knows that I'm not much to look at (thump-thump), but—"

"Guy…"

"No. Agree with me. I'm only telling the truth, here (thump-thump)."

Ann smiled, and I knew if I didn't tell her now, I never would. (Thump-thump.)

"The point of all this (thump-thump) is that (thump-thump), and I know it's wrong (thump-thump), but I've…" my heart stopped…"fallen in love with you."

Ann opened her mouth as if to speak, but I raised my hand to stop her. "I know you don't love me back. I don't expect you to. I'm only telling you this so that you'll know why I sometimes can't talk to you and why it's hard for me to see you having fun with other people." I let out a short laugh. "Especially Heath."

Ann merely stared at me. I had to give her credit; she was handling this much better than I thought she would. In even my best scenarios as I rehearsed this scene over and over in bed at night, she had already run screaming in terror. Instead, still standing before me, her receptive manner encouraged me.

"I also want you to know that you don't need to be afraid of me because of this. I'm not going to start stalking you, and I'm certainly not going to bother you when you're with your friends. I'm not about to give them more chances to make fun of my hair," I smiled.

"I'm sorry about them. They—"

"No, like I said, I'm only telling the truth," I reminded her. "My hair *is* a mess."

"Even if that were true, there's no reason they should have to point it out to you," she apologized for them.

"If pointing out the obvious makes them feel better, then hey, more power to them. When they're married and have kids and are having affairs with each others' husbands and are miserable, they'll still have nothing to talk about except my hair. My hair and the weather and anything else that's obvious."

Ann paused for another second, then finally said, "I wish I could be like you."

I laughed. "No you don't."

"No. I wish I didn't care what other people thought about me. I wish I could just go through life doing what I want to do, not worrying at all about who would still be my friend when I was done."

"It takes a long time to get here, Ann. It's a lonely trip."

"Maybe too lonely?" she suggested.

"Impossible," I smiled.

Then, from completely out of nowhere, my guardian angel hugged me. I welcomed the warmth. Until that moment, I hadn't realized how cold I'd been.

She then placed her mouth close to my ear, and I could feel her breath as she said, "This is important, Guy. I'm going to need this from time to time."

Although I wasn't ready for her to, Ann let go of me. She looked into my eyes and smiled. Unlike after the bus incident a year before, there was no pity in her eyes, only respect, friendship and loyalty. For the first time since Heath had shown me the cruelty that seemingly pumps continuously through the human heart, I was finally able to see that tiny corner that shelters all that's good.

As Ann headed back to the stadium, she turned to look at me, still smiling. I continued to stand between the buses, knowing that it would be best for both of us if no one saw us come out from there together. Ann turned back to look at me a second time, and ran into the fence in the process. She giggled in embarrassment, then disappeared around a bus.

I remained there a few minutes more, staring up into the sky. I didn't want to walk away from what had just happened between us. Somewhat a cynic, I knew something would happen within the next day or two that would again cause me to lose my faith in the human condition.

But I was wrong.

I lost faith within the next hour or two.

CHAPTER 6

Denouement to A Dream

When I was a child, my Aunt Mae sometimes took me ice skating at the park. It wasn't an actual rink, but a frozen parking lot. No kidding. The park people would hose down a parking lot when the weather dropped below freezing and charge the good citizens of the town $3.00 to skate. This drew many heated letters to the editor of our local newspaper, as many people who frequented the park in the winter for ice fishing or sled riding were forced to park their cars on the street. In the end, the head of parks and recreation justified the skating rink by explaining that using the lot for parking in the winter was too dangerous. When asked why, the official statement was simply, "Too icy."

Aunt Mae was a very good skater, so she assumed I should be too. I wasn't. I could never even straighten my ankles in the skates, let alone use them for propulsion. But I wasn't just clumsy, I was clumsy in the company of a hundred other people. Some made it around the rink gracefully, while others failed worse than I did. The better skaters would occasionally help me out; pick me up after a fall or offer me advice. Sometimes the poorer skaters would knock me over or screw up my style just when I felt I was getting it right. The vast majority of the people just skated on by and didn't even notice me.

They were my favorites. Still are.

I mean, of course I wasn't fond of those who knocked me down all the time, but I also found myself annoyed with those who kept offering their advice. They were just getting in my way, interfering with my ability to learn on my own. No matter how good their intentions, they were no more of a help than those who were always tripping me up. It's like this; give a man a fish, and you feed him for a day; teach a man to fish, and you'll piss off the other fishermen.

Or maybe not. I don't know. I just didn't like to skate. ·

Either way, this is why I never seemed to get along with most of my teachers or professors. There were a few who would show me how to F.O.I.L. or mix an acid and a base, then let me have at it. Great. Thanks. But most would then stand behind my desk, wait just long enough to make me nervous as hell, then ask, "How you coming along?" And looking back, Mrs. Patera really wasn't that bad a teacher. Sure, she spanked me for decking Heath Millard, but she also used to place bets on football games with me. That's a pretty cool thing for a sixth grade teacher to do, I think.

Still, I firmly believe the best teachers are the ones who don't fret about their students individually, the ones who present us with the subject and just let us learn it in our own way, at our own pace. They toss the ball out there and teach us the fundamentals—how far we students are able to run with it is up to us.

And then there are those who don't give a damn if we learn anything at all. Those few would include Mr. Bernard.

The week after the announcement that A Daily Planet was being run by Jayson Fayme for my senior year, the staff advisor for the paper resigned from the school. He was also my professor for Shakespeare II that term, so our class was suddenly stranded in The Globe without a bard to direct us. One day he'd assigned us to read all of *Hamlet*, and by the next class period he was gone. We were granted that day off by the head of the department, but were assured there'd be a new professor the following class session.

And good Lord, was there.

Mr. Bernard arrived to class ten minutes late, but he was immediately worth the wait. He was young—maybe in his early thirties—with an amused face. He seemed to squint perpetually, like he was trying to figure something out. His hair was cropped short like that of a marine, but he was built more like a college football player, broad in the shoulders and chest, yet a bit overweight from drinking too much beer with his frat buddies. In fact, looking at him, one could only think of beer.

This was because of his jacket.

Overtop the requisite turtleneck of English professors, Mr. Bernard was wearing a sport coat tiled with the red, white and blue Budweiser beer emblem. His whole torso was nothing but one big billboard gone horribly awry. What amazed me most wasn't that he was wearing such an atrocity, but that he'd actually been able to buy it somewhere. Some company had made this jacket, and there were probably others like it locked in closets across the country. God help us all should they escape and then spring the matching pants.

A couple of girls near me in the back of the room didn't notice his entrance and continued their discussion as he wrote his name on the marker board.

"I really don't think so, Marlena; it's Hamlet's mystery that makes him such an intriguing character."

"This, I realize. It's just that all of Hamlet's inconsistencies can be explained."

"Maybe so, but has it occurred to you that perhaps Hamlet didn't know he was being inconsistent? How can we be expected to explain him when he couldn't even explain himself?"

"Tammy, that's a good point, but it is my belief that Hamlet knew what he was doing all along. It was just a front to—"

"Good morning, college students," the professor greeted, turning from the marker board. "My name's Mr. Bernard, and I'll be taking over this class for the duration of the term. Seems your former professor has," Mr. Bernard held up and wiggled two fingers on each hand to symbolize that he was quoting someone, "resigned. Now I just joined the ball club yesterday, so I haven't had time to prepare a lesson for today. We'll just pick up where you left off, because you college students are paying a great deal of money to attend this school, and I don't believe it fair to you to cheat you out of class time. You and your education are much too important for that.

"Now then, what were you reading?"

"*Hamlet*," Tammy pointed out.

"Oh, I see," Mr. Bernard nodded. "Okay, then, class is canceled for the week."

"You can't do that," Marlena pointed out as three students gathered their books and exited the classroom. Mr. Bernard did nothing to stop them. "We have a test scheduled for Monday. We have issues we need to discuss."

"Are they related to *Hamlet*, or are they more along the line of dating troubles or feminine issues?" Mr. Bernard asked.

"*Hamlet*," Tammy and Marlena replied in unison, both as if to actually say, "You moron."

"Oh, okay," Mr. Bernard agreed with reluctance. "Well, what do you want to discuss?"

"The professor usually leads the discussions," a student in the front row pointed out.

"Well, how convenient for you. Damn college students can't do anything for themselves these days," Mr. Bernard snapped at him. "Okay, then let's discuss Hamlet."

The classroom was silent far longer than it should have been. Finally, a guy from the back corner—someone who hadn't spoken all year, I think—asked, "What about him?"

Mr. Bernard brightened at this. "Good question. What about Hamlet? Does anyone have a response to that?"

Marlena's hand went up, but she didn't wait to be called upon. "Excuse me, sir, but Hamlet is too diverse a character to discuss in such broad generalizations. It is my belief that Hamlet should be picked apart and examined like a dissected animal."

"Which animal?" asked Mr. Bernard. "A perch? A wolverine? A saucy Tabby named Kama who was run over by a school bus?"

"That's not important."

"So then why mention it?"

"I was only using it as an analogy for—"

"Know what's a good analogy?" Mr. Bernard interrupted. "'Like an Italian pastry chef.' It always works, without fail. See, 'Hamlet should be picked apart and dissected like an Italian pastry chef.' Or, 'Holy cow, he sent that ball flying further than an Italian pastry chef.' Jot that down in your notebooks, college students. There will be a…no, wait. Like the Irish Potato Famine. That's better."

Over half the class were writing it down, which was a better ratio than the previous professor ever achieved. One of the students had just now awakened and began to frantically scan the room until he recognized his surroundings and felt certain he was in the correct class. Mr. Bernard, meanwhile, had taken his seat behind the desk at the front of the room. "Now, let's get started. We'll start with Hamlet's name. Now, why in God's name do you suppose anyone would name his kid Hamlet? Any ideas?"

Silence.

Mr. Bernard continued. "Okay, well I theorize that Hamlet was such a nut because he had that stupid name. The kids in junior high probably called him things like 'Pastramilet' and 'Corned Beeflet' all day, asking him if he was honey roastedlet or Virginialet. If anything, I'd say it's his father's faultlet."

"Sir, I really don't think that Hamlet's complexity was caused by his name," Tammy offered.

"Yeah, everyone back then had stupid names," the back corner guy agreed. "I mean, look at this. I can't even say this. Whore…ah…tee-oh. What kind of dumbass name is Whore-ah-tee-oh?"

Mr. Bernard nodded. "I see your point…uh, what's your name?"

"Irwin Schiester."

Mr. Bernard could not contain a quick burst of laughter. "Did your previous professor cover irony yet?"

"I don't think so. Why?" asked Irwin.

"Nevermind," Mr. Bernard didn't explain. "So let me throw out this idea for discussion, class: Hamlet was such a nut because he had only one testicle."

Response from the class was a mixture of laughter and shock.

"In the movie," Mr. Bernard elaborated, "after Hamlet saw his dad...and I mean the old black and white movie, not the Gibson movie. If you're going to see a Mel Gibson movie, see *Mad Max*. It rocks. Anyway, after Olivier's Hamlet saw his dad, he fell to the concrete and shouted out 'Oh, my nard.' Now we all know that in Shakespeare's day, 'nards' was a slang term for testicles, much like the term 'women' actually meant 'hairless, high-voiced boys.' When Hamlet obviously racked himself by falling down, he claimed that he hurt his nard in the *singular tense*." Mr. Bernard leaped to his feet and with a frenzy scrawled those words, "singular tense," on the marker board, underlining them a half dozen times and repeating them in a sing-song matter that sounded not quite entirely unlike the chorus to Rod Stewart's "Infatuation."

He then continued, "It is, therefore, revealed to us that Hamlet had only one testicle and was, in fact, sexually frustrated." Mr. Bernard threw down the marker to his desk as if spiking a football in the end zone, reigning shrapnel and dust upon those in the front row.

Marlena had been searching furiously through her text as Mr. Bernard stated his theory, and seemed a bit peeved when Tammy found it first. "Sir, he didn't say, 'Oh, my nard.' He said, 'Hold, hold my heart.' It's right here on page 56."

Mr. Bernard nonchalantly looked at the book on his desk. "Oh." He then reached into his attaché case, pulled out a sizeable document, and saying, "Well, there goes my thesis," tossed it out the window.

As I watched the pages blow across the lawn and into the parking lot of the oddly busy shoe repair shop across the street, I found myself wondering if this guy was for real or just theatrics, but the scene developing in class pulled my attention back to the stage.

"Sir, if I may bring up a question," Marlena asked. Mr. Bernard waved his arm before him, giving her the floor. "We were debating about why Hamlet didn't kill the King when he had the chance. The ghost of his father and the play within the play were more than enough to convince him that Claudius had indeed killed his father, yet he didn't take revenge when he had the chance. Why?"

Mr. Bernard paused, then asked, "Does anyone care to field this?"

Irwin did. "Because he was a pussy?"

"Correct," Mr. Bernard nodded. "Next question."

"If I may interrupt, it is my opinion that Hamlet did not kill Claudius at that moment because he was praying. To kill someone in the act of praying would be to send their soul to Heaven, which would therefore not avenge his father," an increasingly irritated Tammy explained. I was enjoying this. It's not that I had anything against Tammy or Marlena, I just enjoyed watching the haughty get flustered. "His father was killed with his sins still upon him, so he was doomed to walk the night. Hamlet wanted the same fate to befall Claudius. Wouldn't you concur, Mr. Bernard."

"Oh, you know I would, baby dolls. I'd concur aawwwwwlllllllllll night long"

"But Mr. Bernard, to accept that theory would contradict Hamlet's character itself. Hamlet was an inconsistent, highly impulsive character. He rarely had reason for anything he did. Don't you think that he chose not to kill Claudius because at that moment he lost all trust he had won about revenge through the appearance of the ghost and the play within the play and instead succumbs to the immediate need?"

Mr. Bernard paused for two beats. "You know, if I was younger, I'd probably give a damn. I'm going with the pussy theory, because if there's one thing I've learned, it's that all of man's actions are based on pussy."

"Right on, teach!" Irwin agreed, throwing a triumphant man-fist into the air.

"Here's an idea," Mr. Bernard suggested before Marlena and Tammy could rally and attack. "I'm sure that we can at least all agree that *Hamlet* is best understood when acted out, right? Right. Good. Irwin, you play Hamlet. Marlena, you can play Ophelia. Turn to act three, scene two, and start reading at line...I believe it's one-oh-seven in your Pelicans."

He suggested this passage without looking at the text in front of him; and he was dead on. After a moment, Irwin started in.

"'Lady, shall I lie in your lap?'"

"'No, my lord,'" Marlena followed up.

"'I mean, my head upon your lap?'"

"'Ay, my lord.'"

"'Do you think I meant country matters?'"

"'I think nothing, my lord.'" Marlena sounded angry as she read the line, seeming to get this before Irwin. It was apparent that Mr. Bernard had chosen this passage on purpose. I realized the man knew more than he was letting on.

"'That's a fair thought to lie between maids' legs.'" Irwin laughed. Now he was getting it. He blew Marlena a kiss, but she turned away as she continued to read.

"'What is, my lord?'"

It took Irwin a minute to find his place. "Hold on...uh...oh, 'Nothing.'"

"'You are merry, my lord.'"

"'Who, I?'"

"'Ay, my lord.'"

"'Oh God, your only jig-maker.'" Irwin lowered the book to ask Mr. Bernard, "What's a jig-maker?"

Mr. Bernard explained, "Jig is Old English for jism, so a—"

"That's it!" Marlena shouted as she jumped to her feet. Mr. Bernard stood up to meet her as she continued. "I'm not going to put up with this! You're nothing but a sexist pig with no respect for good literature!"

"Hey, I didn't write it," Mr. Bernard argued in his defense.

"This is sexual harassment! I'm going to report you to Dean Douglas," Tammy threatened. "He'll see to it that you never teach at this school again."

"Oh, get thee to a nunnery," Mr. Bernard called out to them as they stormed from the room. Taking their cue, some other students also starting packing up their books.

"Is class canceled for the day?" Irwin asked.

"Yeah, I guess, but be here Thursday," Mr. Bernard told him.

"Okay."

"Oh, and bring some beer and a couple of babes. And try to make them biology majors. They can help us identify the bugs that have crawled up Marlena and Tammy's ass."

It was going to be a great year. For the first time in quite a while, things were looking up. I left the classroom that day as excited to tell the Arbiter and Rhonda about this excellent new professor as I had been to tell…well, anyone about the night I made love to Ann Penella.

Anyone except for Heath, of course, who would've slapped me six ways to Sunday if he ever found out. Or is it six ways *from* Sunday? I don't know. Either way, it would've been a week full of slapping. Heath made that clear just a couple of hours after I admitted my love to Ann among the buses at Aristotle High School.

That would've made a good movie title, I think. A Sally Field or Meryl Streep vehicle; *Ann Among the Buses.*

I was feeling pretty good about myself after the third quarter had ended and the band members returned to our area of the visitors' stands. I think I can even recall playing along when the band struck up the pep song or "Hang On Sloopy" or some other piece of music that was supposed to inspire our players to the victory they were already well on their way to achieving. Now granted, Ann didn't just drop her life and fall in love with me the way I'd hoped, but—as I said—she didn't run screaming in terror, either. Instead, my honesty and openness sealed our friendship. No longer would I hide from her, and no longer would she have to ignore me. We were friends now. Good friends. For the first time since Terry Hogan moved to Toledo, I had a good friend, and nothing could separate us.

An equation I learned that night: Heath Millard = nothing.

I don't know how he'd gotten wind of it, but it didn't take long for him to learn that Ann and I had spent some time together. It took even less time for him to track me down.

The Fightin' Golden Sandies had beaten the Aristotle Orange Pants 51 to 13, making it one of the greatest victories in the history of our school. Heath was elected MVP of the game, of course, and the Monday write-ups of his performance even went so far as to say that he had been "in the zone" that night.

The zone. Where was this zone, and why the hell couldn't he have just stayed there?

It was almost immediately after the game that Heath launched his first physical attack on me since that incident at his birthday party in sixth grade. We were about to board the buses that would shepherd us back to John Stuart Mill, when I noticed a commotion coming from behind my bus. After a second, Millard came around the corner and shot at me like a BB pellet. I tried to jump through the door of the bus, but it was being blocked by a group of people who were too busy waiting for Heath to kill me to get out of the way. I thought about running, but that would've made me look like both a wimp *and* a coward when wimp alone was good enough for me.

Upon reaching me, Heath grabbed my open uniform and threw me against the school bus. My head slammed first, and I'm surprised

I didn't go down right there. I heard the sharp tone of my skull cracking against the metal, then suddenly Heath's spit was flying into my face as he warned, "If you ever touch my woman again, bitch, I'll put your head through that window!"

He was still in full uniform aside from his helmet, so there wasn't a whole hell of a lot I could do other than scout the area for Ann. I'm not sure if I wanted to actually find her; I just needed to know if she was there.

"You listening to me, dick head?!" Heath continued. He was somehow yelling through clenched teeth. "You faggot. What would a faggot like you want with her anyway? Maybe some mascara tips? Maybe share earrings, faggot?"

He slammed me against the bus again to accent the third "faggot" part. From my right, I could hear laughter.

"I hear you'd rather just jack off on the school bus. What happened to that?"

Oh. So I guess the girl from that night on the school bus over a year ago did realize what had happened. Judging from the laughter of those around me, I realized that everyone was in on the joke. Wonderful.

I still didn't say anything, and my silence seemed to upset Heath even more. He placed the palm of his right hand against my forehead and shoved it against the bus. I again heard that pinging sound as if someone was banging a pipe with a hammer. I clenched my eyes tightly to drive away the sharp pain, but all this seemed to do was produce tears.

"Oh Christ, she's crying," Heath sighed as he released his grip on me. I'd apparently been depending on his support; when he let go, I fell to the ground against the bus. "It's like slapping around a fuckin' cheerleader."

Nobody helped me up after Heath had gone. Nobody came over to see if I was okay, and no one bothered to point out I was no longer wearing my hat. I was midway back to John Stuart Mill before I realized it must still be lying in the parking lot at Aristotle High School. I was certain I'd catch hell for that on Monday afternoon, but I didn't care anymore. I didn't even really care about Heath's threats, either. Ann and I were…

It hit me then; it was a good thing we'd spent the previous school year meeting in the darkness, away from the eyes of her friends and family. Before, we were always just staying clear of possible consequences…but now we had something tangible to avoid. I mean, I didn't so much mind being tossed around by Heath. He'd been doing this to me in one form or another since we'd first met, so I was quite used to it. I'd developed a patience for his He-Man displays, knowing the headaches or stomachaches never stuck around too long. Heath Millard was easily remedied with over-the-counter drugs.

But Ann was dating Heath now, and I wasn't about to compete with that. I would've lost worst than Aristotle High School, so I wasn't going to force Ann to watch that game. It was back to the midnight rendezvous for her and I, which, I can honestly say, was just fine with me. Our affair…albeit still an affair without the sex…would continue.

If our high school paper had taken the turn that *A Daily Planet* would eventually take, then my sordid love life would've made for one hell of a headline.

I should've known the Arbiter had grander plans for *A Daily Planet*—just as with his life in general—then he'd let anyone know. It made perfect sense once I caught on, which is probably why I picked up his cue with little hesitation. It was just a few minutes after I'd told him about Mr. Bernard, in whom he seemed genuinely interested. He suggested he and I conduct an interview with Mr. Bernard to put in the paper, a kind of "new faces" thing. I thought the idea trite for the Arbiter and told him so, but he explained himself by adding that we wouldn't ask Mr. Bernard anything about teaching.

Instead, the whole interview would be based on his life during the Irish Potato Famine.

That Arbiter…always cooking up an angle.

Jayson entered the office at this point, and immediately set off on Rhonda who had been visiting the Arbiter when I arrived.

"Hey, baby, you decided to dump this asshole for me yet?"

"Dump him yourself," Rhonda replied.

Jayson missed it. "Come on, you know you want me more than him."

Rhonda stopped and raised a finger to her chin as if in thought. She looked up at the ceiling for a moment, rolling her eyes from one wall to the other and back again, then responded with a simple, "No."

Jayson seemed genuinely surprised, as if each time he propositioned her would finally be the instance where she'd change her mind. "Why not?"

"Because I don't find you sexually attractive."

I laughed out loud at her response, as did the Arbiter. Jayson's face flushed and he threw himself into the chair at his desk. I'm sure he would've broken something expensive had there been something nearby. Instead, it was all he could do to grab a pencil and throw it against a wall.

Eager to break the silence that followed, I asked Rhonda, "How was badminton?"

"The professor didn't show up again," Rhonda sighed. "What's the point in—"

"Wait a minute," the Arbiter interrupted. "Floodbane College has a professor in badminton?"

"Yeah. He graduated from Dartmouth with a major in racquet sports and a minor in shuttlecock kinesiology," Rhonda explained.

"I've got a shuttle like a cock," Jason spat out, smiling. He then frowned momentarily. "I mean…my cock's in…" then trailed off.

Rhonda stared at Jayson for a moment, then excitedly snapped back towards the Arbiter "I've got news for you."

"Good. That makes my job as a journalist all the easier."

"Remember what you told me earlier about the mascot?"

"Yeah," the Arbiter smiled.

Before Rhonda could deliver the news, Jayson turned back around and practically shouted, "Let me just say this, Vorhees, that if the world was flooded with piss and you were in a tree, I still wouldn't have sex with you."

Rhonda leaned her head forward and squinted at him for a moment before asking, "What?"

"You heard me." Jayson turned back to stare at the wall in front of him.

Rhonda looked to the Arbiter for some sort of explanation, and he had one.

"It's okay. I think that was good news."

"Sometimes I think I'm just imagining him," Rhonda said with a nod towards Jayson. He made no response to indicate he'd heard her.

"What did you hear about the mascot?" the Arbiter asked, getting back to more important matters.

"It's true."

The Arbiter's smile turned triumphant, and he pounded his fist on the plywood desk as he let out a resounding, "Yes!"

Jayson turned back around to see what was going on. "Would you shut your assholes up? I'm trying to design a layout!"

"Sorry," the Arbiter said, still smiling. "Just a little excited over Rhonda's tip." He then turned back to Rhonda and kissed her lightly on the lips. "Thanks, dear."

"What tip?" Jayson asked as the Arbiter turned back to his iMac. "What do you have Rhonda?"

"It's nothing big," the Arbiter explained. "Certainly not front page news. Not as big as the Homecoming candidates article you're working on."

"I'm editor, goddammit!" Jayson shouted. "Tell me what the fucking story is!"

The Arbiter looked up at Jayson and dropped his hands to his lap. "Okay, but then you have to decide whether or not it goes in. This is controversial stuff; we're not supposed to know yet."

"Know what?"

"Guy over there cracked the story," the Arbiter said with a nod and a wink in my direction. My eyes widened at the mention of my name, and my head immediately went to work on the lie I suddenly had to tell. Jayson, Rhonda and the Arbiter were all looking at me with eager anticipation, albeit for completely different reasons.

I thought back to any clues Rhonda or the Arbiter may have already given me. "The tip about the mascot?" I asked.

"Yeah, you were right," the Arbiter continued to smile. "Excellent."

"What about the mascot?!" Jayson was nearing hysterics. "Guy, let me just say this. You tell me what's going on or you're fired!"

I heard a jingling sound coming from Rhonda, so I turned to see what she was doing. She had pulled the change out of her pocket and was sifting through it. It took a moment, but I got the clue.

"Change. They're changing it."

"Again?" Jayson asked, now showing genuine interest. "To what now?"

"You're not going to believe it," Rhonda said, buying me some time.

"She's right," the Arbiter agreed. "You thought the Floodbane College Football Players was bad—"

"—Then there was the Floodbane College 14'ers," Rhonda added.

"What is it?!" Jayson shouted, again losing control.

"Tell him, Guy," the Arbiter suggested. He was having fun with this, and, despite the pressure, so was I.

"Guy?" Jayson pressed.

I blurted out the first thing that came to mind. "Potato Famine?"

Everyone in the room stared at me in disbelief. Even the Arbiter. "What?"

"That's right." There was no backing away from this now. "The Floodbane College Potato Famine from now on." It sounded so weak that I added, "Go Famine!"

Rhonda at this point had lowered her head into her hands so that Jayson couldn't see that she was laughing, while the Arbiter continued to just stare at me.

"You're not serious," Jayson said, but I could tell that he was buying it. Simply amazing.

"Apparently so," I shrugged. "If that's what Rhonda just heard."

"That's what I heard," Rhonda confirmed, suppressing a giggle. "Direct from the coach himself."

The Arbiter was loving this. He was like a karate sensei watching his pupil smash the block of concrete for the very first time. I put the wax on, and I wiped the damn wax off.

"Well then let me just say that I'm writing this article and it's going on the front page."

"You're the boss," the Arbiter acknowledged. "You are the boss."

※   ※   ※

"*I* am the boss," Mr. Bravo pointed out, thumping his finger into his chest. "I don't think you ever fully understood that."

"I did…do, Mr. Bravo," I argued. "I'm telling you, that's not what I was doing back there."

"We have sworn, signed affidavits from all of the bus drivers," Mr. Bravo revealed as he grabbed a stack of papers from his desk and waved them in my face.

"What're those?" I asked.

He looked at them, then frowned when he realized the papers he was holding had nothing to do with me. "It's the score to 'Lullaby of Broadway,'" he resigned only seconds before he came up with a connection, "written on paper, the same material the bus drivers used to write their sworn affidavits that I can't find at the moment. Come on along and listen to me. They saw you under the school buses during the third quarter of the game against the Aristotle Orange Pants. A fine game, too. You should've been watching. That Heath Millard is some ball player. A real blue chipper. Two hundred twenty pounds of twisted steel. One ton of sinewy muscle with a one track mind!"

"Yeah he's amazing," I lied. I wasn't really in the mood for this, but then, when would I have been? I was prepared to defend myself when the missing band helmet was brought up, but it had yet to be mentioned. Mr. Bravo called me into his office as expected, but I certainly wasn't expecting the accusation that came.

"What were you doing under the school bus with that dancer?" he asked again, repeating the first words to leave his lips after I had entered his office.

My answer was the same. "I wasn't under a bus."

"Were you copping a feel?"

"Ex…Excuse me? Was I—"

"You know, did you play with her breasts a little? Maybe rub her nipples with your thumbs, get 'em all hard?"

"I—"

"They like to tell you it's because they're cold, but we know better, right?"

"I suppose."

"Did you kiss her neck? Right there in the hollow of her shoulder? Maybe bite it a little…enough to leave a mark? Do you like that? Does that get your freak on?"

"I don't know what that—"

"Girls like that, you know."

"I don't think that—"

"Did you roll on top of her and march the Golden Sandy?"

"I'm not familiar with—"

"Dammit, Guy, did you pop that bubble?"

I was becoming frightened by this point, but my confusion was still stronger than my fear. "Through a woolen band uniform?"

"Because we don't approve of that type of behavior under school buses."

"I know, Mr.—"

"I know how it feels to love a woman. Don't get me wrong. I know the temptations that teenage girls pose to guys like me...you. Me or you, but mostly you. Not so much me. I see it every day; those girls in their short skirts, their young, pure, innocent eyes open wide with wanton wonder as I wave my baton before me. They follow it as if I were the mighty Sousa," Mr. Bravo was waving his arms as if conducting an orchestra, "commanding their breathing; their tonguing, their fingering."

"Shouldn't you be talking about this on the internet instead of with—"

"But I don't do anything about it, Guy. And do you know why, Guy?"

"I have my—"

"Because, Guy, here at John Stuart Mill High School, we do not participate in the subjection of women."

"That's very noble."

"Yes. Nobility. And you betrayed that nobility."

"No I didn't."

"You don't think that defiling a virgin under a school bus at a football game that your team is winning 51 to 13 is a betrayal of school nobility? 51 to 13!"

"But I didn't defile a virgin, and I—"

"What, do you mean to tell me she wasn't a virgin? You were under a school bus with some skank? More than one? Were you pulling a ho' train?"

"No, I wasn't under—"

"She's not in band, is she?" Mr. Bravo seemed genuinely concerned by this. "I mean, I don't mean to pry into your private life, and I certainly don't expect you to reveal the name of this brazen, bottom-feeding slut, but could you just tell me where…I mean, she's not a flutist is she? She doesn't sit in the front row during rehearsal? She doesn't have dark hair and wear mini-skirts and white ankle socks all the time like an Asian schoolgirl in her sailor uniform?"

He actually started to sweat before finishing his statement, and I felt compelled to calm this man down. I thought he was about to have a heart attack. "She's not in band."

"Thank God," he sighed. "The Mrs. Bravo and I just got settled in."

"In where?"

"Listen, Guy, I think it's best that we just forget this whole thing."

"I'm not sure what—"

"If you need to have sex to…I mean, what I'm saying is that if it improves your performance on the field, I understand. You're not the worst I've seen, after all. Last year, I'm told that one of my students would masturbate on the way home from the games. Right there in front of everyone…no reservations, no inhibitions. The full Paul Reubens, right there in front of the world! I'd sure like to find out who that was."

"I bet you would."

"But as for you, I'd just like for you to not do it where you can get caught, okay?"

I gave up. "Okay."

"Good. Maybe…hey, just between you and me, maybe you can use my van. It's customized for…I think you'll find it adequate. I can park right behind the stadium, and stock the bar for you and put the fish back in the aquarium—"

"I think I can control myself, Mr. Bravo."

"Or that too, if you wish. I really don't even have a van. Well, I do, but it's used for transportation only, for driving people to and fro. Adult people. Only adults."

I turned to leave, but Mr. Bravo called me back.

"Yes, sir?"

"If there's anything you need, Guy, you know, to keep things…pianissimo, you just name it, Guy."

"Well there is one thing I'd like."

"A movie camera? Some tape and a lighting rig?"

"What? No."

"You're sure?" He was sweating again.

"Yes."

"Then name it."

"I'd like a new band helmet. My old one is too tight."

"I'll call the distributor tomorrow morning," Mr. Bravo agreed as he returned to his desk. He looked about nervously, rubbed two pudgy fingers under his two pudgy chins, then sat down and hid himself behind a newspaper. He was obviously feeling self conscious about something, but I wasn't interested in finding out what it was. I was a firm believer that secrets were secrets for a reason. Letting them out usually just led to trouble, and it was even more dangerous to expose the secrets of others.

For a moment I actually felt bad about dispelling the apparent myth that Ann and I made love under that school bus. It might have done me some good, and it wouldn't have been my fault if I wasn't the one who started the rumor. But I quickly realized I'd done the right thing. This was Ann we were talking about, and I had far too much respect for her to let our secrets destroy her social life, especially if those secrets were lies.

It happens after all, right? I'd seen such "secrets" posted in tabloids such as *The Star, The National Enquirer* and *People*. Of course, it's not that I have much sympathy for actors who get upset about tabloid articles written about their nearly fatal drug overdoses or illegitimate Siberian children. Tabloids are as much a part of stardom as the ridiculous paychecks, and getting upset with them was about as logical as getting upset with children for telling body function jokes in Sunday School. And besides, it didn't take long for me to join their ranks when *A Daily Planet* made the tabloid turn thanks to the journalism of one Jayson Alexander Fayme.

❦   ❦   ❦

FLOODBANE ADOPTS NEW MASCOT

"14'ers" no more! For the second time in the past year of the history of Floodbane College, the current athletic department has voted to change the mascot of the college sports collective. What used to be known as the Floodbane College Football Players and the Floodbane College 14'ers will now be known as the Floodbane College Potato Famine!

No one is sure why the change took place, including the athletic department hisself. "This is news to me," said Ms. Backlund, athletic department secretary, senior citizen. "Good thing you young folk today have your little newspapers to keep us informed. I'm all for education for today's youth. Say no to drugs."

Campus opinion on the change is mixed.

"It's a little offensive, don't you think?" asked Sherry Martel, freshman. "Won't it upset the Irish students?"

A quick call to the Admissions Office dispelled this theory as there currently aren't and never have been any Irish students at Floodbane College. The Admissions Office assures us that this is merely a coincidence. "We're making every effort to increase the number of Irish students who apply to Floodbane College," explained one staff member.

When asked about the change, another student, junior Bob Holley, replied with, "We have a football team?"

Other responses to the change have included, "I like potatoes," "I don't like potatoes," "Quit calling me, asshole, I'm trying to study," "Potato Famine, huh" and "Well, it never did seem right to go to a women's volleyball game and cheer for the Football Players."

So how long will this Potato Famine last? All the way to the championship!
—Jayson Fayme, reporting

"You realize that no original material could have equaled this," the Arbiter pointed out as he put down the newspaper and spun around in the swivel chair at his computer. The Arbiter and I were the only two in the office that Monday morning; the papers had already been delivered to the dorms, and the staff had the day off before work began on next week's edition. "Read this article ten times now, and it keeps getting better and better. It's just impossible to purposely write comedy like this."

"So what's next?" I asked. "Piñatas in the chapel?"

"Like that," the Arbiter said with a nod of his head. "Could fill them with rosaries. No, it's not big enough."

"The piñata or the chapel?"

"The possibilities here are huge. Huge! President can't do a damn thing to stop us or he'll lose the Fayme Family Fortune. And Jayson has no idea what's going on. As long as we keep feeding him lies and he keeps printing them, they'll keep happening. We have the power supreme! U-S-A! U-S-A! U-S-A!"

Had this not been so damned funny, I would've been really frightened at how easily the Arbiter had seized control of the whole school. I'm sure that, if he wanted, he could've taken the school for a million in gold bullion and safe passage to Guam. Passive aggressive terrorism. How's that for a new network news catchphrase?

Thank God I was on this guy's side.

That issue of A Daily Planet moved more copies than any other since at least as long as the Arbiter and I had been on staff. Despite the fact the papers are free, a little less than half could always be found left on the distribution tables set up in each dorm and facility. Sometimes they'd disappear by Friday or Saturday night, but we were certain this wasn't for perusal purposes. The students of Floodbane seemed more interested in stoking their bonfires than in learning about how the girls' volleyball team was doing or what some punk sophomore thought of the latest *Evil Dead* film festival.

What they did care about, apparently, was the Floodbane Potato Famine. I have no explanation for this other than they got the joke, which therefore made it entertainment, and entertainment sells better than news. I just hoped the library picked up a copy for archival purposes. In sixty years, I wanted some curious student to get an answer as to how his college's team became known as the Potato Famine, and I wanted that answer to be Jason Fayme.

Whether that would ever come to pass wasn't on my mind at the time. The Arbiter, Rhonda and I were in too festive a mood to think beyond our immediate surroundings. A complete sell-out by Monday evening? That was cause for celebration, and we decided to celebrate at the single best place to eat in the whole town; Panthemom's.

It would prove to be the second biggest mistake we'd make that year.

CHAPTER 7

alt.binaries.pictures. erotica.peanuts

A lot of people don't understand professional wrestling. They just don't get it. Even before I'd learned how to lace my shoes, even before I'd watch wrestling on Sundays after church with my best friend Terry Hogan before he moved to Toledo, I knew it was choreographed. I knew wrestling was scripted before I knew that Santa Claus and the Tooth Fairy didn't exist. Perhaps if the two of them had formed a tag team and fought Conquistadors Numbers 1 and 2, then I wouldn't have continued to wake up so excited the morning after losing a tooth.

That's why I never understood when people felt compelled to point out, "That's all fake, you know. They're not really hitting each other."

"Okay, thank you, because you see, I'm really, really stupid. And while you're being so helpful, could you explain to me how those big men can fit inside that little TV in the first place?"

I mean, when I walked into the room and saw the same people watching repeats of *M*A*S*H*, I never felt it necessary to point out, "That's all fake, you know. Trapper John's not really removing shrapnel from that poor Korean boy's artery. Jamie Farr doesn't really wear women's clothing to work."

Or did he?

It was these people who first made me realize, even before my teenage years, I was beyond most others. It's not that I was smarter than them, but that I *got* it. I didn't go through life missing the point, and, therefore, didn't need to state the obvious in an effort to compensate. I never said things like "Beautiful day, huh," or "Ooh, that acid burn looks painful." What was the point?

I developed a theory at this point which I didn't believe, but I sure wanted to. I theorized that maybe we're each given a certain number of words to say. God, upon the moment we're born, looks at our naked, wrinkled bodies and says, "Okay, this one gets 9.9999998 words to say in her lifetime, and that girl over there gets 6. Choose them well, dear child." This would explain why some people die very slowly at an old age (their bodies slow down before they use up all their words, so their mouth has to catch up) while others die very abruptly in grizzly bear attacks (spoke too quickly).

This is why I refused to ever own a cell phone and instantly hung up on telemarketers.

So, when people pointed out to me wrestling is fake, I had to smile. If they wanted to waste their precious few words on crap like that, so be it.

I wonder, if I'm ever caught and forced to appear in court for killing somebody, could I use this argument to justify my crime? "I'm sorry your Honor, but my victim used up all the allotted words. It was just coincidence that I was there when it happened. I was only doing grunt work for the Lord, makin' the minimum wage."

That's an unfair statement to make, as I never worked for minimum wage in my life. Because my summers were mainly spent watching my little brother, I never joined the teen workforce at Burger King or Sheetz. Band took up my after-schools during the fall, and I guess I was just unmotivated throughout the rest of the year. But then, I was unmotivated for pretty much my entire life. This is by choice, since I've found that motivation just leads to trouble. I mean, say what you like about Ted Kaczynski, but he could hardly have been more motivated.

Of course, I didn't mail bombs to people. I did something much more dangerous to my well being than any Priority Mail explosive. I visited Ann.

A few weeks after Heath Millard dented a school bus with my head, I found myself up at 1:45 a.m. on a Sunday morning watching wrestling. A commercial was on, an ad—like the two before it—for phone sex. A bunch of long haired blondes were letting me know in sultry, breathy voices that they really wanted to "party with me." I normally didn't take notice of such commercials, but it was unavoidable this time. *Every* commercial was for phone sex.

"Man," I thought, "what kind of crowd are they catering to?"

Then I saw what time it was, and I remembered what I was watching, and I knew they were catering to me.

At that moment, I needed Ann.

I quietly slipped downstairs so that I wouldn't wake my brother. I then crossed in front of the darkened dining room and into the hallway leading to my parents' room. They were sleeping, of course, but I knew they'd want me to let them know I was leaving. Dad didn't show any signs of life when I went in, but mom stirred. I apologized for waking her, then told her my intentions. She sighed, but agreed to let me have the car so long as I let her know when I was home. I agreed, kissed her on the forehead, then headed back into the kitchen and out to the breezeway. The night air was cool and dry, and I went back inside to get a jacket. I had a feeling I'd be spending quite a bit of time outside…I wasn't sure if Ann would let me in at all.

The drive to Ann's always took about twenty minutes, and I passed the time listening to some "cool jazz" station on the radio because I liked the DJ. It was a woman, and her voice made listeners think of that cute girl in home room when she wore the Levi's and that little shirt…think of her in that special way. I couldn't listen to this DJ without steaming up my windows, so I had them cracked just enough to let the country air chill the inside of the car. I always preferred to keep the windows down, even if it was cold out. The wind on my face made me feel as if I was going somewhere.

When I finally turned onto her road, I could see Professor Snow's house ahead of me. His porch light was on, and he was sitting beneath it, holding the shotgun in his hands. I'm not sure why, but I slowed down as I passed by. More of that damn motivation, I guess. Snow took this opportunity to shout something at me, but I couldn't hear him. Rather than just drive on past as I would have had I been sane that evening, I pulled to a complete stop in front of his driveway and turned off the radio. Snow stood up as I did this, but he never left his porch.

"Get off the road!" he yelled, still holding his gun. He was about fifty feet away from me, but I could hear him quite well now; could hardly see him though. The only light emanated from the yellow bug light on the porch, but that was now behind him so all I could see was his silhouette. "You'll kill someone on that road! Do you want to kill someone?!"

I almost started laughing. His question sounded like a job proposition. I wanted to ask, "What's it pay?" but instead stuck with the safer, "Not really!"

"Well, you will!" he continued. "It's too late! It happens this late! You get off that road you're on or you're gonna kill someone!"

I wanted to shout something back to him, but I didn't know what. "Okay," was my first thought, but then I considered maybe, "I will, sir." Rather than say anything, I put the car back into gear and continued down the road. Snow shouted something else as I pulled away, but I again couldn't hear him. I watched in the rear view mirror as his porch light disappeared behind the row of trees that separated his property from Ann's, then studied the Penellas' house for signs of activity. A couple lights were on, but not in Ann's bedroom. I thought of turning back; it suddenly seemed rude to drop in on her uninvited…especially this late. Then I wondered if Heath would be there. No way I could go in then. So that would be the deciding factor; if Heath was there, I'd turn around and leave. If not, I'd force myself…

There was no point in defining the alternative. Heath wasn't there.

Knowing better than to pull into her driveway, I drove past to where I always parked when she'd meet me for our late night drives. About a quarter mile past Ann's, I saw the familiar monolithic structure leaning against the night sky; an old, abandoned silo. There remained somewhat of a driveway to the silo, just enough for one car, and I pulled into it. I don't see who aside from me ever used the drive, but the deep ditch that bordered both sides of Ann's road had been filled in so there was no chance of getting stuck. I stopped the car but let the lights paint the silo about thirty feet ahead.

The surrounding farmland was bare at this time of the season, but it was still being used. Apparently the silo was as well…by someone. Near a small opening at the silo's base, there was green graffiti sprayed which read, "Ted NugeNT ROCKS!!!," and another in red claimed that, "Dr. Seuss kicks ASS!" I laughed upon reading the second one; what an excellent pair to be immortalized on an abandoned silo in the middle of B.F.E. I could see the T-shirts from their world tour…"Cat In the Hat Scratch Fever."

I shut off the lights and the engine, then stepped outside to walk back to Ann's. The night seemed to have become even colder from the time I'd first left my house, but this may have been from the lack of buildings to block the wind. From beyond another row of gently swaying trees separating her yard from the farmland shone a light attached to the side of her house. It was aimed towards a shed out back, but it lit the whole side yard and some of the front. It was now nearly 2:30 a.m., yet a couple lights were on inside the house. The one visible from the road was emanating from the living room. The other was facing the back yard. I'd have to avoid that one.

To cross the portion of the yard under the flood light, I hunched down and ran forward like an operative storming the Belgian Embassy. I pressed myself against the house, out of sight of anyone who might've looked outside. I either looked really dashing at that moment, or like a total idiot. Figuring my physical ability, I resigned myself to idiot. Now Heath, he would've looked dashing.

Lord, I hated him.

Ann had two brothers, both of whom were in college, so I had their absence going for me. No dog, either. Just a cat named Doink and her parents who slept on the first floor. Ann's parents, not Doink's. Not sure where Doink's parents slept. I started to wonder who on the second floor needed that light, but not for too long. I didn't want to find an excuse to leave now that I was already in her backyard.

I continued to creep along the house like some kind of prowler, staying out of view of that upstairs window and ducking under windows on the first floor. After a few moments, I made it around to the TV antennae that ran up next to Ann's window.

Without hesitation, I started to climb the rungs of the antennae until I was at the window. Then I froze. I mean, I really froze. I could see inside her window, but nothing was registering. I'd been out there many times before, but never uninvited…and not since we'd had our talk out by the buses. The whole relationship dynamic had changed. Well, probably not for her, but my nervousness that night certainly proved it had for me. It's as if my adrenaline had been racing out of control until that moment, and then stopped abruptly to tie its shoe. What kind of ass was I about to make of myself? What time was it, and where was I, and why was I there? Who did I think I was? Romeo? Cyrano? DeMarco? No way. How could I be considered romantic with a name that doesn't end with "O."

I mean, I'd eaten Toasty-Os for breakfast, and my favorite snack was Tropic-Os, but those didn't count. I needed that "O" in my name. Guyo didn't work. It sounded too much like Gyaos, enemy of Gamera, and knowing that much about daikaiju movies immediately disqualified me from the ranks of the romantics. But then, so did thinking about breakfast cereals while attempting a moonlight serenade to the love of my life.

Lindseyo? No. Maybe if I changed the pronunciation…made it more Italian, like Linzio, bringing up the "Lin," sliding down the "zio" so it almost sounded like one syllable. But even that wasn't right. I kept hearing Lind-see-yo, three distinct syllables, which then got me humming the tune of the song we were taught in grade school:

> Guy-O-Lind-sey-O
> Guy-O-Lind-sey-O
> Guy-O-Linseed Oil
> And Bingo was his name-oh!

So now I had that song, which was hardly "Sexual Healing," running through my head.

I'd say panic then set in, but I think it had done so a good while before that. I was shaking, I was sweating, and still I hadn't turned my head from Ann's window. I was no more than two feet away, and I should've been able to see inside quite well because the moon was shining almost directly into the window that faced the backyard. But I still couldn't make out any shapes. No, maybe I could, but I wasn't able to assign them a name. It was like in French class—that total immersion thing—where a student is shone a picture of an egg while his headphones chant out, "Euf. Euf." The student recognizes the object, but has no idea what the hell the word for it is. He's not only speechless, but thoughtless.

Just like I was when Ann—having just lifted her window—said, "Hello, Guy,"

❧   ❧   ❧

"Hi, Rhonda," I greeted as she slid beside the Arbiter in the booth. She didn't greet him, but instead gave him a quick kiss. He got the better half of the deal, as always.

"Sorry I'm late, I had to pick up my copy of *Antigone* from the theater department," she explained.

"The script?" the Arbiter asked, although I'm sure he knew the answer.

"No, not the script," Rhonda replied with humorous bite. "Why would I need the script? The play's over."

The Arbiter smiled. "I figured you were working·on a one woman adaptation for Off-Off-Broadway."

"I'm neither a feminist nor a gay man, so why would I do a one person adaptation of anything?" Rhonda laughed. God, that laugh was infectious. I knew it was possible to learn a lot of a person by the way she laughed, but was it also possible to learn how one felt about her? "No, it's the videotape of the show."

"I thought you didn't want a copy. Didn't you say it wasn't that good?" the Arbiter asked.

"It's horrid," Rhonda agreed. "The production is horrid. The video production, I mean. We were fine."

"You were better than fine," I complimented. "You were revolutionary."

Rhonda smiled, "You should be a journalist."

"He is," the Arbiter pointed out. "That's the reason for being here."

"Hey, yeah, did you guys order already?"

"Yes," I replied. "Mushroom and green peppers okay?"

"Fine. Anything but olives," Rhonda nodded as the Arbiter echoed her "olives."

Within a few minutes our pizza was delivered and we dug in. After finishing my first slice, I performed my ritualistic "Separation of the

Cheese." Panthemom's pizza was so damn good that I could pull the cheese and toppings off the slice and eat just the crust and sauce, finishing the cheese and toppings separately. The practice met with tremendous public outcry at first, but the Arbiter and Rhonda soon came to accept and even appreciate it.

"So who are you tonight?" Rhonda asked, motioning to the wall-paper on the opposite side of the restaurant. It was mostly a creamy orange, like a bowl of tomato soup made with milk instead of water, but centered on the wall was a faux illustration of dogs sitting at a bar. They weren't playing poker, just sitting there in evening gowns and suits as if from a 1940's detective movie. The illustration stretched about eight feet wide and five or six feet high, all done in green, black, white, and that tomato soup orange. The first time I visited Panthemom's with my parents during freshman orientation, the wallpaper was almost enough to put us off our meals. But Rhonda, as she so often did, took the hideous and made it fun. Every time we visited we each picked the dog that most closely represented our personality that day. There were only nine up there, four of which were female, so it wasn't always that easy to do.

"I'm the big one," the Arbiter answered.

"The lab?" Rhonda asked.

"Is it a lab? I don't know. The one with the medals and the skanks fawning over him."

"I thought you'd go for the enigmatic one in the derby tonight, considering the newspaper success. You know, more clandestine."

"The hat makes him clandestine?" the Arbiter questioned.

"It's not the hat," Rhonda smiled. "It's the way he's wearing it."

The Arbiter smiled. "I guess he does look detective-like."

Rhonda turned to me, "How about you, Guy?"

"The one on the right," I replied without hesitation, speaking of a small basset hound that sat on a stool at the end of a bar with only his beer to keep him company.

"Of course," Rhonda sighed. "You always pick him."

"My mood is constant," I explained.

"I was hoping you'd be a bit more celebratory tonight. The Potato Famine was your idea, after all," Rhonda suggested.

"Well, mine and Mr. Bernard's," I admitted. "He's the one who put the thought in my head. Speaking of which, we should hurry and finish the pizza if we want to finish that interview in time to watch wrestling."

"Have time," the Arbiter said. "Can't rush a Panthemom's pizza. It'd be like running wind sprints through the Louvre."

"I'm sure the French would love to hear you compare the Louvre to a pizza."

"They'd be even more irate when Guy here began separating the paintings from their frame," the Arbiter smiled as I placed a wad of cheese in my mouth.

I nodded reluctantly as I finished chewing, then placed the focus back on Rhonda. "Which dog are you tonight?"

"Well, I don't know," she said as she studied the wallpaper. "I was going to be the skank fawning against the Arbiter's lab, the one in the evening dress with the purse, but maybe not now."

"Doesn't matter," the Arbiter shrugged. "You're not the only bitch in the sea."

Rhonda smacked the Arbiter's forearm, but smiled as she did so. The Arbiter, in turn, shot her a look of disgust and cried, "Ow, hey, I'm having surgery there in a week," as he rubbed the pain away. He was lying, of course, so we ignored him.

"Instead, I think I'll be that little Jack Russell terrier with his paws on the bar. He looks so happy and vivacious."

"Vivacious?" I asked.

"I don't think I've ever heard a dog described as vivacious," the Arbiter pointed out.

"That's because you only hang around with the torpid dogs," Rhonda accused.

"Hey, are you calling me torpid?" I asked.

Rhonda smiled, indicating she was not speaking of me. She could say so much with a facial expression, much more than most people could say in an entire conversation. At times, I became nervous of falling in love with her, but then I'd consider her and the Arbiter and realize I couldn't possibly develop feelings beyond friendship. Anyway, wasn't she like a sister to me? Wasn't she my confidant? Without equal, Rhonda was the person with whom I could most be myself, the woman around whom I felt no insecurities. What's more, when thinking of her, I found myself trying to be a better a person than I knew I was. I tried to be funnier, to be more secure, to be more honest. As I watched her eat, politely chewing with her mouth shut but not afraid to let a little grease drip down to her chin, I knew it was no longer a question of whether or not I'd confess to her that I once killed somebody, but *when* I'd do it. For some reason I still can't comprehend, she made me want to be forgiven.

"I think there was a gang in my grade school that called themselves the Torpid Dogs," the Arbiter recalled, snapping me back into the moment.

"Your grade school had gangs?" Rhonda asked.

"Sure. A couple of them."

"Tough school."

"The Torpid Dogs, the Killer Bs and the Powers of Pain."

"I think you're lying," I countered.

"Good, was hoping it wasn't true." The Arbiter seemed genuinely relived. "What kind of freaky grade school allows that sort of behavior? Hooligans. Should all be—"

A loud crash on the other end of the restaurant startled me to the point that I spilled a bit of pop onto my shirt. In my haste to sit the glass down, I placed it off balance on the edge of my plate and it toppled to its side, sending its contents cascading over the edge of the table. I quickly flipped it back up, and this time managed to rest it evenly as I focused on the commotion in the back of the restaurant. A couple locals were standing over a college student who was lying on the floor amidst a plate of spaghetti. He appeared the type of individual who could normally handle himself, but he'd obviously lost control of this situation. Still sitting at the table was a woman I assumed to be his girlfriend. She was huddled as far back from the scene as the booth would allow, but the look on her face made it clear this wasn't far enough.

"Fuckin' faggot college students," the smaller of the two "townies" spat. He didn't seem to be that tough, but I have the feeling his larger friend boosted his confidence. "Think you can fuckin' come in here every fall and take over the goddam town."

Already, an older man in a stained apron that read, "Don't mess with cook's buns," came out from the kitchen. I thought it was an odd choice, the "cook's buns" apron, seeing that it was a pizza place and there were no buns to be found. I guess for most, humor doesn't need to be accurate to be funny.

"Hey, hey, Matt," said the cook. "You just take it easy, okay? We don't need that kind of—"

"What we don't need is this faggot stinkin' up our town, right Jeff?" Matt asked, not taking his eyes off the student on the floor. He was sitting up now, leaning against the booth, but he wasn't trying to get up. The further from these guys, the better, I guess.

"Fuckin' eh," agreed Jeff. He didn't seem as angry as Matt. To Jeff, this whole scene was just funny. College student lying down in his spaghetti! He could hardly wait to get home and tell his friends.

"Come on, boys," the cook continued. "This couple's just trying to enjoy their dinner."

"Couple? Ain't no way this here's a couple. This boy's a fudge packer."

I guess I'll never understand why when men get into fights, they inevitably paint their opponents to be homosexual. Is this the worst thing they could be? They never insult them with "fuckin' Mason," "dirty polluter," or "asshole who never uses his turn signal." Of all the evils and annoyances that plague this planet, the one that most incites men to brawling is the assumed sexual preference of others.

"You hear that, little man? You're a fudge packer, ain't ya?" Matt continued, much to the delight of Jeff, who's paunchy stomach jumbled slightly under his black T-shirt with the eagle angrily spreading its talons across the chest. Like the eagle, Jeff was balding, and he didn't seem to care. Matt, on the other hand, tried a little harder to present himself. He was dressed like a teenager on a poster display at Abercrombie & Fitch; all good looks and attitude and cotton/poly blend. His hair was curly and blonder than that of his goatee, and his polo shirt would've hung well below his shorts had his shorts not hung below his knees. He was wearing sandals, and I was kind of hoping he'd get spaghetti on his feet.

"What's that like, workin' out at the fudge packin' plant?" Matt persisted, probably assuming that someone other than Jeff was laughing. They weren't. A few patrons had already left, the rest stared dumbly at the scene unfolding before them, much like I was. It's not that I didn't want to help, but that I had no idea how.

Jeff started laughing harder, which only fueled Matt's verbal assault.

"They pay you well out there at the—"

"The fudge packing plant? Actually, it's quite sad," the Arbiter suddenly interrupted, "but they've closed down the fudge packing plant."

Matt and Jeff both turned to see just who the hell had the gall to interrupt them, although I doubt neither knew what it meant to have gall.

"Yep, closed it down just last month. Three hundred employees laid off," the Arbiter continued. "Hard times, my friends. Hard times indeed. There just ain't much call for fudge these days. People are spending less, and fudge is a commodity. Less fudge means fewer packers."

"The hell are you talking about?" Matt demanded.

"Talkin' 'bout fudge, man, what're you talkin' 'bout?!" the Arbiter suddenly yelled, standing from his seat. Rhonda grabbed his arm to sit him back down, but the Arbiter was having too much fun. "Talkin' 'bout how a hard workin' fudge packer can't make a livin' in these United States no more! Poor guy here's been packin' fudge all his life, just like his daddy was a fudge packer and his granddaddy was a fudge packer before him! Hell, his great, great granddaddy started the Fudge Packers' Union—the FPU—and shamed his son on account a he didn't wanna be no fudge packer. He wanted to be a puppeteer and tour the vaudeville circuit, but they don't like to talk about that."

"Are you trying to be smart?" asked Matt. "'Cause if you're makin' fun of us—"

"This ain't no time for makin' fun of people!" the Arbiter continued. He was getting into this perhaps more than he should have, and it was making me even more nervous. He was like the one passenger on the hijacked plane who wanted to counter the terrorists. His heart was in the right place, but his actions could well convince them to just go ahead and set off the bomb.

Rhonda didn't take her eyes off the Arbiter. She seemed certain this was all going to go horribly awry, and she wanted to be ready to fix whatever she could.

"Hell no, there ain't no time for that! This is a time for action! This is a time to fight back! This is a time to tell Uncle Sam, a former fudge packer hisself, that no one ain't gonna take this no more! He may take away the fudge, but he can't take away no one's packer! He can't take away no one's desire! If no one can make an honest livin' packing fudge down at plant 82, then by God everyone's gonna resort to butt piracy!"

Having had enough, Matt forgot about his former target and leaped forward like a rabid dog to get to the Arbiter. Along the way, he grabbed a glass of iced tea from a table and shattered it against a chair, managing to keep a large shard in his hand. He lunged towards

the Arbiter, and Rhonda shoved her boyfriend out of the way, placing her arm in the path of the glass. Matt tried to pull back, but he
was too late to stop himself from slicing her forearm just below the
elbow. She screamed and immediately covered it with a napkin, but
the Arbiter just as quickly pulled it away and began to check it for
slivers. Matt and Jeff stared dumbfounded for just a moment, then
ran out of the restaurant. Someone yelled to call a doctor, but
Rhonda quickly stopped them.

"It's fine," she winced. "It's not that deep. Let's just go home."

"You should really have someone look at that," said the cook, the
telephone in his hand.

"I'll see the campus doctor," Rhonda explained, standing up. She
winced once more as the Arbiter continued to check the wound,
then he placed his hands around it to stop the bleeding. He whispered something in here ear, and she nodded quickly.

"You should at least clean that out," the cook continued. By this
point, perhaps turned off by the blood or—more likely—by the possibility of becoming witnesses, more patrons were leaving the restaurant. Even the couple that was part of the originating fight had
already slipped out of the back door, most likely out of embarrassment.

The Arbiter looked down at Rhonda and nodded, and she allowed
herself to be led back into the kitchen by the cook. After the swinging
door came to rest, I turned to the Arbiter.

"What the hell was that?" I asked.

"Couldn't let that poor guy spend the night lying in his own spaghetti," the Arbiter explained.

"You could've gotten her hurt much worse than that," I told him.
"She could've—"

"Could've gotten you hurt worse, too," the Arbiter shrugged.
"Could've gotten the cook, the fudge packer's girlfriend or anyone
else in here hurt worse. Could've also saved that guy from a serious

beating. Never know what'll happen when you stir things up a bit. Doesn't mean you shouldn't do it."

"I just think the situation could've been handled better," I suggested.

"By better, you mean not at all?" the Arbiter asked.

I didn't answer him. I couldn't. I didn't have an answer for him. He was right. I would've just sat there and watched the whole thing, impassive, as if watching a lion chase down a gazelle on the Discovery Channel. The Arbiter, for better or worse, at least tried to help.

After a couple moments, Rhonda came back out with a bandage on her arm, the cook on the other. She was smiling weakly.

"She'll be just fine," said the cook. "We got ourselves some ointment on there and sterilized it. Better have the doc give her a look-see in the morning, though. Let him rebandage it…put on some of that gauze. That stuff works wonders."

"Thank you," the Arbiter said as the cook passed Rhonda off to him. "Sorry for the mess."

"Oh, it's hardly your fault," the cook shrugged. "That's not the first time those Hardys caused trouble in here. They're good boys, really, just don't know where to draw the line."

"Lot of people having trouble drawing that line these days," the Arbiter mused as we headed for the door. "Just a damn line. Shouldn't be that hard to draw." He looked back at the food, but correctly realized now wouldn't be the best time to show concern for an abandoned pizza.

Before exiting, the Arbiter asked Rhonda if she wanted him to take her home.

"No, I don't want to go back to the apartment yet. My arm is fine, I think. Let's all three stay together a bit longer."

"What do you want to do?" the Arbiter asked.

"I don't know. Just talk."

"Then let's go to the football field, look at the stars," the Arbiter suggested. "Oh, wait. Still got that interview with Mr. Bernard."

"I can do that alone," I suggested.

"No, I want you with us tonight too, Guy," Rhonda stated. It made me feel better than it should have. "You guys do the interview, I've some stuff to do at the library anyway."

"Are you sure you'll be okay?" I asked.

"Yes, thank you, just come get me when you're done...oh, but you'll miss wrestling later."

The Arbiter shrugged. "There's a pay-per-view Sunday, so tonight will just be a bunch of run-ins. I think we can miss this one."

Despite the truth of the Arbiter's remark, Rhonda knew he was only saying it to please her. She thanked him with a kiss.

The Arbiter stopped at the door just as we were about to leave. He looked over at the Employee of the Month plaque then grabbed a pen that was lying on a nearby table. Pulling a receipt from the open trash can in the corner, he scrawled out something on the back of it and wedged it under the plate of the previous month. According to the Arbiter, the new employee of the month was Denny LeRoad.

Rhonda turned to me and smiled. "My boyfriend's insane. Do you really think we should go to a deserted football field with him?"

❧   ❧   ❧

"I'm not sure," I replied. I didn't have my watch, so I couldn't tell Ann what time it was. "It's late."

"Yeah."

I thought I had upset her. It was a pretty stupid thing to do, showing up at a girl's window so late at night without an invitation, but Ann quickly put this fear to rest by inviting me inside her room.

So, of course, trying to be graceful like the actors my mother watched on American Movie Classics, I ended up smacking my head into the bottom of the open window. This would've been fine enough, but—as I wasn't quite in yet—I had nothing upon which to catch myself, and I fell back against the rungs of the antenna's support. Ann reached out to grab me, but my momentum pulled me further from the window until the only thing stopping me from falling off the metal structure was my foot that had become wedged between two of the bars. It was twisted something furious, and I grimaced more out of fear of the inevitable snap than from the pain that shot up my leg like Polaris missiles launched from a crippled submarine.

But then there was a hand on my jacket, and I was swinging back towards the window. As the pain subsided, I realized I was leaning against Ann's breast, and her arms were around me.

My Guardian Angel.

I looked up at her, and she down at me, and then we both started laughing. She was holding a finger to her lips, trying to shush me, which only made us laugh harder. She then guided me past the window and into her bedroom where we both collapsed on her bed and tried to stop ourselves from laughing. No noise escaped our lips, but neither of us could stop our chest from bouncing.

Finally, she whispered, "Are you okay?"

"I think I twisted my ankle," I replied, still snickering. "So much for a grand entrance."

"You're no Errol Flynn," Ann agreed, "but I did always prefer Buster Keaton."

I smiled at her references. "My mom would love you."

She sat up and returned my smile, then replaced it with confusion. "What are you doing here?"

"I don't know anymore," I replied, rubbing my ankle. I guess my mishap was good in that way. Without an injury to divert her attention, I would've had to say, "I was watching phone sex commercials and I thought of you." Girls don't like to hear that sort of thing, I'm told.

"Well, I'm glad you came," she said.

I stopped rubbing my ankle. I stopped thinking. Hell, I think I stopped breathing. "You are?"

"Sure," she shrugged, which disheartened me only until she followed up with, "It's been a while since you've been out here."

It hit me at that point that I was lying in bed with Ann. *I was in bed with Ann!* I panicked once more and tried to stand, but the pressure on my ankle was too much for it. I fell back onto the bed.

"You must've really hurt that," she said with motherly sympathy.

"I've been hurt worse," I told her, thinking of Heath smacking my head against the bus a week earlier. I wasn't about to reveal that incident to her, though.

"Yeah, but that's usually at the hands of my boyfriend."

Okay, well, fine. So nothing's a secret from this girl. I guess it made sense that, being my Guardian Angel, she was also omnipotent.

"Heath brag about me, does he?" I asked, forgetting for a moment about the pain in my ankle.

"You and a few other guys he tends to beat up a lot," Ann explained as she sat up. "That should comfort you. He doesn't just hate you."

Hate me? Never once did I think Heath hated me. I just thought it amused him to slap me around and embarrass me. "Yeah, just don't tell me who they are. I'm afraid to find out who I'm in league with." I then paused a second and turned to look at her. The second window was behind her, so I couldn't really make out any features on her face, just the texture of her hair as it glowed blue-white under the moon. But with the light that shone through it and past her, I was sure she could see me. I wish it had been the other way around. "Ann, if you know he does that…if you know what kind of guy he is, why do you date him?"

"Because that's *not* the kind of guy he is," she replied.

"I see. When he's beating me up, he's faking that whole asshole thing." I realized that I'd just called her boyfriend an asshole. "Sorry."

"No, you're kind of right," Ann conceded. "I know that he's that way with others, but he's not that way with me. He's completely different with me. He treats me with—"

"Yeah, yeah, yeah," I interrupted. I'd heard it all before on the made for TV movies just before the abusive husband…

So now I was worried. "Ann, but that bothers me."

"Why? How does that—"

"I've known Heath a long time, much longer than you," I've explained. "I've seen how the guy behaves around other people, how he can twist around his way of thinking to twist around their way of thinking. Trust me, the guy's always got a—"

"Guy," Ann interrupted, sounding offended, "did you come all the way over here this late to scare me away from my boyfriend?"

"I'm sorry, Ann; it's just that he—"

"Guy."

I backed down. She was right. I'd made my point by now, I'd shown my concern, and that was enough for now.

We sat in silence for a few moments, each of us looking out the window closest to us. Hers led back to the farmland behind her yard, and mine offered me a view back up the road towards Prof. Snow's place. I wondered if he was still out on his porch, and if he'd threatened any other drivers with his—

"He's never tried to touch me."

I turned back to Ann, who was still looking outside. "What?"

"He's never tried to have sex with me."

I didn't know how to respond. I was suddenly overwhelmed with the feeling she was trusting me with something big, with something she'd never entrusted to anyone else.

"Do you want him to?" I asked, hating the question as it came out. I now had to play father figure, full of understanding that I didn't really have.

"No. I don't know."

"Have you told him not to?"

"No. He just knows. He knows I'm not comfortable with it, so he's never tried anything. That stands for something, doesn't it?"

Rather than respond, I took the opportunity to ask the question that could kill me.

"If he hasn't, then have you...ever?"

Ann finally turned back to me. She didn't seem shocked by my question, nor embarrassed, but she also didn't seem sure of answering it. Truthfully, I don't know if I wanted her to. But she did.

"No."

I immediately followed up with another question, making it seem as if I had a purpose to ask her that other than to satisfy my own insecure curiosity. "Is that why you're uncomfortable with him, then?"

Ann didn't answer right away, but I could understand that. "I guess so. And I guess...you know, it wasn't his fault that girl got pregnant. She came-on to him. He was drunk. She knew what she was doing."

Yeah. So did Heath. "That's why it's better that—"

"How about you?" Ann asked.

"What?" I was playing dumb.

"I told you my big secret," Ann said. "Now you tell me. Are you a virgin?"

Fair's fair. "Me, I'm having all the sex I want, I just don't want that much. Now what I really want is the twice baked potatoes," I smiled. "They's tasty."

Ann laughed. It was a well timed joke, greatly relieving the tension that had built up in the room from the point when I referred to her asshole boyfriend as an asshole.

"Why have you waited?" she asked.

Now that was cruel. Really cruel. Why have I waited to win the Stanley Cup? Why have I waited to become the best damn trombone player with which John Stuart Mill High School had ever been graced? Why have I waited to fly to the moon?

"Haven't found that special someone," I replied with a shrug.

"Me too," Ann agreed. I assume she was telling the truth. "I mean, I think that Heath could be the one, but I want the moment to be right. I know that all girls think that. I hate to be a cliché."

"No, that's good, Ann," I told her. "That's the way it should be. It'll keep you…and you know, I really hope it happens that way for you. I really do."

I meant this when I said it, but I wasn't really thinking it, if that makes any sense. My conversation with her was like talking on the phone with the TV on. I could hear what she was saying, and I was responding coherently, but my only thought was, "My God, I'm lying on her bed! She's lying beside me! She doesn't mind! Do I hold her hand? Do I kiss her? I'm on her bed! I'm on her f'n bed!"

I didn't kiss her. I didn't even hold her hand. I just sat with her on the bed until 3:45 a.m., the lights off the whole time, and we talked about everything. I caught up on every conversation I'd wanted to have with her over the summer and into the school year, and she genuinely seemed interested in what I had to say. This wasn't like when we used to just drive around and talk about school and friends (hers, anyway) and our families. We talked more about ourselves than we ever had. We found out we both enjoyed watching repeats of *Too Close for Comfort*, and thought Ted Knight was highly under-rated as a comedic actor. Neither of us had ever seen *It's A Wonderful Life*, nor did we want too. And although it was mainly from her brothers' influence, she not only somewhat enjoyed watching professional wrestling, but was able to name off all the WWE World Heavyweight Champions of the past five years, but not in the proper order.

I learned that her dream was not to become a dancer, but a paleontologist ("I already have a dinosaur named after me," she joked. "The ann-kylosaurus."), and that her favorite author was Yasunari Kawabata, who wrote *Snow Country*. When I asked her why she'd read it in the first place, she said it was because the librarian at the high school told her she couldn't.

"Who's your favorite author?" she then asked me.

"Jon Stone."

"Jon Stone? Haven't heard of him. What did he write?"

I was a bit embarrassed. "*The Monster At the End of This Book.*"

"I've never read it," she admitted.

"It's a children's book," I explained. "One of those Little Golden Books. It's got Grover from *Sesame Street* in it, and throughout the whole—"

"I love Grover!" Ann interrupted.

"All girls do," I suggested. "Grover, Snuffleupagus and Eeyore."

"Oh Snuffleupagus!" Ann somehow squealed and whispered at the same time. "He's so cute!"

I sat silent for a few moments as if scolding her for speaking out of turn.

"I'm sorry," she apologized. "You were saying…"

"Grover spends the whole book trying to stop the reader from turning the pages because he knows from the title that there's a monster at the end of the book. He doesn't want to see the monster, so he begs and begs the reader to stop, but we don't, of course."

"I would've stopped," Ann pointed out.

"Maybe so, but I had to see what would happen to Grover."

"What did happen?"

"Nothing, see? *He* was the monster at the end of book. All that begging and crying for nothing. The last page is a picture of him with his head hung in shame, and he says, 'I'm so embarrassed….'"

"Poor Grover," Ann sympathized. "And what's that supposed to teach our children?"

I paused, looking at the shadowed silhouette of Ann's head. "Grover's a pussy."

I couldn't stop thinking of our conversation as I drove back to my house. I played it over and over in my head, my right and left brain getting into heated debates over whether this was the right thing to say or if I shouldn't have maybe used this word instead of that one. I listened to my brain go at it, thinking all the while that it at least finally had something about which to bicker.

Now if I can extend this absurdity even further, I'd like to say my brain was arguing so fervently that it wasn't even able to process the shouts from Mr. Snow as I drove past. It wasn't until I heard the gunshot that my brain decided to shut the hell up and pay attention to what was going on.

Or at least what I thought was a gunshot. It was as if I'd just woken up to a really loud, sharp noise, but hadn't actually heard it. I could see Mr. Snow still standing out on his porch. It seemed he'd never moved from that spot the whole time I was at Ann's. His gun was at his side, and he was still shouting, but I couldn't make out one word because I had the windows rolled up. I wasn't listening to the radio this time, though. I didn't think that the DJ sounded quite so sexy anymore.

So, maybe it wasn't a gunshot. He certainly wasn't holding the gun in a firing position. Still, I wasn't about to slow down and find out. For the first time in a long time I had something to which I could look forward. Before I'd left Ann's place, she told me she had enjoyed our conversation. She said I made her feel comfortable. Imagine that. I provided her with comfort.

In fact, she said just about everything that night except that she loved me. But the thought of her one day saying those words no longer seemed like a pipe dream, whatever the hell that means. I didn't care anymore. I was giddy. And yes, I meant to use that word. Giddy perfectly described my mood at that point. A thesaurus may have instead suggested dizzy, light-headed, vertiginous, reeling, unsteady and flighty, but they just didn't cut it as did giddy.

(Although, I do now plan to use the word "vertiginous" in conversation sometime before I die).

❦   ❦   ❦

"But how long 'til that?" the Arbiter asked.

"I don't know," I shrugged. "A week? A month? Four years? I don't think that people like you and me are supposed to really know until it happens to us."

"Suppose."

"What's he doing in there, anyway," I asked of Mr. Bernard, getting off the subject. "Rhonda's going to wonder where we are."

As if on cue, Mr. Bernard's office door opened and a disheveled student stepped out. The door shut behind him, and he turned to look at it momentarily, then quickly stepped into the waiting area where the Arbiter and I sat. He rolled his eyes at us and said, "Don't go in there. That guy's fucking nuts."

"Hope he's wearing protection." the Arbiter continued.

❦   ❦   ❦

"Come on, mom, we're just friends," I said in embarrassment as I again kissed her forehead and headed up to bed. Dad, of course, was still asleep. I could've flown home in an A-10 Thunderbolt II with the GAU-8/A Avenger 30mm seven barrel cannon firing and he wouldn't have woken up. On the other hand, mom would wake up to the sound of an ant scampering across shag carpeting if she thought it might upset me. As a kid, this made my mom seem magical to me. If ever I fell out of bed, she would be upstairs before I could start to cry. I can even remember one time when I had a particularly bad dream—or at least one that seemed bad to me at the time. I can't remember all of it anymore, but I do recall being chased across the school playground by a scarecrow who only slightly resembled Andy Kauffman. It had a two tined pitchfork, and I was certain it was trying to kill me with it. I was trying to run from the scarecrow, but I couldn't get my legs to go. I was too afraid to even turn around, so I just kept trying to force my legs to run. Finally, after a few moments, I felt the tines of the pitchfork in my back. I kept calling out to my friends to come and help me, but they were all too busy watching a filmstrip of Rose Bonne's *There Was An Old Woman Who Swallowed A Fly* on the bus garage wall. It was being shown in reverse, so the horse, the cow, the goat, the dog, the cat, the bird, the spider (that wriggled and jiggled and tickled inside her) and the fly were all regurgitated from her mouth. I paused for a moment to watch this freakish event and then woke up with a start as the pitchfork was rammed into my back. To my horror, the pain was still there even after I woke up. I was terrified, but I wasn't about to cry. I was at that point in life in which crying is for sissies only. So, I started to softly call my mom. It was just more than a whisper, but there was panic in my voice. I had to call her only a few times before I heard her footsteps on the stairwell. My call wasn't even enough to awaken my brother in the same room, so I have no idea how she heard me.

She turned on the light above my bed and asked what was wrong, and I explained to her, just now starting to cry a little bit, that the scarecrow tried to kill me.

She picked me up to hug me and gasped when she got her arms around my back. She told me not to move, then there was a sharp pain in my back again. Before I could respond, she showed me a thumbtack. We both looked up at my Hulk Hogan poster and, sure enough, one of the corners was hanging free from the wall. The one stiff blow Hogan threw his whole career, and it was at me. Sure wish they had made a Dynamite Kid poster. Mom pushed the thumbtack back into the wall, then walked me to the bathroom to wash out the wound and apply some Neosporine.

From that moment on, I knew I never had anything to worry about at night. At nighttime, I knew exactly where mom was. It was the only time I truly felt safe.

So, after I told mom I was home, I went upstairs to bed knowing I was the safest man on Earth; my mom right below me and my Guardian Angel always above, both protecting me from whatever catastrophe would happen...

❧   ❧   ❧

"Next," Mr. Bernard called out as he poked his head around his office door. He then saw me and the Arbiter. "Guy. You're not here to interview for the job."

"What job?" I asked. "We had an—"

"Well, enter vous," Mr. Bernard said as he opened the door all the way and turned back towards his desk, activating the screensaver on his computer. I glanced back at the Arbiter and shrugged. He merely raised his eyebrows, and we both stood to walk into Mr. Bernard's office.

Before entering my first college English professor's office, I had a preconceived notion of what it would look like; loads of books stacked haphazardly on shelves, eccentric art from Africa or Egypt, plain black cassette tapes scattered about, certificates and awards lying unframed on top of unused desks, and back issues of *Story* stacked in corners. Mr. Bernard's office was all that without the academia.

On the shelves behind his desk was a collection of beer cans; bizarre beers of which I'd never heard such as Fife & Drum and Old Frothingslosh. To his right, hanging on both sides of the lone window that looked out over the music department facilities, were what appeared to be an original release theatrical poster of the 1954 Japanese version of *Godzilla* along with an autographed photo of who I'd later discover was two-time Democratic presidential nominee Adlai Stevenson with the message, "Don't get any on ya!" Across the room from those was a collection of books and magazines, none of which matched their owner's profession. A quick glance revealed a series of Babylon 5 paperbacks, a stack of *Asian Trash Cinema* magazine and a bunch of CDs lying out of their cases. I couldn't see most of them, but I was able to discern the bands The Dead Milkmen, Paul Simon and Mummy the Peepshow. Mixed in with these were a few video-tapes, all of which were labeled "Frontier Martial Arts Wrestling Bootlegs."

On Mr. Bernard's desk sat a red and yellow lava lamp that appeared to have been on for about a year straight. The "lava" had separated into hundreds of tiny red balls, like bubbles of blood in a bottle of Miller Lite. Next to this was a half empty bottle of Grapeade Snapple and an autographed picture of himself, and open before him was an issue of *Story*. At least I got that much right.

I turned to gauge the Arbiter's reaction to all this, but he seemed content to just stare about the floor. Mr. Bernard seemed as puzzled by this as I was.

"Lose a contact?"

"Looking for shells," the Arbiter explained.

"Try the beach," Mr. Bernard suggested. "Both of you can have a seat. Are you together?"

"How do you mean?" I asked.

"The interview," Mr. Bernard explained. He sat down and took a swig from his Snapple.

"Yes," I replied. Only now did the Arbiter look up from the floor.

"Find any?" Mr. Bernard asked him.

The Arbiter shrugged. "No." He noticed the lava lamp. "Nice light."

Mr. Bernard turned and looked at the lava lamp. "Oh, that's where I put that. Now let's get started. First off, where do you see me in five years?"

"Where do *we* see *you*?" I asked.

"Didn't your fathers ever teach you guys that it's not polite to answer a question with a question?"

"No. He taught me to marry a woman with big boobs," the Arbiter pointed out.

"Your father's a fine man. What do you suppose *he* sees me doing in five years?"

"Actually, Mr. Bernard," I interrupted. "I was under the impression that we were going to be interviewing you."

Mr. Bernard seemed genuinely surprised. "You want to interview me about working for me? You sure are cocky sons of bitches. Full of piss and vinegar and grapefruit juice and other acidic things."

"No," the Arbiter took over. "Guy here called about interviewing you for the newspaper."

"That's right," Bernard beamed, "the by-God *New York Times!* About damn time. Now, I have these documents—"

I interrupted, "No, the Floodbane paper, *A Daily Planet.*"

"What would Floodbane care about the…wait, that's right," Mr. Bernard remembered. "I'm sorry, college students, I thought you were here for the job."

"What job?" the Arbiter asked.

"I'm looking for a personal assistant."

"To assist you with what?" I wanted to know.

"Personal things." Mr. Bernard may as well of added. "Duh."

"What's that pay?" I asked.

"Full tuition," Mr. Bernard replied. He didn't laugh. He didn't even smile.

"How's the dental?" the Arbiter continued as if full tuition wasn't enough for him.

"No dental."

"Not interested."

"I am," I offered. Man, my parents would flip. They were already able to afford my schooling, but they were taking out some pretty big loans to do so. They had never implied that I'd have to help pay them back, but I was going to offer. Having my entire senior year paid for sure wouldn't hurt any of us.

"What are your qualifications?"

"I'm not sure—" I caught myself. Maybe it was Mr. Bernard's immediate negative reaction that clued me, but I suddenly knew I was just supposed to answer him. Even if I wasn't sure of what I would be doing, I had to answer him. "I used to do this stuff all the time."

Mr. Bernard nodded. "I see. Anything else?"

"Yeah, I was really, really good at it. I won many awards and things."

"Excellent. Do you have any tattoos?"

"Yes."

"Can I see them?"

"No, they're still lying on my dresser, back in my room."

"I see. That's fine, because I didn't mean to ask if you have any tattoos. I meant to ask if you're a team player. Are you a people person?"

"No."

"Do you have any references?"

"Oh, yeah. Him." I pointed at the Arbiter.

"And you are…?"

"Him, yes," the Arbiter replied.

Mr. Bernard smiled. "You two are all right. The other students I interviewed had no imagination…no creativity, no ability to think outside the box, and there's an expression I loathe, 'outside the box.' I had an assistant use the phrase 'outside the box' once, and I fired his whole family. The only people who should talk about staying outside the box are toll booth collectors and members of NAMBLA.

"The other applicants thought I was nuts."

"Fucking nuts, actually," the Arbiter told him.

"I still don't know your name."

"You can call me the Arbiter."

"So you're the Arbiter," Mr. Bernard smiled. "You were a pretty hot topic at the last faculty meeting…I'm told. Ain't been to one since they stopped serving the mini corn dogs. I like to dip 'em in cheese."

The Arbiter furrowed his brow but didn't say anything.

"Enjoyed today's *Planet*," Mr. Bernard continued. "First time in fifteen years I've had any interest in it. That Jason Fayme, he's got quite a bright future ahead of him. Not in journalism, though. Maybe in oil skimming or damaged shoe distribution, but a bright future nonetheless. I mean, Mexicans have as much a right to wear Bandolino as we do, right? And Guy, I told you that Potato Famine always works. Thank you for paying attention in class."

He was thanking me? Hell, how could I *not* pay attention to him?

"You're interested in the job?" Mr. Bernard asked me.

"Yeah, sure. For full tuition, sure."

"Then you're hired. Here," Mr. Bernard said as he started searching his desk for something. After he couldn't find it for a moment, he added, "Ummm," and started searching his desk again. I followed his eyes, trying to see something that looked as if I should have it. Unable to find anything, I turned to the Arbiter. He was staring intently at the computer monitor behind Mr. Bernard's left shoulder. While searching for whatever it was he wanted me to have, Mr. Bernard had bumped the table and disabled the screen saver. I recognized that he had YANewswatcher open, but the window had been drawn closed so I couldn't see what bulletin board he was at, alt.binaries.pictures.erotica.peanuts, perhaps. I mean, I'm sure there's something on the net for the nut fetishist. There's something on the net for everyone. I can see the spam now, "Do you want acorn in your mailbox? Barely legal acorn?"

"Here!" Mr. Bernard proclaimed as he lifted an envelope from under his Snapple and handed it to me. He shrugged as if to apologize for the damp, gray circle that had smeared away his address. "Here."

"What is it?" I asked.

"It's a rejection letter," he replied.

I flipped the envelope over. It hadn't been opened. "How do you know? You haven't opened it."

"The idea sucked." Mr. Bernard noticed that the screen saver had deactivated and stared at the monitor for a second. He then pulled the cursor down to the lower left of the screen to manually switch it back on. Within seconds, his screen was taken over by the image of Godzilla stomping through Tokyo, spitting thermo-nuclear breath onto oil tanks. He then turned back to me. "If they accepted it they'll be out of business in a month."

"Who?" I asked. "What was—"

"Easy, George," Mr. Bernard raised a hand to warn me off. "Save that curiosity for Shakespeare class."

"But you didn't seem to like questions in class," I pointed out.

"Hey, there's no such thing as a stupid question, just stupid people asking questions. It's irrelevant, anyway. I won't be your teacher tomorrow. I've been fired." There was no emotion in Mr. Bernard's voice to indicate he cared.

"But...how? You just started."

"It was those two chicks who left early. They filed a grievance with Ms. Muraco. Quick little minxes, those two." Mr. Bernard noticed that the Arbiter had shuddered at the mention of Ms. Muraco's name. "I take it you know her?"

"Had her for Sexism in the Language," the Arbiter pointed out.

"Sex in the Middle Ages?" Mr. Bernard misunderstood. "That may be the most terrifying thing I've ever heard. The contraptions alone...the blood-letting. Do you know how they used goats as torture devices? Sick, barbaric, goat-tongued freaks."

The Arbiter didn't bother to correct him.

Ms. Muraco, aside from being head of the English Department, was also faculty adviser of the Floodbane chapter of Womyn Against Discrimynation, or WAD. I had her the year before for Victorian Literature, and it was the most traumatizing class I'd ever had. I mean, I was the only male in the class, so it already called to mind that school bus ride in high school. I should have known when I read the description for the class that Victorian Literature was not the same as Victorian Underground Literature. I was expecting to read books like *Confessions of An English Maid* and *Fanny Hill*. But instead, I got *Madame Bovary, Jane Eyre* and a classroom full of women who seemed to confuse me with all the boyfriends who had ever done them wrong.

It was the dream that finally did me in. I can't remember where it took place, or even how long it lasted or the build-up. All I can remember is waking up with the horrifying image of Ms. Muraco beating me on the thighs with a yardstick. I would have killed for clown feet then, but I guess that would've made me a repeat offender.

I never looked Ms. Muraco in the eye again. She seemed to like that.

So yeah, it made sense that she'd get Mr. Bernard fired for being sexist. I'm surprised she stopped at that, to tell the truth.

It was the Arbiter who then asked the question I should have. "So if you've been fired, how can you afford to pay Guy full tuition?"

Mr. Bernard laughed. "Good God, do you think I make my living doing this? No, no, no, no. This is only a hobby. Community service."

"Teaching?"

"Pissing people off. I was going to quit anyway. I just took a job with the philosophy department. Bunch of randy bastards over there in the philosophy department."

"At Floodbane?" I asked.

"I start next week. In fact, if I remember correctly, you're in my Tuesday/Thursday class," Mr. Bernard said to the Arbiter. "Can't be too many The Arbiter's enrolled here."

The Arbiter smiled.

"I'll look forward to it, too," Mr. Bernard returned, then looked at me. "Guy, that's going to be a rejection letter from someone.

Respond to it as if you're someone really important, then mail it back to its sender. That's all you have to do."

"You don't want to see it first?"

"Boy, have you got a lot to learn. Just make sure you send it out by the end of the week. Now, I suppose I should start packing up my office."

The Arbiter stood to leave, so I did the same. As I got the door, I turned back around and asked, "What about the interview for the paper?"

"Just make one up," Mr. Bernard said with a wave of his hand. "You guys seem pretty adept."

"Okay, well you had to figure that not everyone on this campus would just let this whole Potato Famine thing go unchecked," Rhonda pointed out now that we'd finally gotten around to telling her about our meeting with Mr. Bernard. It was after midnight that same evening, and the three of us had just returned from the Flood-bane College football stadium. Her arm was well-bandaged now, and—aside from treating it delicately—she didn't seem to be in much pain. I was surprised at how well she was handling what had happened, but I shouldn't have been. This was Rhonda, and it could never be said she wasn't tough.

The three of us probably should've just retreated to our apartments after our discussion at the stadium. We were all pretty knocked out, but we still had an odd energy from the evening's events that wouldn't let us drift off. Rather than fight it, we ended up in the office of A Daily Planet.

"Not really," the Arbiter disagreed with Rhonda. He didn't look up from the Macintosh.

"Don't tell me you honestly believe everyone on this campus to be on the same moronic plane as Jayson Fayme."

"Of course not," the Arbiter continued. "He's pretty much his own little plotted point over there somewhere on the Fayme Family

Axis. But you see, just because people aren't stupid, it doesn't mean they're not morons. What was it, after all, that P.T. Barnum said?"

"'There's a sucker born every minute,'" I quoted.

"No, not that one," the Arbiter dismissed. "That other one he said. Oh yeah; 'If you have to have a football team in this town, may as well name it the Potato Famine.'

"See, no one's going to question it because it's just right."

"I don't mean to step out of line here," I apologized up front, "and I'm certainly not questioning you, but I'm willing to bet the Intercontinental Belt that not everyone shares your opinion."

"Be horrible if they did," the Arbiter shrugged as he once more focused on the computer.

"Does that include Mr. Bernard?" I asked the Arbiter. Only Rhonda seemed to be paying attention at this point.

"As long as it's after your tuition is paid, I wouldn't worry about it so much," she offered. "He may not be a moron, but the guy's lost it, if you ask me."

"Okay, I ask you."

"No one pays full tuition to a student just for answering letters."

"Sure they do," the Arbiter contradicted from behind the soft, blue-white glow of the monitor. "The rich guys, they're all nuts. They're all the time growing their fingernails to about two feet in length, sitting in their underwear, eating a bucket of cold chicken, watching *Family Feud* reruns on the Gameshow Network and yelling 'Pass it to the Hart family! For the love of God, pass it over!' When they set their phobia of germs aside and venture into the world, it's only to pick up bums off the street and give them thousands of dollars for no reason."

"Are you saying I'm a bum?" I asked.

"Yes." No hesitation on his reply. "To him, you're a bum."

"Thanks. I guess that's better than being the bucket of cold chicken."

"Or a contestant on *Family Feud*," Rhonda laughed. She then brought me back to the point by asking, "When do you start?"

"I've already got a letter I'm supposed to reply to," I remembered, feeling in my pocket to see if the letter was still folded in there. "I suppose I should get started on it."

"You've got an article to write first," the Arbiter ordered.

"That's right. I've got to make up an interview." I paused a moment, and looked over at the Arbiter. He was staring intently at the screen, typing in short, furious bursts. "Hey, you don't suppose you could take it for me? You're better at making stuff up."

"Potato Famine was yours," he reminded me. He really liked that idea. I mean *really* liked it. It made me feel proud. "Besides, I'm writing the feature this week."

"What'll it be this week?"

"Thinking Naked Soup Club."

"How can soup be naked?" Rhonda wanted to know.

"No crackers, I suppose." My joke was pretty much ignored, as it deserved to be.

"You'll see when it comes out," the Arbiter replied to Rhonda's question. "I feel like getting the trustees all worked up next week."

"You better be careful you don't push this tabloid turn too far," Rhonda warned. "You're liable to get kicked off campus."

"You don't understand; this will be my life's greatest work," the Arbiter pointed out. "A few words can be much more powerful than a flag on top a radio tower. And even if I did get kicked off campus, it's not like it would affect the colony one way or the other."

"The colony?" Rhonda asked.

"His ant thing," I explained.

"You have an Aunt Thing?" Rhonda smiled. "And I thought my Aunt Moolah had a weird name."

"It's an analogy, not a relative," the Arbiter laughed. "We're all ants; the Earth is our hill."

"Is it now?" Rhonda wasn't buying it. She looked at me with one of her "here he goes again" looks.

"Of course. You see, on this Earth, not one of us really matters in the least bit. That's not a sad thing, really; it's just the way it is. We all pretty much just do our jobs, whether they be construction of the home, nursing the larvae, protecting the queen, charging the turnbuckle, getting kicked out of college…we do what we have to do. That's not to say that we have no compassion for others. If one ant is starving and can't get food, another ant will regurgitate its food to save it."

"Charity's fairly disgusting in the insect world," I observed. "I'm glad we never had to see Whoopi Goldberg puke in Billy Crystal's mouth in any of those Comic Relief things."

Rhonda's face shriveled up and nearly disappeared. "Don't think in pictures."

I smiled an apology to her.

"Comic Relief is a perfect example," the Arbiter continued. "It's all about the members coming together to ensure the survival of the colony. However, we all know we can't stop hunger. Well, we could if we didn't economically view food as a commodity to be bought and sold, but viewed it communally like air or water. We actually grow worldwide way more food than we eat. But that'll never happen, so people will starve every day. Individually, no big deal. But if a whole nation is faced with famine, that's a different story. Likewise, if one ant were to die of starvation, it wouldn't matter because losing one ant is about as painful to the colony as your clipping a fingernail is to your health. There are many others just like it, and they'll serve the queen just as well."

"Are you saying that it wouldn't matter if one of us were to die?" Rhonda asked. She was suddenly less flippant about the Arbiter's theory.

"To the human race as a whole? No, it wouldn't," the Arbiter replied. "We're expendable. But this ant here would be pretty upset if you were to find yourself beneath some kid's magnifying glass."

"That's comforting to know," Rhonda smiled with a roll of her eyes.

"What about serial murderers?" I asked.

"Eight, nine people out of billions? The ants will still go marching one by one."

"Okay, how about the dropping of the atomic bomb?" I asked. "Or what about earthquakes or the plague or the Holocaust? They certainly slowed down our little ant hill."

"They're detrimental, yes," the Arbiter admitted, "but also unavoidable, as callous as that may sound. No matter what we do, no matter where we build our colony, there will always be disasters. There will always be those who feel themselves superior to everyone around them, and will therefore drop all manner of weapons on them from the sky. There will always be disease infested rats waiting to eat your cheese."

"Certainly, you're not asking me to passively accept the Holocaust or Jonestown," Rhonda argued.

"I'm not asking you to accept anything, I'm saying that events like that *will* happen," the Arbiter explained. "Widespread death and destruction? That's just God out mowing the Heavenly lawn."

"I didn't know God owned a mower," I parried. "I always figured He'd just hire some neighborhood minor deity to do it for Him."

Rhonda was taking the Arbiter a bit more seriously. "I disagree with all of this. I don't see how you can fight injustice and tragedy if you honestly feel that you can't win. I think the world can change, we can break the routine sometimes. Even beat it.

"Speaking of which, I'm going to leave before you have a chance to rebut, Arby. It's way past my bedtime, and I want this day to be over."

"You don't want to finish the debate," the Arbiter challenged.

"Arby, we could be here all night debating this. Too bad you didn't bring this up on the football field tonight."

"Let me walk you back," the Arbiter suggested, standing from his chair.

"No, thank you. I've been stabbed once already today. The law of averages says I'll be safe. Give me a kiss, though."

He did and said his good-byes, then the Arbiter and I were alone.

So, it was with thoughts of famines, stabbings, freaks, friends and ants that I opened the letter addressed to Mr. Bernard. This is how it read;

MPGA
Motion Picture Guild of America

To: Bernard
From: Motion Picture Ratings Guild
Reply: H.H. Race

Re: *Leaf Blower: The Movie*

Sir:

Please understand that I am writing in an unofficial capacity, and that my private opinions, as expressed here, cannot be legally held for account to the MPGA.

We (the other reviewers and I) have just finished watching the "director's cut" of your recent "work," "sir," and I feel compelled to give you this advance notice that we will not be recommending that the "film" get your desired rating ("G:" General Audience). Several points led to this decision:

While we sympathize that marketing dollars are short in these economic times, it is unethical to advertise Betty Page in a starring role, when, in fact, she does not appear anywhere in the film.

While the MPGA does endorse a parent's right to discipline his/her child, we do not believe that a fourteen minute computer generated segment of Sybil Danning spanking her "naughty niece" Sylvia Kristel falls under this category.

We appreciate that you were trying to educate pubescent girls about the necessity of breast self-examination. What we do not understand is the presence of the mannequin fashioned after Ron Jeremy, suspended from the ceiling, dressed in a Spartan costume.

It is our understanding that no Girl Scout has ever been sexually attacked by a Douglas Fir, or indeed any plant, while on a jamboree. While we understand that works of fiction sometimes border on the fantastic, the subtitles for the scene ("This part is real! Real! Real! Real!") were misleading and—may I personally add—distracting.

David Bowie and Mick Jagger rubbing their buttocks together was wrong in the 80s, sir, and it is wrong today.

Pink Lady and Jeff. We have fought you time and again on this issue, sir. When will you learn that we will not budge?

Relating to the "docudrama" portion of your "film," I have checked the World Book Encyclopedia, and there is no mention of an Amazon tribe of women who wear high heels and Victoria's Secret panties. Regardless of their existence or nonexistence, however, your constant referral to them as "chicas" was unacceptable.

Nuns do not wear push-up bras, even very progressive orders.

You are fully aware that using a super-telephoto lens is a violation of the 500 feet restraining order placed on you by the Sea-Gals.

On a final note, your advertisement of "May contain offensive material" is indecipherable in six point Goudy Text MT, and unacceptable. Also, the poster material, former professional wrestler Tony "the Dirty White Boy" Anthony sitting on a toilet, is just wrong, wrong, wrong.

Sincerely,
H.H. Race
Chair, Motion Picture Ratings Association

HR/ws

Okay. Well, then—

The Arbiter interrupted any thoughts I hadn't yet formulated with his declaration that he'd finally found what he was looking for on the internet.

"Guy, you might not want to accept Mr. Bernard's money," he suggested.

"Unless he got it from passing Go, I can't see myself making that decision," I countered. The Arbiter did not look up from his monitor. His eyes didn't even float around the screen. No, he was looking at one thing, and he was looking at it intently. My curiosity was piqued. "Why, though?"

"It's dirty."

"The money? Dirty as in stolen?"

"Dirty as in 'Hot, sexy coed wants you to come on her tits— **http://www.floodbane.edu.**'"

At least it had nothing to do with nuts.

CHAPTER 8

Feel Good Hit of the Summer

The Naked Killer. That was the movie to which I'd asked that girl. They were showing it as part of the annual Hong Kong film festival held in our town each year. This and the Menorah placed on City Hall's lawn each Hanukkah were our annual attempts at global sophistication.

But my God, *The Naked Killer!* Who can blame her for turning me down and getting pregnant? The lesson to be learned here is, for a first date, never ask a girl to see a movie about Japanese lesbian hit men.

Third date…no sooner.

CHAPTER 9

Everything Will Happen

"**A**re you happy, Guy?" Ann asked me the week after my first foray into her bedroom.

Ann's bedroom, I should have pointed out by now, wasn't a place to sleep, it was a place to worship. It was a place to idolize Heath Millard, and to dream of an "afterschool" where she could spend her eternity on holy playground with her savior boyfriend; him always throwing touchdowns, her always cheering him on. When I visited her room, I felt like a Baptist soccer mom at a Majick ceremony; the religion made no sense to me.

When in Ann's room, I secretly hoped she'd leave the lights off. Her face in the moonlight was as moving as any masterpiece painting hanging in the Met. It was all I needed to get my minimum donation's worth. But turn on the lights in her room and…well, her face was still art, but the gallery sucked. Imagine a Cézanne hanging in a restroom at Madison Square Garden during a wrestling house show.

At first glance, Ann's room appeared to be decorated just as a high school girl's room should be: a couple of plaques and trophies on the wall to commemorate this and these things, posters of those corporate sponsored, pretty-white-boy rock bands that were always forgotten within two years, and a collection of animals and toys that managed to survive her childhood—some in better shape than others. One of the stuffed animals that hung in fishing nets from the corners of her room was a shark with its teeth pulled out. I felt bad for the shark. What good's a shark without teeth? It'd be like a fork without tines, like something from the Land of Misfit Toys. I wondered who pulled the teeth out, and for what reason. I couldn't help but accuse Heath.

There was also a small collection of books on the shelves, most of them seemingly placed because their bindings were attractive together. No paperbacks here. And, of course, there was the obligatory music box. No dancer on this one, just the box. I would've liked to have known what it played, but I never asked. I didn't want to face the fact it might be the Fightin' Golden Sandies' Fight Song in honor of her boyfriend.

I say that because, aside from what I've just mentioned, everything else in the room was part of a shrine to that fabled Greek god of yore, the mighty Heathus Millardicus. There were news articles adorning every wall (how did she get so much material on him in the short period of time in which they'd been dating?), photos trimmed the mirror and night stands, and a Fightin' Golden Sandie football uniform with Heath's name and number hanging on her door. This confused me, as the school wasn't in the habit of just handing out jerseys. I guess they must've made an exception for our hero Heath. Hell, if he wanted, they would've given him the bus he took to school in junior high…although I'm sure he would've rather had the one into which he smashed my head.

I would spend days theorizing why Ann would pollute her room this way. Eventually I hit the thought that Heath wasn't perhaps a boyfriend so much as he was more of an object…a canvas onto which Ann could paint her Prince Charming fantasies. It was boyfriend as rock star, as TV icon. It helped explain how a girl with her values could associate with someone like Heath. She attached qualities such as kindness, strength and understanding to him the way she would to a teen heartthrob. I mean, girls don't pin up pictures of Chippendale's dancers on their walls, right? It's not about anatomical perfection; they think the guy on the cover of *Teen Beat* is a good guy, that he would care about them in some fashion.

So it occurred to me that Ann may not have known Heath any more than she knew the latest heartthrob the WB tossed into America's living room. She saw what she wanted to see, gave him the qualities she wanted him to have.

But hadn't Ann told me a week before that she had yet to have sex with Heath? I guess that made sense, as I wouldn't have wanted to have sex with my crush, either. At that point, the connection would've become too tight. And what if she didn't live up to my expectations? Worse yet, what if I didn't live up to hers? So no, if Penny from *Lost in Space* were to have magically escaped the reruns to find herself in my arms, she would've left my planet with her virginity intact.

Ah, hell, who am I kidding? I would've done her as if I were about to go off to war.

So what was stopping Heath from making his move on Ann? That was the real question. He was a teenage male, certainly less virtuous than I, so why was he willing to wait for her when so many others would've laid down for him as willingly as a dog craving a Milk Bone? Probably would've rolled over and begged, too, were Heath to have asked. I'd mention that girl again who turned me down for a date in junior high, but now that I remember to which movie I wanted to take her, I don't so much feel the need. *Naked Killer*. Good God.

The answer to why Heath wasn't making his move on Ann was obvious to me. He was hunting, and when hunters are going after big game, they don't charge headlong into the herd with guns blazing. They camp out. They climb up a tree and cover their scent and paint their faces and bang bones together. They wait for the opportunity to present itself. It's the anticipation that makes the kill so rewarding.

He could've had sex with some other girls whenever he wanted, and probably did, but Ann was a rare species. She was smart and wholesome. She'd never been with anyone else. There was payoff at the end of that road. I mean, why do people drive halfway across the country to get to Disney World when the county fair is just up the street?

"No, I guess I'm not too happy," I replied to her question.

"Why not?" she asked.

"I've never been to Disney World."

※   ※   ※

"Don't want to go," the Arbiter said as he closed the door to *A Daily Planet*. It was the Monday after the Panthemom's incident, and the staff of *A Daily Planet* had all left earlier with their assignments. The Arbiter and I stuck around a bit more to shut down the Macs and to discuss the porn site. He'd been oddly quiet about it, saying he was currently more worried about his Naked Soup Club article. When the Arbiter had an idea, it always received his full attention. And when the project was finished, he immediately dove into another. He always had to be working on something. "Besides, can't get in there without a personal invite, won't get a personal invite without fraternity membership."

We started up the stairs that emptied into the lobby of Student Union Student Union. "But you must…I mean, there's gotta be someone in Eta Iota Upsilon who likes you. You're liked by everyone."

"Or hated. And if the hate of the many outweighs the love of the few, or the one, then there'll be no visit to the sorority house o' porn."

We dropped the conversation once we reached the top of the stairs leading to the hallway across from the game room. There were a couple of freshmen, I'd guess, playing the outdated video games inside, but the room was otherwise empty. I didn't even see an attendant at the desk, which isn't all that surprising. Few people ever patronized

Student Union itself, let alone its game room. Were it not for the cafeteria, half the students wouldn't even know there was a Student Union.

We entered the main foyer and stopped in front of reception. A student was sitting behind the counter with his feet propped up on the desk, his head straining at an awkward angle against the back of the chair. His mouth was hanging open, but his eyes were shut. The door to the adjoining office was hanging open only slightly wider than his mouth, and the TV sitting inside (of the door, not his mouth) was casting ghostly shadows across his face. Had he not been snoring, I would've thought that Marty Janetty—or so the name plate of the desk announced—was dead.

As we reached the glass doors that led out to campus, the Arbiter turned to me and said, "You going to answer Mr. Bernard's letter?"

"I'm not sure if I should now," I shrugged. I didn't want to make any money off a guy working in the skin trade. I mean, suppose I were to run for office one day. The killing somebody, I'm sure America would forgive. But the naked ladies…never.

"Do it," the Arbiter responded. "Have to figure out how to break this. Follow the routine until then."

I stared about me for a moment, thinking of what I should do. My thoughts were quickly distracted by the display case on the west wall of the foyer in front of the main desk. The Arbiter followed me as I walked up to it, and neither of us said a thing for a few moments. Finally, the Arbiter pointed to the picture of a girl, her face—as with all the others—framed by the torso of a penguin.

"That's her. That's the girl from the porn promo. Rush Chairman."

"Yep." Pause. "She's much cuter in this photo."

"It's difficult to be cute in amateur porn."

"Probably the lighting."

"Or the sperm on her face." Pause. "Hope she's next." The Arbiter was pointing to the chaplain. "Will try to hack into the full website sometime this week, see if there are any of her."

I was about to suggest some girl on the bottom row when I caught the smell of smoke. At the same time, the Arbiter and I both looked up the hall towards the game room. The two students who had been playing video games were carrying a trash can towards us, billowing smoke. We watched them approach, and they offered a "Whassup?" as they passed.

"Keep it real," the Arbiter mocked as they passed. They didn't respond, and didn't stop walking until they got to the desk. They set down the trash can and stared ahead at the sleeping desk worker for a moment. Although their backs were turned towards us, we could still hear their conversation. They were typically loud.

"Should we wake him?" student one asked.

"Dunno," student two responded.

Pause.

"It's his job, innit?"

"Yeah, but he's sleeping."

"I think so."

Pause.

"Is he dead?"

"He's snoring."

"Dead people snore."

"Seriously?"

"Sure. Why else would they bury them under so much dirt?"

"I figured on account of they smell."

"This one don't smell."

"Must be alive, then."

Pause.

"We should probably wake him. That way, if the whole building burns down, it'll be his fault. Not our fault. His."

"Should be his fault anyway. He's sleeping on the job."

Pause.

"Hey, wake up!" student one asked. "Wake up!"

The desk worker coughed once, kicked his feet off the desk and knocked over a trash can. "What?! What! What."

"Trash can's on fire," student one pointed out. They both then turned around and headed back past me and the Arbiter towards the game room. As they passed, one of them nodded to us knowingly. The Arbiter beat his chest twice with his fist and gave the student the peace sign.

We then approached the desk where the student worker was staring down into the trash can as if he'd just dropped a C note down a sewer grating. We could see the glow of the fire dance off his face, and when he looked up, his eyes were watering from the smoke.

"You know what gets me?" he asked us. "They passed a drinking fountain to bring this to me."

"They've offered you fire," the Arbiter pointed out. "You are a god."

The desk worker laughed. "They could've offered me a virgin instead."

The Arbiter and I both laughed with him as he grabbed an empty coffee mug and calmly left his shrine to collect the holy water and douse the gift of fire. Following his cue, the Arbiter and I left the building. Once outside, the Arbiter checked his watch.

"Going to miss the first match."

"There'll be some interview for the first twenty minutes," I comforted. "Always is. All some of these wrestlers can do is spout catchphrases. Wouldn't know a wristlock from a wristwatch."

"Night after a pay-per-view, though," he reminded me. "Always good stuff after a pay-per-view." He then turned back towards the door of Student Union. "Should probably get a picture of Marty back there. Good article. You want to write it?"

"Yeah." I was starting to enjoy making up the news. A bright career at FOX lay ahead. "I'll write it up tonight."

"After the Bernard letter," the Arbiter reminded me. "Got to keep him on this side. This porn thing could be huge for…Much too huge for *A Daily Planet*."

"Bigger than a story about fire gods?"

The Arbiter shook his head. "Hey, you don't have any classes tomorrow at 11:00 do you?"

"No."

"Good, come to philosophy. Sure Bernard'll let you sit in."

I smiled. Another class with Mr. Bernard at the helm. An offering of fire…or even virgins…couldn't have kept me away.

Well, maybe the virgins.

As the Arbiter suggested, I wrote the letter to the Motion Picture Guild of America first.

To: H.H. Race
From: Bernard

Re: Ratings policy

Sir,

It both saddens and disturbs me that so many films these days laden with violence and corruption can achieve G ratings, while those that celebrate the majesty of the human body are burdened with R or the ticket-sales-killing PG-13. One need look no further than Disney to find evidence of this atrocity. Their history is plagued with films—both live action and animated—that have condoned violence while shunning family values, yet the American public, and indeed, the world, is told that this is acceptable by the G rating attached to the film. For instance:

Bambi. A parent is murdered. G rating.
Fantasia. Blatant drug abuse. G rating.
Escape from Witch Mountain. Satanism. G rating
The Absent Minded Professor. Cheating/poor sportsmanship. G

rating.

Jungle 2 Jungle. Tim Allen. G rating.

Home for Christmas. The very idea. G rating.

Yet still you have the gall to deem a scene inappropriate for children simply because a woman disciplines her niece. Is it wrong to teach our children moral values and that punishment awaits those who do not uphold said values? Should children believe that, as with Arial in Disney's *The Little Mermaid*, disobeying parents leads to happiness ever after? And need I even bring up the phallic undersea kingdom and the immense erection the minister is sporting during the wedding scene?

I can only hope that when this world has reached a state of complete and total anarchy—when violence, drug abuse, Satanism, lying, and bad stand-up comedy are the norm—you'll have not yet committed suicide from the guilt that eats away at you like flies through the festering top layer of a cesspool. I'll want you to wake up every morning, look out your window, and see the hell for which you, sir, are solely responsible.

Good day, sir,
Bernard

B/gl

I was a little disappointed that Mr. Bernard wouldn't be reading that; I was pretty proud of it. He would, however, eventually get to read the news article I wrote the next day before attending his philosophy class.

FIRE GOD EMPLOYED AT STUDENT UNION

Student life at Floodbane will never be the same, not now that Marty Janetty has enrolled. For it would not be altogether inaccurate to say that Marty is one of the most powerful Student

Union Student Union desk workers in the history of the school. One could, in fact, describe his work as "godlike."

"It's a talent I've had since grade school," claims Janetty. "Some students are good in math, others at the clarinet. This is mine."

And what exactly are his powers? Mr. Janetty is peculiarly coy about this question. "Well, I don't like to say that I really have any [powers] per say. It's not like I can ignite objects at will or toss fireballs from my hands, although that'd be really sweet. It's really more that…well…people are always just bringing me things that are on fire. I suppose I could use them as weapons, but I'm usually more worried about just putting them out, and it's sometime hard to hurl a flaming trashcan at mine enemies."

Marty's parents refused to comment on their son's talent, but his father was overheard saying, "What the hell did he ask? Marty caught fire? Twenty-two grand and my boy's on fire? I knew his mother should've let him join one of those pissing fraternities. She babies him, you know. Treats him like a damn third grader."

Marty has learned the difficult lesson that the ability to have people bring him things that are on fire is not always a blessing. Once, when he was in high school, a student caught on fire in a freak lab accident. Rather than place the student under the shower equipped in all the freak labs, the teacher panicked and rushed the flaming student to room 204, in which Marty was learning about faction.

"I got a Saturday detention for that," Marty smiles. "I mean, I saved the student's life, but Mr. Helmsley was angry that we interrupted class."

Did Marty exact his revenge? Did he curse the inconsiderate and malevolent government teacher with burning beds, firestorm spells and hot hail?

"Good Lord, no. He was a pretty good teacher."

But that simple act still haunts Marty. To this day, one can still see the fire in his eyes—the heat in his face—when he's crossed while working at the front desk of Student Union Student Union. This reporter, for one, will be sure not to enter the building without his Floodbane Potato Famine monogrammed fire extinguisher and asbestos laced Potato Famine duffel bag, both of which are available in the Student Union Student Union Gift Shop…which hasn't yet been burned to the ground as of press time.

Nobody noticed the new student sitting in the 11:00 a.m. philosophy class. Or perhaps they did and just didn't care. Either way, I met no opposition as I took my seat next to the Arbiter.

The philosophy classroom was a lot different from the others in which I'd been. The whole building was. Unlike the other halls on campus, most of which had that Victorian style that charms the covers of all the Floodbane propaganda, this one was a shoe box. It was long and thin, with ceilings so low they should've had clearance signs on the doors outside. There were no windows on the walls, so the only natural light filtered in from the glass covered slits along the ceiling on the east side of the room. In the summer, I'm sure this room could've been used as a Vietnamese sweat box. It wasn't too hot in there at the moment, but it was stale due to the lack of airflow. Had I been forced to sit through a class in there, I would've fallen asleep within five minutes each day. Looking around, I noticed a few students already had. This was too bad, because they missed the grand entrance of Mr. Bernard.

He wasn't wearing his Budweiser suit coat today. This one promoted no major corporations, but instead cried out for an era long gone. It was pink with white paisleys playing about, and the lapels were black velvet. It looked like something Elvis wouldn't have worn in even his most misguided of days. Underneath the jacket was a black T-shirt with the cryptic phrase "Shoot, Soundbite, Shoot," written in white letters. This was tucked into white denim Levi's, which were in turn tucked into gray cowboy boots. I wanted to reach out and help him, to be there for him every morning when he looked into his closet and thought, "What today?" but then I thought back to the meeting I'd had with him. I realized maybe these clothes were chosen for a reason. I still had the idea that Mr. Bernard's eccentricity was calculated, that he was testing us or experimenting with us.

I'd been his guinea pig once before, and I felt some comfort in the fact that I was now an assistant.

He didn't speak right away, instead turning to write his name on the board. As he did, the class quieted down, save for a couple students right behind me and the Arbiter.

"No, no, no, you're all wrong," the boy behind me argued. "What Plato meant was that justice was a tool to be used to keep order, like a wrench, a screwdriver, a ball-peen hammer. If there was any unrest, you could bash the people down. Plato agreed with later theorists like H.C.A. Hart who understood that without a strong, firm, government, without an unyielding structure making the trains run on time, freedom was impossible."

"Did you even read *Republic?*" asked the girl behind the Arbiter. Hearing their budding debate, the Arbiter turned to me and smiled. Self-importance amused us. "That's not what he was saying at all. Plato said that justice was giving each man or woman what he or she deserved. Justice can't come via template or morality from a Draconian code; Plato clearly believed the individual to be the master of his domain."

"You missed the entire subtext!" the boy laughed. "If Plato had meant that—"

"Good morning, college students," Mr. Bernard bellowed from the front of the room. "My name is Mr. Bernard, and I'll be filling in for Dr. Strongbow for the rest of the week. He's in Washington D.C. trying to prove that philosophers really do exist. Anyway, we should get right into this. What did the Chief have you discussing?"

"Great western philosophers," the guy behind me announced with uncalled-for arrogance. "We're going to spend the next two weeks analyzing Plato's *Republic.*"

"Never heard of it," Mr. Bernard admitted with a matter-of-factness that quickly silenced the student. "What's next?"

This time the girl behind the Arbiter answered him. I had a feeling these were the only two who discussed anything in this class, and that they did it with verve. "Uh, we're also to discuss Aristotle's *Politics*."

"Uh, nope, missed that one too. Must have been watching a rerun of *The Fall Guy* when that came out. That Lee Majors, aside from being the unknown stuntman that makes Eastwood look so fine, was one crazy mother scratcher," Mr. Bernard reflected with a smile. "Any others?"

"Jean Paul Sartre," the girl tried again. "We read Sartre's *Nausea*."

Mr. Bernard brightened. "Jean Paul Sartre!" But then he dimmed again. "No. I was going to buy that last week, but I was enticed instead by the curves of the women on the cover of *Penthouse Letters*. Kind of curves that make you wanna hop into a BMW and take them at 85 M-P-f'n-H."

The guy behind me finally collected himself. "How do you expect us to hold any sort of a discussion here when you have never read the material?"

"What's your name, son?" Mr. Bernard asked.

"Marc Mero."

"That's your first name?"

"Marc is."

"Well, listen, Marcus, I'm thirty-seven years old. I've been reading all my life. I've got so much wisdom that I'm my own roadside attraction. I'm available just off I 95 next to the world's largest cigarettes and the ninety-six ounce butt steak. Ask me anything. Anything at all."

The girl jumped in first. "What is truth?" she smiled haughtily.

"Truth...truth...truth is...truth is..." Mr. Bernard stammered. For a moment, I was worried for him, but then he added, "Truth is an undefinable term, Miss..."

"Rena."

"Thank you, Miss Rena. You can't quite put your finger on truth, I'm afraid. But it does rhyme with vermouth. Now vermouth, I know exactly what that is. A little gin, a little vermouth...now that's a drink, ladies and gentlemen. Shaken, stirred, served out of a bathtub in '27 or a makeshift tent in Korea, mister do like himself a cocktail."

"What is the meaning of life?" another student asked from the back of the room.

"Yeah, why are we here?" Marc added. "What purpose do we serve?"

"Whoa, call back the troops!" Mr. Bernard laughed as he threw his hands out before him and backed away. "Do you people actually care about this? What kind of pathetic existences can you possibly be living where you have time to worry about such pointless drivel? Don't you realize that in a few short years you're going to have go out into corporate America, put on your navy blue suit and serve the man his french fries? When I was in college, we didn't ask ourselves 'What is truth?' We asked ourselves 'What is vermouth?' Because we didn't have any idea about the positive benefits of a dry martini at the time. All we knew was beer. Lots of beer. Flat, nasty, domestic beer. I's gettin' all misty just thinking about it."

Marc was nearly whining now. "But sir, we're here at Floodbane to learn, to broaden our minds, to experience truth in beauty. It says so right here in the Floodbane College handbook!"

He actually had a copy with him. Unbelievable. It was most likely just me, but I couldn't understand those who got this into anything. People could become so devoted to their school, their religion, their brand of dish washing detergent. Why? To me, that was like buying an album and listening to only one song from it over and over and over again, kind of like my parents' neighbors who once had a "Convoy" party where they drank beer and danced and mingled and blasted C.W. McCall's "Convoy" throughout the neighborhood for four hours straight. To this day, I still break into a cold sweat in the dark of the moon on the sixth of June.

"Beauty? You want beauty? We knew about beauty." Mr. Bernard continued with Marc's thought, smiling as if visiting a far off place about which only he knew. "There ain't nothing more beautiful in this big, blue marble than the sight of a nubile young coed named Pixley, stripped to a black g-string and lying flat on her back in the frat house, the smell of vermouth on her breath; she's yelling 'Take me! Take me now!' while a bunch of your frat-brothers are behind you chanting 'Ber-nie! Ber-nie! Ber-nie!' God, I miss college!"

"This is ridiculous!" Rena spouted. "You're nothing but a chauvinistic pig!"

"Yeah, the pig roasts," Mr. Bernard smiled. He still hadn't returned. "Good times."

"My God!" Rena continued. "You're a prime example of Hobbes' theory on the worthlessness of man!"

"No, that wasn't Hobbes," Marc countered. "That was Nietsche."

"No, Nietsche said, 'God is dead.'"

"What about that?" asked another girl. "What about God? Is there a god?"

"Believe me, dear friend, if there's a Pixley in a G-string, there's a god who put her here. Ain't no way a body like that crawled out of the primordial soup," Mr. Bernard sighed, coming back to us at last.

"Then are we in control of our own lives?"

Mr. Bernard leaned forward on the podium. "Well, I believe it was Hagar who once said—"

Marc was the one to ask, "Who?"

Mr. Bernard excitedly turned and wrote the name on the board, again underlining it repeatedly, causing others in the class to write it in their notebooks. "Sammy Hagar."

"You're comparing Plato, Socrates and Aristotle—arguably the three most brilliant men ever—to a former lead singer of Van Halen?" Marc asked in disbelief. "He wasn't even any good! He ruined them!"

"Hey, I'll have you know that Sammy Hagar was brilliant before, during and after Van Halen. Any man who can turn a song into a tequila franchise deserves our respect. Best of both worlds, indeed. Sammy's insight extends well beyond…well, here. Let's examine this sample from Sammy's study on human impulses, *VOA*." He opened his briefcase and pulled from it a handful of papers. I wondered if Mr. Bernard knew he'd be getting to Sammy Hagar that afternoon, or did he always just have these lyrics with him? As a teenager, I always thought it'd be romantic to write out the lyrics of my favorite songs to give to the girls I liked. This never really worked, however, because none of the girls I like would have accepted such notes from me. More importantly, my favorite songs were all from marching band. Not many women can be wooed by "The Liberty Bell March."

Of course, I doubt many women could be wooed by this particular Sammy Hagar song, either, which was called "Dick In the Dirt." Before I could even get into the lyrics, Mr. Bernard asked us, "Now, what is the focus of Sir Hagar's thesis?"

"That he likes to hump Terra Firma?" some guy towards the front suggested.

"Yes, but that's just scratching the surface of the poem," Mr. Bernard nodded. "Let's dig a little deeper."

"Who's Terry Firma? Is he a guy?" someone else asked. "Is Hagar a fag?"

"Well, look at the first line of the poem. Hagar speaks of a gentlemen named Richard. Who's Richard?"

"Another fag?"

"Read on."

The Arbiter had obviously read further into the song than I had. He confidently suggested. "Richard is Sir Hagar's penis."

"Exactly!" Mr. Bernard beamed. He was finally getting through to us. If he were on a commercial promoting Floodbane, he would've claimed these were the moments that made teaching so worthwhile. "Sammy is stressing the point that no man can really know himself until he knows his penis, and to do so, a man must name his penis. So, hands up! Everyone tell me the name of his penis…except the women. Women can tell me the name of someone else's penis you may have known."

The Arbiter went first. "Springer."

"Good! Yes! Excellent!"

"Pierce!" another guy offered.

"Good!"

"Buster Hyman."

"A first and last name! You can leave now! You get an A for the semester!"

The student left.

"The Allman Brothers Band."

"Abstract. Good. Touring with the Allman Brothers Band. I like it."

"President Franklin Delano Roosevelt."

"Ah, now this bears discussion. Politics; normally not good for sex, unless you're a Kennedy. But, complete this sentence for me; 'Oh baby, slide on down there and have a chat with…'"

"El Presidenté"

"Excellent! Along with the Spanish flavoring, and the chicas do love the Spanish flavoring, 'El Presidenté' yields the power of the position without putting images of sixty-year-olds in your partner's head. And my friends, it's all about the power of the position. The one presidential name that would work, of course, is James K. Poke. A witty derivation of the name of the man who took California from the Mexicans in the 19th century, much like I stole this hot, big-lunged blonde named Shawnae from a Puerto Rican guy back in college." Mr. Bernard shifted gears and pointed to a girl in the front of the room. "Now, you there, when thinking of your boyfriend's penis, what name comes to mind?"

"I don't really have a—"

"Oh, come on. You can't possibly think of it as 'my boyfriend's penis.' It's its own entity. It's separate from the man! Now, when you wake the baby, what do you call it?"

She lowered her head into shoulders, turned red and giggled as she said, "Bronk."

Mr. Bernard nodded knowingly. "Ah, you see, I've actually been doing research on this for a spec. article I'm submitting to *Details*. Nine out of ten women interviewed like to think of their boyfriend's penis as a seventies TV detectives and/or police men…three of those ten liked to think specifically of Jack Palance. I've studied hundreds of women, and it's always the same. Bronk, Kojak, Rockford, Colombo, S.W.A.T., Hawaii 5-O, Baretta until that whole wife murdering thing—"

Marc stood up at this point. He'd had enough. "I refuse to listen to this any longer. You're not a professor, you're a sycophant!"

Mr. Bernard seemed genuinely surprised. "A what?"

Rena joined Marc. "You make me sick! We'll have you fired or shot or hosed down or whatever you need!"

Mr. Bernard threw out his hands to stop them from leaving and fired forth a verbal burst I had rarely heard outside of courtroom melodramas. "So you're saying that you'd like to have me permanently removed from the teaching profession, or better yet, struck down by a lightning bolt into nothing more than a gold filled molar. Correct?"

"Yes!" Rena spat.

"Because I've done wrong! Because I'm an evildoer! Because I'm a wicked, wicked man!"

"Yes! Yes! Yes!"

"Because someone who does wrong must be punished, and someone who does right must be rewarded!" Mr. Bernard reached a roaring crescendo. "Everyone should get exactly what's coming to him! The survival of our very social order depends on it!! Is that what you're saying?!!"

"Yes! Yes!"

Mr. Bernard instantly returned to his customary placidity. "Ergo, justice."

There was silence for a few moments. The Arbiter was trying to suppress his laughter, and I could tell that Mr. Bernard was fighting himself to not look at him. Had he, he probably would've started laughing too.

Marc took a step forward. "That's brilliant. A perfect analysis of Plato."

Mr. Bernard bowed.

"You mean that you made yourself look like an ass in front of the whole class so that we could better understand your point?" Rena suggested.

"Sure, we can go with that," Mr. Bernard shrugged. "Yeah."

"So then next time can we study Aristotle?" Marc asked.

"No, I'm afraid that class is canceled for Thursday. I'm taking my girlfriend up to the lake, and I've got to stock up on Vermouth." Mr. Bernard smiled at Rena as he said this.

She smiled back. "You're a great man, Mr. Bernard. Both in and out of the classroom, you're a great man."

"You don't know the half of it, sister." He then raised his voice for the whole classroom. "You're all dismissed until next Tuesday, and, goshdarnit, you college students think about what I said."

As the others filtered their way outside, Mr. Bernard headed out the door behind his desk, singing Van Halen's, "Hot for Teacher."

꽃   꽃   꽃

Now that's something I never understood. I'd heard of students getting crushes on their high school teachers. I even saw it once; a girl in my American Literature class my freshman year wouldn't leave the classroom until her teacher, Mr. Calloway, told her he loved her. He never did, of course, because that would've gotten him kicked out of school. So the student stayed at her desk until fifteen minutes into the next period when she finally gave up and left.

A few days later, Mr. Calloway received a three day suspension without pay for purposely causing students to miss their classes. Was he bitter? Apparently not enough. Five days after his "student scorned" turned eighteen, which was, oddly enough, the same day I killed somebody, the two of them flew off to Las Vegas and got married by Elvis Presley, I'm told. I never saw either of them again. If we ever do run into each other, they ought to thank me for drawing media attention away from them.

The point of all this? Don't ever pretend to understand how the world works, because it actually doesn't work at all. In fact, I think the only way to get through life sometimes is to believe this…no, not only believe this, but make it a mantra, to say it over and over and over again until it becomes etched in the brain like the jingle of a beer commercial.

Everything will happen.

Again, everything will happen. Feel free to add a lilting melody if it'll help.

The mantra now. Everything will happen. Everything will happen. Everything will happen. Everything will happen.

It's the truth. Everything that can possibly happen on this planet, will. It's the only way modern science, medieval mysticism and blind faith can explain how it is that I was able to make love with Ann Penella.

But again, I'm getting ahead of myself. On my second late night visit to her bedroom, we did nothing more than discuss whether or not I was happy. She asked me that question soon after I climbed through her window (this time without incident, it's not like I injured myself every time I got near the girl) and I honestly thought it was a fairly dumb question. Any question about one's emotions is stupid, I think. Yes, I'm happy. I'm always happy. I'm always sad. I'm always concerned, and I'm always giddy. I don't think it's possible to be just one emotion at any given time. So, I instead said, "No."

I had then brushed off the comment with the explanation that I'd never been to Disney World, although I was actually saying that I'd never had sex with her. Little did I know the airline reservations had already been made.

I'm getting ahead of myself again. I tend to do that with sex.

"What?" Ann asked at my Disney World comment.

"Well, it's true," I smiled to make it a joke. "I've never been there."

"Your parents never took you to Disney World when you were a kid?"

I started to laugh. From my current way of thinking, that was a rather sick joke. "No."

"I went with my parents twice."

"No, don't say that."

"What? I did! Once when I was four, I think, and again when I was nine."

I wanted to let her in on my thoughts so she wouldn't get annoyed, but I couldn't, so I finally suppressed my laughter and changed the subject back to what she'd originally intended.

"I'm content, I guess. Not happy, but content."

"You never seem happy to me," Ann pointed out with a motherly-soft voice. I was amazed at how quickly she could change inflection. "Not from the first night I talked to you."

"After that bus trip?" I reminded her. "Sorry if I wasn't singing 'Zip-A-Dee-Doo-Dah.'"

"You know what I mean. Don't you have anything to be happy about?"

"I've got both my arms," I joked. Ann just stared. "Well, I do, see?"

"I know you've got both arms. Now answer my question."

She was tough, this Ann. Every moment I spent with her, I loved her more. It was starting to get scary, but I couldn't back out of it. It was like being in a haunted house, falling in love; the further into it I ventured, the scarier it got. But I couldn't just backtrack to find my way out. The best I could do was find someone's hand to hold and to keep turning corners—tripping the activators that would throw some new monster at me—until I finally escaped through the final door and back into the light of the outside world, where mom and dad were waiting.

But what a thrill, what a thrill.

"I've got my family," I finally answered her. "I love my family."

"Me too," Ann smiled.

"I didn't think you knew my family."

"I didn't mean...would you cut it out?" she laughed as she slapped my knee.

Hey now, physical contact. Good. Physical contact was always good. I knew that. That I know. Did it mean that she wanted me then and there? No. But it did mean she wasn't repulsed by me, and that was enough to send me flying for the rest of the night. She would soon launch me into flight once more, but then would come the crash.

I mean a big, loud, heard and seen for miles, shrapnel everywhere kind of crash. The kind of crash where, a few hours later on the 11:00 news, a handsome reporter in a London Fog coat would say, "It's a miracle only one person was killed."

CHAPTER 10

"She's A Lady"

*P*eople these days seem confused about pork. Porn. I'm sorry, what I meant to say was porn. People these days seem confused about porn. However, there are a lot of folks missing the boat on pork, too. Keeping kosher is certainly noble in theory, but damn if that bacon isn't tasty.

As I was saying, people these days seem confused about porn. I think this stems from their lack of education on the subject. There's a big distinction between porn and smut that most people just can't differentiate. This is because, for the most part, people learn about pornography from one of two groups; perverts and conservatives. The thing is, neither group gives an accurate reading on the subject. Perverts pretend the Constitution was drawn up so they could hide under drainage grates and take upskirt photos to sell on the internet. I realize our founding fathers weren't the most holy of people (particularly that Alexander Hamilton, he was a stone freak), but I seriously doubt a pantyhose fetish is the reason we breathe free. Conservatives, on the other hand, think the Bible was written specifically to stop God's children from looking at photographs of another of God's children in the buff. Now I don't pretend to have the keenest grasp on modern theology, but I don't see how looking at a collection of cyan, magenta, yellow and black dots pressed onto paper with water and rubber is going to land my soul in hell.

In my opinion, both the Bible and the Constitution are so fraught with ambiguity and contradiction that they should both be replaced by *TV Guide*. Now there's a fine, concise publication full of useful information. I'd much rather know what's on the USA Network on Sundays at 7 p.m. than know what eminent domain means or hear whether or not Saul, son of Kish, son of Abiel, son or Zeror, son of Becorath, son of Aphiah of Benjamin, ever found his father's donkeys. In fact, should I ever get married, I may have the liturgist read from *TV Guide*.

"Could you please turn your *TV Guides* to Saturday, chapter 10 p.m., verses 7, 10, 11 and 19. Walker, Texas Ranger (CC). Repeat. 'Country star Lila McCann plays an aspiring teen vocalist stalked by a rich kid, who's also seeking to control heroin distribution in Dallas. Singer Michael Peterson has a cameo.' Amen."

That makes me think. Perhaps more people would pay attention in church if the Bible lessons had cameos from country/western musicians. Maybe Mel Tellis as Stone Thrower #3 or Shania Twain as Leper in Street. Great fun.

The thing is, if people want to protest porn, then more power to them. They've got just as much right to protest it as I had to look at it on the internet with the Arbiter.

I should clarify this wasn't something we did with regularity. There were always articles to make up, wrestling matches to watch, things to sit and think about. We had no time for the smut. Besides, without spending ridiculous amounts of money for passwords, the quality of internet porn really sucks. This night, however, the Arbiter and I were on a mission.

When Mr. Bernard's screensaver was deactivated during our interview, the Arbiter had seen enough of the host address to get into the newsgroup, "alt.binaries.erotica.sorority." There, he found a message promoting the URL **http://www.floodbane.edu/cmpslife/greeklif/**

sex. There was no password or adult verification device. There was no age warning or link to Net Nanny or Cyber Patrol or Put That Thing Away, Junior or whatever the hell those lock-out applications are called. It wasn't until the Friday evening after the fire god incident that the Arbiter first showed me the Eta Iota Upsilon porn site. I'm not sure at what point he first looked at it, but that Friday night down in the *A Daily Planet* office, the Arbiter launched the website and called me over to his Mac. What we found there would've made Al Goldstein fly the flag with pride (and I'm not just talking about Old Glory). The site was loaded with jpegs of current and former sisters of Eta Iota Upsilon performing the dreams of many a teenager in mid-pubescence. The site was divided, as all respectable internet porn sites are, into various categories: nude, hardcore, lesbian, toys, orgy and financial assistance.

That wasn't a joke. There really was a link from the porn to financial assistance. I found this curious, considering there was no link for Asians. Whoever heard of an internet porn site that didn't offer Asians? Racist bastards. I should point out that the link to financial assistance contained a JavaScript redirect to hide the referring URL. Whoever was doing this knew his or her way around web programming.

The Arbiter and I loaded as many images as we could, trying to identify the women pictured. It wasn't that difficult with most, and a little research revealed that all of the males pictured were Upsilon Iota Eta; Jayson Fayme's fraternity. Mercifully, Fayme was not in any of the pictures—at least in none where faces could be seen.

No other sororities or fraternities were represented.

Questions immediately popped to mind as we looked at the site. Who else knew about it? Who was responsible for its creation? What was its purpose? Did it hurt when the rush chairman of Upsilon Iota Eta got that pierced? Don't we have a weight room on campus? When was Nair invented, anyway? Why do nipples come in so many different sizes?

We wondered if the students photographed even knew they were online. Not one of them was looking directly into the camera, certainly outside the norm of amateur pornography in which women try desperately to give longing looks to the camera, coming across only as stoned and sad. On the other hand, the photographs seemed too clear to have been taken with a hidden camera. No, these shots were of a quality worthy of Bluebird scans.

But what appeared to be bothering the Arbiter most was the level of Mr. Bernard's involvement. It seemed too large a coincidence his newsreader was opened to a newsgroup that happened to advertise the Victorian underground of Floodbane, as it were. Plus, he'd apparently had the newsreader open during the interview before ours. Knowing students would be coming into his office, why didn't he just shut it down? The Arbiter and I were both certain Mr. Bernard was aware of it, but the Arbiter especially wanted to figure out just how much he knew.

And curiously enough, the idea that this discovery might make the front page of A Daily Planet was never laid on the table. At least not until Rhonda showed up.

It was nearing eleven o'clock when she finally came down. I expected the Arbiter to close the web browser when she came in, but he didn't. He left it open to the jpeg of the guy with the Prince Albert.

"Sorry I'm so late," Rhonda apologized as she closed the door behind her. She then glanced furtively around the room, I assume to see if Fayme was there, before descending the final two steps into the office.

"No problem, Rhonda," the Arbiter said, looking up from the monitor. "Guy and I were able to keep ourselves entertained."

I had to hide my snicker with a cough.

"I should say so," Rhonda smiled. "I don't think I've ever come down here when there wasn't music playing. What's been keeping you two so busy?"

"Internet pornography," the Arbiter stated matter-of-factly.

"Mmm hmm. Did they finally upload my movie? Momma needs those residual checks." Rhonda didn't skip a beat, and she never backed down from the joke, even if it was out of character. The Arbiter was so damn lucky.

"Maybe," the Arbiter shrugged as I laughed. "The mpegs were too big to download on this connection, so Guy and I just stuck with the pictures."

"Oh, that's too bad because *oh sweet mother of God!*"

"I know," I agreed with Rhonda as she looked at the picture on the screen. "Makes you think, doesn't it."

"No! No, it doesn't make me think!" She was still yelling from the close-up of the student's pierced penis, and she'd hidden her face in her hands. "It makes me do…it doesn't…no, it stops me from thinking! Oh, ah please, make it go away!"

"I already did," the Arbiter told her.

"I mean from my mind! Someone expunge this image from my mind!"

"I'm afraid that's beyond my abilities," the Arbiter apologized.

"Why in heaven's name was that even there?" Rhonda demanded as she looked up once more at the monitor. To her relief, the Arbiter had collapsed the window. "Is that something of Fayme's? Is it…oh no, that wasn't his…*him* was it?"

The Arbiter paled. "I sure hope not."

Rhonda sighed with relief and fell back into a chair behind me and the Arbiter. She stared hard into the monitor for a second, then shocked the hell out of me by saying, "Pull it back up."

The Arbiter was flabbergasted. "Excuse me?"

Rhonda paused again, still looking straight at the monitor. "Do you know how sometimes you see a horrific image only briefly, just enough to absorb the ugliness of it, but not really enough to remember it?"

"No." The Arbiter shook his head.

"Arby, for the rest of my life, I don't want to keep exaggerating what I just saw. I need to memorize it so my imagination cannot add to the image."

"That may be the…" I didn't want to say "dumbest," because nothing Rhonda said was dumb, "…weirdest thing you've ever said."

"Hardly." Rhonda finally turned away from the screen to look at me. "How long were you looking at it before I came in?"

I didn't answer. Neither did the Arbiter; he just smiled.

"See? That's also why people stare so long at auto accidents and such. It's not because we're fascinated with morbidity, but because we don't want our imaginations to make it even worse."

"No, I think I'm just fascinated with morbidity," the Arbiter countered.

"Pull it up, Arby."

"As you wish."

Although I didn't voice it, I agreed more with the Arbiter. I think we *like* accidents. Accidents, murders, natural disasters, unexpected deaths…as long as they don't happen to us, they brighten our days, give us something to talk about. "Guess who died," is a hell of a conversation starter.

With one click of the mouse, the Arbiter once again filled the screen with the larger than life pixelation of the male anatomy. The three of us stared at it in total silence for a few moments. My facial expression contorted at least every two seconds as a new thought occurred to me.

Able to take it no more, I finally said, "I'm surprised Floodbane let him enroll with that…thing he's done."

"He must not have mentioned it in the personal essay," the Arbiter suggested.

"I'm afraid not even Floodbane can discriminate against someone because of a body piercing," Rhonda explained. "Not even one there."

"Yeah, that'd be piercecution."

We sat in silence for a few moments more before we erupted into laughter over the Arbiter's joke. Somewhere between laughs, one of us screamed to "Shut it off!" and the image was replaced with a more pleasant shot of a woman with two guys. More pleasant? It's amazing how the tolerance level can be raised so high after seeing a man with metal sticking through his...

Sorry, I still don't like to think about it.

Once we'd all settled back down, Rhonda was able to get back to her original question. "Arby, why are you looking at this site?"

"Guy's looking at it, too," the Arbiter pointed out, sharing the blame like a little kid tattling on his younger brother who was also looking at dad's *Playboys*.

"I am not!"

Rhonda and the Arbiter both looked at me incredulously.

I scratched my ear. I don't know why, I just suddenly felt like scratching my ear. I probably would've popped a Life Saver into my mouth if I weren't already enjoying one.

The Arbiter answered Rhonda's question. "It's research."

"For which class?" Rhonda asked incredulously.

"Sex in the Middle Ages," I joked. The Arbiter smiled, but Rhonda didn't respond.

The Arbiter then asked Rhonda to, "Look at the URL."

After a moment, she gasped, "No. No, that's just wrong."

"Wrong as rain."

"How did you find this?" Rhonda continued. "It couldn't have been linked from the main site, could it?"

"Nope. In fact, there's a bot in the source code to stop search engines from spidering it," the Arbiter explained. "It was advertised in a newsgroup I got from Mr. Bernard."

"Mr. Bernard?"

"Yeah, he had it up on his computer when Guy and I went in for the interview. One of the jpegs I downloaded from there advertised this address. Well, it advertised Floodbane, I mean. I had to spend a few hours of trial and error before I was able to pull up…" He gestured at the threesome on the screen.

"We couldn't find any links from Floodbane's site," I offered. I wanted to feel that this discovery was part mine, even though the Arbiter and I both knew that it wasn't. "It's just sitting on the server on it's own."

"Wonder if all websites have a hidden sex page?" the Arbiter mused. "Give '**www.usps.gov/sex**' a try next."

"*They'd* better have Asians."

"This is so wrong," Rhonda pointed out, shaking her head. "This school would be crawling with Feds if anyone found out about this. It'd be a national scandal."

"It may not be the school's doing," the Arbiter suggested. His face lit up as if the gears turning in his head had started to glow red hot. "It's possible that whomever's constructing the website added it without anyone's knowing. Or maybe someone in Eta Iota Upsilon got the passwords and uploaded it herself. For all we know, it could be a hoax; someone outside the sorority could be doctoring the photos and uploading them from his dorm room."

"If that's the case, we could sure use his PhotoShop skills here at *A Planet*," I offered.

The Arbiter dismissed my comment. "And from what I can tell, no one can access it by linking. I did a link search…nothing."

As we spoke, the Arbiter continued to click on different links throughout the site, pulling up enough images to fill a year's subscription of *Penthouse* magazine. After a few images came and went, Rhonda brightened at one.

"Oh! She was in *Antigone* with me!"

"I thought she looked familiar," the Arbiter nodded. "She was very good."

"She's not too shabby now," I added.

After cycling through a few more photos, the Arbiter had finally had enough. He clicked on a bookmark to an internet wrestling league he particularly seemed to like, then turned to face Rhonda and me. "So…what to do."

"Arby, you're not thinking of exposing this in *A Planet,* are you?" Rhonda asked with trepidation.

"Oh good Lord no," the Arbiter dismissed. "Unfortunately, *A Daily Planet* would handicap this. Who cares about pornography in a paper that normally talks about fire gods?"

I interrupted him. "Hey, speaking of that, I meant to ask you what happened to the Naked Soup Club article?"

The Arbiter pointed to the monitor. "Kind of got sidetracked. But see, the soup club, the fire gods? They kind of make porno lose its punch. Can't get that punch back. To make this story work, going to need some pictures."

I didn't know what I was missing here. "I don't know what I'm missing here. I mean…" I pointed to the screen.

"Can't use these pictures; they're copyrighted," the Arbiter explained. I couldn't tell if he was being serious or not. I also couldn't tell if he was serious when he added, "Besides, they're all only 72 dpi, and they're jpeg compressed."

"Yeah," I agreed. "Lord knows we wouldn't want to compromise our integrity by publishing low quality porn."

"Finally, someone who understands," the Arbiter smiled. "No, actually, haven't got a whole lot of options here. This whole site can be deleted in a second. Suppose the perpetrator gets the paper first? The site would be gone before anyone else had a chance to log on. Got to blow the cover off this big time to have any chance of having fun.

"And therein lay the conundrum. Can't go to the school with this. If it is being done by Eta Iota Upsilon, then no big deal. They lose their charter, taking Upsilon Iota Eta down with them, most likely."

"And, in this case, what do we do?" I asked.

"Laugh," the Arbiter replied. "Good and hard. However, if it's being done by President or someone high up there, then it'll probably be about three weeks or so before the bodies are found."

"Whose bodies?" I asked.

The Arbiter just looked at me for a moment before continuing. "Could probably confront Mr. Bernard, but not until he's cleared of any role in this. There's more to him than free tuition, loud jackets and great teaching."

"Why don't we just call the FBI or the DEA or the ASPCA or someone?" I asked.

"Two reasons: One, need proof the site is being created by someone here at Floodbane. Otherwise, what's the point? And two, the story will probably get swallowed by them. Scandals are much more fun when the press messes them up rather than when the government does…bigger snowballs. Got to make sure this story gets the attention it deserves and doesn't become just some filler segment of a second-rate news show.

"So, who's in?"

"I don't know," Rhonda hesitated. "Making up stories about mascots is one thing, but this is serious."

"Yes, it is serious," the Arbiter agreed. "That's why we have to do this, Rhonda. These students are potentially ruining their careers here, their lives, even. For all we know, it's possible they're being forced into this just like Linda Lovelace claimed about 'Deep Throat.' Its our moral duty as citizens of this great country—where at least we know we're free—to ensure that all of our porn is of a higher quality than 'Deep Throat.' So, are you guys in?"

"Sure," I shrugged. "Can't be any more dangerous than climbing the radio tower."

"Yes it can."

"And hey, it could be good promotion. I could get a job offer out of this with some newspaper."

Rhonda looked at me and smiled. "You know Guy, I think that's the first time you've indicated interest in a career? I thought you'd be content to watch wrestling for the rest of your life like the Arbiter here. For which paper would you like to work? *The Times? The Washington Post?*"

"I was thinking more along the lines of *The Weekly World News.* Not quite as prestigious, I know, but I would get to make a lot of trips to the Ukraine to see eighty-five pound babies."

Rhonda deflated as the Arbiter asked her, "How about you, Rhonda? Are you in?"

She shrugged and looked towards the monitor that now detailed the statistics of an internet wrestler named Creed. "I'm still not sure."

"You don't have to, of course," the Arbiter told her as he placed his hand on her arm.

"But you've already got me worked into a plan, don't you?" Rhonda stated.

"I can change it. Plan A involves you. Plan B involves our Guy here getting his penis pierced."

"Hey, hold…wait a minute!" I demanded as I covered my groin with my hands. "Ain't nothing passing through Mr. Kite that could effect his ability to soar freely through the breeze. Understand?"

Rhonda looked at me and smiled, then turned back to the Arbiter. "Okay, being for the benefit of Mr. Kite, what's my role?"

※   ※   ※

That's something I never figured out in life; my role. The only people who really offered any help were my teachers. Of course, with them it was always, "Know your role and shut your mouth…" so I don't think they did much good.

Where I could've really used some input was with Ann Penella. Our friendship seemed to be moving along just fine, as if telling her I loved her removed the pressure of being in love. But despite this pseudo-happiness, I still wanted more. Ann had this power to make me love her more with each word she said to me. She acquired this power by—aside from the whole Heath thing, of course—never failing to exceed my expectations, and she even started to return my faith in the human race.

I'd call it ironic, but sometimes life is too predictable to be ironic. The woman who was rebuilding my faith in the basic goodness of humankind was dating the man who destroyed it. What is it I said before? Everything will happen.

Perhaps the Heath factor was what made it so difficult to accept that Ann and I could not be together. I felt sorry for myself, never a productive start to winning the love of a woman. Still, I furiously thought of ways to win her away from Heath. What could I say or do to make her love me? I mean, all of the words at my disposal (certainly more than at Heath's), the infinite ways in which I could order those words, surely there was at least one phrase in there that would win her heart. "Ann, I love the smell of napalm in the morning; it smells like…victory." Maybe not.

But there was something I couldn't shake. Although still an amateur, I knew enough about relationships to understand that when a guy tells a woman he loves her, she does one of two things, she loves him back or she runs away screaming like a B-movie actress from an army of brain eating zombies. Ann did neither. Why?

I didn't have an answer. No one did, but I wasn't asking for fear of being offered some flippant answer about how she really did value my friendship. Some may have even said she really did love me. But they couldn't know for sure. *I* couldn't know for sure. I don't think even Ann knew for sure, and that's what gave me hope. That right there is why I kept driving out to her house so late at night, week after week. The more I talked to her, the better chance I had of at last putting those right words together.

If not, I could always eat her brain.

I can't recall if I was thinking about this the next time I drove out to Ann's. It was just after midnight when I drove past Professor

Snow's, and, sure enough, he was out on his porch, gun in hand, just as he had been the previous week. I almost smiled as I drove past, despite his prophecies of doom. Life was actually going pretty well. There's something about being in love, even if it's not returned. Just knowing that I had the ability to fall in love was elation enough for the time being.

Perhaps this is why I was willing to make a bold move that night. For the first time in our relationship, I was going to offer Ann a gift. It wasn't anything big. It wasn't diamond earrings or a broach of my grandmother's or tickets to Wrestlemania. It was a book. It was a simple book to say, "I saw this and I thought of you." Of course, that wasn't actually the case. What the gift actually said was, "I busted my ass for the past two weeks searching every used book shop and garage sale within a hundred mile radius to find this for you because I know it's something you might like and will prompt thoughts of me every time you see it."

It was a mint condition copy of *The Monster at the End of this Book—Starring Lovable, Furry Old Grover* by Jon Stone.

So I was feeling pretty good about myself as I drove out to Ann's. I may have even been whistling as I drove up to her house. For all I know, the song could've been "She's A Lady." Why not? Tom Jones. Yeah, it was Tom Jones and all his sexy, Welshman ways with me that night as I drove out to visit Ann.

I fucking hate you, Tom Jones.

I mean, I was in love. Of course I didn't see it. I was on my way to visit my guardian angel, so I'm not expected to take notice of every little goddam thing in the surrounding area. That was Tom's job. That's why he was there. That's why they play him on the radio. I mean, I didn't invite him—sure as hell, I didn't invite him—but he was there nonetheless. It was therefore his job to point out that Heath Millard's car was parked in Ann's driveway.

I drove right by it. I parked beyond her house, as I always did, and the path I took to her bedroom led me around back. Her window was radiating a pinkish ambient light, which struck me as odd. I had never taken notice of anything in her room that would give off such a light.

I chose to focus on this thought as I climbed the antennae. With grim determination, I resolved myself to figuring out what that light was about before I reached the top. I now know why I so desperately clung to such thoughts as I climbed. I'm fairly sure I even knew then. It's because I *had* seen Heath's car. It's because, as I climbed, I could hear the muffled gasps and moans of two people in the throes of passion. It's because I was fully aware of what I'd see when I reached the window.

❧   ❧   ❧

Voyeurism is a sketchy thing, I'd say. I mean, at what point does watching a neighbor exercise in the nude cross from, "Well, it's more interesting than watching *When Good Figure Skaters Go Bad II* on Fox to "I think I'd get a better view from within her closet, and her soup cans need straightened out anyway?"

I guess that, to the misinformed, I probably looked like a voyeur for a while at Floodbane. I couldn't pass the Eta Iota Upsilon sorority house without taking a look up into that window; the one from which we'd seen short bursts of light that could have maybe, possibly, been flash bulbs. After finding the website, the Arbiter and I scouted the sorority house a few times, attempting to verify our guesses on when the girls were "doin' the devil's bidness," as the Arbiter liked to say. All of the action seemed to come from one window only. Curiously, the window faced the street. I'd've thought they would do a little more to conceal their enterprise, but I'd also seen enough of the bastard *Emmanuelle* movies, the ones not made in France, to know those in the skin trade don't always use their best judgments.

On this particular October Saturday night, I wouldn't be heading towards the sorority house with the Arbiter. I was going to be with

Rhonda. Eta Iota Upsilon was having a pre-rush party; their last before the actual rush period began and they had to clean up their act a bit for the Inter Greek Council. Funny thing how that Council could turn any sorority house into a "diverse community of sisterhood dedicated to the creation of lifelong friendships through fellowship and blah blah blah charity work blah blah blah Dean's List blah blah blah spring formal and what blah you." How is it that, even in college, people are already practitioners of the spin doctor?

Amazingly enough, it wasn't my suggestion that I be Rhonda's date for the evening. And sadly, it also wasn't hers. Instead, it was all part of the Arbiter's plan. As I've mentioned, people either loved or hated the Arbiter, whereas they had basically no knowledge of my existence. I could move more freely about the Eta Iota Upsilon house and get more information because people just tended to not notice me. Some would consider that sad, I guess, but invisibility is actually a great benefit; one the Arbiter would exploit to send me out on a date with his girlfriend. Not that I minded, of course.

Don't get me wrong, here. I wasn't about to make any moves on Rhonda; I couldn't do that for numerous reasons. But Rhonda was a lot of fun, smart as heck, and she was great to look at. She inspired so many unique thoughts with each glance, and precious few of them caused any guilt. Plus, from the time she and the Arbiter started dating, we'd spent little time alone together. He and she were willing to let me hang out with them often enough, but it never seemed to work out that she'd be around when the Arbiter wasn't. Just one of those things, I guess, and it was really too bad.

Really.

Rhonda didn't complain when the Arbiter said he'd like for me to go to the party with her. I think she felt the same way I did. Probably. This was going to be fun, the double thrills of hanging out together and of the execution of our mission. And in this situation, at least to me, the Arbiter felt more like a boss than a friend. I had no idea what I was going to do upon arriving at the sorority house, so I at least took comfort from the fact that the Arbiter wouldn't be there watching over my shoulder.

As I've mentioned, this was to be the last party before rushing actually started. Whereas the Arbiter was able to convince Rhonda to pretend to show interest in pledging Eta Iota Upsilon, she wouldn't even entertain the thought of going through the rush process...let alone attempt to become a sister. So, if we were going to bust this porn ring open before Thanksgiving break, we had to get the goods that night.

Distracted by these thoughts as I reached Rhonda's door, I almost made the mistake of knocking. Rhonda had requested of me and the Arbiter that we just walk in so as to not risk alerting Fayme to our presence. I opened the door and started up to Rhonda's place, and she almost immediately appeared at the top of the stairs and waved me to hurry up. I looked at her quizzically and continued at my current pace. When I was within reaching distance, she grabbed my upper arm and pulled me into her living room.

"What?" I laughed as she pulled me beside her on the couch. She was already dressed for the party, wearing Levi's and a soft sweater with erratic purple, navy blue and dark green horizontal stripes. It looked great on her, but what didn't? Rhonda could wear a gown of tinfoil and head cheese and still get the cover of *Glamour*.

"I found this today," she whispered through a smile. I looked around to see from whom she was trying to keep this information, but there was no one else there. I immediately understood her hushed manner, however, when I saw what she was handing me. It was a piece of yellow legal paper with the Arbiter's handwriting on it.

"Read it," Rhonda suggested. I'd already started.

To: Sal Mineo
From: The Arbiter
Re: *Rebel Without A Cause*

You tipped the finish, Mr. Mineo.

Your character Plato's death, to clarify, you gave it away. Sure, it was within the acceptable boundaries of foreshadowing (the longing glances at your photograph of Alan Ladd, the borrowing of Jim's "red windbreaker o' doom," Plato's back story as a puppy murderer, the dead animal being a clue upon which one can almost always make bank), but for at least this reviewer the clues to your eventual demise were given away as freely as the virginity of sixteen-year-old Homecoming Queen Runner-Up Suzie Sue in the back of the rented limousine after the star quarterback has thoroughly plied her with peppermint schnapps.

Know what sealed Plato's fate, Mr. Mineo?

It's the scene at the end of the third act when Jim and Judy almost magnetically touch hands as they look out over the bluff…and standing just behind them…almost framed by their perfect, teenaged, hormonally driven, angst riddled love…is your character, Plato.

Three doesn't work, Mr. Mineo. It's the most shallow of thought—and please forgive the predictability of it—but when the universe is conceptualized it seems to be ordered in twos. Eyes. Footsteps. Heartbeats. Once you consciously attempt to violate that order…the Fickle Finger of Fate is automatically poised to flick you away. It's just easier for everybody that way.

And what's great Mr. Mineo…what's great is that *you* know this…even though Plato doesn't. That's what makes your performance so damn sneaky. The audience is primed to feel sorry for your character when the police gun you down. Plato's death is framed by the picture as gut-wrenching, primarily because innocent, trusting, needy Plato is so…undeserving…of his fate.

But—he's not, of course. He doesn't work; he doesn't fit; Plato only lives so he can stop living. Sweet, sincere Plato is a mere *device* used to teach the audience a very important lesson: Justice is everyone getting what's coming to him. And that's what you were playing, wasn't it, Mr. Mineo? Even in Plato's trusting smile…your eyes were saying something else…your eyes were saying, "It's gotta be me…don't you see…someone's gotta take the bullet…I'm the only one it can be."

Couldn't be quintessential anti-hero James Dean.

Couldn't be ultimate girl-next-door Natalie Wood.

It had to be you. Weak, sad little Plato is the only one strong enough to die for the picture.

To take one for the team.

There was one passage in the film that was so…right…it really needed reproduction here. It's the scene at the Griffith Park Observatory when the lecturer is displaying the exhibit and imparting his "truths" of the vagaries of existence:

> "While the flash of our beginning has not yet reached the light years in the distance, has not been seen by planets deep within the other galaxies, you will disappear into the blackness of the space from which you came—destroyed, as we began, in a burst of gas and fire. The heavens are still and cold once more. In the immensity of our universe and the galaxies beyond, the earth will not be missed. Through the infinite reaches of space, the problems of man seem trivial and naive indeed, and man existing alone seems himself an episode of little consequence."

Yeah.

The universe has no morals. It's aggressively apathetic. Relentless, all encompassing destructive apathy. To the picture, we're all pawns in a game with no strategy…no thought…no hope and no love. Only sacrifice to a Queen who places value on us simply in that we're willing to slave and die for her.

You were the ant, Mr. Mineo. You were the ant for all of us. That is to be respected.

In case no one ever said it…thank you.

I had no idea how to respond to the Arbiter's letter. For some reason, I'd found myself saddened by what I'd just read. Well, I suppose I shouldn't have prefaced that thought with "for some reason." I knew the reason, it just wasn't time for me to deal with it yet.

"My boyfriend's brilliant," Rhonda beamed. She was proud of the letter. I was afraid she was missing the bigger picture, but I wasn't about to reveal it. I was more concerned with how she got it. Certainly it was written within the heavily fortified walls of the "Castle Grayfolder," and it was meant to stay in there until the Arbiter was ready to send it. I'm not insinuating she stole it; Rhonda wasn't that kind of person. She knew of the gray folder, and she respected the Arbiter's privacy. End of discussion, as far as she was concerned. But somehow…somehow, she had the letter. I wanted to ask, but I could tell from her face that that's not what we were to be discussing.

"This is really good stuff," I agreed without lying.

"Have you ever read anything like it?"

This time, I lied. "No."

"He should be doing this for a living. He's such a good writer, a good critic with a sharp eye. I wonder why he doesn't see that. Or maybe he does, and he just doesn't show it. I don't know. I've read many reviews of *Rebel Without A Cause*, but I've never seen a take on it quite like this. It's so personal. You can feel his appreciation and attachment—"

"Do you have anything else of his?" I asked. Then added, "Sorry," for interrupting her.

Rhonda seemed hurt that I had interrupted, but she consented to the change of subject. "Yeah. This and the long lost article on the Naked Soup Club. They were lying on the steps of *A Planet*. Probably fell out of his folder."

"Probably."

"I'll give them back to him tomorrow. I shouldn't have read this, I know, but…"

"He won't care, I don't think," I told her. Not true. He'd care, but he wouldn't let it show. Not to Rhonda. "I'm sure he'd like it back, though."

"It just saddens me, really, that much talented being wasted at the *A Planet*."

"Honestly, I think the Arbiter prefers it that way…for now. He's got bigger plans."

Rhonda smiled. "I hope he does. I always knew he could write, but when he really cares about his subject…I hope that one day he'll be able to write something like this for me."

I cringed. "Believe me, Rhonda. That's the last thing you want."

She looked at me quizzically, but something in my face must have stopped her from delving into my comment. Instead, she put the letter down on the end table next to Wall of Voodoo's *Happy Planet* CD, then turned back to me. "Are you ready?"

"Oh yeah," I replied with exaggerated enthusiasm. "An evening in the Eta Ups. Heaven. Pure, unadulterated, unexpurgated Heaven."

"You don't have it so bad," she said as she put on a dark green Lands End jacket. Rhonda owned no Floodbane College clothing; she wasn't much for free advertising—or school pride, for that matter. "You're not the one who has to pretend to like these people."

"I don't even have to pretend to be there," I explained. "That's the best part of being me, complete and total invisibility."

"I know a lot of criminals who'd love to be your roommate."

I smiled. "Me too. Although a less secure man might be uncomfortable with the thought."

"However, I have to disagree with your view of Heaven. Whereas I don't pretend to be an expert, most accounts I've read of Heaven portray it in a slightly different manner than that of the Eta Iota Upsilon house."

"Accounts?" I asked. "What accounts? Who's been there and come back? Are there travel logs? Captain's logs? Parchment maps to find the mysterious cocoa bean and detailed plans for placing smallpox on a blanket?"

"That's my point. If it were like the Eta Up house, don't you think more people would've fought their way back?"

"Can you do that? Can you escape from Heaven, crawling through the sewage pipes with your good clothes tied to your foot?"

"Why? Do you have friends on the inside?"

"I don't have friends anywhere. That, and I really don't think I'll be joining you guys in Heaven."

"That's a morbid thought."

"It is if you consider Heaven the place to be."

"It's not?"

"Nope."

"Then where?"

"I don't know. Chuck E. Cheese perhaps?"

"With all those robots and kids running around whacking moles? Are you kidding me?"

"Bless the beasts and the children."

Rhonda laughed. "You really don't like God, do you?"

"Okay, here's God's problem. Perfect example; the avenger of blood. You familiar with him?"

"I know that an avenger was mentioned in a few chapters of the Old Testament. Mainly throughout Deuteronomy, I believe."

"I don't know. I just know that God told all those Moses guys that, when they were setting up the cities, some of them should be declared havens from the avenger of the blood. If a man killed somebody, he could hide in these cities and be safe until he was brought to trial. Like an early witness protection program."

"And you want these cities set up again? Do you want people to be able to murder someone and then go have a beer in Memphis?"

"No, I want the avenger of blood again! God's not getting the job done anymore! He's slacking! People are getting away with far too much down here. Decent people have to suffer because God's letting the morons do whatever they want without fear of repercussion. So they'll spend eternity in Hell. Big deal. Obviously, that threat doesn't work. You can't discipline people with abstract concepts. And if people aren't being disciplined, they'll do whatever they want. And it's not even just people committing obvious crimes. It's the way people treat one another and even themselves, justifying it with cliches like, 'Only God has the right to judge me.'

"Well, do you know what? God isn't judging them anymore. He's letting them get away with everything, and Jesus doesn't even come into the picture until after death. So the drug dealer spends an eternity in Hell. Fat lot of good that does the families of all the addicts he created."

"So you're saying we'd all be better off if God were to return to His jealous, vengeful ways?"

"I'm saying that He's God, and He alone has the power to dish out the swift and brutal punishment that so many people on this planet deserve. If He's going to judge us for our actions, why not do it immediately after the action? Maybe then we'd actually learn something."

"I think you're overestimating the power of punishment," Rhonda pointed out. "If you look at the Old Testament, even with the avengers of blood and God's swift retaliation, people were still cruel to one another. The moment a new generation came up, they'd forget all of God's blessings and go right back to being sinners. God could impale the bodies of sinners in the town square and light them afire so the air was thick with the acrid smell of burning flesh and do you know what? We still wouldn't learn anything.

"God realized this, so He adopted a 'hands off' policy. Is it working? I'd like to believe. It may not seem so, but people learn. We may need to have the lesson pounded over and over again into our skulls, but we learn. Every classroom has troublemakers who may hold up the lesson, but there is always going to be a girl in the front row who suddenly understands, and she'll take that lesson with her, hopefully teach it to someone else.

"I can't say if this approach is working for God, but I sure do prefer it. I'd much rather think that people with evil hearts can be converted by a Man who died for us 2,000 years ago. That's such a romantic notion, and naive as it may be, I'd like to hold on to it."

I sighed. She was right, after all. It *was* a romantic notion. And like most romantic notions, it was also an impossibility. I knew that, and perhaps she did too. But faith and hope are powerful, and for some people are enough to carry them through life.

Everyone else, however, needs an avenger of blood.

The argument ended at that point, with both of us sticking firmly to our beliefs just as we had out on the football field that night after the fight at Panthemom's.

I offered her my arm once we were finally ready to leave. She took it, thanked me, and I then rammed the outside of my thigh into the handrail as we started down the stairs. It hurt, but we both laughed as I sat to rub it down. I hoped I wouldn't acquire a limp, since that would draw attention to me at the party. Or worse yet, I hoped our laughter hadn't just attracted the attention of…

"What the fuck's all that about?" shouted a voice from below us. Within seconds, a door opened and shut, and the silhouette of Jayson Fayme was framed in Rhonda's doorway.

She and I both stopped laughing.

"Where are you goin' tonight?" Jayson asked.

"Fayme? I'm sorry. I just really don't want to tell you," Rhonda replied. "It's not that it's a big secret, or some kind of plot against you; it's just that I really see no reason for—"

"Bath house?"

Rhonda and I just stared. We tended to do quite a bit of that when talking with Jayson. I honestly am not sure if it was me or her, but one of us said, "Huh?"

"You *are* going to a bath house," Jayson concluded, putting his hand over his mouth as would a third grader who'd just caught a sibling sneaking a cookie. "You two are like some kind of fucking sex maniac! I mean, I hear you two screaming and moaning up there all the time, but I didn't think you'd get into orgies with all the queers at the public bath. Let me just tell you this, Rhonda Vorhees, I knew you had it in you; I could tell by the way you stare at my ass when I'm not looking. But Arbiter, I wouldn't have…I guess that's how you got the nickname 'Bite.'"

"What are you talking about?" Rhonda asked, shaking her head with each syllable. I chose not to say anything, since he apparently couldn't see us well enough to realize Rhonda wasn't with the Arbiter tonight. Why give him more about which to talk?

"I'm talking about the dirty bath house you're going to."

Rhonda walked further down the steps until she was only about three feet from Fayme. She then talked to him in calm, soothing tones, as if trying to get him to just hand her the gun and release all the hostages. "Jayson, listen. We're at Floodbane College, not in Osaka, Japan. We have dorms here. We have classrooms. We have a library and a natatorium. What we don't have, you see, is a public bath."

"Hey, you believe what you want to, and I'll believe what I see with my own two things," Fayme smiled as if knowing of an underground public bath made him superior to us.

"Thank you, I will," Rhonda smiled. She then turned back to me. "Let's go, Guy."

"Guy?" Jayson repeated. I walked down the steps and into his view. I didn't say anything, and Fayme just stared at me as I walked by—his mouth agape.

"Holy shit," he claimed after Rhonda and I were at least ten feet past him. Rhonda and I kept moving, hoping that would be the end of it. But it wasn't. With Fayme, that was never the end of it. He apparently was having trouble coming up with another of his witticisms, and finally settled with, "Holy shit," only louder this time.

Afraid he was going to follow us, Rhonda turned around. "Oh, what?"

"Nothing," he lied, then added, "I just can't picture Guy at the bath house. I had more respect for you than that."

"You did?" I asked.

"No," Fayme laughed. "I was lying!"

Unlike the Arbiter, I wasn't that good at dealing with such conversations. I guess I'm too easily baffled by the incomprehensible.

"Does the Arbiter know you two are bumping uglies?" Fayme continued.

"Bumping what?" Rhonda asked.

"Bumping uglies." Fayme repeated with a pelvic thrust, managing to come off as condescending with the phrase. Amazing. Most people need at least a full sentence for that.

But I wasn't about to reward him by turning this into a conversation. "I've heard of them. They're my favorite country/western comedy duo."

"…Who?" Fayme asked.

"Bump and Ugly!"

"I love them too!" Rhonda chimed. "They're those puppets, right? The ones with the big mouths?"

"Yeah. They had a hit song a couple years back…some novelty song; it was always on the radio…Irlene Mandrel played drums…shoot, what was it called?"

"Public Bath," Rhonda offered.

Fayme was starting to feel left out. "I loved that song. We played it down there all the time."

"I bet you did," Rhonda said, rolling her eyes. She then took my hand. "Let's go, Guy. I want to get this over with."

"Okay, I'll see you guys later," Fayme warned us. He then walked back into his apartment, allowing the screen door to slam shut behind him. See us later? Not likely.

I was oddly happy for a moment, and it took a second for me to realize why. Jayson had believed that Rhonda and I were a couple. He had actually placed us together, and although it was just Fayme, it pleased me. For the first time in my life, I knew what it was like to feel the pride of being with a beautiful woman…and to have her hold my hand. Damn, brother she was holding my hand. It felt good, and I started to hope people at the party would see us the same way Jayson did.

Rhonda and I didn't speak for a bit as we walked down her street. Her silence soon forced me to concentrate on other things, like the sky ahead of us. Clouds were rolling in heavy and thick, making the twilight darker than normal. The setting sun was struggling to offer a pleasant display of color, but these clouds would have none if it. They took nature's normally beautiful exhibition of over-saturated reds, yellows and oranges and beat them into a big black, blue and purple bruise on the forearm of the heavens.

I was about to point this out to Rhonda, when she spoke. "I just don't like Jayson."

I laughed. "And I don't like world famine or the number 17. Them's the breaks."

"I'm serious," Rhonda scolded. "I know you and Arby find him amusing, but I don't. He annoys me."

"He annoys everyone."

"Yes, but I'm not annoyed by his mannerisms. He's just a vulgar Jerry Lewis in that aspect. I'm annoyed by the fear he causes me. I just know that any day now he's going to climb the bell tower and start picking off coeds one by one."

There was something in her voice that I'd heard before. I recognized it immediately, if only because it was the second time I'd ever heard it; need. That night, Rhonda needed me. Not in a "damsel in distress" way. Not in a "weak vs. the strong way." But just in a "hear my concerns and understand them" way. And it may be selfish, but it made me feel good. Frightened by the responsibility, but good. Better than even Jayson's misunderstanding of our relationship. I only hoped that this time I'd do a better job of playing the role of comforter and protector.

"I still say there's nothing to fear about Jayson Fayme, but then there's usually nothing to fear about the dark, either. I guess I understand. Just forget about Fayme and let me and the Arbiter watch the bell towers for you.

"With Jerry Lewis, however, you're on your own. That sumbitch is bonkers."

Rhonda smiled as she gently squeezed my hand. Was it her touch that sent the shiver up my spine, or was it the chill of the wind as it swept over us?

CHAPTER 11

The Doppler Effect

I'm not sure when I realized I was no longer holding *The Monster at the End of This Book*. My hands were gripping the bars of the TV antennae so tightly that the rusted metal was scraping into my palms. It burnt as if the circulation had been cut off and the blood was only now rushing back, but despite the discomfort, I wasn't letting go.

I'd like to think I had a good reason to climb that tower in the first place—whether it be to ensure Heath wasn't forcing himself on Ann, or even to still figure out what that pink light was. But those weren't the reason. Truth be known, I couldn't locate one for climbing the tower. Trying to was impossible. Thoughts and emotions were churning through my mind like piranhas in a feeding frenzy. I couldn't see them individually, only their boiling mess, but I was aware of what would be left behind.

My question about the light was answered the moment I looked in Ann's window. She had turned on the lava lamp that adorned her dresser at the foot of her bed. The liquid was clear, and the lava was purple. The combination of this and her salmon wallpaper gave the room an unnatural glow with an almost blurry edge—as if I were looking at it through onion leaf paper. Everything in the room appeared to be floating and morphing like the lava itself, objects melting into one another only briefly before splitting apart to join another's rhythmic pulse. I know I couldn't have been right, but it seemed the only stationary object in the room was Ann.

She and Heath were above the covers, affording me a .view of everything they were doing. The headboard of the bed was against the wall and beside the window through which I was looking, so Ann's head was no more than three feet away from me. She was lying on her side, her back to Heath and her head turned down from my position, not that I was worried about them seeing me. They didn't seem too worried about their surroundings.

Ann was wearing only a sweater, underwear and socks, and I couldn't make out colors in the weird light of the lava lamp. Everything seemed a shade of pink. Heath was behind her, his stomach pressed into her back, and he appeared to be fully clothed. He had one arm under her neck, the hand reaching down the top of her sweater. The other arm came up her side to reach up the bottom. Against him, Ann was curled almost in the fetal position. Her eyes were shut and her mouth was open slightly, but her legs were clamped.

For the first time in my life, I was jealous of Heath. It never occurred to me before that I should envy him, even when I first saw him kiss Ann. I only hated him, because to envy him would've probably caused me to hate myself.

I still hated him, now more than ever, but I was jealous as well. As I watched him slip his hand closer to her panties, I could only pretend I was in his clothes right now, that it was me grinding against Ann's hips. Lord knows my body thought it was me. I was as erect as I assume Heath was.

Heath's mouth was hovering close to Ann's ear, and he was whispering something I couldn't quite discern. I think I heard the words "touch you," but I couldn't tell if it was a statement or a question. Either way, Ann turned her chin up to him, and Heath nuzzled his lips in her neck. She seemed to soften up at this, and her legs opened just a little. This was enough for Heath. He immediately moved his hand between her legs, albeit still over her underwear. It looked to me as if Ann tried to move away, but Heath used his arm under her sweater to pull her closer. Ann's legs clamped shut again, but this only applied more pressure to Heath's hand. Ann moaned again and began to move her hips with his fingers.

After a moment of this, Heath tried to reach under Ann's underwear. This was apparently too far. She reached for his hand and clearly stated, "I don't know, Heath. I'm not ready."

"Yes you are," Heath argued, not moving his hand.

"Please, Heath," Ann continued.

Heath moved his hand at this point, but only to grab hers. He slid it over her underwear and made her touch herself, saying, "Feel how wet you are. You're ready."

Heath started to use Ann's fingers on herself through her underwear. She didn't appear to be pulling away from him, but she didn't seem to be getting into it, either. I wasn't sure what to make of her actions, or of my reaction. I suddenly found myself back on the school bus, only this time as an observer. That night, I couldn't understand why no one came to help me until Ann finally stepped up to the plate. Now Ann was on the receiving end, so why wasn't I taking a couple practice swings? I didn't want to think it was fear of another pummeling from Heath, I didn't want to think it was any kind of voyeuristic inclination, but I knew it was both of those. It was the combination of those with my feverous hatred of Heath and my love for Ann. My love for Ann that was presently being beaten out of my chest with the force of a sledgehammer. The physical pain was sharper than the night Heath had nearly given me a concussion off a school bus for simply talking to his girlfriend. What would he do if he found out I'd been sneaking off to her house at night? And Ann...my God. How many nights did I lie awake dreaming of the scene that was now opening before me? As much as I didn't want it to be Heath in there, and as repulsed as I was by my state of arousal, I wasn't leaving. The emotions were too varied, too intense, leaving me numb, unaware of anything save for the sweat that moistened my neck and face and my breathing that was coming in spurts.

"You've touched yourself before, haven't you?" Heath asked as he continued to manipulate Ann's fingers.

She didn't reply.

"You like to do it, don't you." Heath stated this as fact, not as a question. "Don't you, Ann."

After a long pause, she finally breathed, "Yes."

Heath raised his head to look down at Ann, and I could see his pink face smiling. It was the same smile he shoved my way when I agreed to not narc him out for shooting me with the BB gun. It was his victory smile; his "You stupid morons can all kiss my shiny ass" smile. Through it, he added, "When you're touching yourself, you think of me.

"You wished that I was there with you, didn't you Ann," Heath continued. "You wished that it was me with you instead of just you."

"Yes, Heath," Ann moaned. "I wanted it to be you."

That was enough for Heath. He pulled Ann's hand away, rolled her onto her stomach, then slid her underwear down her legs. She raised them slightly to assist him, and he kissed the small of her back and tops of her thighs and he pulled them off. He then rolled her back over and kissed her on the stomach, lightly at first, but then with more power. He roughly manipulated her breasts as he did so, then looked up at her with that smile again. If he wanted to, he could have easily seen me in the window. I didn't move. Maybe I wanted him to see me, or maybe I couldn't stop watching. I don't know. I don't think I want to.

Ann was now looking away from him, up towards a corner of the ceiling. I found myself hoping her thoughts were somewhere else; that she was thinking of that lava lamp or snow peas or the cross-face chicken wing, anything other than Heath and what he was about to do to her.

I may have been right. When Heath lifted himself atop her, she suddenly snapped out of her fantasy. "Heath, wait. What are you—"

"I want to feel myself inside of you," he said with emotion thick like sludge.

"Heath, please. Can't we just—"

"You've dreamed about this your whole life. Let it happen."

And she did. Caught up in the moment, with no one there to serve as the voice of reason, Ann succumbed to that rat bastard. And as she whispered a relenting, "Okay," the room lost its pink luster. It started to glow brighter as if it were nearing explosion. I felt I was watching footage of an atomic explosion, the blinding flash of light and the swelling of the cloud even before the sound could reach me. But no sound ever arrived. Quite the opposite, it seemed to roll away. I could no longer hear what Ann and Heath were saying. I couldn't even hear the wind or the amplified thump-thumping of my heart as in similar scenes in movies...or when confessing love for a girl amongst school buses at high school football games.

I knew this wasn't right. Yes, I loved Ann, but what was happening to me made no sense. I still had the wits to realize the room wasn't really about to explode. I knew the wind hadn't suddenly stopped blowing and that my heart hadn't...

Maybe it had. Maybe the blinding light was the tunnel of which so many people speak. I was dead; I was certain of it. To prove it to myself, I looked back into the light in Ann's room. But I was no longer there. I was no longer on the TV antennae. I hurriedly looked around to get my bearings, but all I could see were trees. I was lying on my back in some kind of wooded area, and Ann's house was nowhere in sight. I wasn't worried at all about where I was, but rather about how I got there. My inability to explain it caused me to fear that perhaps I *wasn't* dead; maybe I really was just losing my mind and that I'd never been to Ann's house in the first place. But then I looked at my hands, and in the puddles of moonlight that dripped through the trees, I could see blood on my palms. Like that of a drowned man, my skin was pale blue in the glow of the moon, and the blood was black against it.

Black and blue. How many times could Heath bruise me before this whole thing came to an end? I had no answer. I stood to look around. My hands ached as I pushed myself up, and I suddenly realized how badly they hurt. They were ringing as if I'd just smacked a metal pipe into a concrete wall…or perhaps someone's skull. I ran my fingers over my palms, causing them to sting more, but the blood didn't smear. It was already dry.

I could see no artificial light in any direction, only the ghostly highlights of the moon on the trees and leaves. I wondered if I'd blown my chance to get into the afterlife when I didn't walk into the light at the end of…Ann's bedroom.

The thought of her and Heath having sex hurriedly snapped me back to reality. I wasn't dead. I had no idea where I was, but I knew I wasn't dead. Was Heath? Is that why there was blood on my hands? *My God, that's why I can't remember*, I thought. *I killed somebody.*

I'm not sure what it says about me, but that thought didn't horrify me. I stared at the blood on my hands, envisioning them around Heath's throat. Or had I stabbed him? I pictured myself in the scene as if it were on TV, and we were all actors. I looked pretty good, if I must say so myself. I'm sure the murder would garner me no Peoples' Choice Awards, but I was after critical acclaim, not media success. Besides, I already had my reward; I'd finally beaten Heath. After being shamed and tossed about by him since grade school, I'd finally climbed back into the ring and pinned his proverbial shoulders to the metaphorical mat. 1…2…3!!!

The excitement and joy was too much, and I had to let everyone know. I had to shout from the rooftops…

❦   ❦   ❦

"Pull up your fuckin' pants!" some girl yelled from across the room. Rhonda and I turned to see what was going on, but our view was blocked by the hoard of cackling partiers who had gathered around the spectacle.

I still have no desire to ever get drunk. I can't imagine willingly consuming anything that would cause me to lose control of not only my basic motor skills, but my cognitive skills as well. I had spent over twenty years developing them, and—although some would certainly argue—I was quite proud of my progress. I had no desire to be an infant again, completely at the mercy of those around me. Yet others seemed to, and with alarming frequency.

Surely I'm not the only one startled by the number of phrases Americans have for getting drunk and/or its aftereffects, am I? Trashed, wasted and bombed are the three unimaginative terms that come to mind immediately, none of which are very flattering. The first two call to mind spoiled vegetables, dirty diapers or used lard, while the third makes me think of Dresden or Hiroshima. What gets me even more is the amount of pride people have in their ability and need to make asses of themselves, getting sick in the process. How many times have I heard people proudly proclaim, "Man, I got so fuckin' wasted last night! I puked in my roommates shoes!"

People don't brag about puking because they got food poisoning or couldn't handle that last ride on the Rotor at the county fair. I guess they feel that drinking all that tequila and doing shooters means they've earned the right to be sick. It's an accomplishment; a goal to which we all should aspire.

At the Eta Iota Upsilon party that night, some guy was about to reach greatness. Despite the early hour, he had already become ine-briated enough to conclude that we all wanted to see his privates. Breaking through the crowd that had formed around him, the student stumbled his way across the living room of the sorority house and ran out the front door.

Perhaps "privates" was a poorly chosen term.

The crowd behind him laughed as they followed him outside, but I was struck by something else. As he passed, I caught the unmistakable spectral highlight of gleaming metal.

I turned to Rhonda. "Did he have—"

"I didn't need a face," Rhonda shuddered. "Dear Lord, I didn't need a face."

At least now I knew we were in the right place. I was now looking forward to what I'd turn up. This evening was going to be big.

As his adoring admirers flocked behind the naked, pierced guy, one woman stopped in front of me and Rhonda. According to her nametag, her name was Elizabeth. I had no reason to not trust it.

"Rhonda!" Elizabeth sang with the pep of a high school cheerleader; a position from which I'm sure she wasn't too far removed. "It's totally great to see you here again!"

"I've never been here before, Beth," Rhonda corrected.

"Elizabeth, please, thank you. Oh, come on; sure you have!" Elizabeth argued. "Everyone's been to the Eta Iota Upsilon house! We've totally got the highest GPA of all the sororities on campus!"

"That's great." Rhonda's acting was so good that I almost believed her smile was genuine. "Do guys always run around naked here?"

"Oh no, of course not," Elizabeth responded, still smiling. "We support three charity organizations."

"Which ones?" Rhonda continued to keep up that smile.

Elizabeth paused, looking at the painting behind us. It was a framed reproduction of those little cherub angels looking up at something. Rhonda and I both turned to follow Elizabeth's gaze, but were pulled back abruptly when she suddenly claimed, "Good ones. Ones that do good."

"I'm sure they are, Liz," Rhonda agreed, winking in my direction. First she held my hand, and then she winked at me. What a night! All it would take was a light kiss on the cheek and a, "I had fun tonight, I'll call you," and it would have been a date. A date with Rhonda.

"Elizabeth please thank you," Elizabeth corrected, snapping me out of my reverie. "That's a totally good thing for a charity to do...something good, I mean."

"Do you think so?" Rhonda asked.

"Yeah, we all thought so. We took a vote. That's why we chose them. Voting is very important here, since it's a good way to make sure we do what most people would do. Would you like anything to drink?"

"Yes, thank you, Liza. Can I get a Diet Dr. Pepper?"

"Elizabethpleasethankyou. I don't think so, but we do have a drink that totally tastes like Dr. Pepper. It's really cool because it catches on fire."

"Wouldn't that burn your lips?"

"Only when you forget to blow it out. Want one?"

"No thanks. Guy might, though."

"Who?" Elizabeth asked.

"My date," Rhonda explained as she turned to face me.

Elizabeth jumped as if I'd just sprung from the closet wearing a hockey mask. "My god, you scared me! How long have you been standing there?"

"About five mintues," I replied.

Elizabeth's chipper disposition suddenly soured. "How did you get in?"

"Through the front door."

"We are *so* going to get that checked." Elizabeth turned sternly to Rhonda. "If he's bothering you, we can call security."

"He's my date," Rhonda reiterated, a little slower this time. "Why don't you call security on the drunk who just exposed himself?"

"Because Albert's not causing any trouble."

"And Guy is?"

"It's no trouble, really," Elizabeth persisted, watching to ensure I made no sudden movements for a gun or my privates or something else equally deadly. "Security knows right where the house is. We're very proud of that aspect of our sisterhood. Other sororities have to give directions sometimes, so it takes a really long time for them to like get there. That, and our annual Ferrets for the Elderly Festival is just another reason you totally should consider pledging Eta Iota Upsilon." She stared me down throughout her entire sales pitch. Amazing.

"It's okay, really," Rhonda tried once more. "Thank you, though, Shirley."

"Elizabethpleasethankyou. I'll go get you that drink now." She turned to head off to the kitchen, but stopped abruptly and turned back to me. "I'll be watching you."

"Thank you," I said with a slight nod. "That's totally kind of you."

Elizabeth looked me over once more, glanced up at Rhonda, then headed back towards the kitchen. By this time, the naked guy's spectators had started to filter their way back into the house. I guess it's not surprising the naked guy wasn't with them. He was probably halfway to the town square by now, and would soon be sitting atop the statue of Andrew Jackson.

Frightening as it may seem, there's history behind that comment. Floodbane had a strict policy against hazing, but attempting to stop fraternal organizations from hazing is like attempting to shovel the driveway during a snowstorm. Upsilon Iota Eta was especially notorious for its hazing stunts, the most popular of which involved pledges posing naked behind Andrew Jackson atop his horse.

And they say homo-eroticism is dead. Viva le Fraternity!

Luckily, none of the other partiers seemed interested in talking to me and Rhonda. Most were divided between the kitchen (beer) and the living room (dancing and beer), and the rest seemed to take turns in the upstairs bedrooms with their partner. The occasional loud crash and laughter could be heard, which somewhat saddened me. Aside from the ugly and predictable decorations—mainly poorly framed, horribly shot photos of drunken sisters from parties past—the house was gorgeous. It was a huge Victorian structure with ceilings that seemed to reach into the third storey and flourishings adorning every inch of exposed wood. When newly married couples dream of their first home, they dream of the Eta Iota Upsilon Sorority house—minus the coeds and the pierced penis…hopefully. At that moment, however, the house was more suited to the dreams of a teenage male in health class.

As the crowd inside multiplied, I focused my attention back on Rhonda. That was always so easy to do. I could've been in the middle of the running of the bulls, less than five feet from a charging stag, and Rhonda still would've had my full attention. I couldn't help but think back to that night at Panthemom's when she showed the deftness and courage of a firefighter, shoving the Arbiter out of harm's way despite the obvious danger to herself.

I sometimes wonder why the Arbiter hadn't moved on his own. If Rhonda hadn't pushed him, he may have been cut up pretty badly. Did he know Rhonda would help, or did he just not care what would happen to himself? I never fully understood that, but if it didn't bother Rhonda, why should it bother me? Especially now that the Arbiter had left me alone with his girlfriend. It charged me the same way as that night on the football field when I rested my head on Rhonda's stomach.

Of course, with Rhonda, I got that charge whenever she looked at me. I don't want to say it was sexual, but then I also sometimes don't want to say that I have hair growing on my shoulders. One can't change truth, one can only shave it.

I have no doubt that Rhonda knew of my growing attraction to her, just as the Arbiter must've. Hell, who wasn't attracted to her? But she knew as I did I wasn't about to act upon it. What she didn't know were the reasons why. I'm not even sure if I knew the reasons, although I could certainly harbor a well educated guess. But it almost felt good to be attracted to someone and not have the pressure of ever having to do anything about. It was liberating. If only my attraction to Ann had been the same, I wouldn't have ended up killing somebody.

As much as I wanted to keep the curtain open on this evening, I knew the Arbiter was eagerly awaiting his report. I turned to Rhonda and asked if I should begin my mission.

"Probably," she replied. "I don't want to spend any more time here than is absolutely necessary."

"What, with all these naked men and flaming Dr. Peppers around?" I joked.

Rhonda smiled.

"Are you coming with me to help look?"

She shook her head. "I'd better stay down here. There's less chance of us getting caught if I watch your back. Plus, now that I'm Elizabethpleasethankyou's new best friend, I can maybe get some information on this end. If so, I'll come find you."

"Okay. I'll try to make this quick. I'm afraid that if I take too long these women will brainwash you into actually pledging."

"Oh, good Lord," Rhonda laughed. "I'd just as soon kill myself."

"I thought you Christians aren't allowed to do that," I smiled.

"Of course we can. We can do whatever we want; we just know that we have to suffer the consequences. Anyway, I'll be down here if...here comes Elizabeth."

I turned to see that Elizabeth was approaching with two flaming drinks in her hands. She was smiling as she approached and handed one of them to Rhonda.

"We were all out of the stuff to make those drinks that taste like Dr. Pepper, so I just added something to a real Dr. Pepper and lit it on fire. Make sure you blow it out first."

"Thanks. That's lovely, Elizabeth," Rhonda said as she took the drink, "but I think I'll let it cook some more."

"I see that creepy guy that was harassing you finally left."

I wasn't standing more than two feet from Rhonda, and she turned to me to point that out. Elizabeth didn't seem to notice, so Rhonda smiled and nodded for me to get started. I smiled back, and I swear to God I almost kissed her. The opportunity seemed so right, the kind they show on TV where the guy doesn't kiss the girl and I just think, "What an ass, how could he have blown that?"

I don't know if I really blew anything at that moment. Kissing Rhonda would've been disastrous to my friendship with both her and the Arbiter, but it would've somehow saved...I still don't like to think about it.

I reluctantly turned away from Rhonda and headed upstairs. The last words I heard before reaching the second floor were, "Ow, shit! I have totally got to stop forgetting to blow these things out."

The stairwell opened into a hallway adorned with murals of sorority sisters past. Many years were missing, the earliest I could find was 1939. I seem to recall that the sorority itself was much older than that. As I scanned the cracked, fading gray images of the Eta Iota Epsilon alumni, I couldn't help but think two things; most of these women are dead, and I wonder if any of them ever posed naked.

There were six doors leading out of the hallway, only one of which—the restroom—was open. There was some guy in there slumped over the toilet, rolling his head across the seat. I was pretty amazed he'd been able to get that drunk already and was thankful I wouldn't have to listen to him brag the next day. There certainly are benefits to being a loner.

Looking back down the stairwell, I tried to get my bearings. The Arbiter and I had seen the flash bulbs popping in one room only, so I needed to concern myself with just that room. Making a guess as to the layouts of the house, I headed left. From what I figured, there were two possibilities; the door directly in front of me at the end of hall or the one just to the right of that. I put my ear up against the door on the right, but couldn't hear anything over the music pounding its way up from downstairs. It was Jimmy Buffet singing about a cheeseburger or a peachy lean muffin or some other nonsense. I wondered what that must be like, being able to make a living singing about fast food. Poets used to find inspiration in nature and God and love. Jimmy Buffet found it in ketchup and tropical drinks. Nice.

Wanting to get this over with and join Rhonda downstairs, I opened the door. Someone walked upstairs just as I did, and I paused momentarily to see if I'd be caught. It was the pierced guy—who had only gotten so far as to put his underwear back on—and one of the sorority sisters. They were equally drunk. The couple started my way, but I just stood there with the door cracked open. They wouldn't notice me, of course, unless they ran into me.

Which they did.

"Wha' the fuck?" slurred the guy. "Sorry, man. I di'n see you."

"No problem," I said.

"You usin' this room?" he asked.

"Yeah," I smiled. "My girlfriend's already inside."

"She startin' wi'hout you?" the guy asked, much to the delight of the woman with him. They both laughed hysterically, then she fell down. And stayed down.

"Fuck!" the guy yelled. He didn't try to help her back up. "I can't fuck if she's cunconsience."

"I'm sorry, if she's what?" I asked.

"That's date rape. I arspect women tooooooooo mush to do that shit," he declared, pounding his fist into the wall to emphasize "mush."

"You're very noble."

"You really sink so?"

"Yes, I really sink so."

"You're the bess, man. I know I don' say this often, but you're the bess brother a guy ever had. You my dog! You my fo-fuckin' dog! We all 'bout...just...dogs."

"Thanks."

"No, I mean it. Sorry for bustin' a light on your bike when we's kids. I used a pull some wrong-ass shit."

"You're forgiven."

The guy gave me a look like he was going to try to kiss me, but then turned to look back at the woman unconscious on the floor. She had fallen with her back to the wall, and was drooling on her shirt. "Damn! I really wanned to take her to Boneville."

"Where?"

"Why's she just all layin' there like that?"

"Well, if I could hazard a guess, I'd say she's drunk."

"No shit, I can see that…but why's she so drunk?"

"Could be that she's spent the night drinking like a fish in water."

The guy turned to me, puzzled. "Did Chrissian warriors drink a lot?"

Now I was confused. "Who?"

"Damn, I wan be a Chrissian warrior."

"Marching as to war?"

"Don' matter. I do' wanna know marsh…wear…marshing what?"

"It was a—"

"Listen me a goddam minute, will ya? This is 'portant. All I know is I do' even wanna fuck her anymore. She's a goddam mess."

"Yeah."

"Funny how you don' wanna fuck a shick what has spit all over her shirt."

"Yeah. Funny."

"Goddam, I'm horny. I need another beer."

"Get me one, too!" yelled some guy from inside the room I had been about to enter. "Bud!"

"No prob, Steve," the pierced guy called back, and then he turned to stumble his way back downstairs. Realizing I wouldn't be finding anything in that room for the moment, I closed the door and went up to the one at the end of the hall. Hoping these beds were empty, I stepped inside before anyone else could see me. I groped for the light and turned it on.

The room was large, containing three normal beds and one Floodbane College standard-issue bunk bed. Despite the three large dressers sitting against the walls, the floor and furniture were covered with clothing, including a wild array of "unmentionables." I couldn't see any camera equipment, but I wouldn't figure they'd just leave it lying around. Despite the mess, one corner at the far end was completely cleared out. No desk, no bed, nothing. Just an empty space with a blank wall.

I'd found the studio.

There were two computers in the room, both of which were PCs. I chose the one nearest to the window, and fired it up. As it started to load, I went back to the door to shut off the lights; I didn't want anyone outside to see I was in there. By the time I got back to the desk, the computer had already locked up.

Well, that makes my job a little easier, I thought as I turned on the other computer. This one started okay, but it was password protected. Before I could even begin to think of possibilities, I noticed a pink Post-It™ note on the monitor that read, "Password: EIURewlz."

Nobody's that stupid, I thought, but I was wrong. They were that stupid. The password worked.

I immediately launched Windows Explorer and did a search for "*.jpg." The list it brought up was far too large to cycle through, so I started a manual search of folders on the hard drive, hoping to find a folder called something like "My Pornography," I guess. It wasn't there, of course, but then a thought occurred to me. If I were uploading illegal porn on the internet from a room shared by at least four other girls, I certainly wouldn't keep that porn on my computer. I could see in Explorer that the computer was also on the campus network, so I was quite certain I would be finding no evidence on the hard drive.

There were quite a few CDs scattered about the desk, none of which appeared to be writable. I was about to start rifling through the drawers when I got an idea to verify if I even had the correct computer. After looking through the Start Menu for a moment, I found a program called CuteFTP, which I cleverly deduced to be an FTP program, software used to transfer files between locations. I launched it and did a quick survey of the domains that had been listed. I could see nothing for either the sorority or Floodbane, but another name caught my eye.

"**douglas.com**"

I double clicked on the folder, and CuteFTP connected me to the Floodbane Server. Within seconds I was looking at a folder containing jpegs with titles such as "bigboob3.jpg," "butshot.jpg" and "preslez8.jpg." Following the hierarchy revealed that the smut was in a folder called "bovary" three subfolders deep in a bogus English department section. No wonder the network administrator hadn't found this stuff; who'd go looking in there?

To the left of the network window was the source information, which only indicated that the files had been uploaded from the D:\ drive and that the disk was currently not present. I finally smiled at my success, but then had another thought. After poking around CuteFTP a bit more, I managed to find the menu for setting file permissions online. I checked the read, write and execute permissions on a few pictures, and found they had all been shut off, even the readables. This meant that currently no one could view the pictures online. Why?

I was into this now. I was suddenly Columbo, calmly and coolly solving the crime and restoring peace and justice to the world. I was proud of myself, and I wished that Rhonda was up there with me.

My thoughts of her took me back to the evening after the Panthemom's incident, the evening we spent on the football field of the Floodbane College…what were they at that point? The Potato Famine? The Fire Gods? The Allman Brothers? I get so confused.

We were lying like tiles in a Scrabble game, my head on Rhonda's stomach, hers on the Arbiter's for a double word score. He was stroking her hair, which he often did in such scenarios. Rhonda had told the Arbiter a couple times how much she liked when he did that, and he was happy to oblige. However, Rhonda was not touching my hair. That was probably for the best, as the grease trouble I had in high school had only grown worse. I greatly looked forward to the day when I could shave it off and just not be bothered with it anymore.

Surprisingly, we weren't talking about Rhonda's "stabbing" at Panthemom's earlier that evening. We were instead magnifying fear that at least Rhonda and I had felt. She was, after all, the one who asked of us, "Okay, what's the scariest thing that could happen right now?"

I heard her okay, but for some reason I needed to hear the question again. "What?"

"Look around. What's the scariest thing that could happen to us at this moment, in this situation?"

I raised my head, as did Rhonda, so we were now sitting upright in the center of football the field. The Arbiter had merely propped himself on his elbows. Had he a long blade of grass in his mouth, he would've looked like some kind of country bumpkin on *The Beverly Hillbillies* or another similar show. The grass was damp beneath us, and a cool breeze blew across the field. The stadium looked somewhat eerie in its emptiness and echoed the chatter of the insects who shared the field with us. It made me wonder how many grasshoppers or katydids had died senselessly, trampled under the cleats of men as they defended their goal line from the enemy's onslaught.

What if they were to rise up against us, those katydids? What if they were to decide they'd had enough? Scary enough for Rhonda's game, but then I scanned the area about me. The various floodlights from the stands and the surrounding park area cast solid shadows across the bleachers as if purposely hiding from us certain areas. It was from these areas that I drew my inspiration.

"I don't know. Like maybe a pack of wild dogs would come charging out of the corner over there and attack us."

"Your biggest fear in life is of dogs?" the Arbiter asked.

"No, I was just trying to think of something that could attack from that corner over there where the concession stand is." I pointed to an area in the shadows. "Dogs were all I could come up with. Other than katydids, I mean."

"So then actually your greatest fear in life is of concession stands," the Arbiter corrected himself.

I laughed. "Ever had them nachos? That cheese, it's scary, scary stuff."

"Take the salsa! Take the salsa! For God's sake, take the Salsa!" the Arbiter screamed. It seemed to be a reference to something, but Heaven only knows what.

"I think it'd be more frightening if the nacho cheese were to attack," Rhonda added.

"Like in *The Blob?*" I asked.

"Yeah, only *The Blob* wouldn't go as well with broccoli," the Arbiter suggested. "Found that most '60s horror movies don't so much. Too runny. Texture's all wrong. But mix *Earth vs. the Spider* with a nice hollandaise, now there's a meal."

Rhonda laughed lightly. "You know what's odd about those '60s horror movies? They used to terrify my brother. He could watch anything else, wander through our woods at night, rush headlong into those campy haunted houses at Halloween—but show him *The Blob* or *The Tingler* and he'd have to sleep in my room."

I was taken by this. "I didn't know you have a brother. How could I know you this long and never hear about him."

"'Cause apparently he was a wuss," the Arbiter claimed, somewhat rudely, I thought. "Would you speak about a brother afraid of *The Blob?*"

Rhonda ignored the Arbiter. "My brother's name was Wes. That's what we all called him, anyway. He died when I was seven."

"Oh, I'm sorry." I was embarrassed, but my morbid curiosity again took over. "Not to seem rude, but can I ask how he died?"

"So many people ask me that, it's weird," Rhonda pointed out. "I guess that's just what most people find interesting about the matter."

"No, I mean, I feel bad for you, but—"

"It's okay. It was a long time ago, but do you know, I don't tell people how he died. I don't want the most interesting thing about Wes to be the method of his death. It doesn't matter to me anyway. I'm still sad sometimes that he's gone, there's so much about living right now that I know he would've loved, but how he died is so completely unimportant."

"That's only because he wasn't eaten alive by sharks," the Arbiter suggested.

"Of course, the sharks," Rhonda laughed with a trace of guilt. "Had he been eaten by sharks I would've had T-shirts made."

"Yeah, something like, 'My brother was eaten by a shark and all I got was this lousy T-shirt,'" I offered.

"Or, 'One girl's brother is another shark's chum,'" joked the Arbiter.

Rhonda face twisted in the most wonderful way as she looked at the Arbiter in disbelief. I really didn't understand these two. At times, the Arbiter seemed so completely insensitive to Rhonda's feelings, and other times he could show more compassion than an elderly woman for a child with a really bad cold. And what's more, Rhonda never objected either way. The Arbiter apparently knew her so well that he could take chances with jokes that would've landed him a few month's worth of sensitivity training were he in the work force. "'Another shark's chum?'"

"Yes, chum. They use it to—"

"I know what chum is," Rhonda interrupted as if offended, "I just haven't heard anyone use it to describe a friend since *Batman* back in the '60s."

"Hey yeah, *Batman*," the Arbiter smiled. "How do you suppose he'd go with a nice cheese sauce. A Batman fondu."

"Isn't that the dance he did in one of the episodes? The Batman Fondu?" I asked, standing to do the "Batusi." Rhonda actually looked around to see if she should be embarrassed for me, while the Arbiter just shook his head.

"Wouldn't know. Never seen the show."

"You've never seen *Batman*?" Rhonda couldn't believe it.

"You can watch a few episodes, you know. Liberace's dead," I suggested. "A couple others, too. Cesar Romero…"

The Arbiter didn't say anything, he didn't even move, and I immediately realized my error. Yes, he knew I was aware of his habits, but Rhonda was not. For his privacy, and more importantly my own well being, I was really hoping she'd missed it.

"Wait, what?" Rhonda asked. "What does that have to do with anything?"

No such luck.

I was hoping the Arbiter would cover my goof, but he was making no indication. I assume he just didn't want to lie to her. Knowing a pause would only add to the importance of what I said, I tossed out the first explanation that came to mind. "That's how I decide everything these days."

"How?"

"Liberace's death," I continued. "You know, 'Are you going to watch the game tonight?' 'Don't think so. Liberace's dead,' or 'Hey, Guy, what would you like for supper?' 'Let's see…I had a sandwich for lunch, and Liberace's dead, so I think I'll go with the hearty beef ragout.'"

Rhonda paused. "You are so weird."

"You don't know the half of it," I smiled.

"Okay then, what's weirder than that?" Rhonda asked. "What best exemplifies your freakishness?"

"I thought we were talking about the scariest thing that could happen to us," I reminded her, but she was having none of it.

"That topic ended days ago. Now I just want you to tell me what's the weirdest thing you've ever done."

"Good Lord, can't we ever just talk about the movies like normal people?"

"Normal people?" the Arbiter chimed in. "Normal people talk about how much they enjoy movies about talking pigs. Had a man once tell me that a talking pig movie taught him how to be human. You call that normal?! Learnin' 'bout humanity from a friggin' talkin' pig?! You can't learn how to be human from a talkin' pig, you can only learn how to be a talking pig!!"

"What are you talking about?" Rhonda asked.

"Pig talkin' lovin' talkin' pig moron!" the Arbiter exploded one last time. He then turned calmly to Rhonda. "I really don't know. I just suddenly felt all this anger locked up inside of me, like it's been building up for about eighteen years, the compression getting heavier and tighter, squeezing my soul, smashing my very being, until it just now had to burst its way out of me in a fiery explosion of confusion and hostility."

"And that was it?" I asked. "Seventeen years of pent up anger became a tiny rant about a talking pig?"

"Don't underestimate the nefarious evil of a talking pig movie," the Arbiter warned. "Besides, wanted to hurry up and hear what you think is weird about yourself."

"Well, I'm sorry to have diminished your moment of self knowledge."

"That's okay," the Arbiter forgave me. "Your obvious lack of interest in those around you has already become the foundation for the next explosion."

"I hope I can be there," Rhonda requested. "In the meantime, get on with it, Guy."

"Okay, the weirdest thing about me. Well, having no time to think, I'd have to say that it's…I'll say it's probably that, when I was in junior high or high school, yeah, I think high school, I used to wrap Twinkies in cheese and dip them in ketchup."

There was silence.

"Why?" the Arbiter finally asked.

"To eat," I explained, adding a resonant "Duh!" in my mind only.

"Oh, thought maybe it was for a science project or some kind of abstract art class."

"Twinkie art? I suppose there's a calling for that."

"Hey, if people buy photos of babies dressed up like bees and flowers and cabbage, they'll buy Twinkie art."

"Do people really buy photos of babies dressed up like bees?" I asked.

"Sure do," the Arbiter replied. "Can't seem to get enough of them bee babies. Calendars, posters, greeting cards…put a little hat and some wings on a baby and you've got yourself a licensing machine. Ain't nothin' sells easier, except for maybe lesbian porn."

"Okay," Rhonda interrupted, "I don't think I want to hear about how you acquired that knowledge. Why don't you instead tell us what's the weirdest thing you've ever done."

"Because I've never done anything weird," the Arbiter told her.

Rhonda laughed heartily. "By who's standards?"

"I'm actually the bastion of normalcy," the Arbiter continued. "There's nothing weird about me at all."

"Please," Rhonda laughed.

"It's true. It's documented."

I remained silent through all of this. Radio towers? Letters to dead actors? Did the Arbiter really consider this normal behavior or was he just playing his game.

"Come on, there must be something," Rhonda persisted. She reached over to squeeze the Arbiter on his side, just where his ribcage ends. He immediately jumped away from her touch and tried to suppress a laugh. The Arbiter, ticklish. I would've never guessed. I had to smile at the tenderness of the scene.

"Okay, well, if only to quell the uprising, I once bought personalized license plates."

"That's weird?" Rhonda asked.

"Yeah, a lot of people do that," I seconded. "That how I know when I'm behind 'MS MATH' or 'BLK BEU T.'"

"Like the horse?"

"I never saw her face, so I can't really say."

"Well, there's the submission. Personalized license plate. Take it or leave it."

"What did it say?" Rhonda asked. "'ARBITER 1?' '4 RHONDA?'"

"'AGP 7472.'"

I thought about it for a moment, but had to ask, "What's it stand for?"

"Nothing," the Arbiter replied. "Random collection of letters and numbers."

"Wait," Rhonda ordered. "You paid the money for a personalized license plate but didn't come up with anything personal? Can I ask why?"

"I couldn't come up with anything clever," he told her. "Besides, random letters and numbers are much harder for the cops to remember than 'WALKAWAY' or whatever."

"So if you weren't going to get a personalized license plate, why bother getting one?" I asked.

"'Cause they're super cool!" the Arbiter barked, raising both thumbs in the air, and I could tell that in his mind he was spelling "cool" k-e-w-l.

"Sometimes you make absolutely no sense to me," Rhonda said as she rubbed his forearm.

"That's not the worst of it," the Arbiter smiled.

I chose to play the set-up. "What could be freakier than buying a nonsensical personalized license plate?"

"I didn't own a car."

Is this thing on, ladies and gentlemen?

Rhonda sighed heavily. "I wish my mother had warned me about guys such as you."

"About what type of guys did she warn you?" the Arbiter asked.

She smiled slyly at me. "The shy, quiet types."

It took me a minute to realize she was talking about me. "Hey, wait, I'm neither shy nor quiet."

"He's right," the Arbiter agreed.

"Thank you."

"He's reclusive and despondent."

"Much more accurate, yes," I agreed.

"Well, whatever," Rhonda laughed. "I'm not the one to make that judgment."

"Actually, if anyone, I'd prefer it be you," I told her.

"Oh, no, I don't care to have that job, thank you," Rhonda refused with a shake of her head. Her hair bounced lightly as she did so. It made me wish she were my daughter so I could take a picture of her and show it off to the guys at the factory. "I'm not qualified."

"Who is? And don't even tell me Jesus," I warned her.

"Well, yeah, now that Liberace's dead," the Arbiter interrupted. "Jesus is all who's left."

"If Jesus is the only person allowed to judge me, then why do so many of His followers do it for Him?" I asked.

"They're fools," Rhonda said. "If I may make this argument easier than it should be, there are two types of Christians in the world. There are loving Christians, and there are hateful Christians. Some of us like to believe we've learned from the words Jesus taught. We try to follow His example and to be good people, and we accept the faults in others because we know that we have faults ourselves. That's the reason Jesus was sent to us, after all, and the reason He died for us.

"But other people…rather than follow Jesus, they try to become Him. Rather than try to gently guide people down His path, they blindfold them and shove them. They use the teachings of Christ only to further their agendas. Despite the fact that God gave us the ability to make our own choices, and that He sent His son to forgive us when we make the wrong choice, some Christians want to remove that. They want to deny us a freedom given to us by God, the freedom to be wrong sometimes, in essence making them more powerful than God."

"So if it's not what God or Jesus wants, then why do They allow it?"

"Because people change, Guy, it's that simple. Because people can learn, and they can grow. God knows this. He gave us that ability. And no matter what we've done in the past, we *can* make amends. That's why we can't judge people. Although I may know what you've done, I can't know what you might one day do.

"So when people judge you, Guy, it's only because they're on some kind of power trip, not because Jesus wants them to."

"Either that, or because it's just funny," the Arbiter said, "because you are one freaky, talkin'-pig-lovin' motherfucker."

I laughed out loud upon recalling the Arbiter's comment, but immediately suppressed it. The last thing I needed in the Eta Iota Upsilon bedroom was to be caught because of one of the Arbiter's jokes. His mission failed because of his own joke? He wouldn't have been able to live with himself. It wasn't even that funny.

Getting back to my mission, I opened a drawer to my right and started looking around for the Zip disks that would hopefully contain the porn. Not in that drawer. I opened a cabinet in the hutch above the particle board desk, but nothing but old papers and nudity-free photos of sorority parties long past. *Come on, Guy, what would Columbo do?* I asked myself. *What would Columbo ask himself?* And then it hit me. *Columbo would ask himself—*

❧   ❧   ❧

What the hell are you doing? I kept asking myself. I didn't expect to come up with an answer, but I had to keep my mind working on something, anything, to distract me from the fact that there was no way I'd be able to beat the train.

I can't say exactly what led me to that point. I'd like to think it was the guilt of having killed somebody, but I knew that wasn't the case. I felt no guilt for what I'd done to Heath, only that I hadn't done it sooner, before he had the chance to violate Ann.

That was the reason. It was Ann. Our relationship would never be the same now that she'd had sex with Heath. I could no longer be the guy she turned to with fears about the first time or questions on where her relationship with Heath would lead. It's not that I enjoyed those conversations, no guy likes to be the "supportive friend." Right after the sucking and gripping reflexes, it's the first thing newborn males understand; showing a woman that you care for her feelings while she's in love with someone else opens no doors. So knowing this, why did I so readily accept the role with Ann? Simple; it at least gave her a reason to talk to me. Now, this reason was gone, those fears of her first time had all been allayed.

Considering the fact that I, the supportive friend, had killed the very need for my support, I'd say it was a safe bet Ann would never speak to me again. I could be wrong, but I was always under the impression that women don't speak to those who kill their boyfriends...unless the killer has a really nice ass, of course.

It wouldn't matter with me, though. In a few moments, chances were that I wouldn't even have an ass, it being scattered across the countryside along with the rest of myself and my mother's car.

Well beyond the tracks, the sun was now rising. I had no idea how long I'd been wandering in the woods, but I was eventually able to find my way back to my car. I took a different route home, not wanting to drive past the scene of the crime. Since I wasn't even sure of how I'd killed Heath, I also could not be sure of who—if anyone—had seen it. Perhaps the police had already been called in. I was thankful I'd parked far enough away from the house that I could drive off without being noticed.

I was on the road only a few moments when I passed a cemetery located beside an old church. Out of habit, I held my breath as I drove by. One of the old wives' tales my dad—making it an old husbands' tale, I suppose—had imparted was that I had to hold my breath when we drove past a cemetery or I'd lose a day of my life. As I started to breathe again after I'd passed, a thought occurred to me; could I kill myself by driving back and forth past a cemetery without holding my breath? It'd be an interesting way to do it, because I'd know exactly how many days I'd wasted by choosing to end my own life. Most people who commit suicide never know just how much they'd missed, but I would. Wild.

By the time I'd completed that thought, I'd reached the train tracks. There was no warning signal at this crossing, and I didn't stop to look for a train until I was directly over the tracks. I started humming "Leader of the Pack," as I sat there, wondering if anyone would cry over my death. Probably not. Chances are it wouldn't even be investigated. My parents would be sad, and there'd be a small write-up in the local paper just below the firemen's pancake breakfast, but even that would focus more on the damage done to the train than on the boy who was killed.

Before I'd finished the first chorus of "Leader of the Pack," a light appeared in the distance to my left. I watched for a few moments as the train rounded a corner, and I wondered if it could even see me yet and how long it would be before it was too late. I immediately turned on the radio and began searching frantically for a station that was playing one of those suicide songs by Judas Priest or Ozzy Osbourne so they could get blamed for my death; I knew that humming "Leader of the Pack" wouldn't be enough. Funny how Rob Halford and Ozzy caught so much flack for their lyrics, when '50s and '60s songwriters such as Jody Reynolds, Mark Dinning and Ray Peterson never so much as received a summons. Good thing there was no PMRC in 1958.

Although I was unable to find any appropriate suicide songs, I did happen across "MacArthur Park." Lyrics that bad could certainly drive one to suicide with more violence and frenzy than any musical suggestion from Ozzy or Rob, but the poetry of the moment wasn't there. So as the train chugged closer, I backed off the track. I continued to reverse for another couple hundred feet or so, popped my last LifeSaver, then—for no discernible reason—I threw the car into drive and started to speed forward. The train was quickly approaching the intersection, and I was sure I had no chance to beat it. I had the gas pedal pressed to the floor, but the car's engine was taking a while to catch up to my intentions. The wind was whipping around my head, doing its best to drown out the deep whistle of the train and the roar of its wheels on the track. My mother always used to play a Paul Simon song in which he sang that everyone loves the sound of a train in the distance, and it made me wonder if everyone also loved the sound of train smacking headlong into the side of a car.

By this point, I wasn't really so sure if this was a good idea. What would Ann think? What would mom think? What would Paul Simon think? But I was committed. Trying to stop now would only slow me down enough to smack into a box car half-heartedly, as opposed to into the engine with conviction. And what had I always been taught? "If a job's worth doing, it's worth doing right."

I had my eyes shut at this point, expecting that, when I opened them, I'd once more be looking into that bright tunnel of light; only this time, it'd be for real. But then I felt the car's engine suddenly grab hold, and I could almost hear it chanting its mantra, "I think I can! I think I can! I think I can!" as it dug in and shot me up the slope to the tracks. As we reached the top, I turned to the left and opened my eyes.

There was the light. There was the tunnel. Only I didn't have that sense of calm about which people often speak after having an out of body experience. My only sense was that this light was two seconds away from splintering me to oblivion. The train's whistle screamed at me with the mixture of confusion, anger and fright of a mother yelling at her kid for running into the street, but then it was behind me. An eternal moment later, my mom's car landed heavily at the bottom of the tracks like something out of a car chase in a Dirty Harry movie, and I somehow managed to keep it on the road.

I didn't turn around to face my beaten foe, but instead listened to the horn fade out under the clamor of the following freight cars. The conductor laid on that horn for a good, long time until he was sure he'd driven home his point. But like the troublemaker in the back of the classroom, I wasn't paying attention. As the last rail car crossed the intersection and the whole event rolled off into the distance, all I could think of was poor Jimmy Webb and that damn wet, metaphorical cake of his.

God, I hate this song, I thought as I turned off "MacArthur Park." In the silence that followed, I listened as the train faded mournfully away, and I thought, *If I ever start a rock band, I'm going to call it The Doppler Effect. When VH1 Behind the Music asks where I came up with the name, won't I have a great story to tell?*

My hometown didn't have a Sunday paper, so there was nothing in the press the next day about the death of Heath Millard. I considered driving out to Ann's to see how she was taking it, but I didn't think it wise. So, when life went about as normal that day, I wasn't surprised. It wasn't until the bus ride to school the next morning that I noticed something was amiss. Word should have gotten out by then, so I half expected to see my peers crying all the way to school. No one did. Most stared blankly out the windows, a few slept, and the rest made fun of the fact that I was reading a book. "Hey, nice book. Book reader. You're a real book reader aren't you? Book reader." I swear, it wasn't the taunting that bothered me as much as it was the poor craftsmanship. If you're going to be a bully, then show some pride in your work. Put a little elbow grease in it. "Nice book." Unbelievable. I guess one girl was crying about Heath, but only because he'd apparently stood her up again that weekend. According to her, Heath stood her up every weekend. I smiled, knowing that Heath would be standing her up for a long time to come.

The situation grew more alarming once I reached school. There should've already been banners up in the hallway, mourning his passing and celebrating his life. There should've been one in the cafeteria that we all could sign to express our love and sorrow to…someone. Not Heath. The principal should've choked out, "God must've needed a quarterback for the great pick-up game in the sky," during morning announcements. There should've been guidance counselors coming into our classrooms asking if the sight of his desk was too upsetting and whether we should remove it from the room.

"Can I have it? I can't see the board from back here," I was set to reply.

But there was nothing. There wasn't even an announcement over the PA system or a forced moment of silence for the tragic hero of John Stuart Mill High School. Could it be that his death still hadn't been discovered? Good Lord, what had I done with the body?

Then I realized it; there was no body. There was no killer. I didn't kill somebody after all. The son of a bitch must've kicked out at two. Whatever happened during the period I repressed after seeing Ann and Heath having sex, it certainly didn't involve the killing of Heath Millard. But what about the blood on my hands? I noticed Sunday that my palms were red and severely scrapped up, but I thought then that maybe I'd strangled Heath with a rope or even beaten him with a rusty pole. Now I knew the truth. More likely than not, I'd really only scraped them up when I was clutching the rusty bars of the TV antenna.

My fears were confirmed at lunch when I saw Heath in the cafeteria, his entourage following him around like Elvis Presley's goons. In fact, if I used my imagination, it almost sounded as if Heath's friends were referring to him as "E."

"Sonny…Red…bring me some of that puddin'. No, the whole tub. Thankyouverymuch."

I would've been disappointed to see Heath alive and breathing were I not so used to his victories over me. This one was two fold; not only had he made love with Ann, but I had somehow come out of it with skinned palms! Kicked out at two? I never even got Heath's shoulders anywhere near the mat. Where was the justice? Why couldn't Heath just follow E's example and have a heart attack on the toilet?

More important was the immediate realization that Ann wasn't with him. Whereas they were normally inseparable throughout the school day, they were now ignoring each other…or at least one was ignoring the other. Either way, this was my time; I knew that. I'd had my foot in the door for the past couple of years, and it was finally time that I kicked that damn thing in. By that Friday, I'd finally mustered up the courage to do so and stopped Ann in the hallway. I wanted to speak with her sooner, but I wasn't sure how to approach her. That and I had no Life Savers handy. By the time I got around to buying a pack, word had gotten out about what she'd done with Heath. He'd been dating her for quite some time, so he wasted no more of it in letting everyone know he'd finally conquered Ann Penella. Class act, my buddy E.

To their credit, most of her friends stuck by her…including her fickle cheerleading buddies. I had thought most would take the opportunity to shack up with Heath, but that didn't come to pass. I was glad to see Ann wasn't alone. Losing her virginity was tough enough, I'm sure, but metaphorically losing it before the whole school…Heath may as well have made an afternoon assembly out of it.

When I finally did stop her in the hallway, I still had no idea what to say. I could tell just by looking at her that she wasn't her former self. She tried to force a smile when she saw me, but she may as well have made one with crayons and notebook paper and taped it to her face. It looked that bad. Still, I forced one as well. I wonder if mine was as cartoonish as hers.

"Hi, Guy," she greeted. "How are classes?"

How are classes? That may have been the first time she ever dared small talk with me. That hit me harder than her forced smile.

"I don't know," I replied. "The same. How about yours?"

I couldn't believe I was doing this. What would we talk about next? The weather? Our work day? Our golf games?

She shrugged. It was obvious to me that neither one of us were ready for this conversation. I felt bad for her; I at least had a pack of Life Savers. I would have offered her one, but I wanted no more detours from the conversation we needed to have. It was odd, as if talking about the first time was actually harder than doing it. Plus, we were at school where she obviously was no longer comfortable. My next suggestion seemed the only logical route to take.

"Okay, I'm not sure I want to talk to you in the hallway. I mean, I want to talk to you though, so I was wondering if I could come out again this weekend."

Ann paused a moment, looking straight into my eyes. "Of course you can. You don't have to ask that. You know that."

"I know, it's just that I thought that Heath…" It was a dumb thing to say. Ann seemed to shrink ten inches at the mention of his name. I wasn't sure if I hated myself more for implying that he'd be there, or him for making her feel that way about anything.

"He won't be there," Ann said weakly, turning away. "You don't need to worry about that."

"I'm sorry, Ann, I didn't mean—"

"Don't worry about it. Just please come out. I'd like for you to."

I smiled and thought about touching her, only I wasn't sure how to go about doing it. Should I touch her hand or her upper arm? Should I pat or rub it or even just rest my hand there? It was too unnatural an action for me to take, so I opted to force a smile again. "I'll be there Saturday night. Same time as last week."

Stupid. Stupid. Stupid. Stupid. Stupid. Stupid. St—no, actually this was a really...no, it was stupid. Stupid. Stupid. Stupid. Stupid. Stupid. Stupid. Stupid. It was almost as if I could see the words leave my mouth and float to Ann's ears, but I was helpless to stop them. Her face dropped at my statement, and I concentrated hard on making sure that mine didn't. Did I mention yet how stupid I was?

"Last week?" she asked. It was impossible for me to gauge her emotions. There seemed to be too many happening at once.

"Yeah, last week. Not this past week, I mean, but the week before that. The last week...before this week...past. Want a Life Saver?" Weak. A desperate attempt, but it was the best I had. Ann looked at me for another moment, then finally relaxed. Her next statement floored me.

"I wish you had."

Stupid. Stupid. Stupid. Stupid. Stupid. Stupid. Stupid. Stupid. Oh, who was I kidding, I never could have...nope. It was stupid. Stupid. Stupid. Stupid. Stupid.

So I did blow it. I had my chance to be her hero, the knight in shining armor that all men want to be for the woman they love, and I completely blew it. All that rationalizing I'd done to stop myself from interfering...what a waste. What a cowardly waste. If only I'd listened to my gut instead of my head. I promised myself right there that I damn sure wasn't going to make that mistake again.

"I'll be there this week," I told Ann. "I promise."

"Good. Thank you. I'll see you then."

"Okay." We both stood there for a bit longer before leaving. It was the last time we'd ever see each other this way, and perhaps we both knew it. Perhaps we could feel it, much like people can feel storms gathering on the horizon. But this storm was welcome. It had been brewing for quite some time now, and was finally going to bring much needed relief. By the time it had passed, Ann Penella and I would have made love.

As I made the ritualistic midnight drive to Ann's house that night, I still wasn't thinking about sex. The tense atmosphere from the day before weighed heavily upon me, and my only concern was cutting through that. Yes, it was partly for my sake, but mostly for Ann's. I wanted to return her to her old self; to the type of girl who helps out nerdy kids on school busses and discusses wrestling with the social misfits. That was the girl who had become my guardian angel, and I didn't want to lose her.

Professor Snow was out on his porch again, but he didn't shout anything at me this time. His shotgun was in hand as he watched me drive by, but he didn't raise it and he uttered no prophecies of doom. I took that as a bit of encouragement. It was like he'd given me his blessing tonight, and I was grateful for it.

I parked in my normal secret spot, but I didn't make the usual production out of sneaking to her room. Somehow, I don't think it would've mattered if I'd been caught that night.

When I scaled the antennae to Ann's window, I found it already open despite the chilly evening air. I noticed immediately after entering that the room was decidedly different. All the pictures of Heath had been torn down, and many of the stuffed animals were missing; I assume the ones bought or won for her by Heath. This left her room decidedly bare, but clean. Pure. She would soon be ready to redecorate, and I was excited to see what she'd put up. Her choices were endless, and maybe we'd get to make them together.

"Hello," Ann greeted after I'd climbed in. She didn't seem back to normal yet, but she did sound better than the day before.

"Hi," I said as I turned around to shut the window. Looking out at the TV antennae, it suddenly occurred to me that I had never retrieved *The Monster at the End of this Book*. Did someone else pick it up, or was it still down there? I didn't see it before I climbed up, but I hadn't been looking for it, either. If someone in Ann's family had found it within the past week, then she would've known for sure I had been out there, and I was afraid of how she'd take it.

"What are you looking at?" Ann asked.

I didn't turn around yet, not until I was sure every trace of guilt was removed from face. "Nothing."

"Then come here," Ann requested. I obliged and sat on the edge of her bed. She was sitting up against the headboard with her legs under the covers. They weren't the same sheets she normally used, and I guessed that she'd changed them after Heath had been there with her. She was wearing full, flannel pajamas instead of the sweater from the previous week, and open on her lap was a hardbound edition of C.S. Lewis' *Prince Caspian*. Her hair was pulled back in a ponytail, and she looked so cute I almost felt ashamed for being there. "I'm sorry I didn't talk to you this week, Guy," she said as she inserted a book mark and closed the book. "I had some things—"

"I know," I interrupted. "I understand." Ann hung her head and didn't say anything, so I added, "You don't need to be ashamed."

She looked up at me again. "I'm not ashamed, really. Just sad."

"Why?" I asked.

"I don't know. I guess because my first time is over," she shrugged, getting right to the heart of the matter. "I always thought it'd be something more than that."

"You mean he wasn't very good?" Dumb question, and I wanted it back. Of course Heath was good. He was legendary. The King of Rock 'n' Roll. Luckily, Ann wasn't offended.

"I don't know…it's not that. It's just that…girls tend to plan these things, you know? We have dreams of what our wedding day will be like and what it'll be like when a guy asks us to marry them. And we think about our first time. We wonder where it'll be and who it'll be with. We have all these ideas, and…Heath didn't live up to them.

"It's not his fault, really. Maybe I had my dreams set too high. Maybe no one could've."

"What were they?" I asked.

Ann shook her head. "I don't know. It doesn't matter now. It's done." She paused a moment, lightly brushing the cover of the book with her finger. She then turned to me and added. "There is one thing that upsets me more than most, though."

"What's that?"

"I thought it'd be him telling the whole school about it, but I guess I can handle that. Most my friends understand. And it's not like I'm a slut, right? I waited this long, and even now it was only once."

"You're not a slut, Ann," I agreed. "Even if you'd done it more than once, having sex with one guy doesn't make you a slut. Now Heath, on the other hand…now *there's* a slut. Damn, dirty skank."

Ann didn't acknowledge my joke. "What bothers me most about it is that…this'll sound dumb, but what bothers me most is that it was with Heath."

I was shocked. "Why? I thought you loved him."

Ann shrugged. "But I'm not sure that he loves me."

"Then…" I stopped, wondering if I should ask this, but Ann had been open to answering everything else. "Then why did you do it?"

"Hope," she answered immediately. She had obviously known the question was coming. "I wanted something beyond it." She paused again. "I wanted…no, it sounds too simple."

"What's too simple?" I asked.

Ann didn't reply. Instead she leaned over…and she kissed me. With God as my witness, Ann Panella, the girl with whom I'd been infatuated, with whom I'd been in love for so long now, leaned across the bed and gave me a kiss. Not on the cheek, not as friends do, but on the mouth. It was quick. It was short. I don't think I even felt it, but that wasn't the point. I had wanted this for so long, only to…I'll liken it to an amateur wrestler training intensely for ten years to go to the Olympics and win the gold, only to get there and have the medal handed to him because his opponent forfeited.

I won't say I was in shock, but I sure wanted to be. It would've explained my response—or lack thereof—to her kiss. "Are you saying I'm simple?"

Ann smiled, and I tried to read through it. Maybe she was just as surprised by the kiss as I was. Maybe it was an impulse thing. But did I want it to be? Dammit, she'd just kissed me! Why the hell wasn't I reacting?

"Do you still…do you still love me, Guy?" Ann asked.

Ooh. Well then, what to do about this. Okay, she'd just kissed me, which I didn't get, and now she wanted to know if I loved her, though the answer would've been obvious to even that fraternity piss boy while in the murkiest depths of his coma…if comas do indeed have depths. Why did she ask me this now? Why ask me at all? Dammit, Guy, stop thinking and kiss her back!

Seeing that I couldn't answer her question, Ann added, "Because Heath doesn't."

Okay, that helped. Now I sort of understood. Not her action, but her motivation. This was okay with me, as I always found it easier to understand motivations than actions. I mean, wanting to walk out of the bank with bags full of other people's money makes perfect sense. But actually going in with a gun and leaving with dozens of people lying on the floor counting to one hundred by Mississippis, that I don't get.

I considered not answering Ann. I also considered lying to her. But how would that look? If my feelings had suddenly changed, it could only have been because of what she and Heath had done in this very room, on this very bed, a week before. I didn't want to appear that shallow, and I didn't want to lie, either. I would also say I didn't want to ruin my chances, but I knew there were no chances to ruin. The kiss that came and went as quickly as a comet would not be lighting my night skies again in my lifetime.

I took a moment more to answer because I needed that time to raise my voice above a whisper. "Yes."

At my reply, Ann smiled briefly then asked, with a feeble voice and tears welling in her eyes, "Will you make love to me?"

Looking back, I'm shocked that I was able to say anything at all. Knowing myself and the way I handle things, I should've just sat there and stared at her blankly, maybe talked some wrestling until she grew bored and fell asleep. But something inside of me was able to grasp the situation for what it was and assign the proper importance to her words. This part of me was suddenly so primed for the occasion that it even knew not to ask her, "Are you sure?" which was my first inclination. It would've been the right thing to do, but I'd been doing the "right thing" with her for far too long. Now I wanted to do something else.

It was obvious she only wanted this to help put Heath behind her. True as that may have been, I was more than happy to oblige her. If I was the guy who helped her through this difficult time, then shouldn't I also be the guy who reaped the rewards? And why the hell was I over-analyzing this? I'd done that the week before; tried to do what I thought was best for her. Instead, I only failed her miserably. My gut was telling me I loved Ann, and she needed someone to love her right now. Why even contemplate backing out?

I leaned in to return her kiss, and this time it was more passionate. We stayed there for a while, exploring each other's taste. I had thought about this moment for so long, knowing in the back of my mind that it would never happen.

Everything will happen.

As I reached to put my arms around her, she pulled back just long enough to ask me again, "Do you love me?"

"Yes," I whispered, my lips brushing hers.

"Tell me that you love me."

"I love you, Ann," I said as tears welled up in my eyes now as well. I leaned forward to kiss her neck because I didn't want her to see me crying, but she put her hands on either side of my head and pulled me up. Seeing my tears, she smiled and lightly rubbed them away with her thumbs. I took one of her hands and kissed her palm as I repeated, "I love you," and she then lay back on the bed.

Looking down at her, I suddenly felt as if I were looking down at some wood planks, a few screws and a couple of gears, having just been ordered to, "Build this clock and make it tick." I had no idea where to even begin. I'd heard so much about erogenous zones and G-spots and batters boxes, yet I had no idea where any of them were, let alone what to do if I found them. What if I did this all wrong? What if I was so bad that she'd never let me do this again? What if I was so bad that word got out and *no one* would ever let me do this again? It's a lot of pressure for a man. It's hard to make a clock.

But then a phrase popped into my mind. It was from a movie, some '90s soft core smut on late night cable that no doubt starred Tanya Roberts or Shannon Whirry, or maybe both. I don't remember that much, but I do remember a woman seducing another, and as she unbuttoned her blouse she purred, "Women know what women want."

I had no argument with this, it made perfect sense. And the line gave me an idea; to make sure that Ann was happy, I just had to make love to her as if I didn't have a penis. It being my first time, my penis would be pretty much useless anyway. I wasn't going to last long, so I needed to use that precious time wisely.

As Ann laid before me, I started to remove her pajamas. She put up no resistance, even assisted. Two times she reached to remove my shirt, but I stopped her both times. I had to remain dressed for as long as I could. So in a manner of moments, Ann was lying naked while I was still completely clothed. I couldn't tell if she found this awkward or not, but she still made no motion to stop me.

The lava lamp was not on that night, so I only had the ghostly glow of the flood light outside by which to see. It reduced Ann to nothing more than abstract shadows, but it was enough. I was acting more on instinct and touch than on sight. Old Obi-Wan and Yoda would've been proud of their young Jedi Knight.

I continued to kiss her wherever I could find skin amongst the tangle of sheets. This went on for quite a while because I never wanted it to end. I kissed and touched her entire body, committing to memory every taste and smell. After a while of fighting the sheets that had by then entangled us, I grew frustrated and threw them to the floor. With nothing to stop me now, I became bold. I touched her breasts, and I believe it gave me more shivers than it did her. I still couldn't believe that I'd reached this point, but I certainly wasn't about to waste a second of it.

Within moments, I was tasting her breasts. It was probably just me, but the skin tasted sweeter there. I'm not sure how long I lingered, moving between her breasts and neck, but I eventually worked up the courage to move down further. My body was shaking at this point, so I made sure to not raise myself with my arms. I didn't want Ann to think I was having a stroke. Instead, I rested my chest on her thigh, allowing her body and the bed to absorb the energy that was trying so hard to force its way out of me. I wanted to move slowly, but my inner coach kept pointing the shot clock, yelling at me, "Go for the three! Go for the three!"

I certainly didn't want to let down Coach, so I moved my hand between Ann's legs and was relieved to see that she was ready for me. I rubbed my fingers back and forth as Ann swayed her hips to my rhythm. After a moment, Ann let out a sudden gasp which led me to believe I'd found the part of the woman many men apparently miss, if those glamour magazines and sex psychologists are to be believed. I continued what I was doing as I liked the response it was getting, but suddenly Coach was shouting again. "The box! Get in the box! Go for the lay up!"

I didn't like basketball. I'd never even been to a game. I mean, all these musical terms at my disposal, all these trombone analogies about double tonguing and the spit valve and my F trigger, yet my id was going for the basketball comparisons. No wonder so many guys watch Sports Center even when their team didn't play the night before.

For Coach and the highlight reels, I slid my hand down a little further and reached inside of Ann with my middle and index fingers, continuing to rub her with my thumb.

Ann was moaning now, answering any questions I may have had about my technique. Coach was gone now, replaced with some hip, well-dressed sportscaster spouting catch phrases on ESPN: "You can't stop Guy, you can only hope to contain him."

From the light outside, I could see that Ann had one hand over her neck, the other clutching the sheets on the side of the bed. Her eyes were shut, and her head was tilted back against the pillow. Seeing her this way almost made me try for the fade-away jumper right there. But no. I started to kiss her stomach, inches away from my hand. The position was too awkward for me, however, so I slid off the bed and pulled Ann over to the edge. She quickly obliged and opened herself to me, so I returned her urgency.

"Guy is givin' some restaurant quality loving," the ESPN sportscaster continued overtop the highlight reel.

It's odd how sex looks so different from the way it feels. To watch it on TV or even hear it described, it always seems so…smutty, really. Dirty. Perhaps that's because of pornography and the way women are presented there, because of the picture fundamentalists paint to illustrate how ugly and sinful it is. But as I kneeled there before Ann, a girl with whom I was madly in love, who was the most beautiful person I'd ever met, I could only think, *My God, I hope I make this work.*

I first noticed the aroma. It was heavy and sweet…nothing like what I'd expected. I wasn't sure if I liked it or not, but I knew I never wanted it to go away. I hovered there for a few seconds like a man about to make his first parachute jump, frightened and frantic but loving the entire experience. Then I tasted her, and it was wonderful. I couldn't get close enough to her, and I found myself spreading her legs wider to gain better access. I used my lips, my tongue…even my teeth to please her as much as I could, and I altered my cadence whenever I remembered to do so.

"It's Guy's world, we're all just livin' in it."

I remember thinking that my music abilities were finally paying off as it was so easy to pick up on her movements and stay within her rhythm. Mr. Bravo would've been proud. Hell, Mr. Bravo would've wanted pictures. I was determined to stay down there until the buzzer sounded or until Ann finished. And if that didn't happen, I would just go as long as I could. An hour. Two. August.

I was paying such careful attention to Ann's movements and reactions that I had no idea how long it was before she pulled me up so that I was laying directly on top of her. I wasn't about to wait for her to tell me what to do next.

"Can I make love to you?" I asked, only because I already knew the answer. If there was any doubt that she'd say yes, I wouldn't have taken that chance.

"Yes," she agreed.

"Guy must be butter, cause he's on a roll," quipped the sportscaster.

"I have no condoms," I pointed out, having just realized it myself. I wanted to kick myself for bringing it up, knowing that this may have ruined my chances after all, but I also had no desire to risk impregnating her. And more selfishly, who knew what manner of rare and exotic diseases Heath had contracted.

These fears were all put to rest when Ann pointed to the dresser and said, "Heath left his. They're in the second drawer from the top."

Okay, I know this was a little creepy; not only was I making love to Ann to help her forget about Heath, but I was now using Heath's condoms. Why would she throw out his pictures but keep his condoms? It was all so painfully wrong, I knew it, but I was still desperately seeking a victory over Heath. Actually, I don't like the way that sounded. I would've made love to Ann even if there had never been a Heath. In fact, I would've preferred it that way. But because he was real, and because of our past, I have to admit that there was an extra thrill in this. I'm not saying I'm proud of it, just being honest.

I had never used a condom before, of course. I'd never even seen a package out of the box. There was a time when I thought it would be a good idea to go to the local drugstore every week and buy a box just so the cashier, at least, would think I had an active sex life. But I didn't have the money...and the cashiers at the drugstore weren't really the type who should be thinking too much about sex. Not unlike elementary school teachers:

"One of my students stood up today," Mrs. Piper would've said, "a boy named Guy Lindsey, and he said—"

"Yes, I know his parents," Principal Steele would've smiled, carefully nodding his head in that polite principalesque way. "Fine people. Salt of the Earth."

"Well, their boy stood up in class today, and he said, 'Mrs. Piper, I'd really like to buy myself some condoms. Trojans. Lubricated and with the spermicide, if you please.'"

"Hmm," Principal Steele would've still been nodding his head, practicing for the parent/teacher conferences. "Interesting life for a five-year-old. Did he say who he was going to engage in this inappropriate behavior with?"

"With *whom* he was going to engage in this inappropriate behavior," Mrs. Piper would've corrected.

Luckily for me, putting on a condom is not all that difficult; if it doesn't unravel, turn it over. So it didn't take long to get it on and position myself for the shot.

And then it hit me like an elbow from Charles Barkley. I was about to lose my virginity, and I was going to lose it to the most incredible woman I'd ever met. What had I done to deserve this? How had all of this come about? The path that led up to this moment certainly wasn't one I'd ever want to walk again, and looking back at it did not fill me with pride. So instead I looked ahead, and that frightened me even worse. My friendship with Ann had settled into a comfortable pattern, and we were about to change that drastically. For better? For worse? I had no idea. My future suddenly wasn't so bleak, but it also wasn't as controlled.

I was shaking uncontrollably now, both from fright and anticipation and from the pressure of having been propped above Ann for a few moments now. I tried to steady myself, but Ann made it clear I should be concentrating on other things. She grabbed my shoulders as if to steady me. "Guy, I'm ready."

The sports announcer called from the booth, "Guy is going deep, and I don't think that one is playable."

Good enough for me. As Ann moved her hands to my hips, I lowered myself on top of her. Being new to this, however, I couldn't find where to enter. I knew where the basket was, of course, but I was shooting up above the backboard. After a couple of attempts, she finally reached down to guide me in.

At first, I didn't move. I just laid on top of her, savoring the moment. I had let go of so much in that one motion, and it almost seemed a disappointment. I was expecting to be overwhelmed by a sudden sense of guilt over my loss of innocence, but the whole thing effected me in much the same way that burnt toast affects the local fire department.

But then Ann started to move her hips, and everything changed. Pressure was applied to me with every movement, and I quickly started to move with her. I can't begin to describe how it felt, but it's not like I had been afforded much time to come up with clever analogies. Maybe fifteen seconds after it started, I was finished.

"All the girls who aren't having sex with Guy are left to drool the drool of remorse into the pillow of regret." My sportscaster was getting very cerebral.

I continued to lay there heavily, spent, still inside of her. She had her arms around my back and was breathing with me. I had taken my "first step into manhood" without the confidence of being ready for the journey. I felt I could put the start on hold as long as I didn't let go of Ann, but I also knew it must be uncomfortable for her. I carefully pulled myself out, holding onto the condom to make sure it didn't slip off. I rolled over beside her. She continued to lay on her back, but she turned to look at me.

"Thank you, Guy," she smiled.

"No, don't thank me," I said. "It's not like I loaned you a pencil."

"But that's not—"

"I don't think I did well enough to deserve a thanks anyway."

"You did just fine," Ann smiled.

"I didn't think I lasted long enough for you to finish."

Ann laughed and said, "Oh, I finished long before we started that part."

The sportscaster summed up the highlight real with one final line; "Guy is King of the Lovin'! Bring him the finest meats and cheeses in all the land!" then he was off to cover the Yankees/Indians doubleheader.

Suddenly, I was ten feet tall. I was worried about how I was going to fit back out the window. I didn't know the Arbiter yet, and I still have never owned a high bouncing ball. But had I the opportunity, I would have tossed a hundred of those little guys straight into the air.

"I thought you said you'd never done that before," Ann continued.

"I haven't," I confirmed with pride.

"Well, you were better than…" I knew Ann wouldn't be able to finish the statement, but that she even thought it was good enough for me. Trying to cover, she added, "Most men apparently can't ever get that right. How did you learn that?"

"You can thank Tonya Roberts."

I took the new route home again, but I raced no trains that night. I guess there are two reasons for not driving the regular way; I didn't want any death threats from Prof. Snow to cloud my sunrise, and I wanted the juxtaposition with the previous week.

Ann and I had talked for quite some time before I left. We didn't discuss what we'd done, but quickly settled back to talk of wrestling and movies and children's books. I guess I should've remembered to check for *The Monster at the End of this Book*, but my mind was too removed from myself. I almost turned back for it, but figured it wouldn't matter if someone found it now. In fact, I was hoping someone would find it.

I was so far gone at that point that I didn't stop before crossing the railroad tracks. I didn't even slow down or look for oncoming trains. The road was clear and open ahead of me, and I wasn't concerned with anything else. There were no suicide races that night, but had there been, it wouldn't have mattered if I'd lost. I had a place to go now, and it would take something much bigger than a freight train to stop me from getting there.

It would take Heath.

CHAPTER 12

Up On the Roofie

I suddenly couldn't remember what was the capital of Burkino Faso. I sat in front of the computer in one of the bedrooms of the Eta Iota Upsilon sorority house, rattling my brain to try and remember the capital of Burkino Faso. I have no idea why it was bothering me so much, but it was all I could think about at that moment. I knew the answer was out there, so it was just a matter of finding it. If I couldn't do so through memory, I would find the name of the capital through the process of elimination. If I started putting together sounds and syllables, then I'd have to accidentally stumble across the word eventually. It's that whole "an infinite number of monkeys with an infinite number of typewriters and time will eventually write the complete works of Shakespeare" thing. It's rumored that one of those big schools with the trustee money and government grants took this theory to the lab. Oddly enough, after only three days, a less than infinite number of monkeys with a handful of Apple eMates produced four Ephron sister movie scripts; Hanging Up twice. The project was immediately scrapped. The notes, destroyed. The monkeys, quarantined.

Of course, as with the monkeys, my process of elimination theory was flawed. If I couldn't remember the name of the capital, then how would I know when I accidentally stumbled across it? If the monkeys don't understand what they're typing, how would they know when they had Shakespeare?

There's something I learned about myself at one time in life, I'm sure. Let me talk long enough and eventually I'll contradict every point I make.

And I was just procrastinating, after all. Having searched for ten minutes, I had yet to pull up any sort of proof of a sorority porn ring. There were no cameras or camera equipment to be found, no pictures or negatives strewn about the floor. In fact, the only photos I could find were a few of some children playing near a backyard swimming pool. They were older photos, no doubt of one of the sorority sisters in her childhood days. She had blonde hair that lay flat and wet against her shoulders, and a pudgy little stomach hidden somewhat by the inflatable dolphin she was carrying around with pride. Beside her were a couple of older boys, perhaps her brothers, and a man whom I assumed to be her father was sitting on a lawn chair in the background. He was wearing a straw hat, holding a glass of lemonade or iced tea or something, and watching his children as if all was right with the world. It was a nice photo, and I understood why the owner would want to keep it with her all this time.

Burkino Faso. How could I remember a name like that and not remember its capital? Burkino Faso City, perhaps? No. And was I even in the right room? Maybe this wasn't the room from the which the Arbiter and I had the seen the flash bulbs popping. I wondered what the Arbiter was doing right now; when not with me, he was usually with Rhonda. Perhaps he was writing another letter to a dead actor. I still couldn't figure that out, but I seriously doubted I was equipped to do so. I couldn't even recall the capital of Burkino Faso.

Unable to concentrate on the task at hand, I stood to search the room one more time. I looked outside the window once more to verify I was in the right place, trying to reverse my point of view so I was on the street looking in. It seemed right, but there was nothing here.

Just as I was about to look under a bed once again, the door to the room flew open and a couple stumbled in. I recognized the girl from around campus and from the photos hanging in the house, but I didn't know her name. The guy, on the other hand, was quite famil-iar to me.

"Hey, 'su 'gain," he slurred as he came further into the room. "You ever bang that chick?"

"Which chick?"

"Th'un out there in the hall." When he pointed behind him, he lost his balance and fell against the wall. His legs came out from under him as he did, catching those of the woman he was with. She also lost her balance and fell, managing to get an arm up to stop her head from cracking the wall. It worked, but she apparently found the floor comfortable enough to finish her evening there.

The guy who brought her up poked and prodded her a bit, but to no avail. "Goddam, I'll never goin' get some laid t'night," he whined as he stood and trudged back out of the room. "I need another beer."

After he was gone, I decided to do the humane thing and check on the girl. "Are you okay?" I asked, kneeling beside her. "Do you want to get on the bed?"

"Too far away," she whispered. "I can't afford it."

"I'll cover it this time," I suggested. It's so easy to be chivalrous to those who are drunk. Any offer of kindness means so much to them.

"Thanks," she smiled as she turned towards me. "My bed's over there."

She pointed at the bed by the window, but my gaze didn't make it quite that far. Hidden between the computer desk and the wall was a manila envelope.

"Just bring my bed over here," the girl requested as I walked over to the desk. Without answering her so she wouldn't look my way, I grabbed the envelope and opened it to reveal two unlabelled Zip disks and a third with a few words crossed out so that it now read,

"Sexism in the Language." I laughed out loud, causing the girl on the floor to agree, "Yeah, that's a good one."

She reminded me vaguely of my father who would often fall asleep in his lounge chair while watching the news or a football game. When my mother and I would talk near him, he'd awaken just enough to hear the conversation and say, "Mmm hmm," assuming we were talking to him.

"Just go back to sleep," mom and I would tell him, and I told the girl the same.

"Okay, I'll get ready in the morning," she said softly, then nothing.

With her out, I felt safe enough to check out the Zip disks I'd just recovered. The Sexism in the Language Disk was just that…a bunch of WordPerfect documents that appeared to be labeled as class assignments. I ejected it and popped in the first blank one, and I immediately knew I had something. Every file was labeled either .jpg or .png, with a few .txt files to round it out. There were also a couple of folders labeled with what appeared to be last names, so I opened one of them and launched an image. Internet Explorer started up to read the image, and there she was, none other than Elizabeth herself. Her wrists were tied to those fake pillars people use at proms, both of which had vines crawling to the top. A closer look revealed it was the vines that bound her, although somewhat haphazardly. They were simply wrapped a few times around her wrists. Elizabeth was completely naked save for a lei around her neck and a couple more wrapped around her ankles, and she was doing a poor job of trying to look frightened. On the top of each pillar were a few candles in an attempt to simulate tiki torches or something like that.

Man, I thought, This woman really should hook up with the Fire God at the front desk of Student Union Student Union."

I was struck by the similarities between the photo and the scene from King Kong in which Fay Wray is offered to the mighty beast by the inhabitants of the island. I almost smiled as I closed the picture and opened the next, revealing that this was a series. The first few showed Elizabeth struggling to break free of her captive state, but it wasn't long before Kong actually did appear in the form of a two foot, black, stuffed gorilla. The whole thing was oddly comical, watching this woman being terrorized by a rather cute, stuffed monkey about one-third her size. It begged the question, if an infinite number of stuffed gorillas did an infinite number of photo shoots with an infinite number of college coeds, would I ever understand why the natives in King Kong built such a large door on their island? I'm talking about the one that Kong broke through in an attempt to retrieve the lovely and talented Ms. Wray. Why was that door so big? If the natives wanted to keep Kong confined to a certain area, why not just build a complete wall and put a door at the bottom just large enough for the natives to get through? Did they sometimes want Kong to get out? Were they thinking they'd eventually want something else to get in? It made no sense.

Pretty impressive wall, though.

Leaving Kong and Elizabeth to their privacy, I opened the next folder and started glancing through those photos as well. This one contained a blonde and two guys in a much less imaginative series. It was your basic hard core amateur porn shoot, with bad lighting, unattractive models and disgusting close-ups. I thought it odd that I could get aroused more easily by a woman with a stuffed toy than by real people having real sex, but then I froze. I mean everything froze: my hands, my gaze, my brain…the cars and the people and life outside. On the screen before me was obviously the same girl from the family photo hanging on the computer desk, the one taken near a swimming pool. Her features were exactly the same, only matured. She had the same flat, blonde hair, the same pudgy belly. But in the new photo, she was holding something other than an inflatable dolphin.

The dolphin wasn't all that was missing, however. The girl had lost her smile. She had lost it not only from her face but from her eyes as well. There was no joy in them as there had been back in that photo where she was content to play with her brothers and her dad...

Her dad. I couldn't stop looking at him in the family photo. He seemed so thrilled with life, as if everything he'd wanted out of it was playing before him. He seemed so proud and so hopeful. And yet there on the computer monitor was his daughter less than fifteen years later in circumstances that would've crushed his pride and his hopes. Every memory of days such as that in the photo, ruined by the push of a button and the flash of a light. He would blame himself, I'm sure if it. Who else could he blame? To whom could he point his finger and say, "It's your fault my daughter made this decision. It's your fault she wasn't raised to avoid this path." I was certain it wasn't his fault, but he wouldn't accept that. Not this man with the straw hat and the lemonade.

I couldn't do this to him. I couldn't take this disk to a newspaper and expose what his daughter had done. Maybe they would both eventually get past it, but maybe not, and I couldn't take that chance. I looked over at the porn shot on the monitor and I felt sorry for the woman as well. She had once been her daddy's little girl, she'd been this man's daughter. If that bond were to be broken, then I wasn't going to be the one to do so. Damn the Arbiter and his grandiose schemes, I wasn't going to be part of this one.

I smiled to myself as I reached this conclusion. It wasn't a smile of victory, but of contentment. I felt relaxed. It seemed that by defying the Arbiter and not turning in this woman, I was in essence forgiving her. I know, I know she'd done nothing to me, but that didn't matter. She'd done something that was obviously wrong, and I was forgiving her for that. It made me feel good, and I now understand that people don't have to always be forgiven by the person they've wronged. Forgiveness is an amazing thing no matter from whom it's coming, and I needed that amazement. I needed forgiveness, and I knew from whom I needed it.

I ejected the Zip disk from the drive and turned the computer off without completing the shut-down process. I put all three Zip disks in my pocket, but pulled the one from the Sex in the Middle Ages class back out and returned it to the envelope. I then stepped over the girl on the floor. Hadn't I put her on the bed? No time now. I headed downstairs.

Although the stereo was still playing, the house was deserted save for a couple students passed out on the furniture and a few others milling about. I looked around for Rhonda, calling her name a couple of times, but she didn't answer. She wouldn't have left the house to follow everyone else, I was sure of that.

Before I had a chance to worry about her, Jayson Fayme emerged from the kitchen.

"What are you doing here?" I asked. Before he had a chance to answer, I changed the question to, "Have you seen Rhonda, Jayson?"

"Listen, asshole, I didn't know what it was," he blurted out, seeming exceptionally nervous. "They told me it was roofies. It's not my fault."

"Roofies? What are you talking about?" I asked.

"Roofies," Jayson repeated with a fear I hadn't seen in him before. "I put it in Rhonda's drink."

"I…you what?" I asked. "You did what?"

"I mean, I didn't do it. I didn't do a goddam thing. I didn't know what it was," Fayme explained as if that relieved him of any guilt. "I thought it was a roofie. That's what the guy fuckin' told me. It's not my fault."

I found myself thinking of the bat the drunk guy had used to smash up my door my freshman year of college. I wanted that bat right now. I would've broken both of Jayson's legs right there if I hadn't been worried about something more important than his intentions with Rhonda.

"You thought it was…so then what did you give her?" I asked.

"How the fuck should I know?" Fayme replied. "It sure as shit wasn't a roofie."

I lost it. I'd had enough of people not giving me straight answers, and I freaked. I jumped over to where he was standing, grabbed him by the collar, and shoved him against the wall, driving my forearm into his throat. By now, a couple others had come to the dining room to see what all the commotion was. None interfered. "What the hell did you give her?"

"I told you I don't know! I thought it was a roofie!" Fayme yelled. I'd never seen him this nervous before.

"You gave somone rohypnol?" asked one of the girls that had come to see what was going on. "You son of a bitch." She gave him a look that revealed more than it should have, then dropped her beer to the table and went to the phone just inside the kitchen door.

Rohypnol. I knew that word, and I remembered that roofie is slang for it. The date rape drug.

"It's not my fault!" Fayme cried once more as he blinked the beer from his eyes. "I wouldn't do anything to hurt her."

"Like rape her?! What the fuck did you give her?!" I yelled, slamming Fayme into the wall once more. His eyes clamped shut as he winced in pain, and they were wild when he opened them again. "They told me it was a roofie, but it wasn't. She started freaking out. She was yelling about things that weren't there, something about the Arbiter, about climbing up to see him, and then she just took off running."

"Climbing up…?" I looked at Fayme for another moment, then threw him into a cabinet. "You asshole," I yelled as some cups and framed photographs fell on top of him. Lying on the floor there, he looked no different to me than he had the day the Arbiter knocked him off his bike. I was so furious that I was unable to move, afraid of what my first action might be. I remembered what happened the last time I felt like this, and—despite what I'd always believed—I suddenly knew I was capable of that again.

But then I heard the girl on the phone, talking to whom I'd guess was security. She turned to me and asked, "What was the name of your friend?"

My friend. Yes. Rhonda really was my friend. "Listen," I said frantically to the girl. "Call the Arbiter. He's at 1571 and tell him what happened. If he's not there…shit. If he's not there, try him at the Daily Planet office. Tell him Rhonda's in trouble and we have to find her. Her name's Rhonda."

I started to run towards the door, but the girl called out, "What's the Daily Planet number?"

I told her, she repeated it, then I raced out of the house. Jayson yelled out, "If you see her, tell her I'm still free tonight!" I paid no attention to him, just as I paid no attention to the rain that was suddenly beating down in torrents. My clothes were soaked in a matter of moments, but I kept running. I had to find Rhonda. Ahead of me, I could see a mob of people purposefully making their way towards the fraternities. I considered following them, and then stopped cold. In the distance, a brilliant flash of lightning burned up the sky. In that instant, I saw the Floodbane radio tower reaching up like the arm of a skeleton from the grave. "Climbing up to see him…" I knew where Rhonda was heading, and I knew where I had to go.

Ann's place, of course. It was Saturday night, after all, and it had been a great week for us. Unlike when some other couples have sex for the first time, there was no tension between us. In fact, our relationship had actually improved since that night a week earlier. We talked in the hallways at school without fear of what others would think. And, for the first time ever, we actually spoke on the phone. I had called her, asked her dad if she was home, and then spoken to her for nearly an hour.

And then there was me, just me. I don't want to say I was bouncing, but that week I found myself watching sitcoms on prime time

TV and giggling. Giggling! At one point, I may have even been over-heard saying, "It's funny 'cause it's true!" I stopped to read the spirit signs hung up in the hallway and actually made a note of which cheerleaders signed them. When tickets went on sale for the big dance after the last home game of the season, I...no, I didn't buy any. Give me some credit here. I just looked to see how much they cost.

I'd like to think it wasn't the sex that made me feel like a Marvin Gaye song, although it was certainly sex that made Marvin Gaye feel like a Marvin Gaye song. I suddenly understood why there are so many songs about "makin' love, baby." To be able to have that feeling and make money off it? Now that's America. Land of the free, baby dolls.

I felt no guilt about what I'd done with Ann. I'd been told I would, but no. I couldn't even imagine why anyone would. What had we done that was so wrong? Why would sharing that with one another destroy our lives? I read once that when teens have sexual relations and then split up, it affects them worse than divorce affects adults. Maybe so, but that pain ends, I'm sure. To love someone and never share it? That dull, throbbing pain can't be cured. It can be lessened, perhaps, but never cured.

So no, there'd be no Saturday evening confession from me. Ann and I both felt good about what happened, and it made our relation-ship more comfortable. Perhaps that's why I didn't feel awkward driving out there so early. It was only 9:30 p.m., and I usually wouldn't have made that trip until after midnight. I didn't tell Ann I'd be coming so soon, but she had mentioned her family would be going to a movie that night and she'd be staying home. She had some things to do that she hadn't been able to get to while dating Heath.

Me? I figured that now was the time to find The Monster at the End of This Book and, provided it was still in good shape, give it to her. Well, that and I really wanted to have sex with her again.

I was actually somewhat happy to see Professor Snow out on his porch, gun in hand. I even almost waved as he shouted his predictable predictions of gloom and doom. They seemed funny to me now, which made me take note of my mood. Professor Snow never really changed what he said or how he said it, yet I took it differently every time I drove by. Sometimes I laughed, while other nights I'd drive miles out of my way to avoid him. Odd how a crazy man on a porch could have become so important to my life. It's as if he'd become an amalgam of everyone who had an effect on me, a position I'm sure no sane man would have wanted.

So I didn't wave at him, afraid my gesture would've been taken as mockery. I merely drove by, intent on getting to Ann's. Who knows? If the night went well, maybe I'd ask her to be my girlfriend. It was too soon, I knew that. But it sure felt good to think about such things with a degree of realism.

That changed, and it changed hard. Heath was at Ann's. His jacked up, black truck with the oversized rear tires and the "No Fear" sticker was parked in the drive, and there was no Tom Jones on the radio to distract me from seeing it this time. It was Heath. I could feel my face turning red as emotions I didn't know I had forced their way from my gut to my brain. What was he doing here? Was he going to force himself onto Ann again? No. Not with me there he wouldn't. No fucking way. I wasn't going to be a passive bystander this time.

I pulled my car into the drive instead of heading up to my normal parking spot. I also ran up to the front door instead of climbing the TV antenna. I raised my fist to knock, but then paused. Her family wasn't home. If something was going on that needed to be stopped, a knock on the door wouldn't do it. I'd have to go in and stop Heath myself, and the only chance I had of taking him out involved surprise. I lowered my hand and tried the door. It was open, but that wasn't unusual. Where we lived, most people never locked their doors...even at night. There was no need to. It's not like there were any killers stalking about.

I opened the door and slipped my way through, careful not to make any noise. A part of me wanted to rush up there, grab Heath by the neck and slam him against the wall. But the real me wouldn't allow that to happen. I had to fight that part of me to even enter the house, so my calculated attack would have to suffice. The lights were on downstairs, but the neatly and conservatively decorated rooms appeared empty. It gave the house the dreary, helpless effect of a funeral home. Or maybe that was just me.

I found the stairs to the second floor just off of the living room area. There was an entire history of family photos framed on the walls of the stairwell. Had I been there under different circumstances, I would've been thrilled to see photos of Ann as a child standing next to Snoopy or dressed up as a pirate for trick or treat, to see her in a baseball uniform surrounded by little boys who were jealous of her throwing arm.

But then I envisioned her with Heath, and my heart again started thumping in my head, throwing emotions at me faster than I could handle. I ascended the stairs as quickly and quietly as I could, and scouted the doors for signs as to which was Ann's. Only one was closed, so it was safe to guess. Approaching it, I began to hear movement and muffled voices coming from inside. I stood against the wall so no one would be able to see my shadow under the door.

I shouldn't have waited. Despite my true self, I should have just charged right in and laid Heath out, lifted Ann onto my horse and rode off into the sunset. That would've been the perfect ending. It would've been the Hollywood ending. But instead, I again hesitated. I hesitated long enough to hear Ann say, "Heath, make love to me."

No, what? That couldn't have been right. She hated him. She told me so last week. She finally realized she wanted me instead. I pressed me ear to the door to see if I could understand anything else that was said, and I heard Heath ask, "Do you still love me, Ann?"

"Yes," she replied without hesitation.

"I'm sorry about how I behaved over the past couple of weeks," Heath continued. He sounded phonier than a three dollar bill, but I knew Ann wouldn't hear that. "I just care about you so much, and I got scared. I didn't want to lose you."

"You won't lose me, Heath," Ann promised. "You'll never lose me."

And then there was silence. I could hear sheets ruffling, but nothing else was said. It looked as if the hero wouldn't be needed tonight. His valiant deeds weren't required, so please go home.

I broke. I felt as if I'd finally climbed the mountain, only to be shoved from the top to shatter on the jagged rocks below. So many pieces of me had been torn off that there was no way I could be put back together. Unlike Steve Austin, they could not rebuild me. It's not that I wasn't hurt or angry, but that I was tired. I'd been fighting Heath for so long, spending so much energy on trying to achieve the impossible, and I was spent. All I wanted to do was sleep. I wanted to go outside, lay in the ditch, and let the wind and the rain slowly carve away at me until there was nothing left but fossil and sand.

I left the house as quietly as I had entered. I lightly shut the car door and I didn't turn on the headlights until I was out of the driveway. But as I drove off, I looked over my right shoulder and saw the TV antenna that I had climbed so many nights before. I stopped the car right there in the road and walked to the antenna. There were no lights on in Ann's room—not even the pink one—but that's not why I went over. It took me only a few moments to find The Monster at the End of the This Book. It had fallen behind a shrub, and could only be seen from behind. I picked it up and dusted some dirt off the cover. It was warped and damp from the dew and the one rainfall we had since I'd left it, and the last few pages were stuck together.

Grover finally got his wish.

CHAPTER 13

✿

The Wisdom of the Moon

*R*unners often speak of getting their second wind. They talk about how, when running marathons, they suddenly drum up a reserve of energy that propels them towards the finish line.

I think it's a crock. I had barely made it past the educational facilities and to the dorm area of campus before my sides started to ache as if an alien inside was about to claw its way out and kill everyone on the spaceship. Coincidentally, the pain first hit at about the location where the Arbiter had first met Rhonda. I stopped momentarily to catch my breath amongst the shrubs, allowing the rain to continue to flow off my already drenched clothes.

I could still see the radio tower ahead of me, it's red warning light slowly pulsing off and on like that of a firefly attracting a mate. I began to question if this really was where Rhonda would be heading. I mean, those omnipotent moments where people suddenly "know" exactly what someone is going to do…they don't really happen, right? But the debris of drunk party goers scattered about the sidewalk like the dead of a military caravan on a march through enemy territory led me to believe I was on the right path. Some of those who'd followed Rhonda had now given up and were staggering back to the source, while a few gave entirely into their stupor and just laid down in the grass. Far ahead, a large group of people was just now making its way past the row of fraternities that separated the main campus from the baseball diamonds and the radio tower.

I started forward once more, trying to pace myself so I wouldn't cramp up even worse. Looking up at the radio tower, I half expected to see a silhouette framed by the light like the Bat-Symbol in the skies above Gotham City. I sure could've used Batman right then. Batman, Iron Man, Son of Ambush Bug…but I knew they weren't coming. For now, at least, I had to play the role of superhero. The thought terrified me, but it made me move more quickly.

More people had joined the hunt by the time I reached the frat houses. Men and women alike were leaving their parties with beer cups in hand or bottles hidden behind brown paper bags. Unlike the party I'd been attending, not as many of these students seemed drunk.

Passing through two buildings, one of which was the Upsilon Iota Eta house, I heard someone call out, "Hey, you rushing?"

"No," I responded without slowing down. A concrete wall guarded by rottweilers couldn't have slowed me down.

"Oh. Okay. Wanna beer?"

"No." I never turned my gaze away from the tower.

"Come on up, we'll have a beer and listen to some Floyd."

I didn't take him up on his offer, but I desperately wanted to. I wanted to be in a situation where, if I wanted, I could have just dropped what I was doing to have a beer and listen to "some Floyd." I wanted my life to be that simple.

The student asked another question, but I couldn't hear him now. His voice was drowned out by the rain and…and the scream. I couldn't make out what was being yelled, but it was definitely coming from the radio tower, and it was definitely a cry of fear. As fast I could, I ran towards the tower.

❦ ❦ ❦

But then I slammed on the brakes; enough to actually squeal the tires and fishtail the car to the left hand side of the road. I sat there a moment, staring through the passenger's side of the front window towards the road ahead. Aside from the idling of the engine, the night was completely silent. This time, however, I knew I wasn't dead. This time I had my faculties about me, and perhaps that's why I did what I was about to do.

I backed the car to my own side of the road, then turned into Prof. Snow's driveway. Sitting on his porch as always, he stood and raised his shotgun as I drove down the stone lane, the gravel crunching under the tires of my parents' car. His gun was trained on the windshield, and I hoped he wouldn't shoot because I didn't want mom and dad to have to pay for auto repairs. He didn't, and I stopped the car before his garage. With purpose, I walked up to his porch and stood before him, in some way knowing he wasn't going to shoot me. When I was close enough to see his face at the end of the barrels, I saw that his eyes were betraying him. Although he was the one with the gun, he was also the one who was afraid. It made me feel powerful.

I reached my hand out to him and said, "Give me your gun."

Prof. Snow didn't move, neither did I. We stared at each other over the barrel until he finally sighed with a closed mouth and lowered the weapon. He then handed it to me, even turning it around so I could grab the handle. It was heavier than I'd expected, and I afraid of looking foolish as I raised it to my shoulder. Taking what I'd learned from TV, I tilted my head to the right to place the sight between my right eye and Prof. Snow's chest.

Prof. Snow didn't move. Perhaps he was just waiting for me to pull the trigger. Maybe he'd been wanting me to all along, and that's why he kept threatening me. Who was I to deny him this request? Who was I to tell this sick, messed-up bastard, "Sorry, but even though it's obviously what you want, and even though you've done nothing but torment me and probably Ann as well every single time we've passed you by, it's not my role to pass judgment on you." Nope. By giving me the gun, he had assigned me that role.

"You've threatened me an awful lot, Professor." I think I was trying to be cool. It's as if there was a camera somewhere nearby, and I had to look good for my legions of fans. Or perhaps when this whole scene was dramatically reenacted on *America's Most Wanted*, I just didn't want the actors to be cooler than I had been this night.

I stood there thinking of something the action film villain would say, and I had it all ready to go when Prof. Snow said, "I was in love once."

It was the first time I'd heard him utter anything aside from his prophecies of doom, or perhaps this still was. Using a normal voice and speaking of love, he sounded crazier than ever. I continued to stare at his chest over the barrel of the shotgun, and I wondered how long it would take for me to actually pull the trigger. Not the physical process, of course, but the time it would take for me to summon the courage.

"You drive out to that girl's house nearly every weekend. I see you do it. At all hours of the night, too. A man doesn't do that less he loves someone."

"What do you know about it?" With the gun still aimed at his chest, I raised my head to look him squarely in the eyes. In the yellow haze of the bug light, he looked unnatural...almost alien. Perhaps that's why he went crazy. Maybe it was aliens that had caused him to crash that night, and they'd taken over his mind. Killing him now would save the entire human race. I pressed my finger against the trigger.

"About love?" the Professor asked. "Not one man alive out of junior high who doesn't know about love. That girl in the second row with the denim skirt. The way the hair falls over the shoulders of that girl in front of you. Even the way the teacher's slip rustles as she walks by to make sure you're not cheating on the quiz. I may be more dead than alive, but I know about love."

I again raised my head to look at him, trying to figure him out. "You sure speak well for a man who's crazy. Melodramatic perhaps, but—"

"I'm crazy now?" Professor Snow smiled. For the first since I'd arrived he turned away from me. He looked towards the road, and his smile faded. "No, I'm not crazy."

"If a man sits on his porch night after night with a shotgun and a police scanner, yelling at cars that go by…he's crazy. I'm sorry, but those are the rules."

Again Professor Snow smiled. "Rules. See, if you have rules, there must be a game. So whose game are we playing? Can you answer me that?"

I had no answer for him, but he expected that, I'm sure.

"If you can't tell me whose game we're playing, then you probably can't even tell me when the game will be over, or whether or not we're winning. And if you can't tell me that, then I don't really think we're playing a game. If there's no game, then we've got no rules."

Or maybe I could just kill him because he was pissing me off.

"And none of this changes the fact that the woman you love doesn't love you back."

How do the crazy people always know so much? I wondered as I finally lowered the gun. Just as I did, I jumped as the scanner spat out something about a woman reporting domestic violence. Had my finger been on the trigger for two more seconds, Prof. Snow may well have been dead.

"You don't know that," I quickly told Prof. Snow once my heart settled back to its assigned place.

"I know that I've never once seen her drive out at this time of night. Seems to me that you're the one doing all the work here. And I also know that your car is not the only one I see driving by." The Professor nodded up in the direction of Ann's place as if to remind me why I was on his porch and not in Ann's bedroom. Then it hit me as if my head had been slammed into a school bus. I may have even winced from the pain of it.

Ann was no longer a part of my life.

It wasn't her decision. It wasn't mine. It was the result of the actions we'd taken. The night we made love, I'm sure she was convinced Heath would never talk to her again. I was her replacement. Her scab. But when Heath came back, she tore me off with one painful scratch. Ann was too kind to not be embarrassed by tossing me out like that, and that would preclude her from any longer showing me friendship or respect.

And Heath…how many times had I figured he'd won his final battle over me. He'd had my shoulders pinned to the mat so many times now, but he kept lifting me up to offer more punishment, to showboat in front of the crowd. Big pop.

I started to cry at that point. Not a big, sobbing cry, but tears and sniffles like at the end of a sad movie. Professor Snow could see that.

"There's the moment," he sighed. "The worst moment in boy's life. It's not her fault. Don't blame her. The Moon once told me that a pretty face don't make no pretty heart. Truer words may have never been spoken."

The moon. This guy was too much. Had I known he was this entertaining, I would've visited months ago. Using my sleeve to wipe the tears from my face, I sat down on his bench. After a few moments, Professor Snow sat down beside me. Neither of us spoke. We just listened to the remaining insects continue their conversations after my squealing tires had so rudely interrupted them. They worked through their own love troubles and let the cold but gentle wind wrap around me and Pref. Snow as the scanner occasionally hissed its updates about the domestic violence situation in town.

Listening to the troubles of others while sitting in the calm of country isolation was soothing. It made me feel better than it all, or at least far removed from it. "I understand why you stay here."

Prof. Snow shot me a look of frightened confusion that somewhat made me nervous. "You hear them?"

"Hear what?" I asked, making sure I was still the one with the gun.

The Professor relaxed, realizing that I wasn't with him on this one. "That's fine. You shouldn't be able to."

"Voices in your head?" I asked. It seemed like a logical question.

He looked at me as if I was the one who was nuts, then shut off the scanner. He walked to the end of the porch and studied what little of the landscape he could see in the darkness. Without turning back, he repeated, "It's not her fault. It's this road."

"The road?"

"My wife and kids are out there. The road took them away. This girl of yours is out there too, and you can't see her either. It's because of the road. A man has one real job in life, to protect his family. You make promises to God, to fate, or whomever you can that you'll do the right thing as long as your family stays safe…stays protected. You go to work to protect them from hunger. You go to doctors to protect them from sickness. You pay taxes to protect them from war. You buy deadbolt locks and guard dogs and alarm systems and houses in the country and shotguns and police scanners to protect them from all manner of evil the universe can create, but you can't protect them from the road. The road took my family, and the road took yours."

From the direction of Ann's house, I heard a truck starting up. The tree line separating her property from Professor Snow's was suddenly bathed in a ghostly light, and I followed these ghosts as they glided from tree to tree.

"No," I told the Professor as I stood up and grabbed the shotgun. "It wasn't the road."

       ❦   ❦   ❦

It was the drugs. Rhonda had made it quite clear to the Arbiter and I that nothing would ever make her climb that radio tower. But there she was, much higher up than I had gotten. I paused briefly, the rain flowing down my face as I looked up at her. The crowd—most of whom I recognized from the party—were oddly quiet as they watched her climb. I could hear some people debating over what they should do; climb to get her? Send for help? Someone else pointed out that campus security had already been notified. Beside me, a woman who wasn't at the party asked who it was. When someone answered that it was Rhonda, the inquisitor responded, "Damn, I didn't think she was this stupid."

She's not, I wanted to tell her. *This is Fayme. This is all Jayson Fayme.* But I didn't. I couldn't. I was growing numb to everything going on around me as if the rain were an invisible cloth trying to filter everything out. Or maybe this was a play at President's Performing Arts Center for the Performing Arts, and Rhonda was acting again. She was Antigone, and I was an admirer in the audience.

No, that wasn't right. I could've remained a coward behind that thought and just waited for help to arrive. But when I looked up at Rhonda once more, I noticed something I hadn't before. As she approached that first set of lights, I could see she was *on the outside of the tower!*

Not even the Arbiter was daring enough to attempt that, and certainly not while it was raining. My numbness was overtaken by fear, and I found myself scaling the fence that barricaded the radio tower. Was that a piece of Rhonda's jeans I saw snagged by the barbed wire? I didn't stop to check. I didn't even stop to see if I'd cut myself as I flipped over the fence and fell to the ground below. I was sure I had, as I could feel a sharp pain, but I was too caught up in what I was doing to even tell where the pain was. I think I heard someone—or maybe even a couple people—ask, "Who's that guy? What the hell's he doing?" At that moment, I couldn't have correctly answered either question.

The tower was slicker than I thought, and my foot slipped off when I first attempted to climb. I fell only a few feet, and my chin cracked down on one of the bars. A bolt of pain shot up through my teeth and into my head, but it cleared quickly and I once more tried to pull myself up past the point where the tower tapered to the ground. This time I got my footing, and I started to climb. In a way, being on the outside almost made it easier. It was less claustrophobic; more like climbing a ladder…or a TV antenna.

Looking back towards campus, I could see even more people coming to participate in the media event. None of those making their way to the tower appeared to be from security or the fire department or whoever is responsible for getting people off of radio towers, just more bored students. And where was the Arbiter? Had that girl reached him? He was the one who should've been climbing this tower. For Rhonda, he should've been the one. But that's not the way the world works, obviously. So fates and vertiginousness be damned, I continued my climb up the tower.

It was taking me far too long. I made sure that each hand, each foot was firmly placed before pulling one of them off and moving it up. As eager as I was to reach Rhonda, so did the weather seem eager to prevent me from doing so. The rain wouldn't let up; I could see layers of it breaking through the glow of the street lamps on campus. Sometimes the wind would shift suddenly and I'd find myself blinded by the water that covered my eyes. Without letting go of the metal bars, I'd wipe my face on my soaked sleeve and continue upward. Very quickly, my thigh muscles tightened. I knew that despite the adrenaline wave I'd been riding since leaping the fence, I wouldn't be able to make it much higher. In an effort to figure out how far I had to go, I called out to Rhonda. To my shock, she answered right away.

"Hurry up," she called, but not in fear. She sounded more like a child coaxing her parents to the giraffe or Colobus monkey display at the zoo. "Hurry up, we're almost there."

"Hang on," I yelled, thinking it may have been the dumbest thing I've said. We were a hundred feet above the ground by that point, and here I was telling her to hang on. While I was at it, why not suggest that she continue to breathe?

"Come on," she beckoned. "We're almost there. We're going to make it."

"Make it where, Rhonda?" I continued as I forced my tired muscles to climb another rung. And another. And another. "Where are we going?"

"Up," she replied simply.

"Down is nice," I suggested as I looked up to see her. She was past the three middle lights, but not much further ahead of me. I was amazed at how I'd climbed, but was starting to fear that I didn't have the strength to get back down.

"But he's up here," Rhonda explained as I watched her climb higher.

"Who?" I asked. Whatever Jayson had given her was really playing with her mind. Damn it. Why can't the government just hurry up and make marijuana legal so the morons could do that instead of seeking out the heavy stuff. Instead of tripping out and climbing towers or killing their classmates, people would just sit up in their bedroom, smoke a joint and *talk* about climbing towers or killing their classmates. "Who are we going to see?"

"The Arbiter," Rhonda called back. I was disheartened with her answer. If she would've said Jesus or Napoleon or Clifford the Big Red Dog, I could've attributed that to the drugs. But the Arbiter...the Arbiter brought it too close to home. We were now back in our circle, and I didn't want to be there. I wanted to be so far removed from all of this...but hell; for all I knew at that point, the Arbiter may have really been up there.

Where the hell are the helicopters, I thought. *Aren't there supposed to be helicopters or a crane or something to get us down from here?*

"Rhonda, I have the evidence," I told her. It was all I could come up with that might interest her. "I've got everything we need on a Zip. Come on, let's go take it to..."

Mistake. I couldn't very well suggest we take it to the Arbiter when Rhonda believed that he was at the top of the radio tower. I had to take a different approach...something to get her down.

"The Arbiter will want that," Rhonda said. She was shouting to be heard over the wind and rain, but her voice somehow still sounded gentle. "Come on. We'll take it to him."

"But the computers are back down in the office," I pointed out. I tried to climb closer to her, but my legs were no longer cooperating. I had to get her back down to me, and where the fuck was security? Where was the Arbiter?

"We can't go there without Arby," Rhonda pointed out. This was fine. As long as I kept talking to her, I could stop her from climbing any higher.

"Sure we can. I've got a key. Remember? The Arbiter told us to meet him there after the party. We don't want to break his plan."

"But he's up here now. He changed the plan. At the party, he told me to come up here. He said to meet him up here. Come on, we should give him the disk."

There I was, risking my life on a radio tower in the midst of a driving rainstorm, and all Rhonda could think about was whether or not the Arbiter would be pleased. I was so damn tired of hearing about the Arbiter, but at that point I was tired of everything. I was tired of freaky professors who paid me thousands of dollars to write letters to people who probably didn't even exist. I was tired of moronic students who stooped so reprehensibly low as to give the date rape pill to possibly the sweetest, most genuine woman I'd ever met. I was tired of a best friend who was always launching schemes to humiliate others just to further his agenda in life...whatever the hell that agenda was.

I was just tired. I closed my eyes and hung there, waiting for one or both of us to fall and let this whole thing be finished. I'd heard people with terminal diseases talk of the calm that fills them when the final moment comes, when they realize they're going to die and they finally accept it. I wanted that calm. I tried to relax and accept my coming death, but I felt no peace. I tried harder. I even relaxed my grip on the tower to prove to everyone I was ready to die, but I felt no rush of euphoria.

Damn it, I've accepted it! Where's my peace! My God, why haven't thou forsaken me?!

"Guy, come on, the Arbiter's waiting," Rhonda yelled down to me. "Come on."

I was crying again. It was all I had the energy to do. "I can't," I told Rhonda, giving in to the situation.

"What?" she asked. "Guy, I couldn't hear you."

I lifted my head up, looking past the red lights, "I'm too tired, Rhonda. I can't climb anymore."

"Okay. Okay, I'll come get it," she suggested. "It's okay."

I could make out her form as she started to descend past the lights. I don't know how she had the energy to move, or if she believed she could make it all the way to the top. These first lights we were next to were only halfway up the tower. But considering the head start she had on me, I figured she must've rested periodically during her ascent. I had caught up to her pretty quickly, after all. But I'd used everything I had just to get there, and there was no way I was moving any further up or down.

I slowly started to regain my composure as Rhonda came closer to me. I used my sleeve to temporarily wipe the tears from my face, but quickly realized Rhonda would not be able to see them through the rain. My chin stung as my arm brushed against it, so I touched it lightly and held my fingers in front of my face. Even in the red glow of the warning light, I could tell they were stained with blood. I tried to wipe it off on my pants because I didn't want to get any on Rhonda.

She was only a few rungs above me now. If I wanted to, I could've reached up and grabbed her ankle. But I knew that wouldn't be smart. I didn't want to startle her, nor did I want to throw myself off balance. And what would I have done after grabbing her? I hadn't the energy to hold her there, and there seemed to be no help on the way. My only chance was still to talk her back down.

"Hello, Rhonda," I said as she stepped further down. Her left foot was now only one rung away from my hand. "Heard any good jokes lately?"

"Hurry, Guy, Arby's waiting," she urged as she reached her hand down. It was still too far for me to reach.

I devised a plan. "Oh, Rhonda. Shoot. I must've left the disk at the party. We'd better go back and—"

"No!" Rhonda shouted. "You said you had it. You told me only a couple moments ago that you had it, and the Arbiter wants it. Give me that frigging disk!"

Frigging. Even in this situation, out of her mind, Rhonda wouldn't swear. My God, I loved this woman. "But Rhonda, I'm telling you the Arbiter's—"

"Give me the disk! The Arbiter wants the disk!"

The Arbiter wants the disk. Christ. This wasn't going to work. I obviously couldn't talk her down when she was thinking this way, and I would not be able to stall her until help arrived. I only had one other option. "Okay, Rhonda, but I can't reach you. You'll have to climb down a little further."

She did, and was now standing on the rung next to my head. For the first time since I'd left her at the party, I could see her face in the red light the warning beacon afforded us. Her hair had been flattened and tattered by the rain, and it appeared to be jet black. Her sweater and jeans hung heavily on her body, and she was shivering furiously. Despite her assuredness, I knew she wasn't making it to the top.

"Okay, can you reach me?" she asked as she lowered her hand.

"Yes," I replied. I wrapped my left arm around a tower rung, tightening my elbow over it, then reached into my pocket. The Zip disk was there, and I cautiously pulled it out. It would be safe from the rain in its plastic case. "I got it right here, Rhonda. All of the evidence is right on this. The Arbiter will be so proud of us."

"I know," Rhonda agreed, I think with a smile, as she grabbed at the disk. But just as she did, I let go. The plan was simple enough. With no disk, she had no reason to keep climbing. In fact, we'd have to hurry back down to get it before anyone else found it. It would probably be broken, but we'd have to be sure.

Simple enough. Right? I mean, I wasn't wrong in thinking that, was I? For the rest of my life, that's how I'll justify my actions that night. That's how, right there. But common sense will always argue to the contrary. I was over a hundred of feet off the ground, maybe two, clinging to the outside of a radio tower during a rainstorm, trying to talk sense into a woman who was on a drug of unknown origin while I myself hadn't the energy to even move my legs. In such a situation, nothing is simple.

When I let go of the disk, it fell to my shoulder where it balanced for just a moment. In an attempt to save it from falling, Rhonda lunged out to grab it. She lost her grip on the tower and slammed down into me. Had I not wrapped my arm around the tower rung, I would've also lost my hold as Rhonda's shoulder collided with mine. I felt her grab at me as she fell past, and I swung my arm behind me to grab her. But there was nothing there.

This happened so quickly that it seemed as if it hadn't. I felt as if I'd just awoken from a nightmare and was waiting for my senses to come back to me. But they didn't. The nightmare kept going as I watched Rhonda fall. Something had to happen soon. It was taking far too long for her to reach the ground, so I knew something had to happen soon. Either I would wake up or her feet would get really big or Andy Kauffman would start reading *The Great Gatsby* or...or the Arbiter would suddenly jump over the fence, run for the tower and leap into the air to catch her like Superman.

But none of this happened. When Rhonda hit the ground, there was no one there to help her, no one to hold her.

For a few moments, no one moved; not me, and not anyone in the crowd that had gathered around the tower. Their screaming had stopped, leaving only the unforgiving wind and rain and the swaying trees to show any sign of life. But then a few people turned away from the scene and a few others jumped the fence to check on Rhonda.

"Don't pick her up," I cautioned them with a voice no stronger than a whisper. "Don't pick her up."

      ✿   ✿   ✿

I wanted her to stay where she was, safe in her house as Heath drove away. Had I believed she was in the truck with him, I would've stayed right there on Prof. Snow's porch. Ann had been hurt enough, and she was never going to be hurt by me. Not that night, not ever. But Heath wouldn't be taking Ann anywhere. He'd had his fun with her, and now it was time to go home.

Prof. Snow made no move as I backed out of his drive. He seemed confused about my sudden course of action. Had I thought about it, I probably would've been as well. What was my intent, after all, to ram Heath's pickup with my mother's car? What would that accomplish, other than to piss off my mom and Heath?

Yet, it's what I did. I reversed out of Prof. Snow's driveway as fast as the car could go, more than once misjudging my angle and cutting into the yard. I could see Heath's headlights coming towards me, but mine were out. Hopefully, he wouldn't see the car until it was too late. I considered briefly that, because I was reversing out of the drive, he'd hit the passenger side of the car. At least one thing had worked to my advantage.

As Heath got closer, I was reminded of racing the train. I'll freely admit I wasn't thinking too clearly the night I had pulled that stunt, but at least then the goal was to *not* get hit. Tonight I wanted Heath to ram me. Maybe Prof. Snow was right about that road.

Just as I was about to enter the road, I realized I'd pulled out too quickly. It wasn't going to work. I slammed on the brakes and came to a rest stretched across both lanes. Heath was still bearing down on me, and the glare of his headlights made me panic. All of the sudden, getting broadsided by a pickup truck didn't seem like such a great idea. "No Fear," Heath's windshield taunted. But as I groped for the gearshift, Heath betrayed his sticker by swerving. I could hear the squeal of rubber on asphalt, and his headlights were no longer facing me. Heath's truck had fishtailed and rolled over.

As it rolled towards me, I finally got the car in gear and pulled back into the Professor's driveway. Heath's truck had stopped rolling by that point and slid past me on its side, finally coming to rest in the ditch across the road from Prof. Snow's house, its headlights illuminating the field beyond. I sat in the car for a few moments, trying to catch the breath I hadn't realized I'd lost. On his porch, Prof. Snow stared blankly at the overturned truck and then dropped to his knees. He clutched the bench and pulled himself against it, and I realized how hard it must've been for him to watch an auto accident happen on his property. I felt bad for him, but in a few minutes I'd feel even worse.

Grabbing the shotgun from the seat, I stepped out of the car and walked over to Heath's truck. There were no cars coming, so I made no attempt to conceal the weapon. Good thing, too. Where does one conceal a shotgun? Come to think of it, Heath might have heard that line a time or two, "Is that a shotgun in your pocket or are you just glad to see me?"

Heath had already pulled himself out of the truck when I got there, but he was doing so with pain. He was favoring his left arm, and he couldn't seem to stand. Watching him try to get up reminded me of Bambi's first attempt to stand in that old Disney movie, only Heath wasn't surrounded by cute little skunks and rabbits.

Although he could see me standing in the road, he couldn't yet tell who I was.

"What the fuck were you…" He couldn't finish his sentence, so he changed his tone once he gathered the breath to speak. "I need help. I'm hurt, man. Shit, it hurts."

"Good," I replied. "What's it feel like, being hurt?"

I couldn't believe I was spouting this crap. I made a mental note to never again laugh at the ridiculous dialogue of Chuck Norris.

"What?" Heath asked. "Listen, man I think it's broken. I can't stand up."

"So I bet your football career's over then, huh. And you had such great potential."

"What are you…" Heath stammered. For the first time since I'd known him, he seemed genuinely frightened. "Who are you? What's going on?"

"I'm about to kill you," I replied.

Heath didn't respond. I was waiting for that "Is this some kid of joke?" line that people always ask in the movies, but Heath had figured out this wasn't a joke. Give him that much. "Fuck. No. I can't move. Please, just give—"

"No, Heath. No. No charity from me. I'm afraid that…I'm afraid we're past that point. We've been past that point since grade school."

"Grade school, I…Guy? Are you Guy?"

"Hard to recognize me when you're not slamming my head into buses, I know. I get that a lot."

He was still trying to stand, but couldn't even reach his knees. I'm surprised he didn't try to climb back under the truck, as the depth of the ditch afforded him at least a foot of crawl space. Instead, he tried to pull himself up out of the ditch. I watched him struggle for a few moments, smiling at the poetry of the moment. "Keep it up, sport. Give it a hundred and ten percent."

Sport? I'd never called anyone "sport" in my entire life. I really had absolutely no grasp on this whole action hero thing. It was somewhat disconcerting.

"Come on, Heath," I continued, "the whole school's behind you. Hell, the whole town! You can do it, buddy, you just gotta believe. Pain is temporary. Pride is forever!"

"Shut up!" Heath yelled, but I could tell he was crying. To this day, I still wonder if it was from pain or from fear.

"That's right! You gotta want it! Show us your Fighting Golden Sandie spirit!"

"Shut up!"

"If you've got spirit, let me hear it!" I chanted, mimicking the cheerleaders.

Heath didn't respond. He was now halfway out of the ditch, so I finally raised the shotgun. Heath began to claw and kick harder at the dirt and weeds around him. I pointed the shotgun at his back and hoped that Prof. Snow had loaded and cocked the thing. Imagine my embarrassment if I'd had no bullets!

"You know, I'm only doing this because you deserve it," I told Heath. "People say that we're not supposed to judge one another, but guys like you, you make it okay. You make it easy. Do you know that? It's true. And do you know what else? Ann loves you. She really does."

"I know," Heath replied. He was no longer fighting his way out of the ditch, so I figured he must've responded to my comment to try to stall me until he got more strength. He was a clever one, that Heath Millard, but I wasn't going for it. To literally be on the other end of the shotgun, it felt…different. I'm sorry I can't do better than that, but that's all I felt. Different. I didn't feel powerful, I didn't feel vengeful. I was, after all, just doing my duty. Heath had been such a bastard his whole life. Clear back in grade school, he had a selfishness and cruelty about him that it takes most people half a lifetime to develop. If, at this age, he could already disdain everyone and everything around him, who knows how deeply and intensely it would develop.

He gave one final *old football try* to climb his way out of the ditch, and I knew he wasn't going to make it. He never would. I calmly told him, "This is the point where I'd yell at you for screwing up my life. And not just mine, but everyone's. But I'm too tired, and I just want to go home and go to bed, so I'm just going to shoot you."

The night swallowed the clap of the gunshot. It sounded pathetically unimpressive compared to the pumped of resonance of a gunfight on TV. It was more like the snapping of a leather belt, but the result was satisfactory.

Heath flinched backwards as the spray of pellets tore into his back. He feebly tried twice more to kick his way out of the ditch, and then fell still. I kept waiting for him to pop up suddenly and start slapping me around. Any minute now his friends would jump out of the pickup truck and start laughing at me, or Principal Steele would walk out of the cornfield with his paddle. But not this time. Heath didn't get the better of me in this situation.

I didn't even care that I'd won my war with him. I just cared that it was over. I didn't even bother with the three count.

From the glow of the truck's headlights, I could see that Heath's blood was starting to stain the back of his varsity jacket. I wondered if he would have been as proud of this blood as that which sometimes stained his uniform after a game. Would he have shown it off in the cafeteria, and would anyone have been impressed? Of course. To the faculty and students of John Stuart Mill High School, Heath was Jim Jones. And the only way to stop them all from drinking the Kool Aid was to make sure it was never made, right?

I didn't look both ways as I crossed the street back to Prof. Snow's house. Through the wall of trees that separated Ann's house from Snow's, I could see that no lights had been turned on. If she had heard the gunshot, she at least hadn't discerned what is was, or was perhaps frightened by it. I thought momentarily of turning off the lights on Heath's truck, but it seemed too symbolic a gesture…like closing Heath's eyes or giving him a proper burial. Nope. Heath's car battery could die as well.

Professor Snow was still sitting next to the bench when I got back to the porch. Without saying anything, I handed him the shotgun and thanked him. He took the gun, but he still didn't break his gaze from the pickup in his ditch. Looking back at Heath, I almost felt bad leaving him there. But in all fairness, I had told him I was tired.

I listened to the radio on the way home. Cool jazz. I was almost afraid the tranquility of it would put me to sleep in the car, but it didn't. I made it home safely, crawled into bed, and fell immediately into a deep, peaceful sleep.

❀

CHAPTER 14

Avenger of the Blood

I awoke in a hospital bed. I first realized this not from the lack of décor, but from the smell. It wasn't necessarily foul, but distinct. In much the same way that grandma's house smelled like all the pasta sauces, cherry pies, casseroles and soups she'd cooked over the years, so do hospitals smell like all the babies delivered, kidneys removed, livers transplanted and room deodorizers sprayed to cover it all up.

Before I had a chance to remember what placed me in this aromatic jubilee, I heard a voice from the end of my bed.

"There, I told you he wasn't dead."

"I never said he was dead."

"I'm afraid you did. In fact, you stated it just like that. You said, 'He's dead.' You said it twice. 'He's dead. He's dead. He's double dead.'"

"Yes, but that was fifteen minutes ago. At the time, he looked quite dead. But I've since changed my mind since then."

"Sure, now that he's alive."

"Aha! There! '*Now* that he's alive.' See, even you admit that he was dead."

"He was never dead."

"You sure seem to think so."

"Now why would I stay here as long as we have if I felt that he was dead? Obviously, waiting to talk to a dead guy isn't an efficient way to manage one's time."

"Unless…unless one were waiting for said dead fellow to come back to life."

"Okay, but how many times has that happened?"

"Eight."

"I see."

I found myself hoping these men weren't my doctors.

"Welcome back to the land of the living, young man" one of them said to me.

"It's good to be back," I replied with more strength than I figured I would have. Whatever had happened to me, it obviously wasn't that bad.

"Your roommate, however, will be disappointed. No four point for him."

"Unless he was already getting one," the other guy pointed out.

"No, we have a new policy," the first guy argued. "Since we instated the policy that a student who's roommate dies gets a four point, then it only seems fair that students whose roommates don't die can't get a four point. Each is given an automatic B+ in badminton."

"I'm not sure I understand."

"It's simple. Roommate dies; four point. Roommate lives; no four point."

"Won't that encourage those students who have the potential to get a four point to murder their roommate?"

"Well, yes, that would be the flaw, but no policy is perfect. I mean, look at Seward's Ice Box."

"Whose ice box?"

"Seward's."

"And did this Stewart have a four point?"

"If so, he must've killed for it."

"Like our students do."

"Exactly; which is why we've been training the R.A.s on how to handle the murderous lechers."

"That's an excellent program, I'm sure. As always, Floodbane is on the cutting edge of social conscience and emotional acceptance. But I don't see how an R.A. will be able to prevent murders. Aside from policing every student in danger of getting a four point, they couldn't—"

"Oh, heavens no. We're not training them to spot and prevent a murder before it happens, we just want them to be able to pick up the pieces afterwards. In times of crisis such as that, students can suffer various psychological effects that can effect them psychologically. They could turn to drugs or alcohol or poetry, and that could, in turn, affect enrollment. So it's important that our R.A.s be able to add the proper amount of drama to the event."

"Perhaps we could hire this Stewart to speak to them."

I'd realized by now I was dealing with Dean Douglas and President Tunney, and I was hoping to confuse them into leaving. "So, if a student kills his roommate, does he get another one?" I asked.

Unfortunately, President parried my ploy with, "Son, didn't we just cover that?"

"We're glad you're up," Dean Douglas said as he rose from a chair at the end of the room and made his way to my bed. He sat down and took my hand, and I noticed at that point I had no I.V.s or anything sticking out of me. I must've been okay.

Well, except for the fact that a fifty year old man was holding my hand. I promptly pulled it away.

"Why?" I asked. "Did you come to offer me a four point?"

"No, sadly, your roommate is still alive." Douglas sighed. "But we would like to offer you a diploma."

"A diploma?"

"You can pick any major you like. Ecology. Physics. Organizational communication—"

"General studies," President added.

"You don't have majors in any of those," I pointed out.

"Didn't I explain to you already that there's a flaw in every plan?"

"No."

"Well, that would be the flaw in my plan, which only proves my point. QED."

QED. I think I heard my mom say that once. I didn't know what it meant then, I didn't know now. Feel free to look it up.

"Why are you offering me a diploma?" I asked.

"We offer diplomas to all of our students," Dean Douglas explained.

"Don't most of them have to graduate first?" I persisted.

"Yes, but it's our view that not all students *need* to complete their educations in order to be recognized for it. You have learned enough, young man. Our meager school has nothing more to offer to you. If you will, look at it like a prison break, only with the blessings of the warden."

"Does this have anything to do with the radio tower?" I asked.

Dean Douglas responded, "If a man sitting in the electric chair suddenly gets a pardon from the governor, he generally doesn't stop to question the governor's motives," but I wasn't listening to his response. The thought of the radio tower suddenly yanked me out of the hospital room and back to reality. The image of Rhonda lying on the ground below…people crowding around her. I was sure she was dead, but I guess I still needed verification.

"What degree did Rhonda pick?" I asked.

President and Dean Douglas looked at each other, then turned back to me. "Rhonda?"

"Rhonda," I repeated. "The woman who was on the tower with me."

Dean Douglas leaned in. I could smell his breath as he spoke, and it reminded me of canned peas. "I want you to listen to me very carefully. This college has had more than enough of its share of bad press due to the death of its students. Is it our fault kids get drunk and fall out of fraternity windows? No. Is there anything we can do to stop drug addicts from climbing radio towers at all hours of the night? Huh uh."

"What happened to Rhonda?"

"Is there anything we can do to stop the biology department from dumping toxic waste into the creek and producing behemoth ticks that terrorize the campus?"

Dean Douglas and I both stared blankly at President for a few moments before the Dean turned back to me.

"I don't care about the problems of your friend," he stated without sympathy. "I don't care about *your* problems. What I do care about is this school. If you get out of this hospital and start talking about faulty barbed wire or ineffective fences, then the press is going to hop all over this like something that hops on things."

"And now I'm hearing rumors of one of our sororities marketing pornography."

"Really?" President brightened.

"What happened to Rhonda?" I asked.

But Dean wasn't paying attention to either of us. "Problems like that, they're sometimes hard to solve. Too many distractions. But problems like you, they're easy.

"The doctors have said that you're fine. You've been treated for exposure, and you're free to go once you feel up to it. Once you get back to Floodbane, I want you to continue to go through the motions. It shouldn't be that hard…it's what most students do anyway. You continue to go to classes, and you continue to play in your little basketball games."

"What happened to Rhonda?"

"It doesn't matter if you do any of your assignments. You will pass, and you will graduate. The rest of your tuition has also been covered."

So it seemed that neither Dean Douglas nor President knew of my agreement with Mr. Bernard. And if they didn't know of that, then they also honestly didn't know about the Eta Iota Upsilon porn scam. In a way, it made me feel sorry for them. They really did believe they had control of what was going on at their school. I could empathize.

But what had happened to the Zip disk?

"Now, are we agreed?"

"What happened to Rhonda?"

Dean Douglas leaned in closer, perhaps in attempt to intimidate me. "Are we agreed?"

I nodded. "Yes."

"You're a smart man," Dean Douglas smiled. "I'll see you on graduation day."

And with that, he and President got up to leave the room. As they disappeared into the hallway, I heard President ask, "About this porn ring…which sorority?"

Unable to process all that happened since…how long had I been in the hospital? I looked around to try to get some idea, but there was nothing to provide any clues. I thought about getting up, but decided against it. It was all too surrealistic at the moment. It was as if I were still in that state when one wakes up from a dream and can't yet discern the dream from reality. Only this time, it was reversed. It was reality that violently shook me awake, and I didn't want that. I wanted to be asleep where I could still pretend to not know what became of Rhonda. But before I could even shut my eyes, my door was thrown open and in walked Mr. Bernard. He was carrying a bunch of those Mylar helium balloons, each sporting a picture of Ziggy.

"Hey, monkey boy!" Mr. Bernard greeted as he carried the balloons over to my bed. Instead of floating to the ceiling when he let go of them, they dropped, stopping where their string hit. They were at that odd state where the helium could no longer lift them but was still powerful enough to stay aloft with the extra support of the string.

I understood the feeling.

"Glad to see you're okay. We've been worried about you."

"Who's 'we?'" I asked.

"Did I say 'we?' I meant 'me.' Actually, I didn't even mean that. What I meant to say was that I'm hungry. Can you believe the hospital cafeteria isn't open at 3:30?"

I looked at the clock on the wall. "It's 10:45."

Mr. Bernard stared at it for a moment, then looked back at me. He then looked at his watch. "I'll never get used to that. Anyway, how are you feeling?"

I knew he wasn't really concerned about my health, so I switched to something that mattered to at least one of us. "What happened to Rhonda?"

"I thought you were there," Mr. Bernard replied. "That's what the Arbiter reported."

"The Arbiter?"

"The Arbiter, in *A Daily Planet*. Nice article. He's a talented young man. Get that boy an agent and a muse or two, one Asian, one Latin, teach them to dance, and you've got yourself the next John Dos Passos…or am I thinking of Judy Blume? I have the article here. Want to read it?"

"No. No, I don't. Just tell me what happened to Rhonda."

Finally someone answered me. "Rhonda was pronounced dead when the paramedics arrived."

I knew that. I knew that from the way she landed, from the way she lay at the base of the tower. This is why my reaction was so calm, why I didn't burst into tears. From the moment she fell, throughout the entire duration of unconsciousness (how long was that?), to this moment, I'd been able to prepare for the official announcement.

But there was something else, too. There was another emotion tearing feelings away from Rhonda's death. It was anger.

"He wrote an article about it?"

"It's right here if you want to read it," Mr. Bernard said. "Very professionally done."

"He wasn't there," I muttered more to myself than to Mr. Bernard. My former professor asked what I'd said, but I continued muttering. "He couldn't show up to grant Rhonda her final wish, but he could report it." I turned back to Mr. Bernard. "Did he mention the disk?"

"Disk."

"Anything about pornography?"

"Damn, are you a randy fellow! Been in a hospital bed for the better half of a week and you want to watch a little *Dirty Debutantes vol. 6!* I knew I liked you for some reason. I should take you to New York with me."

"New York?"

"NYC, baby. One of my movies is being produced by a student at NYU, some genius, no doubt, and I want to oversee the project. Don't trust the rotten little bastard. Probably wants to add puppets, or maybe even monologues and puns. Can't trust anyone, my friend."

"Which movie?" I asked. I'd never read any of his scripts, but judging from the response they garnered, I couldn't imagine anyone with the slightest degree of decency would want to film one.

But then, we *were* talking about NYU.

"Doesn't have a title yet. We'll work on that later. It's the tender story of a Jewish pirate who's afraid to love. Lot of special effects shots and musical montages. We even have a catch phrase that'll carry us through the sequels; 'Oy! Matey!'"

I chose to ignore this at the moment. "I had the proof on the Zip. I had the photos from the Eta Iota Upsilon's porn site."

For the first time since I'd met him, Mr. Bernard turned serious, but for only a second. He looked at me with a degree of surprise, but this was immediately replaced with what I presumed to be a mixture of sorrow and pity. As quickly as this came, he switched back to flippancy. "Well, enjoy the balloons. Ziggy. They were fresh out of Rex Morgan M.D."

"No, wait. Tell me what you know."

"Take too long, I know a lot. You rest up."

That did it. I snapped. "Dammit, listen to me! Rhonda is dead! Don't any of you care?! *You* don't care, *President* doesn't care, the goddam *Arbiter* doesn't even care! She's dead because of some freakin' joke you all thought would be funny. In the process of trying to destroy lives, you completely wiped one out. Now I want to know why! I deserve an explanation!"

"Boy, have you got a lot to learn," Mr. Bernard sighed. He stood and walked to the doorway, but then turned around. "I like you, Guy, so listen to me. Not everyone thinks as you do. Not everyone processes information the same way you do. And just because you want something, even if you should have it, even if you've busted your ass and slaved for it for years on end, you'll rarely get it. Look at me…I'm still waiting for a Climax Blues Band reunion. Think that'll ever happen?

"You don't get to decide in life what you deserve. Too many other people are going to make that decision for you. Incorrectly, most likely. Don't be wrong with them."

And he left. I wanted to chase after him, or at least try to find some kernel of usefulness in the "wisdom" he'd imparted. But despite my intentions, it was easier to just fall back on the pillow and return to unconsciousness; the only place where I could make sense of what was going on around me.

❦   ❦   ❦

I wrestled with the thought of whether or not I'd actually killed Heath when I awoke the following morning. I didn't want to get my hopes up, after all. I'd been down this road before. But I didn't even need to wait for school on Monday to learn of Heath's fate. It was everywhere. My parents were the first to let me know, as it had apparently been prayed over heavily in church already that morning. People in the congregation were actually crying, mom reported. She didn't seem to be too broken up about it, at least not past the "Well, that's a shame…his poor mother," point. Dad was more interested in the football games and at what time mom's fried chicken and rice were being served. At one point, after watching some professional player throw a 56-yard touchdown pass, he muttered, "I wonder if Heath could've made it this far?"

That made me happy. Although I hated Heath, I certainly didn't want to think my dad was some kind of callous bastard.

Curiously enough, as the day went on, I heard no deliberation over who was the murderer. Everyone in town, and even the reporters on the news, seemed pretty sure of who it was.

Professor Snow.

I couldn't believe this. Apparently, he was found immediately after Heath, still sitting on his front port clutching the shotgun. Never mind the fact that Snow had no car to leave those tracks in his driveway and front yard. Don't even wonder why Heath's truck was overturned. And why bother seeking out a motivation? There's a crazy man with a gun, and there's a dead, teenage hero in the ditch in front of his house. The public wanted vengeance, and they wanted it now…before football season ended.

I felt bad for Prof. Snow, both because he was now labeled a killer and because he spent the whole night outside and had probably caught a cold. In all of the reports and hearings that followed, I kept waiting for him to say that he didn't do it and to reveal the true killer.

But he never did. He just kept saying over and over again that it was the road. It was the road that killed Heath, and that it will kill again.

I eventually started to consider turning myself in. Freaky as he may be, I didn't want Prof. Snow to be punished for my crime. But before I was able to consider this too strongly, something amazing happened. Finally, Prof. Snow was deemed unfit to live on his own, and he was put in a psychiatric ward. This man, who had once been forgotten by everyone except for the church volunteers who brought him groceries and cleaned his house for him, was finally getting the attention and help he needed. And who knows; maybe once he was away from the road that claimed the lives of family, maybe he could sort of "get it back together."

Whether or not that would come to pass, it was the only incentive I needed to remain silent about the killing of Heath Millard…unlike back in town. I was prepared for an outpouring of emotion from the community, but my god did they take it to the extreme. School was cancelled on Monday, and half of Tuesday was spent in an assembly honoring Heath. Every student who wanted to eulogize him was allowed to get up in front of the school and do so. Teachers, students, janitorial staff…even cooks got up to deliver speeches through teary eyes and runny nose.

"I'll never forget how Heath'd always used to steal an extra slice of pizza. He'd hide it under his first slice. He'd put it right there underneath it and smash it down all flat so that it would only look like one slice. We always thought it was so funny, and we'd let him do it because of all he did for this school and its lunch program. And to honor his memory of him, we've decided to now sell two pizza slices at a special price; $1.20 because 12 was his number, without the oh, because there's no room on a jersey for three number unless they made them too small, and if we sold two pizzas for twelve cents, we'd have to fire more helpers on account of making up for the lost money.

"This Heath special starts tomorrow, and after voting on it with the kitchen, we've decided to call it the Heath Special in honor of his death. Now, whenever you take a bite of our pizza with 100% real cheese and Mae's homemade tomato sauce, you can think of Heath.

"Thank you, and God bless Heath."

Huge pop from the school. I, on the other hand, was extremely disappointed, no more school pizza for me.

But that wasn't it. At the request of Heath's parents, it was decided Heath would be buried *under the football field*. I swear I'm not making this up. The day after the memorial assembly, the school was once again let out early to attend the service at the stadium. It was packed despite $8.00 a ticket, the money from which would be donated to Heath's favorite charity once the school board figured out what that was. And to make matters worse, the marching band had to dress up and play the funeral dirge as his casket was carried by the team captains from the locker room to the field. People who couldn't get into the stadium lined the streets to bid farewell to their fallen hero, and many band members had to be helped to the field because they were sobbing so hard. It was like Lincoln being taken to Springfield.

Once at the field, we stopped and came to attention near the end zone. The goal posts had been wrapped in crepe paper and adorned with floral arrangements, and a huge portrait of Heath's face hung between them. The scoreboard was lit up to reflect every touchdown Heath had ever scored, and the clock continually counted down from 12:00 to 0:12, then reset itself to symbolize "Heath leading eternity to victory," as the head of the athletic department later explained. The priest was wearing a referee's shirt and whistle around his collar (was Heath even Catholic?), and all of Heath's fellow players were in their football uniforms, as were the cheerleaders. The dancers weren't on the field, so I couldn't see how Ann was taking all of this. In fact, I hadn't seen her at all since Heath's death. Was she even in school?

If the school memorial assembly was over the top, then this one was over the top, back down the other side and halfway up the next peak. To start off, the flag twirlers, who sometimes marched with fake, wooden shotguns, tossed them all into a bonfire because they now wanted to be a "non-violent dance troupe." I think the symbolism of this gesture was diminished by the fact that they continued to refer to themselves as a dance *troupe*.

After this, the co-captain and coach of the football team each made his own announcement. First the captain dedicated the rest of the season to Heath, "...because Heath was a winner and he would like us to win."

Of course, they went on to lose every game by an average of 32 points. At the end of the season, the coach stated, "Our boys should be commended. They laid down this season in honor of Heath to prove to the community and themselves just how important he was to the team. To make that kind of sacrifice and lose that badly week after week...that's something special."

The day of the funeral, however, the coach had a different announcement to make. After a ten minute speech that was about as relevant and coherent as an MTV Video Music Awards acceptance, he concluded with, "From this day forward, in honor of the memory of Heath's death and all he did for this football team and its school, we will now be known as the John Stuart Mill High School Fighting Golden Heathies!"

Oh Lord, no. I wanted to laugh so badly that I nearly bled from biting my lower lip. The people in attendance applauded and wept at the gesture, but I felt bad for poor Sandie. It had never occurred to me before, but that's probably how John Stuart Mill got its name; some girl or guy or maybe even a dog named Sandie had died, or possibly even done something great, and the name was immortalized by a sports collective. But now Heath had wiped out that memory forever.

Bastard. Even in death...

Heath was buried in his jersey. I guess that was appropriate, if not the most intelligent thing to do. When the school decided to retire his jersey the following year, they realized they had nothing to hang in the gymnasium. Why another jersey wasn't made, I have no idea, but the city instead decided to exhume the body and remove the jersey. It was in surprisingly good shape, but football jerseys are made to last, I suppose. I wonder if they gave Heath's corpse another shirt to wear, or if he's down there half-naked.

But that's not the only thing worth mentioning about Heath's burial. I mean, I guess I shouldn't be surprised with this. It was fitting, if not creepy as well. But, if a sailor can be buried at sea, then a football player can be buried in the end zone. It's all true. Right there in the center, probably next to Jimmy Hoffa. To many, this was a fitting tribute to their local hero. To me, it was high camp. But again, the community missed the symbolism of it all. From that day on, each time a player performed his touchdown celebration at that end of the field, he would be dancing on Heath's grave.

After the community mourning period had ended, I finally was able to think about what I'd done. I ran through the whole Dostoevsky *Crime and Punishment* debate over and over again, arguing over whether it was okay to kill this guy who was a blight on humanity. Could he have redeemed himself and actually done something good for the world? It's possible. But what could he become that would compensate for what he'd been? Knowing Heath as I did, I knew he'd only become worse, and would probably acquire power along the way. I couldn't let that happen. Was it my right to make that decision for humanity? Well, God was obviously wafling on the subject, and someone had to step up to the plate.

Although I found myself without remorse for having killed Heath, I did pity Ann. Imagine that…I pitied my guardian angel.

There was certainly no public lack of interest in Ann after Heath's murder. Everyone knew he had been out visiting her, and they all wanted to know what he'd said; what she'd said; what they'd done. There were typical moronic news reports about her…

"When Ann Penella said goodbye to Heath Millard that night, she had no idea that it would be their last."

No kidding. I need a news reporter to tell me that Ann had no idea her boyfriend would be murdered? Do news reporters have to actually get an education, or do they get their jobs based on the clothes they wear?

As a result, Ann became quite withdrawn. I was happy to note that—despite quitting every extra curricular activity,—she did continue to get good grades and eventually received a rather nice scholarship at a school far from our little town. I can't say I blame her. She wanted out, and she made that happen in the best way possible.

She and I never talked after the murder. Well, not in the actual sense of the word. A couple months after the incident, we happened to be in the library together. I saw her sitting in the V aisle, and I took a seat at a table nearby. Although we hadn't spoken, after all, it's not as if we were avoiding each other. We were simply avoiding a conversation that we never wanted to have. Funny how the fear of a little thing like one conversation can completely destroy so much.

Of course, my killing her boyfriend may have been slightly responsible as well.

But as I sat there reading *The Rime of the Ancient Mariner*, I could feel eyes upon me. I turned to see that she was looking at me with an expression I couldn't place. It wasn't anger or depression, but more like curiosity. She looked like she was trying to figure something out…or maybe remember where she'd left her keys or something like that. I didn't know how I was to react, so I didn't. I just simply returned her gaze.

We remained that way for a few moments, when her face suddenly brightened like that of a child who for the first time laces his shoes by himself. Whatever had been puzzling her, she now had figured out. She looked at me a moment longer, then left the library.

To this day, I have no idea what that moment meant to her. I'm sure she knew from the day after it happened that I was the one who'd killed Heath. And although she never talked to me about it, she also never told anyone else. I guess that it was her last duty as my guardian angel, protecting me in that manner. I loved her for that, but then I already did, didn't I? For the rest of my life, though, whenever I think of Ann Penella, I'll think of that moment in the library when she told me something I couldn't understand.

❧   ❧   ❧

Being confused was nothing new to me, of course. Especially in the presence of the Arbiter, I'd been confused countless times before. But not like this. Whereas it was mostly more of an amused bewilderment, this confusion was that dangerous mixture of anger and pain.

"He's gone," the Arbiter repeated. "Left. Asked him if your tuition was still covered, and he said he's pretty sure you'd have no trouble with that. Did you get a deal from the school?"

"Yeah," I replied. It was more of an automated response than an answer. My thoughts couldn't get beyond the image of Mr. Bernard fleeing town in a beat-up convertible, the law hot on his tail, maybe some teenage runaway he'd picked up at a truck stop crouching down in the front seat with a pistol in her hand.

A thought occurred to me. "Mr. Bernard visited me in the hospital. Didn't say much, though. Nothing useful, anyway. He said he was going to New York, but I didn't think it would be so soon." I paused. "Do you think he was part of the porn thing?"

"Doubt it," the Arbiter replied. "Not sure how he found out about it, but he was nothing more than a repeat visitor."

"Any ideas then? Who is running the site?"

"Was. It's gone now." The Arbiter looked away from me and seemed to take notice of the stereo in Rhonda's apartment. He walked over to it and started sifting through the CDs that were lying about.

It was odd being in Rhonda's apartment that night. After the accident at the radio tower, it had somehow become the responsibility of the Arbiter and I to clear out her things. Rhonda's family had yet to return to Floodbane, although there was really no reason to. Her body had already been transported to her hometown, and I'm sure the last thing her family wanted was to return so soon to the place of her death. So, whether he had offered his services or they had been solicited, the Arbiter was now in Rhonda's apartment boxing up the items she'd chosen to carry with her through life.

"The disk was the only proof, but it shattered when you dropped it from the tower," the Arbiter added as he placed a Wall of Voodoo CD in the player. The familiar beat of "Far Side of Crazy," started pumping through the apartment. I wondered how long it would be before Fayme came complaining up the steps, and I hoped he would. I was sure the next time the Arbiter saw him, he'd do more than knock him off his bike.

Then I realized what the Arbiter had said. "Wait. Everything that's happened, and you're worried about…" I decided to switch gears. "Have you seen Fayme?"

"Yes."

I kept waiting for the Arbiter to elaborate, but I eventually had to prompt him. "And what did you do?"

"Didn't do anything."

"You didn't do anything?"

"Well, obviously did something. Stood there. Processed thoughts. Didn't kick his ass, if that's what you're getting at."

I could feel my face starting to burn. "But didn't…this was all his thing," I pointed out.

The Arbiter looked at me as if I'd just told him that his mother was a turtle. "His thing?"

"The whole tower thing," I elaborated. "He was trying to—"

"Know what he was trying to do. If he'd been successful, would've kicked his ass. But he failed as badly as—"

"Failed? Failed!? My God, Arbiter, if it hadn't been for him Rhonda wouldn't have climbed that tower in the first place!"

"And if the radio had never been invented, there would've been no tower."

"I think that Jayson was a little more directly involved than Marconi."

"So were you. How many people do you want to blame for this? How about the school? How about the ISP that hosted the damn site in the first place?"

I had no idea how to respond. Rhonda was the only person for whom the Arbiter had shown genuine affection since the first day I'd met him. Aside from the planning and execution of his grand schemes, she was how he spent his time; doing things with her, doing things for her. And now that she'd been torn violently away from him, he didn't seem to care. Perhaps that explained my intensity. I had to react for the both of us.

"No! This was Fayme's fault! He killed her! He's the one who put whatever-it-was in her drink! He's who sent her up that tower!"

The Arbiter slumped back onto Rhonda's couch. "Fayme."

We were silent for a few moments, letting Andy Prieboy of Wall of Voodoo dictate the conversation.

"So what'll we do?"

The Arbiter looked at me blankly. "Clean up Rhonda's things, then head down to *A Daily Planet*. Already have some ideas for next week's edition."

"Next week's edition? Jesus, Arbiter, He killed Rhonda! You know the college isn't going to do a damn thing about it! If you ask them, he wasn't even at the party! My God, Arbiter, we can't just..." I stopped. I had no right to say what I was thinking at that point.

"So you want to go downstairs and do what? Break his knees? Cut off a few fingers? Or are you going so far as to suggest that—"

"What I'm saying," I interrupted, "is that he did something wrong. And it didn't just...end wrong. The entire act from start to finish was wrong. And as always, he's not going to get punished for it. Not even a smack on his ass from his parents."

"And you're his punishment, you're suggesting? Fayme should get what's coming to him? 'Ergo, justice,' the whole bit? No, see, that's not your job. It's not your job anymore than it's your job to be the mark of a policeman's bullet. Such endings aren't yours or anyone else's to write. Fayme's not a killer, he's a plot element. He furthered a story that was already being written, propelling to an ending that was already decided. He ultimately is no more important than Mr. Bernard or Dean Douglas or the fire god. Their actions, feelings and problems are trivial and naïve, and their roles, separated from the story, are of little consequence.

"No, you don't get to make such decisions. That right belongs to one person only."

"No. Don't you start on God at this point. See, God stopped caring about injustice a long time ago. God stopped caring about *us* a long time ago. He has better things to do with His time than dole out punishment to those who deserve it."

"Interesting theory, but unrelated. Wasn't talking about God."

"Then who?"

"The Queen."

What was I saying before about confusion? "What, of England? Canada? Hearts?"

"Of the colony."

Which explained nothing, of course. But then it came to me, and I was disgusted. "This whole ant thing again?"

"'Thing?'" the Arbiter repeated somewhat insulted. "Don't know why you can't understand this. Loved Rhonda."

"Then where the hell were you that night?" I was interrogating him now.

"Where do you think?"

"I think you weren't where you should've been! You weren't where Rhonda needed you to be!"

"Was *right* there, actually," the Arbiter explained in a manner that let me know he would go no further with that thought.

But I wasn't going to let it end. "You weren't in our apartment. You sure as hell weren't in the office."

"Was right there," the Arbiter repeated. "Can't be blamed that she didn't get there."

I stared at him in disbelief. I was dumbfounded. The Arbiter had loved Rhonda, hadn't he? Hadn't he just said so? His apathy threw my emotions out of whack, and the only one I could even remotely latch onto was revenge.

I calmed back down and tried to reason with the Arbiter. "Listen. We have to do something about this. We're the only ones who—"

"No!" he snapped, finally displaying an emotion. It was neither the one I'd expected nor hoped for. "Come on, Guy, how well did you even know her? She had two dogs back home. Do you know their names?"

I didn't even know she had pets.

"What was her favorite movie? *Labyrinth*. What word did she misspell to lose the sixth grade spelling bee? Unparalleled. She misspelled unparalleled. She put an 'I' in there. All you knew about her was what she offered, and do you know why that is? Because that's all you *needed* to know. Learning any more may've dropped her down a rung or two, may've shattered the image of perfection. You learned all you needed in order for you to play out your role in the colony; to figure out how you two fit into it together."

"Damn it, Arbiter, this isn't an ant colony!" I was shouting again. "We're not just a bunch of workers serving a fucking queen who just spits out more ants all day. Rhonda may not have mattered to everyone, but she mattered to me. So I didn't know her life story. Big deal. I know that she made me feel better when I was with her, that—"

"Would you listen to yourself?" the Arbiter interrupted. "You don't believe that. It was your attitude towards her that made you feel better. With you it was Rhonda, with others it's tapioca pudding. The point is that everyone's here to serve the colony. Rhonda's gone, so there's nothing she can offer anymore. Harming another member of the colony won't help anyone."

"Unless that member has already harmed others," I suggested.

"So it's back to Plato again? Been there quite a bit lately, too. No desire to go there with you now."

"Yeah, it seems you've had no desire to go anywhere as of late."

"Listen, if you think you've got the right to make that decision, then do what you must. But you will be wrong."

"I'll be wrong?" I laughed. "Listen, sport, I don't think I've ever been right."

The conversation pretty much ended there. I was too angry with the Arbiter to go any further, so I released my frustration by packing up Rhonda's things. It's odd, almost oppressive, packing up items for someone who's dead. I found myself being overly fastidious about where her belongings were placed and how safe they'd be. I worried about what Rhonda had liked the most and what she simply hadn't managed to throw out yet. It's crazy, but more often than once I found myself going into the other room to ask her.

It took longer than we expected, so I wasn't surprised when the Arbiter suggested we blow off the paper that night. I'm not sure of his motives, but I didn't complain because I had absolutely no desire to work with him. It was only for Rhonda that I was even able to stay in her apartment and help him at all. Damn the paper. For all I cared, there didn't need to be one for the rest of the year.

But that night, I couldn't sleep. I could only think of Fayme. He was probably at the fraternity house, getting drunk with his friends and making up stories about how he'd done Rhonda at the party before she took off for the tower. Or worse yet, he was using her death to get the sympathy of another woman so he could slither his way into places with her that Rhonda would never let him go.

Then I started to think about what the Arbiter had said; how it wasn't my right to decide who got punished and how he received it. Was he right? When I murdered Heath, did it end up being better or worse for the community?

Sorry, Arbiter. For the *colony*.

And where was the Arbiter when Rhonda needed him? I can't say exactly, but I know a lot of time passed from when the girl first attempted to phone him to when Rhonda...well, a lot of time passed. The Arbiter said he was right where Rhonda needed him to be. Where was that? Not his apartment. Not the office of *A Daily Planet*. So where? Panthemom's? The sidewalk where they first met? The tower?

My God, the tower. What if he really was up there? What if Rhonda knew something I didn't? What if he was up there and if I'd just let Rhonda go ahead she wouldn't have...

No, this wasn't my fault. No matter what the circumstances, I was not to blame for what happened to Rhonda Vorhees, to the woman who that night was going to at last be the one to forgive me for killing somebody. I was not to blame, but I knew who was.

I thought back to Mr. Bernard teaching Plato in philosophy class and of the lesson I learned that day. Justice. Justice is everyone getting what's coming to him. But despite the Arbiter's claims, one can't have justice without someone willing to enforce it. I thought of the Arbiter's critique of Sal Mineo, the appreciation he showed Sal for bowing out so the dynamic would not be thrown off balance. What about that? Why was the Arbiter not showing the same appreciation for Rhonda. Simple; because she wasn't the one who was supposed to bow out. That role was forced on her, and I was all too aware of who made her accept it. I couldn't let such arrogant interference go unpunished.

My first thought was that I didn't have Prof. Snow's gun. I'd need another weapon this time, and the only thing I could think of was a knife. We had a bunch of them in a kitchen drawer, which I never really understood. Neither the Arbiter nor I ever cooked.

We had no butcher knife, but there was one that was particularly long and jagged. I pulled it out and studied it in the soft, green glow of the digital clock on the microwave. I wasn't filled with anger like some killers say they were at the moment of attack. I hadn't completely whited out or lost sense of who and where I was. If anything, I was sad. No, sad is not exactly right. Melancholy, perhaps. Defeated. I didn't want to be the one to do this. I didn't like the roll that God had forced upon me. But I'd spent so much time questioning His ability to get things done that He apparently gave me one of those "If you think it's so easy, do it yourself," responses. I thought back to how I'd felt after killing Heath...how it felt *to* kill Heath. Know what? I couldn't remember. I had no idea. In the manner that some women say they forget the pain of bringing a life into the world, I forgot the pain of taking one out.

I didn't want to do this, but it wasn't my decision to make. It was the Queen's, as the Arbiter would say. With that in mind, I walked softly into the Arbiter's bedroom and thrust the knife into his chest.

He woke up quickly, of course, and looked about as if he knew something was wrong but couldn't figure out what. My eyes had grown accustomed to the dark, and the red light of his alarm clock was enough to afford me a view of his face. He coughed violently, and then seemed to realize what had happened. He placed his right hand over mine and the knife, and with his left he reached forward to touch my leg. Surprisingly, he didn't fight what was happening. He didn't even seem frightened. It was a much more respectable death than was Heath's.

Heath. If ever there was a chance, now was it. "I once killed somebody," I confessed.

The Arbiter laughed…or spasmed. I'm not sure. But just before he lost his grip on my hand, the Arbiter said, "I know."

It was his own fault. That's all I could think as the Arbiter died. It was his own fault for not caring, right? His complacency, justified by some ridiculous allegory of ants, angered me more than even Fayme's actions. I mean, he'd spent his life manipulating people, somehow getting even his enemies to do exactly what he wanted. That kind of control, there's just no need for it. It's dangerous, and it had to be ended. Justice. Justice is everyone getting what's coming to him. The Arbiter disagreed because he knew on which side of justice he stood.

Mr. Bernard, on the other hand, understood justice. He saw the result of our scheme, and fled to the immunity of New York City. To me, this remorse indicated he had feelings, that he was human. But the Arbiter, he just didn't care. He would learn nothing from what had happened, and would therefore make the same mistake again. In that aspect, he was no different from Heath.

As I walked out of the room, I caught a glimpse of the Arbiter's folder on the desk. For a moment, I thought of taking it with me. But wouldn't reading its contents be like dancing on his grave? And what would I find, anyway? More letters to dead actors? Maybe this time to Peter Sellers? Ted Knight? Divine? Maybe James Dean, maybe Natalie Wood. More than anything else, this habit of his proved his insanity…that I was right in what I'd just done.

For that reason, I decided to take it. It was evidence in my defense, and I needed that.

I didn't turn on the lights as I entered the living room. I was too geared up to go back to sleep, but I also wanted to do nothing more than just sit and think. There was a lot to work out now, decisions to be made. While making my way to the sofa, I bumped hard into an end table and knocked over a jar full of high bouncing balls. I heard them softly hit the carpet and I thought back to a time I didn't care to remember. Not right now.

I decided to not flee from my crime. Just as I had done with Heath, I'd let the events play themselves out. Eventually, someone would come to check on the Arbiter's absence, and I'd be there waiting for them. I actually hoped they'd come soon. That night, I handed in my official resignation as Avenger of the Blood.

As I waited for the discovery, I turned on a light and opened The Arbiter's gray folder. I felt guilty doing so, but all feelings were immediately swamped under the name at the top of the legal pad wedged inside:

To: Ms. Rhonda Vorhees
From: The Arbiter
Re: Antigone (or "I Don't Believe in Beatles, I Just Believe in Me")

Antigone was a selfish bitch.

Now, that's not how you played her, of course, Ms. Vorhees. You played her like every other half-decent actor has played Antigone over the last 2400 years; earnest, spirited, resolute, righteous, martyred Antigone, standing alone against the deluge, a one woman Army of Justice carrying the natural rights banner for all who are rolled over by the dictates of tyrannical positive law. Your performance celebrates the triumph of the one over the many.

The poster girl for principled civil disobedience.

Like Ghandi with tits.

I dropped the folder to the couch and jumped over to the TV. Resting halfway in the VCR cassette slot was a videotape labeled in neat, green handwriting; *Antigone, PPACPA.* I stared at it blankly, afraid to turn back to the Arbiter's final critique. But I did. I had to. I had to at least give him that. I sat back on the couch and looked towards his room, half expecting him to come out and catch me.

Absurd as it was, it still made me uneasy.

And you served the Sophoclean vision, Ms. Vorhees. I'm certain there's not a person who saw this filmed production who wouldn't consider defying Kingly decree and burying her dead, traitorous brother. I'm sure every young woman immediately identified with her plight as the offspring of the incestuous marriage between a murderous father and his widowed mother. I know that each person who had to dab the moistness from her eyes as Antigone wailed, "Woe for me, the word I hear comes hand in hand with death!" firmly believes that if she ever finds herself arranged to be married to her first cousin that she would sure be giving those Theban Gods the whatfor!

Do you see? Do you see what you've done, Ms. Vorhees?

Do you know why Plato hated the theater, Ms. Vorhees? Plato hated the theater because he thought it was phony...no, it's worse than that, because Plato said the world in which we live was phony; Plato said theater was destructive because it leads us further and further away from the truth. He said art was at best at the third remove from the essential nature of things...Plato said that art was designed to strip away the primacy of man's reason and allow him to be ruled by misleading and deceptive emotions.

He said art was a goddamned lie. Your performance, Ms. Vorhees, was a goddamned lie.

The truth is that Antigone was a petulant, inbred child, willing to sacrifice the needs of the living to placate her jones to avenge the dead. The truth is Antigone totally disregarded her sister Ismene and her fiancé Haemon. "The last of your King's house" is how she referred to herself, Ms. Vorhees, the last of the lineal descendants of the Theban King Labdicus. But what about Antigone's sister? Her poor, slow sister Ismene who Antigone left alone to bear the brunt of the family curse after hanging herself in the cave? What about Haemon? Haemon, Ms. Vorhees, Haemon who she damn well knew would defy his father and attempt to come to her aid; Haemon who she knew couldn't live without her, who wouldn't want to live without you, who would slice himself open at the sight of your broken body.

The truth is you signed his death warrant. He couldn't go on. He just…couldn't.

That's the truth.

What do you suppose all your fans think about King Creon, Ms. Vorhees? What do you suppose they think about the author of the law that led to the destruction of everyone for whom he cared…his wife and son, dead…his sister and brother-in-law, dead…his nephews and niece…dead. His Kingdom in tatters, his work destroyed, his life in ruin…all by his own words…his own will…his own need…all that is left for him is to beg…to plead for death, "Is there none will deal a thrust that shall lay me dead with the two hand steel?" Do they feel his pain? Do they recognize that he was doing the best he could for his people? Do they realize that, as leader of a nation, he had to make unpopular choices with a cool head that went unbetrayed by a warm heart? Do your fans understand that sometimes the needs of the many really do have to outweigh the needs of the few?

Or the one?

Did the people who watched your performance understand that it's the one left to live who really suffers? That in the cold light of an endless day the only hell that really exists is the one in which unreasonable men are left alone and accountable for their unpardonable sin of thinking without thought? The sin of putting temporary desires ahead of reasoned reflection? The sin of truly believing it's all really about you?

Antigone changed the world, Ms. Vorhees. Her death brought down a King and displaced an entire society. She was uncommonly uncommon.

She was not an ant.

But try as they might to identify with her, fundamentally, your fans are ants. Ms. Vorhees. It doesn't matter how high their hopes are, in the real word ants don't move rubber tree plants and ants don't bring down entire societies with their deaths. No blood oaths, no wrathful vengeance, no dress pins in their eyes, no overly referential multipage monologues in mournful reflection…in the real world we carry on.

Because, Rhonda, the truth is that the rest of us are ants.

Even if you weren't.

> The dream is over. What can I say?
> The dream is over, yesterday.
> I was the dream weaver, but now I'm reborn.
> I was the Arbiter. But now, I'm John.

And so, my friend Guy, you'll just have to carry on.

But not me. I've got a date.

See you around, Ms. Vorhees. I've got the funniest story to you.

S'long,
Arby

Oh, I am so embarrassed….

0-595-23683-9